D8 With F8

D8 With F8

Anthony P. Jones

Brown Bags Books LLC. Publishing company

Brown Bag Books LLC.
9962 Brook Rd. #629
Glen Allen, VA 23059-6501

Library of Congress Cataloging-in-Publication Data
Jones, Anthony P., 1958-
D8 With F8 / Anthony P. Jones
p. cm.
ISBN 978-0-9715899-1-9
1. Journalists— Fiction. 2. Washington > (D.C.) — Fiction.
3. Charlottesville > (VA) – Fiction. 4. Serial murders –
Fiction.   5. FBI— Fiction. I. Title II. Title: D8 With
F8.   III. O'Grady, Schaffer.

Manufactured in the United States of America

For:
Jim, Jeff, Janice and Michelle

Acknowledgements

I believe this is the most difficult section of any book to write because inevitability, I will forget to mention someone. Before moving forward, there is something I need to clear up; I was asked by the members of a book club if I meant what I said on the first line in my acknowledgements from *Operation Smokeout*. Once again, allow me to thank God for my talent and overactive imagination. In the business of writing, belief may be the only thing that gets you to the next day.

As I began researching just how twisted the human mind can become, I gained a new appreciation for the FBI and the men and women, who make it their business to hunt these people down and get them off the streets. Jim Clemente not only did this for a living, but he also made sure *D8 With F8* followed some logical course, while making sure my "literary license" didn't stray too far a field.

I certainly could not have gotten this book finished without the help of a skilled editor and Vicki Moore is the best I've ever worked with. Vicki is also a dear friend that I've known so long that I've stopped counting the years.

Likewise, readers are very important. In addition to Jim and Vicki, Sybil Scott is a consistently reliable reader, who shoots her feedback strait; my personal feelings aside. To date, she is the only person, who has read every word I've written including eight additional completed manuscripts and two additional ones in the works.

D8 With F8 has been reviewed by several "players" within the Hollywood circle. This would have been impossible without the help of Ken Mathis, a fraternity brother and long-time friend. Along with his brother-in-law, Dan Harvey, these guys have placed this work in the hands of people I could only dream of reaching.

If you're reading this, it means that the cover grabbed your attention and that credit goes to the same two gentlemen, who worked with me on *Operation Smokeout*; and are also friends, Lee Brauer and Scott Sherman. If you're trying to get a book to market, you'd be crazy not to look these guys up. They take words and put them to pictures that make people want to see what lies within the covers.

My medical school experience continues to provide me with benefits, including contacts within the medical community. I met my BEST friend at Meharry Medical School in 1980. Dr. Raphael Wilson and another close friend, Dr. Clarence Scranage were my go-to guys for much of the medical events within this book. Scran's work as an ME (medical examiner) and Ray's knowledge about drugs gave me the needed insight to make this story work. I received additional drug help from my cousin and pharmacist, Marie Powell Daly and one of the FBI's Hazardous Materials Specialist, Michael McCarthy.

Anyone reading my books will unmistakably notice my love for Xavier University of Louisiana. The nurturing I received at Xavier is in many ways responsible for my determination to succeed. Likewise, the University of Virginia pushed me to write and develop my craft. I could not have completed any of my works without the input from both these schools and the many people I came into contact with.

There are two organizations, which were critical in my development, The Hurston/Wright Foundation and the James River Writers. Every writer can benefit from networking and interacting with others in the business; these two organizations provide unprecedented access.

There are some other talented individuals, who have helped to bring this book together; Sue Young singlehandedly brought my web site, brownbagbooksllc.com to life. She has a keen eye, which brought my vision to life. Sue and her husband, Paul are dear friends, who I owe more that I can ever repay. Ed Jones, my uncle, computer expert and, whose knowledge of software made him the perfect go-to guy to get the book properly formatted. When I told my brother, Chris (my producer and long time member of the film industry) that I wanted a video to go along with the book, he showed up with a film crew. Rubin Rios is the exceptional director and editor responsible for the film. Jason Parks lent his skill behind the camera to capture the concept. Curtis Harmon, John Rappole Jr. and Scott Russell put the original music together to keep your attention focused on the action. None of this would have worked without my actors, Stacy Young, Leilani Torralbas, Regina Brown, Ben Myers,Sylvia and my family actors, Sylvia, Cassidy, Alex and Mike. Paul and Julie Weissend and their kids allowed me to disturb their peaceful home for the filming of the video. I can't thank all you guys enough!

Chris, Mike and Nick Jones along with Wilbert Bailey jumped in with a big hand to help bring this all together. I couldn't have done this without your support.

I have been blessed to have such a supportive family; without them, none of my books would have been possible. Nick. Morgan, Alex, Cassidy, as well as, my sisters and brothers and extended family, keep me motivated to continue writing.

Juana, if I'd never been curious to find out what was so interesting in the books you constantly read, I'd never have picked one up. I've never put them down since, thank you. Sylvia, thanks for the twenty. I may not understand life, but I know it will trudge its own course. I wish you nothing but the best.

The blurbs you find on the back of this book represent my "Dream Team." Their accomplishments in their chosen fields of entertainment continue to engage fans and impress their fellow colleagues. In addition, they have provided me a source of inspiration and nurturing in my journey as a writer. You guys are the best!

My most important "thank you," goes out to my readers; without you, the words I've put in these pages would remain silent. If you would like to host an in-person meeting, visit www.brownbagbooksllc.com; I will make every effort to visit your group.

Prologue

Dr. Dirk Gerard reexamined the crumpled scrap of paper in his hand then looked up to make sure he was at the correct address. The apartment would have been hard to miss with the multitude of blue and red lights whirling atop the emergency vehicles that were just outside the front door. Dirk walked into the apartment near the University of Virginia Law School where the corpse waited for him. As the state's leading forensic pathologist, the Governor personally requested that Dirk handle the case when the Governor's niece was found dead by her study partner and occasional convenient lover, Michelle Perkins.

Dirk was meticulous, and to date solved every case that he worked on. Little had been said about the fact that he assigned the more questionable cases to others in his office to protect his track record. Everyone involved in the current investigation expected nothing less than the "master's" best. The weight of the task at hand pressed heavily against his psyche and shoulders making his next step forward a struggle.

As he crossed the door seal of the bedroom he set down his black forensic bag and removed his shoes. The coldness of death rushed to meet him causing him to visibly shake. Death was his business, but the young dying still disturbed him. He rubbed his hand across the rapidly retreating hair on his head. Before he stepped forward, he looked around and noticed how neat and orderly the room was. No clothes were on the floor, bed, or loveseat. All her dresser drawers and closet doors were closed. The picture on her nightstand of her hugging a dog was still facing her pillow and was straight and dust-free, as was the framed artwork on the walls. Dirk viewed her neatness as obsessive— nothing was out of place.

He bent down to see if any footprints remained in the carpet. They could be very helpful in determining who might have been present at the time of the victim's death. The Berber carpet left little hope of finding footprints, nevertheless, he moved along the edges of the walls to reach the area where the corpse lay.

Standing next to the four-poster bed, before looking at the victim, Dirk reached in his shirt pocket for the notes from his interview with the Governor. Sarah was a second year law student at UVA. She had the second highest GPA in her class and was breezing through law school as

ANTHONY P. JONES   D8 WITH F8

if she had been given copies of all her exams. Firms had already begun to compete for her even though she was still in school and had yet to pass the bar exam. Sarah's death was going to be front-page news tomorrow and Dirk wanted to get a head start on solving the case before the press started to hound him for information.

Dirk stared at Sarah. Even in death, her loveliness commanded his attention. Curly mahogany hair gently held her face and deep green eyes, which once held the joy of life, stared back at Dirk with the unmistakable vision of death.

On the bed, Sarah's 300 thread count Egyptian cotton sheets were only wrinkled where the weight of her body forced them to bend. He stopped for a moment, struck by a thought. He could see that Sarah had the perfectly decorated room, perfect grades, perfectly expensive sheets on the bed, and the perfect body. Sarah had the best of everything money could buy. Even so, she could not prevent the inevitability of death.

Dirk kneeled down to look for evidence. He immediately noticed hairs that belonged to someone other than the victim around the pillow and on the sheets. He used a pair of tweezers to lift the hairs and place them in a zip-lock evidence bag to be processed later.

"Well Miss Sarah, it seems you either enjoyed several partners at the same time or you didn't change your sheets very often." Dirk looked around the room, again noting the cleanliness and order; and he knew the sheets must have been changed regularly, probably every few days. He pulled out a white sheet of paper and placed it between Sarah's legs, which were sprawled to either side of the bed. He removed a comb from his case and gently stroked it through her pubic hair. "If you were with several partners last night there will be hairs from each of them tangled with your own." As expected he found several foreign hairs. Dirk gathered the hairs, placed them into a bag and labeled it. Back at the lab, he would determine their origin.

Dirk had begun snapping pictures when he walked in the room. He looked around and realized there was nothing else to shoot and put a digital camera back in his case, the entire scene had been photographed in excess. Experience taught him that often the answers he sought were right in front of his face. Having pictures of the crime scene would allow him to view things without the tension or emotion that surrounded the actual sight. He would download them this afternoon and have them cataloged by tonight.

Dirk looked around the room again. He covered his mental checklist one last time. There was nothing else he could do until some of the evidence was processed, so he called to the police waiting just outside the front door. "Okay boys, bag her and get her to Richmond as quickly as possible. From the rectal temperature reading, I'd say she's been dead about six hours. The sooner I have her in the lab the better for our case. Let's get moving!"

The officers scurried in the room pulling on purple nitrile gloves as they entered. A collapsible metal gurney was rolled next to the bed. The younger of the two officers, with no experience in matters of death, was at the foot of the bed. He grabbed Sarah's ankles and immediately let them go. He was surprised by the cold stiffness of her skin. Skin that just a few hours ago, he would have longed to caress. Dirk looked at the officer and noticed that the color had left his face. Dirk knew that he had to intervene, or the crime scene would be contaminated with vomit.

"Don't think about what you're doing. That's not a person, it's a corpse, just get it into the bag and get it out of here."

The young officer was sweating profusely. The top half of his uniform was soaked. He reached down and grabbed Sarah's ankles again and in one motion they lifted her body onto the gurney before he ran out of the room. The older officer then zipped Sarah in a body bag and rolled her out of the apartment to the coroner's van that would transport her to Richmond.

Dirk leaned his five foot nine inch frame against the wall letting his head fall back until it came to rest. He watched as the policeman bagged the body, when he finished and began to roll her out, Dirk's eyes drifted towards the ceiling. He was momentarily amused by the heaving sounds the young officer made giving up the breakfast he'd recently eaten. Dirk closed his eyes slowly letting his head fall forward. Then as if jarred awake, he jerked his eyes towards the bed. In the mirror he saw one of his assistants enter the room. "Thomas. I didn't hear you come in."

Thomas Brothers was a medical student at the Medical College of Virginia. He was sitting out his third year to assist Dirk and earn the extra money needed to finance the cost of his final two years of medical school. "Dr. Gerard, you look like shit. Is everything okay?" Dirk nodded. "What can I do to help?"

Dirk could hear the sobs and crying of the people just outside the front door as the lifeless body of a former friend passed. He sat down on the floor pulled his hands to his knees and began to reflect. "Isn't it strange that a person's death touches us more than their life? When someone we know dies, we search for the goodness they possessed while during their lifetime we looked only for their faults. These types of scenes cause so much pain." He stood staring into Thomas' eyes through the mirror.

"That's probably true Dr. Gerard. However, there is only one true solution to pain— death."

Dirk gazed intensely at Thomas realizing that the person he saw reminded him of himself twenty years ago. "I realize you've been through a difficult time the past few months, but time will heal those wounds and cure your cynicism. Maybe you should use the upcoming research break to take it easy for a while. The lab will be fine if you're not there."

Thomas let a cynical laugh escape as he shook his head from side to side. "You know I can't do that."

Dirk tried to smile; his eyes expressed both sincerity and sadness. "I'll make sure the checks keep coming. You need the time off."

"Look who's talking— no, Dr. Gerard. I'd rather be here. It helps me to forget my pain." Unable to engage Dirk's eyes directly he looked at his mentor's reflection in the mirror and repeated his earlier statement. "Death is still the only permanent solution to pain." The pain that Thomas felt was not contrived, or manufactured by his actions, it was real. Work would only dull it for a few hours. Jack Black, as in Daniels would take it away shortly after he got home but the morning sun would bring it back again. He had been told by the few people he associated with that as the days wore on he would feel the pain lessen its grip on him. It had been months now, however, and the pain was worse than ever. Each day the dawning sky gave him one less reason to live and another pound of hatred for Victoria. The pain had to end. The necessary sacrifice of life was irrelevant; death would have to do— for everyone.

◆

Back at the lab in Richmond, Dirk had almost completed the autopsy. The white walls, bright lights and stainless steel tables gave a sanitized appearance to the gruesome job of dissecting a human. Sarah's hollowed out body lay on the table in front of him. Adjacent to her body was a mobile table containing all of her organs. He weighed each of them using a metric scale that could have just as easily been used in the produce section of any grocery store. Then he took tissue samples to analyze later. The final step of the autopsy was to peel forward her scalp, remove her cranial cap, and take out her brain. Many secrets could be held in the coils of jelly-like gray matter. Many times the cause of death waited there to be discovered. Dirk turned on the autopsy saw that would be used to cut through the skull when his chief assistant walked into the room waving several loose papers.

"Dr. Gerard, I have the results from her stomach contents." The assistant yelled above the whine of the saw while waving the paper in the air.

Dirk turned off the saw and set it on the table next to Sarah's head. "Let me guess, large amounts of alcohol."

The assistant looked at one of the sheets of paper. "On the contrary. Actually, if she'd been drinking it might have saved her life. She'd been popping Ecstasy all night. The alcohol would have diminished the effects of the drug." He paused, shuffling the reports in his hands. "Also, she seemed to have had an affinity for oral sex. I'm running tests now to see if the DNA profiles in the semen samples match those of the hair samples you found at the scene."

Dirk crossed his legs and leaned against the table. "Five bucks says you'll find a match." He looked down at Sarah. "The poor girl probably thought she was doing the right thing by avoiding alcohol. This is one of the few times the opposite is true. Were you able to determine if there was more than one semen sample?"

The assistant hit the paper with one finger. "Yes. And both match the blood types of the samples we found in her vagina."

Dirk twisted his mouth and blew a heavy sigh. "The Governor is not going to like our findings. His perfect little niece liked the multiple-partner mattress mambo." Both he and his chief assistant laughed and shook their heads. Dark humor was often used to lighten the mood in the autopsy room. It helped them get through the grisly task at hand. Especially, when they worked on someone so young, or as important as the Governor's niece.

Silence settled over the room as the weight of their charge still loomed. The chief assistant was the first to break the silence. "I guess all we have to do now is to profile the DNA and determine whether Sarah took the ecstasy on her own, or if it was forced on her."

"My thoughts exactly." Dirk lifted the saw and his thumb danced back and forth across the switch as if he were anxious to turn it on. "In this case the Governor is going to want to know the source of the drugs as well. That shouldn't be too hard. Most of the Ecstasy that reaches the U.S. comes from Israel. Complete your tests and then we'll go over our game plan. We're going to have to tell the Governor's people something soon." The drone of the buzzing saw ended their conversation. Dirk watched his chief assistant leaving and briefly let his attention fall to

Thomas.

Thomas was working on physical evidence found at the crime scene, but had stopped the moment the chief assistant walked in. He was inconspicuously sitting near the glass that separated two different autopsy areas. He listened intently to the conversation between Dirk and the chief assistant. Thomas' attention strayed from the conversation the moment the chief assistant mentioned Ecstasy. The missing portion of his plan was so simple that he had overlooked it. Plugging the perfect drug into the puzzle would make things perfect. He looked at the digital clock above the table where Sarah lay and spoke into the autopsy recorder to mark the exact moment. "Wed. Sept. 24th 2:45 and 12 seconds p.m." Thomas knew if he worked late tonight he could complete his profiles so that the police could begin to narrow their investigation by tomorrow. He could then take Friday off. The weather forecasts called for rain all weekend, including Friday. Rain was perfect, it was an integral part of Thomas' master plan to end his pain; executing it to perfection was the final step. By Monday morning he would have a new reason to live.

The chief assistant turned leaving the room and heard excited words rise above the cry of the saw. He paused a moment to see if Dr. Gerard had called again. He let the door close and grabbed another assistant who was in the lab. "There he goes again, talking to 'Thomas' the wonder assistant. I think we need to give Doc a referral to Dr. Kenard over in psych." They both laughed and walked off.

Chapter
1

Schaffer O'Grady woke Friday morning still holding his copy of *Mind Hunter*. The book read like a novel, but it was completely true. John Douglas, the author, is known as the father of profiling for the FBI. His book is about serial killers. Douglas and his colleagues interviewed a number of incarcerated serial killers to determine how their minds worked. His research became the bible for the FBI's Behavioral Analysis Unit.

Schaffer's dreams were filled with events similar to what he read before falling asleep. More than once he awoke last night sweating and jumping uncontrollably because of what he viewed in his dreams. The torment he felt during the dreams had been so real that he was relieved when his coffee maker came on this morning waking him from the fretful night.

The smell of fresh brewed coffee gently lifted Schaffer's eyelids and caused his taste buds to dance with excitement. As for his anxiety, only time would be able to relieve what he was feeling. He was still troubled by the abject cruelty humans were able to inflict upon their fellow man. In *Mind Hunter*, John Douglas gave his readers meticulously detailed accounts of how several serial killers executed their victims. One case that troubled Schaffer was that of a teenage boy who started to rape women after his girlfriend broke up with him. One of his early victims, unbeknownst to him was a prostitute who attempted to please him rather than fight. Her consent enraged the teenage assailant because he felt she was attempting to control him. For her acquiescence, the teenager brutally killed the woman. Schaffer found it even more disturbing that the teenager had an IQ above 120 and let something so mundane trigger his entry into the world of killing for pleasure.

Descending the stairs, he heard movement in the kitchen. "Good morning Gretchen," he called. The dog ran over and pounced against his body. Even though he expected the greeting, his six foot frame and two hundred pounds were no match for an excited dog that was about half his height and one fourth his weight. The dog made a mad dash for the back door. "All right girl, I'm coming." He opened the door and let her out for her morning run, then went back to get a cup of coffee. Before pouring the coffee he retrieved the four newspapers that were delivered to his doorstep daily. He'd have to wait for the other four that came in the mail.

ANTHONY P. JONES   D8 WITH F8

With coffee and papers in hand, Schaffer walked out on the deck and took a deep breath of the fresh air. About half a mile from the deck the Blue Ridge Mountains rose majestically from the horizon. The leaves were hinting that they would soon paint the mountains with the vibrant colors of fall. His first autumn in Charlottesville promised to be a beautiful one, despite the harshness of the earlier drought. The edges of the leaves were already kissed with color.

Today Schaffer had to go back to Washington to meet with Joe DeApuzzo before he spoke to a gathering of newspaper journalists tomorrow. Joe wanted him there because of some special assignment that he would only delegate in person. Schaffer knew it had to be connected with John Douglas' book that Joe had sent him.

Schaffer had fallen in love with this area ever since Joe sent him to Charlottesville to cover a story at the University of Virginia. So much so that he returned to Georgetown only long enough to pack his belongings and have the house converted to a duplex. One side, he rented and the other he kept for himself in case he ever needed to stay in DC for an extended period of time.

He received his assignments via e-mail, except when Joe felt it was very important, or when Joe was attempting to fix him up. For the past week Joe had been dropping hints as inconspicuous as a giraffe in downtown DC. Schaffer knew Joe could not keep a secret and that this was just another attempt to fix him up with someone. Assigning him to the story was just a cover for Joe's real agenda.

Aah Joe, you got to love him. At least his heart is in the right place. But, Schaffer couldn't say much about Joe's choices of women for him. He didn't need anyone as badly as Joe thought he did, especially the women Joe had a tendency to pick out for him. Schaffer had no problem being alone. Relationships, at least the ones he'd been in since Doran, required too much effort and returned nothing that he cared to discuss.

Schaffer unfolded the papers and placed them side-by-side on the deck table. The *Richmond Times Dispatch,* the *Washington Post* and the *Charlottesville Daily Progress* all ran the same lead story, **Governor's Niece Found Dead at the University of Virginia**. The *New York Times Washington Edition* buried the story in the 'Nation' section. He began to read the story, but was interrupted when he heard an outburst of frightened birds taking to the air.

Gretchen came back to the deck hurriedly. She jumped up and down excitedly, barking and wagging her tail watching the frightened covey of quail fly to a safer location. After the birds disappeared Gretchen leaned against Schaffer's leg holding her head high and continuously beating her tail.

"Good job girl. Are you ready to go in yet?"

She looked back at him as if to say, *never*. After a second thought centering on food, she reluctantly followed Schaffer through the screened-in porch to the house.

He fixed breakfast for them both, high protein dog chow for her and high cholesterol sticky bun for himself. Later, he would have a couple of glasses of Hendry Cab to reverse the effects of breakfast. Right now though, he had to get a move on so that he wouldn't be late for Joe's meeting. Maybe this time Joe would have something really exciting for him, especially if Douglas' book was any indication of what was to come. His thoughts immediately reverted to the story in the papers that lay across the table on the porch. He wondered if the governor's niece was the victim of a perverted killer's lust for death.

Schaffer headed upstairs trying to decide which suit would best represent him at the luncheon. He remembered someone once saying that pinstripes made a person look smarter so he decided to wear his double-breasted gray pinstripe. To maintain individuality, he decided to add a dark purple shirt with white cuffs and collar and a solid gold colored tie.

Within a few minutes Schaffer was dressed and headed out the front door. Gretchen whined when she saw the door open and realized she was not invited to come along.

"Don't worry girl. I'll be home tomorrow afternoon. Then I'll run with you outside. You're going to stay at Donna's until I get back." Her stub tail wagged enthusiastically when he patted her head.

As he drove down the driveway, Schaffer took time to examine the grapevines planted on either side. One day he wanted to place a sign out front, Welcome to Schaffer's Vineyard, all five-point two acres. At least it was a start. He wished he could say it was his idea to plant the vines, but they were there when he bought the place— five point two acres of vines and ninety-five more of beautiful scenic countryside. Schaffer's neighbors on either side owned hundreds of acres of land with at least twenty-five acres planted in grapes. Students from the University of Virginia were brought in as interns to practice the craft of wine making. Their reward was three easy credits; his neighbors however, were able to place several cases of wine in their cellars to relax until maturity. Schaffer couldn't wait to get in on the act.

◆

ANTHONY P. JONES   D8 WITH F8

The drive to Washington on Route 29 was lined with mountains, rolling hills and farm pastures containing all types of vegetation. Even though he'd made the drive numerous times, Schaffer still found it breathtaking. He always managed to see something new on every trip. The one constant was the cows standing on the same hills, in the same positions they were always in as if they had been painted onto the hillsides.

The heavy rains that came about two months ago began to quench the parched earth. Hurricane Isadora dumped more rain in a couple of days than the area usually gets in three months. Even though no significant amount of rain fell since then, Isadora had done her part for the fall leaves.

Two hours after Schaffer began his drive he pulled into the *Washington Post's* headquarters. He turned the engine off but kept the radio on so that he could hear a selection from *Kind of Blue*. The string bass thumped the rhythm laying the groundwork. Eight notes later, Miles' trumpet and Bill Evan's piano added a syncopated beat, followed closely by the saxophone with its melodious overtones. Miles Davis always touched Schaffer deeply. The "Smooth Jazz" stations finally got it and began playing more cuts from the Masters. Schaffer thought Miles and most of the other great Jazz artists were just too heavy for the average jazz listener. But, once converted to an aficionado, one couldn't help believing that an appreciation for the jazz Masters made most of the other music played on this station seem like "jazz light." Still, it was better than anything else the airwaves had to offer.

After not having to come into the office for so long the walk to the front door felt as if Schaffer was voluntarily re-entering prison. As soon as he entered the building, it started with the security guard and janitorial staff.

"Hi, Schaffer, welcome back to the big house."

"Hey big guy, congratulations on your last Pulitzer."

"Schaffer, you headed up to the warden's office? How'd you ever convince Joe to let you out of the cage?"

He politely waved and walked down the hallway as quickly as he could to get to Joe's office. The pressroom was filled with reporters hiding behind cubicles. If they were not busy, they at least wanted to appear to be since the blinds covering Joe's ten-foot window were open. Schaffer made it to Joe's office without being stopped and when he walked through Joe's door, Joe began grinning. Immediately, Schaffer had a vision of a birdcage door standing wide open and Joe having yellow feathers all around his mouth.

"Oh shit!" The words left Schaffer's mouth before he had a chance to think.

"What? I didn't even say anything. Joe's smile faded, but the wrinkles in his forehead remained.

"A shit-eating grin on your face one second after I walk in the door means you're up to something."

Joe placed his hand over his heart. "How could you say such a thing?"

Schaffer couldn't stop the smile that crept across his face watching Joe's actions. A month ago he and Joe went out for a drink and had too many; Schaffer asked Joe what Pigmy tribe he was from. Joe didn't speak to him for a week. This was the first time they'd been face-to-face since that night and seeing Joe's little hands reminded Schaffer of that night. Through his smile he took the bait. "Okay. Who is she? Oops, I'm sorry. What assignment do you have for me, Boss?"

Joe rocked back in his chair and put his feet on the desk. "You think you're so smart. Who is she? You could fuck up a pervert's wet dream."

Schaffer took a seat in front of Joe's desk. "I'm sorry. Did I ask the wrong question?"

Pleased with himself, Joe folded his arms behind his head. "I simply have a great assignment for you. If you're lucky, you may even get a side story and a book deal like that Harris guy who wrote *Silence of the Lambs*. Then I won't have to listen to your smart-ass remarks when I give you an assignment."

Schaffer saw a copy of Douglas' book on Joe's desk. He reached over and picked it up. "Does your assignment have anything to do with this?" Schaffer waved the book.

Joe let his feet fall to the floor and put his elbows on his desk. "The FBI is holding a session of the National Academy for policemen from all over the country and a group from the state of Virginia will be there as well. It's going to be held on the Marine Base at Quantico under the direction of an Agent Duplechain."

Schaffer looked surprised and didn't let Joe get another word out. "Duplechain? That sounds like a New Orleans name."

"Well it should, smart ass. Agent Duplechain is a graduate from your alma mater. That's why I was smiling. I thought you would like dealing with someone from Xavier. So much for your fucking theory."

Joe looked as if he would poke his tongue out at any minute.

Schaffer slid Joe's book back on his desk. "Well, Joe DeApuzzo. It seems like I didn't figure you right— this time."

Joe made the biggest fist possible with his little hands and pounded it on his desk. "Goddamned right you didn't. I just wanted to put you together with a schoolmate and you act like I'm arranging some stupid high school fix-you-up. I remember how crazy you are about 'Xavier University of Louisiana,' as you're so fond of saying. Agent Duplechain graduated after you so maybe you'll have a chance to catch up in as much as you were there during the Jurassic period."

Schaffer saw Joe's hand again and suppressed his laughter, still thinking about the Pigmy comment. "I look forward to it."

"Good because I asked Agent Duplechain to join us for the luncheon tomorrow. Afterwards, you'll have the opportunity to do a one-on-one interview to help you prepare for the training session, which starts Monday. We want you to be comfortable, especially since it's been a while since you've been a cop...of sorts."

"Secret Service."

"Secret Service, cop— what's the difference?"

Schaffer shook his head exasperated knowing further comment was useless. "So, that's your big surprise?" Schaffer asked, wondering why Joe didn't just have him come to the house before the event.

Joe's face held a look of satisfaction, as if he'd just won a war. "Fucking A! Now you may go. Some of us still have to work to collect a paycheck. I'll see you at the Four Seasons." Joe moved his hand in the air as if sweeping Schaffer away.

The friendship between them was reflected in both their faces. "Thanks Joe, I really appreciate you looking out for me."

"Yeah, yeah. Now get the fuck out of here!"

"Before I go, why did you have me read Douglas' book? Is that a prerequisite for the National Academy?"

"Ask Agent Duplechain when you see her."

"Her?" Schaffer looked at Joe. Noticing Joe's attempt to hide his smile, Schaffer knew that it was useless asking any more questions. He turned and left the room, this was another one of Joe's set ups.

Chapter
2

Early Friday morning Dirk held a live press conference to deliver his findings on Sarah's autopsy. He took time to warn the Governor what he would be saying so that his Honor wouldn't be caught off guard. Just before the conference began, Dirk's assistant ran in with a cell phone.

"Dr. Gerard. They found it. The detective is on the phone now." He handed Dirk the phone.

"This is Dr. Gerard."

The detective began speaking immediately. "We found the stash of Ecstasy about one foot from the end of the bed between the mattress and the box spring. That was a good call."

"Thanks. I guess I should really credit the medical student working in my office, Thomas actually made the call." Dirk looked towards his office. There he could see Thomas' reflection in the glass as he finished his assignment for the day.

The detective continued. "I've got some more good news. Two freshman boys came in with an administrator from UVA first thing this morning. They admitted to sleeping with Sarah last night. She was alive when they left, or so they say. I've got some men checking out their alibi."

Dirk looked out into space, dumbfounded. "Damn! She liked them young. I hope this doesn't get messy."

"Yeah. It could be tricky."

"College has changed since I was there, Detective. Men used to be considered the aggressors." Dirk checked his watch.

"I guess it's the girls' way of getting back at us, Dr. Gerard. It's a new kind of 'women's lib,' dominate and control, two at once even."

"I'm all too familiar with the concept of domination. Thanks for the information, Detective. I'll use what I need for the press conference. I don't want to embarrass the Governor." Dirk handed the phone back to his assistant and took the podium.

Cameras flashed as Dirk leaned towards the microphones. "Thank you for coming ladies and gentlemen. I'm going to make this very brief. Sarah Phillips died from an overdose of 3, 4-Methylenedioxymethamphetamine, commonly known on the street as

Ecstasy. The investigation is ongoing, so that is all that I am at liberty to discuss at this time."

The questions began at once from the press.

"Do you have any suspects?"

"We heard she was raped. Is that true?"

"You should check your sources. Really, those are questions for the police. However, I'm sure I can speak for them when I say the investigation is ongoing. When we have more, we will share it with you. Thank you for coming. That's all for now." Dirk waved his hand and walked from the podium stopping far short of what he'd expected to say. Scores of people snapped pictures and shoved microphones in his face still asking questions. He escaped to the solitude of the morgue.

Dirk walked over to a small table next to Sarah's body. There, Thomas had a box packed and taped. Routinely, Thomas carried items from an investigation to his completely furnished home lab, which was in the basement of the house where he lived. There, he could work late into the night without having to worry about the drive home.

Normally, Thomas would make sure one of the other assistants was present at the time he packed any box. Today however, he packed it while everyone was busy preparing for the press conference. Thomas hated Dirk's chief assistant. The guy acted like he didn't trust Thomas the way Dr. Gerard did. He always complained that taking things from the office could compromise the chain of custody of the evidence. Fuck him; Dirk wouldn't question what was in the box. Since they were leaving together, he would wait to tell Dr. Gerard then.

Dirk walked to the room where his chief assistant was working. "Igor, I'm headed home."

"Yeees master." His assistant answered in usual form. Everyone who worked with Dirk appreciated his sense of humor.

Dirk and Thomas walked to the underground garage attached to the morgue. Dirk liked the protection the garage provided from nosey reporters that might have been waiting to ask him more questions if his car had been in an open lot. When he pulled out of the garage, just as he expected, the reporters rushed towards his car. He wondered why none of them were ever around to charge his car when he worked on bodies of the lesser known. They were just as dead and their deaths just as tragic. Dirk pushed down hard on the horn and hit the gas. None of the reporters followed him from the lot. About ten blocks later he stopped at a small parking lot and Thomas emerged from behind the tinted glass of Dirk's BMW with his box of supplies in hand and got into his waiting car.

♦

Forty-five minutes later Thomas pulled into his garage and was through the door and into his house before the garage door had completely closed. He snatched the TV remote from atop a stereo speaker just inside the door. He pushed the power button and the TV came to life. After seeing that the noon weather report had not yet come on, Thomas took a second to look around. The house was just as empty as yesterday, just as empty as it would be tomorrow. All that remained in the family room was a newly purchased stereo, TV and a raggedy-ass leather chair that he claimed was an antique.

When hurricane Isadora left the area two months ago his wife, three children, dog and all his furniture blew out with the storm. Thomas didn't care about the possessions or his wife for that matter. He could replace the furniture, but he missed the kids and the dog had been his best friend. Thomas knew that she took the Aussie Terrier out of spite because she never liked the dog. He figured she probably dumped him on the highway somewhere between here and wherever she was headed.

Daddy's little bitch. Thomas referred to Victoria in usual form. *Until the day her father died, he called her Princess.* The thought enraged Thomas every time it came to mind. *That's why he gave her that fucking regal name, Princess Victoria, just to piss people off. No one could make that bitch happy, not even her asshole father. Shit, she could make Jesus lose his religion."* Thomas thought.

Thomas moved to his chair in the middle of the family room. He sat down and reached over the side for a book that was leaning against it. He lifted the book, read the title again and ran his hand over the cover, *The Enneagrams.* While he waited for the weather report he opened the book and began to read.

The Enneagrams are a personality typing method that dates back hundreds of years. A Sifu in China theorized that there are only nine different personality types, which he assigned to a point on a star. By using his theory and understanding each of the nine points, people could interact more productively. Many people have written about the Enneagrams in recent times, but Thomas chose Helen Palmer's book. He thought that getting a women's point of view would help him to understand them better. He did understand one thing, no one that was the same type as his soon to be ex-wife deserved to live. Since he couldn't find her, the next best thing was to find women like her. An understanding of the Enneagrams made finding these women far easier.

For the past six weeks, Thomas prepared for his next move. Almost everything was ready. The organophosphates and LSD was prepped, the envelopes treated, the clothes bought and the fake mustaches made from hair he collected from two of Dirk's autopsies that he'd assisted on. He'd even selected his first few subjects. The only thing that was missing was something to get his subjects 'in the mood.' Ecstasy gave him the idea, but there was something better, liquid ecstasy, gamma-hydroxybutyrate, or GHB. Not only would that put them in the mood, but its interaction with the LSD would also make them willing participants in Thomas' plan.

Thomas found it amazing how receptive people were after going through similar circumstances. In Charlottesville, VA a group of separated and divorced Catholics openly welcomed the chance to find out more about themselves. In helping them interpret their Enneagram data, Thomas made a note of any female "number eight's". On this particular evening there was only one.

Lynda Goodwin, a twenty-eight year old architect, started her own firm after none of the larger firms offered to pay her what they did the males they hired.

After all, I finished first in my class at UVA and my work has proven itself innovative, was Linda's mantra.

Thomas still heard her words bouncing off either side of his skull. She was too pompous making the announcement the night of the meeting. Thomas suggested she learn to play 'the game' if she wanted to gain status and respect. She responded by telling him that she never kissed anyone's ass. He decided at that moment that he would prove her a liar.

The only factor left for Thomas to be able to carry out his quest was rain. He emerged from a trance-like state just as the weather report began. Not very much longer he heard what he'd waited for.

"There's a ninety percent chance for rain all weekend beginning this afternoon."

Thomas rocked back and forth in his chair howling like a madman. Rain would wash away all evidence outside of his victim's houses and usually; he would be invited to come inside rather than having to stand in the pouring rain. As soon as the screen went dark he jumped from his chair and ran up stairs covering two or three steps per leap. He tossed his newly purchased clothes in a duffel bag then quickly ran out to the car to get the box he'd brought from the morgue.

The jars inside the box made a clinking sound as he took them to the basement and set up the apparatus he needed to synthesize GHB. In a few hours the configuration would be complete. Thomas' hands wrapped around an Erlenmeyer flask full of colorless, tasteless liquid. He started singing. "Love potion number nin-e-ine." He reached in the box and pulled out several glass vials, which he filled with the liquid and tossed into his duffel bag. He continued packing the bag with several oral syringes, which were normally used to administer medication to children.

GHB was initially manufactured around 1969 and once was used as an alternative anesthetic for surgery. Its use was discontinued because of its unpredictability. In the 1980s, GHB was widely available over the counter in many health food stores as a substance that stimulated growth hormone release. In turn, the growth hormone would reduce fat and promote muscle building; as with its surgical use, the result was volatile and unpredictable.

Thomas knew that GHB would enhance his subject's sense of feeling, spike their libido and cause them to want to be touched. The LSD would heighten these effects making the women he selected hornier than they had ever been in life. He also knew that in sufficient amounts the GHB would cause them to fall into a coma-like state where they would be helplessly unable to move. Their brains would be working overtime sensing everything around them with no ability to control physical movement. This was exactly the effect Thomas wanted. He wanted to be in complete control, rendering any female helplessly subject to his fantasies.

With the duffel bag packed, Thomas applied one of the many fake mustaches he stored in his work area. They were odd looking because he made them from hair he collected from two different autopsies, one Black female, the other White. Upon closer examination, one could see the combination of straight and wavy hair. With the mustache set, Thomas slid on a pair of rubber gloves that were so transparent no one would notice that he wore them unless they touched the latex. He pulled a fifty-dollar bill from his wallet, laid it in a dish and poured the organophosphates and LSD over it. Using a wooden clothespin, he hung it to dry. After it dried he slid the treated fifty into a plastic sleeve which he then placed in the inside breast pocket of his jacket.

Five minutes later, Thomas was on his way from Fredericksburg, VA to Washington, DC. Almost an hour later, at 5 p.m. he cruised into the Four Seasons hotel and checked in under an assumed name. He paid in cash and tipped the clerk one hundred dollars so that he would not insist on having a credit card to secure incidentals. Once in his room, he slid the

ANTHONY P. JONES   D8 WITH F8

treated fifty-dollar bill from his breast pocket. After putting on a fresh pair of rubber gloves he slid the bill from its protective sleeve and placed it on one of the pillows on the bed. On the way out he hung a Do Not Disturb sign on the door and let it shut.

Thomas walked out the front door of the hotel and immediately a doorman hailed him a cab. He opened the door and slid in.

"Where to, Sir?" The cab driver asked in a heavy Jamaican accent.

"Let's cruise 14th Street." Thomas answered.

"I know a better area if you prefer."

"That's okay. It's been nine months since I've had a piece of ass, so a hundred-dollar hooker will do as well as a thousand-dollar one. Maybe I'll get lucky and find a neophyte." Thomas noticed every person they passed.

"Yes, sir. They're easy to pick out. Most of them don't know how to shake ass with just the right wiggle yet, so they stand out. I know the perfect spot. How young do you want her?"

Thomas stopped to consider the question. "Hmm, mid twenties should be just about right."

The driver pulled onto 14th Street a few minutes later. He went to an area of the street that the pimps used as a recruiting office. "The pimps don't usually get here before 9, so you should have plenty of time to make your pick."

The driver's words were barely out of his mouth when Thomas' eyes fell on a beautiful young girl. She was wearing a long black dress that was split up one side. Around her neck was a choker with a dream catcher dangling from its center. Her dark satin black hair dangled loosely about her shoulders.

"There, right there." Thomas pointed, noticing the innocence on her face.

"Wow. She's a real looker."

"Pull over quickly!" The driver spun around in the middle of the street ignoring the horn blasts from oncoming traffic. When he pulled in front of the girl, she took a few steps backwards. Thomas rolled down his window. "Hi, you look as if you've just come from the Kennedy Center."

"I'm sorry. This is all I had to wear." She looked frightened and pensive. "I've never done anything like this before."

"That's okay." Thomas looked around. "You're not a cop are you?"

The girl's head quickly darted from side to side. "Where?"

Thomas laughed. "No, no. Not 'a cop!' Are you a cop?"

"You scared me to death!" She placed one hand over her heart. "I thought you said a cop. No, I'm not a cop are you?"

"Hell no! I just want the company of a beautiful woman tonight." Thomas opened the door. "Get in."

She didn't move an inch. "I'm sorry, but you'll have to give me the money up front."

"Stop apologizing. How much do you need?" He flipped through a stack of large domination bills.

She swallowed hard and as convincingly as possible she said, "one-hundred dollars, as long as it's just straight sex."

Thomas nodded as his eyes filled with lust. "Okay, I'll give you fifty now then we'll go to dinner. If we still like each other after that I'll give you the other fifty."

She stood looking at him for a moment remembering that an experienced hooker warned her never to get into any car without getting all the money first. But she was desperately hungry and needed every penny she could get her hands on.

Thomas smiled and extended the fifty. Hesitantly, she reached out for it and stuffed it into her purse.

"Take us to the best restaurant near the Four Seasons." Thomas held out his hand, helping her into the car.

"I know just the place." After a totally silent fifteen-minute ride, the cab driver pulled in front of the Mendocino Grille and Wine Bar.

Thomas handed the driver fifty dollars. "Keep the change."

"Thanks!" He said and put the money into his shirt pocket instead of the lock box.

As they were stepping out of the cab Thomas turned to his date. "You know I forgot to ask your name. I'm Thomas."

"Rachel." She almost gave her last name then remembered another piece of advice, no names. She tried to smile but she was still very uneasy.

Thomas didn't press. "Well Rachel, shall we go in?"

They entered the restaurant, which was unusually quiet tonight. Seating them took less than thirty seconds. Thomas held the chair while Rachel took her seat.

Rachel looked around. "This is a very lovely restaurant."

"Yeah, the cabby knew what he was talking about." For the first time all evening, Thomas began to feel nervous. "Why don't you take a look at the menu while I run to the restroom?"

"Okay." Rachel watched Thomas as he walked away. Even

though she knew this evening had nothing to do with love, she couldn't help but feel Thomas was different from someone who picked her up for a quick fuck. He had treated her with respect so far this evening. If she had not needed the money, she would have spent time with him because he seemed to be a nice guy.

A few minutes later, Thomas returned. "What looks good on the menu?"

"I decided to wait for you. I haven't even opened it yet."

"Why thank you. May I get you a drink?"

Rachel hesitated, folding her hands. "That depends."

"On what?" Thomas stood behind the chair waiting for an answer.

Rachel appeared to be peaking from behind her hands. "Are you having one too?"

"Absolutely. And I don't like to drink alone." Thomas sat down. "What would you like?"

Rachel momentarily looked like a little girl. She hunched her shoulders and scrunched her nose. Almost apologetically, she answered, "I'll have a champagne cocktail."

"Excellent choice." Thomas noticed their waiter was standing by to take their drink orders. He turned and placed the orders. "The lady will have a champagne cocktail and I would like a Gin Ricky. Would you also bring escargot for starters?"

The waiter committed the orders to memory. "Very well, Sir."

Rachel was so hungry that everything on the menu made her mouth water. Right now she could eat anything as long as it eased her hunger pains. Her eyes continued to pan the seafood selections. Each time she saw an entrée that looked good her eyes drifted from left to right to examine the price, which all seemed too expensive to her. One price startled her to make an audible point, "wow!"

Thomas lifted his eyes to Rachel. "Something must look really good."

"Everything looks good. Some of them are just a bit—" Rachel didn't want to sound unsophisticated so she let her voice trail off.

Thomas picked up on Rachel's concern and he wanted to put her at ease. "Oh, I see. Everything on the menu looks good and since they're so inexpensive you want to order more than one. Go for it." Thomas was touched by the fact that Rachel was concerned with how much she was costing him, especially since he had picked her off the street. She seemed different than most women he interacted with, which was a refreshing change. Thomas knew she wasn't anything like Victoria.

Rachel looked into his eyes and smiled. "Thank you."

"Beauty and grace. Those are rare qualities, hard to find in the same person." Thomas sat back in his chair.

Tears began to well in Rachel's eyes. Less than an hour ago, she was just another hooker on 14th Street in DC looking for clients. The man in front of her was being kind and considerate, not at all what she expected from someone who just wanted to use her body as a depository. She wanted to be cautious, but something pushed her onward. "Thank you. You're being very kind. To be honest, I really don't understand why. I haven't done anything to deserve it."

"Sure you have. You agreed to come to dinner with me. That took trust, even given what you say you have chosen to do for a living. Let me tell you how I see it." Shyly, Rachel nodded for him to continue. "I believe you when you said this is your first time. Your eyes still hold their innocence even though there is great sadness there as well. Until we arrived at the restaurant, you were very tense. Since we have been here, you have not one time rushed. If your profession was that of the others I saw on 14th Street you would be rushing me, or you would have demanded much more money for the evening. I think you're a victim of circumstances. You didn't choose to be out there tonight, you just had no other choice. How am I doing so far?"

She moved her head up and down. Finally, past the lump in her throat she answered. "So far so good."

"What I don't know is what brought you to this point. Would you like to talk about it?"

Still struggling, Rachel swallowed hard. "I guess it'll be alright. Just give me a minute." After dabbing her eyes, she looked into her glass, avoiding direct eye contact. Her fingers rolled the champagne flute back and forth. "I left home a few years ago in the hopes of finding a new life. Things there had not been pleasant for some time. I just couldn't take it another day, so I left the Creek reservation in Alabama and came here to Washington."

Rachel struggled to get her next words out. Several times her mouth opened but no sound ever made it to her lips. "I was abused by my father since I was sixteen. He even brought my brothers in to watch once in a while. If anyone tried to say anything, he beat us, especially my mother." Pain and confusion covered her face. "Still, she should have defended me. I guess she wasn't strong enough to help. He convinced her he was acting within his missionary rights. If he is a representative of God, then I want no part of it." Tears streamed down the sides of Rachel's face.

Thomas reached across the table and brushed away her tears. "Somebody should rip that son of a bitch's heart out and send him back to his God. He doesn't deserve to live." Thomas didn't try to hide the rage on his face. After a few seconds his expression softened. "I do know what you're feeling."

Rachel shook her head. "I'm not sure anyone knows what I'm feeling."

"I do." Thomas insisted. "I had to endure something similar. My mother abused me until my father found out."

Rachel looked up. The look on her face turned from one of despair to concern. "What happened?"

Thomas looked away. He seemed to be lost a million miles from their table. Hearing her question caused him to relive his ordeal, although he had only been silent for a few seconds, it seemed an eternity. Still looking away, he began to speak. "It ain't worth talking about." He put his hand over his mouth and sat a while longer. "Suffice it to say she really had me messed up for a long time. She almost ruined my life."

Rachel reached out for his hand. "Oh my God! I'm sorry, Thomas."

He slid his hand in hers. "You don't have to be. You didn't have anything to do with it."

"For the moment, Rachel forgot about her own problems and concentrated on Thomas'." "I don't understand how any parent could abuse a child. What's worse is the other parent letting it happen."

Thomas played with a knife in his free hand. "In my case, Dad didn't let it happen."

Rachel was looking at Thomas, but he continued looking off in the distance. Her tears were flowing rapidly, as much for Thomas as for herself. Rather than saying the wrong words, she squeezed his hand tighter. After seemingly being stuck in space, his eyes returned her gaze.

"You see, I do understand." The muscles in his face tightened, contorting his face in what seemed to be as much in anger as in pain.

"I'm sorry, Thomas. I didn't know you had suffered something similar to me. I guess we're two of a kind."

Thomas didn't answer. He just looked at Rachel and smiled.

The waiter who had been watching their exchange now saw an opportunity to move in and take their orders. "Hello folks. Here is your escargot. I hope you're finding everything else on the menu to your liking."

Thomas welcomed the change of subject. "We certainly are. Rachel is so hungry that she may want to order more than one item."

"Thomas!" Rachel's voice rose as if she was offended, but her face was red with mild embarrassment.

"What ever she wants she can have. What's your favorite item on the menu?" Thomas asked the waiter.

"I'm partial to the seafood items." He quickly answered.

"Great, then bring us three of your best dishes." Thomas handed him their menus.

"Yes, sir." The waiter left to place the orders.

"Who's the third meal for Thomas?" Rachel asked playfully.

"It's just in case you don't like one of the other two."

They watched the waiter walk towards the kitchen.

"So, what do you really want to do in life?" Thomas asked bluntly, even though he appeared more visibly relaxed.

The question caught Rachel off guard. She looked down at her hands unsure why Thomas had asked this question. Her dreams of a better life consumed her thoughts and a gleam came to her eyes. She lifted her face to answer the question. "I want to go to college to study Psychology. After getting my doctorate I want to help kids that are helplessly caught in abusive relationships. I think it would help me to heal myself while I help others at the same time."

"That's an admirable ambition. What's keeping you from getting started?" Thomas could see that his question stung.

Rachel tried to laugh and again looked down. "Money, a school that will accept me, a different line of work, take your choice."

"Maybe I can help." Thomas offered.

"Yeah, right. That's why you picked me up tonight." Rachel's voice was sharp with sarcasm.

Thomas ignored her response. "Of course, I'll have to know how to get in touch with you again." Before he could finish his thought he looked up and saw the waiter approaching. "Aah, here comes dinner. I'll wrestle you for first bite."

"I'm starving. You won't stand a chance against me." Rachel raised her fork like Anthony Perkins raised his knife in *Psycho* and offered her best imitation of the sound effects.

Thomas put his hands up. "Okay, you win. You can try all three before I lift my fork."

Rachel almost drooled as the aroma of the food hit her nose. The waiter barely got all three plates down before she began to take a bite.

"This is heavenly."

"Is it safe for me to take a bite yet?" Thomas finally asked, holding his fork a safe distance away.

Rachel scooped up another bite of food. "If you want any you'd best dig in."

They ate, laughed and talked like two old friends that were trying to catch up on the past few years. When they finished Thomas paid the bill and they stood to leave. They reached the sidewalk and dark clouds seemed to envelope them. The short walk to the hotel was completely silent. Rachel attempted a smile to reassure Thomas during their elevator ride to his room, but his demeanor had totally changed. Repeatedly, he clinched his teeth flexing his jaw muscles. His brows nearly unified as he drew them together tightly in a frown. Even his walking movements became stiff.

Thomas opened the door to his room. He began speaking, all care removed from his voice. "Your other fifty is on the pillow. I'm going to take a shower, fix yourself a drink if you'd like to." He walked towards the bathroom without looking back

For the first time since she entered the cab, Rachel felt dirty. She wrapped her arms around her body attempting to comfort herself with a hug. The deed was now at hand. As wonderful as she felt earlier, at this moment she was just a whore. Her hands were shaking as she opened the liquor cabinet. "Shall I fix you one also?"

"Yeah. Throw me a Jack Black on the rocks." Thomas answered emotionlessly before closing the bathroom door.

Rachel sat Thomas' drink on the nightstand and walked around to the other side of the bed where the fifty-dollar bill laid waiting. She sat on the side of the bed and took a sip of her drink. The tears rolled down her face as the warm liquor raced down her throat. She gulped the rest of the drink and rose to fix another. She sat back down on the bed and reached down to remove her shoes. Then she looked down at the money on the pillow. Hesitantly, she reached for the bill as if she sensed it was too heavy to lift.

Thomas stood just behind the bathroom door with his ear pressed against it. He was waiting for any sound that indicated Rachel had touched the bill. Then he heard a glass hit the floor. He rushed from the bathroom still fully clothed. His initial look of concern was replaced by jubilee. His victim took the bait and it worked perfectly. Rachel fell crosswise on the bed and still had the fifty-dollar bill in her hand. Thomas rushed over and took her pulse. She was alive. He reached into his pocket, pulled out surgical gloves, an oral syringe and a vial containing the GHB. He slid on the gloves and took the fifty from Rachel's hand and placed it into a plastic zipper bag. He filled the syringe, opened Rachel's mouth, inserted the syringe and depressed the plunger.

Rachel coughed as the GHB slid down her throat. Thomas felt his hardness strain against the zipper of his pants anticipating what would come next. He ripped her clothes off and grabbed Rachel's head tilting it back and opening her mouth. "Now bitch you'll get exactly what you deserve. I'm going to fuck you until you choke."

A pitiful whining sound escaped Rachel's mouth and tears again slid from her closed eyes. The anger on Thomas' face melted into a look of pain. He gently laid Rachel's head back on the pillow and sat beside her on the edge of the bed. He slammed the heels of both hands against his forehead and slid them down his face. "What the hell am I doing? She has seen enough pain for four lifetimes, she doesn't deserve this."

Thomas rose from the bed and returned to the bathroom to seek relief from his tension in the shower. He was accustomed to relieving himself, though each time he did his hatred for Victoria grew even stronger. "If I ever see that bitch again I'm going to push this up her ass until I see the head come out of her mouth." He stood in the shower letting the water pelt his body until he had regained control over his senses.

Thomas returned to the bedroom and found Rachel asleep on top of the covers. He tucked her in and climbed in beside her, pulling her close to him. He kissed her on the back of the neck and looked at the clock, 2:00 a.m. In four and a half hours, he had to be up and headed to Charlottesville to go over Sarah's crime scene for the second time. Instantly, he fell asleep.

Chapter
3

The Four Seasons Hotel, located in historic Georgetown, rose from the ground with the look of old world red bricks. The angles and peaks formed by the bricks were as precise and lavish as was the interior of the hotel. Schaffer arrived an hour before he was to speak and walked into the Corcoran ballroom. The room was immaculately prepared to receive the invited guest; everywhere his eyes fell was a reminder of the hotel's grandness. Oriental rugs graced the floors and the tables in the ballroom were set so exact, Miss Manners would have to think twice before reaching for something on the table.

Rather than going to his seat at the head table, Schaffer sat at Joe's table to review his speech. He never liked to speak from an organized paper, however today he wanted to make sure he covered several topics. The note cards were just there to make sure he didn't miss any important issues about his time in Cuba.

After fifteen minutes Schaffer was about half way through the speech when he heard footsteps and a voice from behind. "Is this Joe DeApuzzo's table?"

Even though intrigued by her deep throaty vibrato, he didn't immediately look up, but answered. "Yes it is."

"Wow, that's some pen. Where'd you pick that up?"

"Thanks, it's a David Oscarson, Celestial. I get all my pens from Paradise Pen." Slowly, Schaffer turned from his speech in the direction of the voice. His eyes strained to remain on the papers even though his head had already moved.

Schaffer did a double take when he saw the face that accompanied the voice, her smile lit up the room. "Oh, I'm sorry. How rude of me." He jumped from his chair; totally losing his composure he looked more like a schoolboy than an award-winning reporter. "I'm Schaffer O'Grady. Please have a seat."

Schaffer began memorizing everything about the woman in front of him. Her café au lait colored skin was smooth and clung to her five foot nine inch body. He looked into her deep brown eyes that were filled with life and the wisdom of an old soul. Her nose and cheek bones left no doubt of her Native American Heritage. His eyes caressed beautifully formed lips, noting that the bottom lip pouted slightly as it rested above her chiseled chin.

The woman graciously nodded towards Schaffer. "So, you're the person we've come to hear. From what I've been told you won't disappoint your audience. I look forward to your presentation."

"Thanks. Can I get you anything?" Schaffer fumbled with the cards in his hands. He fidgeted, moving his arms from a folded position to putting one hand in his pockets then finally, letting both arms rest by his sides.

She smiled at Schaffer's schoolboy charm. "I've heard the Four Seasons is known for great service, but I thought that was a waiter's job. Not the guest of honor."

Schaffer helped her with her chair as she sat down. "I don't think I got your name."

"Now look who's being rude. My name is Renita Duplechain."

Even though Joe gave Schaffer Renita's name yesterday, the stupefaction brought on by her allure prevented his immediate recognition. "So, how do you know Joe?"

"We met at my office a few years ago. He's a nice guy, so we've remained friends. I even bought a house in his neighborhood."

"Joe's always liked being friends with beautiful women, but I've never heard anyone call him a nice guy. I guess he tried to turn on the charm around you. What kind of work do you do?"

Renita smiled. "I'm an FBI agent."

As if someone had just turned on the electricity in his brain Schaffer responded. "Oh-my-gosh!"

Renita tilted her head to one side and her eyebrows raised slightly. "Is something wrong?"

"Not at all! Joe mentioned yesterday that he had invited an FBI agent to the luncheon. I just hadn't expected—"

Renita's face was more serious now. "A woman?"

"No, no. He said you'd be a woman. He just didn't elaborate." Quickly, he changed directions. "He did say that you graduated from Xavier. So, I guess we have something in common."

"Oh, is that right?" Renita's smile was even more brilliant. "When was the last time you were on campus?" She asked.

Schaffer sat down. "It's been years. I need to get back."

"Yes you do. I try to get back for homecoming every year. Of course, I call it a recruiting trip. It helps when my rich uncle pays for it." Renita held up her FBI shield.

"I'm going to have to make it a point to get back this year. Has the school changed much?"

"Other than buying up all the surrounding land and putting up several buildings not much has changed." Renita tried to sound as pleasantly sarcastic as possible.

One of the waiters for the afternoon saw them sitting at the table and walked over to offer his services. "May I get you something while you wait for the others to arrive?"

It was difficult, but Schaffer managed to take his eyes off of Renita and look at the waiter. "Absolutely. May we have two glasses and a bottle of your 1997 Hendry Cab?"

"Excellent choice sir. I'll get it right away."

Schaffer held up one finger keeping the waiter in place for a moment. "I'm sorry. I forgot to ask if you were on duty, or if you even liked red wine."

"It's okay. I love red wine and I took the day off." Renita folded her hands and placed them on the table in front of her. "Are you a connoisseur?"

"Huh?" Schaffer's face wrinkled with confusion. "Oh, you mean the wine." Renita nodded. "No. I just stumbled over this one and it was great. It's from a small vineyard in California. Boy do they make a great Cab even though they're known for their Chardonnays. I asked the hotel to have this one for today. For years, the Hendry Ranch Vineyard had supplied grapes to Opus One. Luckily, George finally decided to make his own wine."

"You're on a first-name basis with the vintner? I can't wait to taste it."

The waiter promptly arrived with the wine and glasses. After he poured both of them a glass, Schaffer raised his glass towards Renita. "Here's to new friendships." Just as he finished his toast he saw Joe enter from the back of the room.

"Well, I see you two have hit it off." Joe managed not to look pleased as he shouted across the room.

Schaffer looked at Joe then back to Renita. "Would you excuse me for a moment?"

"Certainly." Renita took a sip of her wine and lifted Schaffer's pen to take a closer look.

Schaffer left the table to intercept Joe before he reached the table. When they met, Schaffer he threw his arm around Joe and spun him in the opposite direction. "Why didn't you give me a heads-up about Renita? God, she's beautiful!"

"Damn Schaffer! She's too young for you. You said you don't like them young. Just keep it strictly business. I told you this is not a fix-you-up."

"You said she finished Xavier ten tears after me. She can't be that young."

"I didn't say when she finished. Besides, she's not your type. Don't you remember?" Joe paused. "I have no taste in women? You're just here to meet with her about your next assignment."

"There's something you're not telling me. What's the downside?" Schaffer asked with some urgency.

"Shit, you mean to tell me the great reporter, Schaffer O'Grady hasn't figured it out yet? You're already buying the woman drinks. I would have thought you would have gotten the woman's pedigree by now. You must be getting too old for the job." Joe freed himself from Schaffer's grasp.

"Alright— I'm your bitch!" Schaffer threw his hands up in surrender. "I know I said I didn't want you to try to fix me up again, but she's special. Come on Joe, I can see it in her eyes."

Joe pushed his finger against his cheek. "I'll have to think about it. I'm not sure she would believe me now— no it just won't work."

"What do you mean?" Schaffer asked with a hint of panic in his voice.

"I already told her that you were a self-centered worthless piece of shit. I'm not sure I can undo that. I'm very convincing you know." Joe took tremendous pleasure in Schaffer's anguish.

"Gee thanks."

"What the hell did you expect? Everyone else I've introduced you to you acted like 'Jack Fucking Frost.' Renita is too nice a person to be hurt by the likes of you. Don't you think we should be getting back to the table? I don't want to leave her alone too long. The guy I invited to meet her should be here soon. I'm sure she's got to be tired of listening to you babble." Joe started walking towards the table.

"Yeah, let's go." Schaffer followed. "Take care of me Joe."

Joe waved Schaffer off as if he was dismissing him. Renita was glad to see them return and hoped that Schaffer had some interest in her.

As soon as they reached the table Joe opened his arms wide. "Hello sweetheart." He kissed Renita on the cheek and gave her a bear hug. For the moment Schaffer wanted to be in Joe's skin.

"Joe, you always did give the best hugs. What's new?" Renita hugged him again.

"From the looks at this table, I'd have to say you two."

"Oh, stop." Renita lovingly put her hand on Joe's chest.

Joe noticed Schaffer's pen in her hand. "Oh, God, don't tell me you wrote with that pen; he'll have a conniption."

Renita admired the pen a moment longer then held it in Schaffer's direction and turned her attention to Joe. "Joe, he's right to protect it; you should never let anyone else use your fountain pen, it could damage the nib."

Schaffer cocked his mouth to one side, folded his arms across his chest and looked at Joe out of the side of his eyes. Just as his mouth started to open, Joe's hand rose.

"Wan, wan, wan. You should stop your bitching. If that pen is so precious leave it at home."

Renita put the pen in Schaffer's hand. "You're missing the point, Joe."

Schaffer edged his way back into the conversation. "Just ignore him Renita, he's a big kid."

Joe didn't turn Renita loose. He looked at Schaffer and hoped he was filled with envy. "Well, you know what they say."

"What's that?" Schaffer crossed his arms.

"Kids always call it like they see it. I leave you alone with my girl for a couple of minutes and you're buying her wine, making goo goo eyes with her and hell, you even let her touch your precious pen." Joe kissed Renita again hoping to add to Schaffer's envy.

She held Joe's arm and laughed. "Give him a break Joe. Schaffer's a nice guy."

"Listen to the lady. If you don't she'll have to run you in on abuse charges." They sat down at the table. "I would ask you if you wanted a glass of wine, but I think you've already been tilting the bottle at your desk." Schaffer motioned to the waiter to bring another glass.

"How'd you know about my abusiveness? And here I thought I'd hidden it from everyone. Sure, I'll have a glass of Ripple with you." Joe joked.

"Sorry, Renita. You can dress them up but you can't take them out." The glass arrived and Schaffer poured Joe a teaspoon of wine in it.

"Okay boys. I'm impressed with you both." Renita touched each of their shoulders. "There's no need for one-upmanship. Let's play nice."

"Alright, but only because you say so." Schaffer filled Joe's glass. "Now I know why you've been hiding her. I'm calling Nina, 'as in Simone' right now." Schaffer lifted his IPhone and pretended to dial.

Renita looked at Schaffer puzzled. "As in Simone?"

"Yeah." Schaffer answered. "That's how Joe first mentioned Nina and I've called her that ever since."

"Go ahead." Joe said confidently. "She's got Tina at the zoo. Good luck finding her." Joe took a gulp of wine.

Renita sat back in her chair and looked at Schaffer. For the first time since they'd met she became apprehensive. She knew the question that Schaffer was about to ask. He looked at Joe and then towards Renita. "Who's Tina?"

Renita turned her attention to Joe. Her eyes seemed weak and pleading. Joe flashed his best shit-eating grin and answered the question. "Tina is the beautiful young daughter of a certain FBI agent friend of mine."

Renita held her breath waiting for Schaffer's response. Most men still ran from women with children, especially in DC where they outnumbered men three to one. Extra baggage just wasn't in the equation when the pickings were so bountiful.

"I see." Schaffer looked at Renita as if she lost her luster. "Of course, she would have to be beautiful, just look at her mother. How long are they going to be at the zoo?"

"I told Nina we would call her after we were finished here. Then we're going to meet them for ice cream." Joe said proudly.

"I'll drive! Oh yeah, but since the Vette only seats two, you'll have to ride in the trunk, Joe. After all, the top's down. I wouldn't want to get all four of your hairs out of place Joe." Schaffer laughed and winked in Renita's direction.

Renita laughed too, but tried to hide it behind her hand. "Thanks, Schaffer. I'd love to ride with you."

Schaffer tried to think ahead. "Do we need to make arrangements to come back and pick up your car?"

"No. I took the subway. Joe met me at the station and dropped me off here. Excuse me boys, I need to go to the lady's room." Renita sensed they needed some time alone, Schaffer probably had questions for Joe.

Both the men stood and watched Renita as she left the room. Schaffer punched Joe's shoulder. "Joe DeApuzzo, you sneaky bastard! I thought this wasn't a setup?" His voice danced with excitement.

"It wasn't my idea." Joe sat down and clutched his wine glass. "Nina came up with the entire plan. I told her you couldn't be bothered with kids. She said, nonsense! Renita is the nicest girl we know and Tina's the perfect kid. Not like the bimbos I usually fix you up with.

However, I have to warn you."

Schaffer cut him off. "So you admit the other women you introduced me to were bimbos, or were those Nina's words?" He paused a second. "Why do you want to warn me?"

Joe's face held no sign of amusement and his voice conveyed his absolute seriousness. "If you hurt her I'll personally cut your nuts off."

"I'm not worried about you old man. Renita is the first stable woman you've ever introduced me to. All the others had all the boobs and ass a man could want. They just forgot to go through the brain line before coming to earth." Schaffer jammed his finger to his head. "Renita's beautiful and smart." He looked down, turning his attention to the glass in his hand. "I've only believed in love at first sight once, until today. It's crazy, I keep hearing Etta James singing *At Last*."

Joe dropped back in his chair, shaking his head from side to side. "This is just fucking amazing! Nina said this would happen."

"Mom always said when I found the right one I'd know. I haven't known Renita for an hour yet and I'm sure she's the perfect woman."

Joe threw his hands in the air. "This is unbelievable!"

"What's unbelievable?" Renita asked as she returned to the table.

"This guy across from me. He's a real piece of work." Joe halfheartedly tossed his hand in Schaffer's direction.

Schaffer looked around the room. He had been too wrapped up in the notion of Renita to notice all the people arriving. "I guess I'd better get ready. Renita, I can't wait to get ice cream." Schaffer started towards his place on the stage.

Renita's face was filled with anticipation and pride. "I can't wait to hear you speak. Break a leg, or whatever you're supposed to say."

"Thanks. Please keep that old man out of trouble and out of your hair until I get back." Schaffer walked to the head table.

Joe pointed towards the stage. "Get your butt up there where you're supposed to be. Hurry before your head swells some more and you need someone to carry it for you. It's so big now no one will be able to sit next to you."

"I love you too, Joe. I'll see you two in a few minutes." Schaffer stepped onto the elevated podium separating him from the people on the floor.

He was barely out of listening range before Renita's questions began. "Do you think having a daughter frightened him?" She leaned her head against her hands, which were clasped to one side.

"If his nose opens any wider small children and pets better not get close when he inhales." Joe unfolded his napkin and threw it in his lap.

Renita looked confused. "What are you talking about?"

Joe leaned on the table. "Don't tell me you've never heard that expression before."

"I can't say that I have." She moved her hands to the table.

"Suffice it to say that describing him as smitten is a gross understatement. The real question is what do you think?" Joe took a drink while looking at Renita curiously.

"If everything you and Nina said is true, I'm going to cuff his wrist to mine and throw away the key." She gestured as if throwing a key over her shoulder.

"I think I'm going to puke." Joe put his middle finger in his mouth. "All bullshit aside, I love him like a son. He's a great person, even if he is weird." Joe laughed and grabbed Renita's hand. "If you ever repeat what I just said, I'll turn you in for perjury."

For a moment she even let herself dream about the possibilities of a relationship. "Not to worry; your secret's safe with me."

During their conversation the room had filled with people. Schaffer was introduced to the enthusiastic gathering. He started to describe his time in Cuba and the room grew so quiet he could hardly hear a fork touching a plate. Schaffer's attention however was focused on the beautiful young lady next to his boss. He couldn't wait to really get to know her and her daughter, Tina.

This day started off beautifully and was only getting better. Nina's plan worked flawlessly, Schaffer was hooked.

Chapter
4

At twelve noon, just as Schaffer began speaking to his gathered audience, Rachel slowly awoke in her room on the fourth floor. The drugs, alcohol and stress of her life kept her out cold all night.

The grittiness in her eyes glued them together. Rachel raised her hands to wipe away the sticky deposit of the night's sleep. Her eyes began to focus and she looked around before sitting up. The room appeared larger than she remembered. There was no sign of Thomas. No sounds emanated from the bathroom, Rachel assumed that she was alone. She sat up and held the covers over her bare breasts. Softly, she called out. "Thomas, are you here?"

There was no answer. Rachel reached for the thick terrycloth robe that waited for her at the foot of the bed and placed it around her body. She looked in the bathroom to confirm that Thomas was not there. She walked back to the bed and sat on its edge. The last thing she remembered was fixing a drink and sitting on the side of the bed. The absence of memory sent a chill across her causing her to rub her hands over her arms to ward off the rapidly approaching goose bumps.

Rachel walked over to the window and peaked out. One memory rushed to her consciousness, Thomas brought her here to have sex. She placed her hand down near her crotch; internally she felt none of the lingering sensations of intercourse. They had not had sex. For the moment she was puzzled. She looked around for her clothes, but saw nothing.

Rachel opened the curtains and light fell across the room. Looking around she saw an envelope that had been placed under the front of the door. It looked as if someone had pushed it beneath the door during the night. Walking towards the envelope, she noticed her name on the front.

Rachel squatted down and lifted the envelope. For a moment she just looked at her name. She couldn't imagine what it could be and gave it a squeeze as if she was trying to determine what was in a Christmas present. Her long narrow finger easily slid behind the envelope flap. Gently ripping it open, she reached in and pulled out a note and another envelope. On the outside of the note, "read me first" blared in bright red.

Rachel sat on the floor in a lotus position. She leaned back against the bed, opened the note and began to read.

"Dear Rachel,

Thank you for a beautiful night. It felt good to hold you throughout the night without further expectations. I would love to see you again if you would do me a favor. Sorry to put a condition on this, but I feel it is important.

I want you to get off the streets and follow your dreams. I have left you a little something to get you started. Oh yeah, your clothes tore when I was taking them off last night so there's a package waiting for you at the front desk. Call down when you want them brought up.

I paid for the hotel room for a week. Find an apartment near Georgetown University, and then contact Fr. John in the admissions office. He'll help you with school.

Call me if you would like to. My number is (804) 554-4736. I hope to hear from you soon.

Thomas

Rachel held the second envelope clutched to her breasts for a long time. Her heart beat franticly with anticipation. Finally, she opened it with one quick rip. Pulling her knees to her chest, she held the envelope in front of her face, slid in her thumb and forefinger and lifted its contents. A check slid out, Thomas Brothers was in the upper left hand corner, no address, and no phone number. She continued to pull the check out, seeing the dollar figure written on it, all the breath left her body and her head fell to her knees.

When Rachel lifted her head she could not control the flowing tears. She held her hand over her mouth. "Oh my God, Thomas. Forty thousand dollars." This was the kindest act anyone ever did for her. She jumped up and ran over to the phone and punched in Thomas's number. She expected to leave a message and was surprised when he answered.

"Hello."

Her voice was quiet and still a little shaky. "Hi, Thomas. I really don't know what to say. Thank you."

"That sounds just fine to me. So do we have a deal?" Thomas smiled, relieved that she sounded happy.

"Believe me I never want to see 14th street again!" Rachel said. Then struggling for the words, she continued. "I'll pay you back as soon as I can."

"You'll pay me back by becoming a psychologist and of course, staying in touch." Thomas flashed a prideful smile.

"I'm going to be hard to get rid of. Let me know if I'm calling too much. Oh, God, Thomas thanks. I can't wait to get started. I'm going to open a bank account and look for an apartment this afternoon." Thomas had answered her prayers and given her dreams wings.

"Get a cell phone too. Don't forget to give me the number. I've got to go now. There's a lot of traffic out here. The road needs my full attention; the rain is coming down in sheets. Call me in a few days."

"I will. I'll talk to you soon." She paused. Then she said the words he had hoped for, "Thomas, I love you."

"Great. Bye now." Thomas hung up the phone.

Rachel looked outside at the sun and wondered where Thomas was in the rain. Dismissing the thought she pushed the numbers to call the front desk. This was better than any Christmas she could remember or wanted to remember. Desperation gave way to redemption, now she would be able to begin again— as long as the check didn't bounce.

Chapter
5

The crowd that had listened to Schaffer began to thin. Off to one side in the front of the room, he stood finishing his last television interview with Channel 4.

Out of the corner of his eye he watched Renita and Joe as they waited patiently near the entrance at the opposite end of the room. Renita talked to Joe laughing and smiling. They had only met about two hours ago and already Schaffer couldn't wait until he could see more of her smile.

A reporter from channel 4 asked, "You've thrilled us with your stories from Cuba and your all too short time at the White House. What's next on your agenda?"

Schaffer smiled, he felt his next words should be, *I'm going to Disney World.* Instead he pointed towards Joe. "See that man over there. He gives me all my assignments. However, that lady next to him has invited me to get an ice cream cone. So, right now I'm going for ice cream. Thanks for coming guys."

"Wait! Is she a love interest?" The reporter shouted still trying to get more.

"We just met a couple of hours ago. How does one tell in such a short time? That's all guys. My ice cream is waiting. I'll talk to you all later." Schaffer waved and walked over to Renita and Joe. "Let's get moving before someone else stops us."

"That was an interesting exchange. Why was he pointing his camera over here?" Renita nodded in the direction of the cameraman and reporter, who was still speaking into his microphone.

"He wanted to know if you were my love interest." Schaffer answered flashing a toothy grin as he touched her arm.

"What did you tell him?" She asked wondering what he thought.

Schafer managed to look serious. "I told him that I had to go because you two wanted to take me out for a quickie."

Renita's face turned red. "No you didn't!"

"Don't worry, I told them we were getting ice cream first. And of course I told him that the quickie thing was off the record." He held out his hand for Renita and Joe to lead the way.

Renita punched Schaffer in the chest, playfully. "I should break a couple of your ribs."

"Naw, what you should do is pull out your Glock and give him a new asshole." Joe put his arm around Renita. "Come on, the girls are waiting."

Schaffer felt a hand grasping his shoulder. "Where do you think you're running off to— Sugar?"

Schaffer stopped cold and all humor left his face. Renita turned to see who was there. Schaffer placed both hands on his hips. "My dear General Roseboro, what did I tell you about calling me that?"

Schaffer spun and threw his arms around Dee. They laughed, hugged and exchanged a brief kiss. "Dee, you look great. How are things at the 'Big House?"

Dee held on to his arm. "It's not the same without you there to stir things up. But, judging from this scene, I'd have to say that you're doing just fine." Dee nodded towards Renita.

Schaffer reached out for Renita's hand. "General Deidre Roseboro, this is Special Agent Renita Duplechain and the short bald guy there is my boss, Joe DeApuzzo."

Renita took Dee's hand. "Pleased to meet you."

Dee didn't immediately answer, but instead looked at Schaffer. "Is this your girlfriend?"

Schaffer let his gaze alternate between the women. His twisted lips and evil eyebrow raise let everyone know mischief was waiting to free itself. "If there is a God! But, we haven't had a chance to discuss it; we just met a couple of hours ago."

"Well, Sugar, you never did take long to make up your mind." She turned back to Renita." He's a good man— a little paranoid at times, but his heart is in the right place. Be good to him. If I were about eight years younger, I'd wrestle you for him."

Renita smiled warmly. "It wouldn't be a fair fight. You're much more adept at matters of warfare than I, I wouldn't stand a chance."

"I like her, Sugar. We should all get together sometime. I'll give you a call." Dee left for the White House.

"She's quite a pistol."

"That's an understatement!" Schaffer started walking towards the exit.

Schaffer and Renita both looked at Joe, who was unusually quiet. "What?"

"Just making sure you were still here. It's not like you to stay so quiet during such an interesting discourse." Schaffer winked at Renita.

"What did you want me to say, she's the damn Chairwoman of the Joint Chiefs of Staff." Joe picked up his pace. "Let's get the hell out of here before we get stuck here all night."

They entered the elevator for the short ride to the lobby. Two floors later, the doors opened. As Renita stepped from the elevator a young woman ran into her knocking her back into the elevator.

"I'm sorry. I wasn't paying attention. I should have waited until I was sure there was no one coming off before I barged in." The young woman reached out to catch the door.

"Are you okay?" Renita asked the woman. "You seem a bit upset."

The startled woman's eyes darted back and forth, scanning the people that filled the lobby as if they were chasing her. "I'm fine, thank you."

Schaffer looked over at the young woman. "Rachel? I thought I recognized that voice. What are you doing here?" She seemed shocked at the question. He quickly recovered. "On second thought, don't answer that. I shouldn't be so nosey."

"Hi, Schaffer. Can I talk to you for a moment?" Rachel took his hand giving it a firm squeeze.

"We're just heading over to pick up Renita's daughter and get some ice cream. Would you like to come?" Schaffer asked trying to calm her jitters.

"I can't, but thanks for asking. What I really need is your advice. Do you mind if I call you later?"

"Not at all. Do you still have my cell number? She nodded that she did and Schaffer looked at his watch. "Call me around four. I should still be in town."

"Thanks. I'll talk to you then."

She tiptoed and kissed him on the cheek. Renita looked very uneasy, unsure of the problem and moved in a little closer searching for information. Schaffer could also see Joe getting pissed— his eyes could never lie. They watched as Rachel got on the elevator and the doors closed.

Before either Renita or Joe had a chance to question Schaffer he put his arm on Renita's shoulder. "She's going to be alright, she's just had a difficult life." He turned and started walking to the front door of the hotel. "We met about two years ago when I was researching my story on DC's hookers."

"What kind of research were you doing?" Joe asked too abruptly to be viewed as anything other than an accusation, even though he had approved the story.

"Take it easy, Joe. She had just hit the streets when I began my research. I was her first client, of sorts. I took her to get some food and listened to her story. It was the saddest thing I have ever heard. Her dad and brothers sexually abused her for years. After she couldn't take it any more, she ended up here. With no skills she couldn't find a job. Unfortunately, she remembered how to do one thing and knew she could get paid for it. I paid her for the week and kept her with me during my interviews. I told everyone she was my assistant. The truth is, I wanted to keep her off the streets. I gave her some money to help while she looked for something else. Rachel dreamed of going to college to become a psychologist. It doesn't look like she made it." Schaffer shook his head and looked at the ground.

"Is that the girl you had me get the job for at the warehouse?" Joe's expression softened.

"That's her. She hasn't been in touch lately. The last time I heard from her, her roommate had just moved out and she needed some extra cash." Schaffer continually shook his head.

Joe interjected. "Looks like she got a promotion; how else could she be spending time at the Four Seasons."

"Stop being so cynical, Joe. I gave her the money because I wanted her to feel as if someone cared. Hope is all she had— if you take that, what's left? I doubt she still has any of the money left I gave her, it's been a while."

Renita glanced at Schaffer looking concerned, but not about Schaffer's interaction. "Remember guys, I'm a profiler. Something is disturbing that young lady and it's not the fact that she spent a night at this hotel with some man who could care less."

Schaffer wanted to change the subject. "I guess I'll find out at four. For now, let's get the cars. I need some ice cream."

They walked out the front door and Joe and Schaffer handed the attendant the keys for their cars. Two young men bolted from sight to fetch the cars. Seconds later they could hear the familiar roar of the Vette's engine.

The Vette came out first. The valet held the door for Schaffer. "She's beautiful, sir. If you ever want to get rid of her please give me a call." He handed Schaffer a card with his name and numbers written on it.

"I can't let her go. We've been together too long." Schaffer handed him a ten and walked around to open the door for Renita. When he got in he raced the engine a couple of times and looked over at Joe. "Want to race old man?"

"Trying to show off again? You can't impress Renita that easily. Besides, if you break the law she'll have to arrest you. Not that that's a bad thing." Joe's tires squealed as he bolted from the Four Season's driveway into the always-heavy DC traffic.

Schaffer followed and by the time he hit third gear Joe could only be seen in the rearview mirror.

Renita looked over to him smirking and shaking her head. "Boys, muscle cars and testosterone...what a combination."

Chapter
6

Renita and Schaffer pulled into the National Zoo's parking lot. Sixty seconds later, Joe arrived and parked next to them. "What took you so long old man? Did you forget to sit on your pillow?" Schaffer leaned against the side of his car.

"Don't ask me to bail you out when you get arrested for speeding." Joe slammed his door; his face was red with anger. He felt jealous even though he only wanted to be friends with Renita.

"You forget I'm chauffeuring a cop around." Schaffer tilted his head towards Renita.

Renita begged out, waving her hands like a referee indicating an incomplete pass. "You boys are on your own. I'm not getting pulled into your game, snipe-for-snipe."

"See Joe, I don't need your help, I'm winning." Schaffer looked around the parking area for Nina. "I believe there are two other young ladies waiting for us. Let's join them before you get into trouble." Schaffer grabbed Joe's shoulder.

"You seem very anxious to get some ice cream, or to meet my daughter, which is it?" Renita asked Schaffer, truly interested in his answer.

Schaffer stopped walking and focused ahead along their path. "Both."

"Why?" Renita looked at the side of Schaffer's face noticing the far-off look.

Slowly, he turned to face her coming out of his trance. "Well, the ice cream speaks for itself. As far as meeting your daughter is concerned, kids don't lie because they still operate on instinct. Their first impressions are usually correct, so once Tina meets me you'll know you can trust me." Schaffer placed his hand over his heart.

Renita raised her eyebrows. "Her instincts are unusually good. I guess she inherited that from her mom."

"Mommy!" Tina yelled and ran towards Renita as fast as her long, thin legs could carry her.

"Hey baby. Are you having a good time?" Renita wrapped her arms around her daughter.

"Yeah. Can we get some ice cream now? Nina said we could as

soon as you got here." Tina tugged Renita's hand leaning her weight to encourage movement.

"That's Aunt Nina to you young lady! Aren't you being a little rude? You haven't said hi to Uncle Joe and you haven't met—"

"Hi Uncle Joe. Mommy, I know who he is, Schaffer. Oops, I mean Mr. Schaffer. Aunt Nina told me all about him." Tina pulled Renita close to her and whispered in her ear. "What do you think about him? He seems pretty cool to me."

Renita laughed. "Oh he does, does he? You are too much! What am I going to do with you?"

"Remember, you said I was a good profiler. Since I've done my job I would say ice cream is in order." Tina stood her ground, waiting to be rewarded.

"I never could refuse such a beautiful intelligent young lady." Schaffer held out his hand for Tina. "I would be honored to take you for ice cream. Lead the way." They started and the others followed.

A few steps later Tina stopped. Wiggling her narrow index finger, she beckoned Schaffer closer. "Take mommy's hand too. You don't want her to feel left out."

He did as he was told and leaned closer to Renita. "How old did you say she is?" Tina giggled placing her free hand over her mouth.

"Six going on forty." Renita answered as she looked down at her daughter.

Schaffer could almost feel Renita's heart beating through her hand. Her warmth radiated into his hand on its way to his heart. After a few steps she interlocked her fingers with Schaffer's. He squeezed down a little to let her know that he approved.

Joe threw his arm around Nina, then as if crying he said. "This is beautiful man." He pretended to wipe a tear from his eye.

"Joseph! Mind your business." Nina cut her eyes in Joe's direction and smacked his hand.

"They are my business. And don't you forget it." He kissed Nina on the cheek. "I guess you were right."

Nina smiled and kept her voice low when she answered. "When you put two good people together only good things can come of it."

Schaffer heard what they both said and decided to let it pass for the moment. He only met Renita a few hours ago and already they were holding hands and acting as if they'd known each other for years. Joe and Nina already had them married. Love at first sight always seemed to be too fairytaleish to Schaffer. However, he did have to admit that the woman holding his hand made it seem like reality.

"Here we are ladies. The ice cream is on me, get whatever you want." Schaffer reached in his pocket for his money clip.

"I want one about this big!" Tina held her hands about two feet apart.

"Then that is what you shall have. What's your favorite flavor?" Schaffer peeked at the menu on the door while waiting for her answer.

"Pralines and cream. Although, their pralines aren't as good as mommy's, she makes the best ones in the world. You should come over and try her cooking. She's a great Cajun cook, I gau-raun-tee!" Tina used her best Cajun accent.

"If she can make crawfish etouffe I'm camping out on your doorstep." Schaffer said looking first at the waist-high matchmaker then at Renita.

Renita stood tall and cleared her throat. "That happens to be a specialty of mine."

"Then put a pillow on the porch I'll be there until you fix some for me."

"Can you buy fresh, live crawfish around here?" Renita asked.

"It doesn't matter. I'll have them flown in from New Orleans. What day would be best for you?" Schaffer slid his cell phone out and looked at the calendar.

"Today is Saturday." Renita looked up moving her fingers and counting. "I should finish up the class by next Thursday or Friday, so how does next Saturday sound?"

"It's a date. I'll make the red beans and rice." Schaffer put his hand on his chest.

Joe jumped in. "We'll bring the wine."

Schaffer turned and looked at Joe. "Be quiet old man. Nina's welcome, but I don't recall your name being mentioned."

Tina frowned at Schaffer. "You can come too Uncle Joe, Mr. Schaffer's just joking."

"Hiding behind a child again Joe? Have you no shame?" Schaffer hung his head and poked out his lips in jest.

"Oh stop, Schaffer. You boys are so bad." Renita patted Schaffer's arm.

"Don't pay them any attention. They always act like this." Nina added hopelessly and tossed her hands in the air.

Schaffer did his best Rodney King imitation. "Can't we all just get along?" Everybody got a quick laugh. "Hey, don't the Redskins play

Dallas next Sunday?"

Joe instantly answered. "Absolutely! And don't start asking me for tickets."

"But, Joe." Schaffer said. "I wouldn't dream of it. Actually, I have a better idea. Since we're going to get together on Saturday anyway, why not meet at my house on Friday evening and make a weekend of it and have dinner on Saturday or Sunday? Gretchen would love the company."

Renita looked at Schaffer as if shocked by his statement. "Who's Gretchen?"

"She's his German stub-tail leg humper." Joe laughed.

Nina hit Joe on the shoulder and shot him a nasty look. "Joseph, watch your language! Tina is here. Don't let me have to remind you again."

"Sorry." Joe hung his head like a scolded dog.

Tina looked in Joe's direction. "That's okay Uncle Joe, I've heard worse."

"That's enough, young lady!" Renita said sternly.

Schaffer patted Renita's arm. "You'll have to forgive him. He suffers from Turret's as well as idiot's syndrome. Gretchen is my German Short Haired Pointer. She loves visitors. I'm trying to teach her to bite Joe on sight, but she hasn't mastered that yet."

"Your house should be beautiful now that the leaves are starting to change." Nina turned to Renita. "He has a breathtaking view in the back of his house. There's a large field that ends at a brook. Then the mountains rise up from the water. It's just beautiful."

"Wow! This sounds like some house. I can't wait to see it. Where's it located?" Renita asked looking at Schaffer.

"Charlottesville. By the way Nina, I just had the vines pruned back and I plan on adding five more acres to the vineyard. Next year I will be able to get a Senior Intern from UVA to work with a pro to make the wine." Schaffer beamed with pride.

Joe looked pissed. "Showoff! You can't buy Renita and Tina's affection with grape vines."

"I don't know Joe. It sounds like a good down payment to me." Renita's face blushed after making her statement.

Tina came alive. "Grapes! I love grapes. They're my favorite fruit. Do you have a lot of them Mr. Schaffer?"

"Not as many as my neighbors Tina. But, I'll have plenty of them around for you next weekend. There may even be a few left on the vines that we can go pick ourselves." He was rewarded with a look of pure astonishment on Tina's face.

"Can we go mommy? P-leeease?" She pulled on Renita's sleeve.

"I don't see how we can refuse such a wonderful invitation." Renita answered with approval, flashing Schaffer her stone-melting smile.

Tina clapped her hands. "Yesss!"

"Great! Then I will expect all of you next weekend. Don't forget to bring bathing suits for the hot tub. Try to get out of DC as soon as possible. I want you to be able to enjoy all of the weekend." Schaffer hugged Tina.

Before anyone else had the chance to speak Joe abrasively changed the subject. "Where's my damn ice cream?"

He waved his hands through the air pushing everyone towards the counter. After the ladies went by, Joe grabbed Schaffer's arm. "Don't you think you should slow down a bit? The last thing I want to see is the ladies set up for a letdown. Your track record with women isn't that good."

"Joe, I've never met the right one before." Schaffer answered confidently.

"What the hell are you talking about? You just met her a few hours ago." Joe protested, holding Schaffer's arm securely.

"She's different, Joe." Schaffer tapped his chest. "I can feel it. Next weekend should help me to see things even more clearly. Don't worry. I'll be on my best behavior."

"You'd damn well better be!" Joe snorted and released Schaffer's arm.

"Come on guys. You've got to pick out what you want." Nina said impatiently.

"We're coming honey." Joe answered like the dutiful spouse. He stepped in behind Schaffer and patted him on the back. "I trust you, Schaffer. Don't let me down."

Chapter
7

Saturday brought the start of a new weekend, a rainy weekend, a weekend that would spawn the birth of a new killer, a killer who knew how to remain anonymous.

Thomas started to sing an old Carpenter's tune changing the words to suit his needs. "Rainy days and killing eights always gets me up." The murderous feeling crept over him like sunlight over the Earth at dawn. He lifted his cell phone to call Rachel, and then hung it up. No, he didn't want to talk to her, at least not yet. She would only make him feel warm and fuzzy. He needed total concentration to make sure that everything went perfectly. He needed anger, hate and rage, only they could sustain him through his quest.

Driving across Virginia Highway 3 Thomas began to frantically search the skies because the rain stopped around noon and had yet to return. He saw a Costco and quickly pulled into the right lane which was always a parking lot at this time of day, especially on Saturday. Costco sold everything in bulk and bulk was what he needed. Once inside, he quickly strolled down the isles in search of *Nads Hair Removing Gel*. He tossed a gallon-sized container into his cart, followed by Cheerios and cold cuts. Fifteen minutes later he was back in the car en route to the ABC (Alcohol Beverage Control) store. Lately, it was his most frequent shopping location. Inside he knew the way to the Jack Daniels Black blindfolded. Thomas picked up three fifths; just enough to make it through the weekend. Then he walked to the counter and began to look around the shelves covered with various liquors.

"Can I help you find anything tonight?" A clerk asked.

"I believe you can. Don't you guys carry Virginia wines?" Thomas looked over the shelves as he waited for an answer.

The clerk pointed to the back wall. "We sure do. Which one were you looking for?"

"Naked Mountain Chardonnay." Thomas said with emphasis, letting the clerk know there was no substitute.

The clerk led Thomas to the wine display. "It's right over here. How many would you like?"

"Make it a case." Thomas turned his back to the clerk and moved towards the front counter. "Two for me and ten for my women."

When the clerk reached the counter he sat the case next to his register. "Do you need anything else for your party?"

"Now that you mention it, grab me another couple bottles of Jack."

"Yes, Sir." He hurried off to get the liquor and returned seconds later. "Will that be cash or charge?"

"Cash." Thomas pulled a wad of hundreds from his pocket.

The clerk rang up the sale. "If you pull up to the door I'll load these for you."

"Where did you go to customer service school? I know a lot of people who could benefit from your training." Thomas walked towards the door. "I'll be right back."

The clerk waited for Thomas with a hand truck just outside the front door of the ABC store. Thomas motioned that the trunk of his BMW 750i was unlocked and the clerk placed the packages inside. When he completed his task he waved and turned to reenter the store.

Thomas opened the window. "Just a second please."

"Yes, Sir." The clerk answered, turning his head.

"Listen, I really appreciate your level of customer service." Thomas said holding out two twenty-dollar bills.

"Any time, sir, Any time." He answered, politely taking the bills and grinning from ear to ear.

A short drive later, Thomas arrived home. At the end of the long driveway sat his five thousand square foot house. Two hundred yards behind the house a twenty-foot cliff jutted out hovering above the Rappahannock River below.

Thomas unpacked the car and headed inside to listen to the weather channel. He wanted to know when the rain would return so that he could be precise with his preparations. He couldn't afford even the slightest deviation from his plan. He wasn't about to let anything interfere with his revenge, not even God.

Once convinced that the rain would be back by nightfall, he retreated to the basement. There he made eyebrows to match his false mustaches. Momentarily he wondered why he had never distilled anything to rid himself the 'queen bitch.' Oh yeah, she loved him and he her.

Saturday evening crept into Saturday night and Thomas was much too restless to sleep. He still had to prepare if he was going to begin his quest of death the following day.

Thunder had been rolling across the sky for the past hour. But by 11 p.m. not one raindrop had fallen from the clouds. He would not complete the last phase of his preparations until he was certain the rain would come.

Thomas stood in his room with only the darkness to cover his body. Looking out the window he resembled a child waiting for a parent to return after a long trip. His only companion for the evening was an ever-diminishing bottle of Jack Daniels whiskey that he held cocked off the side of his naked hip. By 3 a.m. he still had not moved except for the arm movements necessary to take a periodic drink from the bottle. A sharp bolt of lighting slashed across the darkness commanding the thunder to roar for several seconds, making everything in its path tremble. Total silence followed, then a subtle pecking against the windowpane. Thomas blinked and shifted to identify the source of the noise, moving his head for the first time in several hours. The next combination of lighting and thunder sped the rush of blood through Thomas' body. His glum expression was replaced with exhilaration as the raindrops tapped a steady rhythm against his windowpanes. Each successive bolt of lighting and clap of thunder pushed the rain harder from the heavy clouds, causing the blood to pulse through his veins even faster.

The pounding raindrops seemed to outwardly soothe Thomas. The opposite was true. The harder it rained, the greater the beast inside him grew. His smile turned sinister— the process was now complete. Saturday's lack of rain slowed his quest, but now he could begin. The only thing left was to prepare for battle.

Thomas retreated to the bathroom where he used electric hair clippers to remove as much hair as possible from his entire body. First, his head, then his chest and everything else down to his toes. He worked diligently. When he finished clipping, he covered his body with *Nads Hair Removing Gel* and turned on the shower. He let the water heat to a level that would scald. Steam billowed from the shower letting him know that it was ready. He closed his eyes and stepped inside. He gritted his teeth as the hot water washed away the remaining hair from his body. His eyes were fixed on point somewhere off in the distance. His mind was living the fantasy.

Thomas stepped from the shower cleansed of hair and any remaining human compassion. He walked into his dressing room, stood in front of a three-sided full-length mirror and turned on the lights for the first time since the sun left the sky. His skin glowed red from a combination of the scalding water and the chemical hair remover. . He turned to examine all angles of his body. Not a single hair remained. There was no hair on his head, arms, legs, or torso. No eyelashes or

ANTHONY P. JONES   D8 WITH F8

eyebrows. He even took extra care to remove the hairs from his nose and ears. A lesser-trained killer would never have even thought about those areas, but Thomas would be the *master*.

After his skin cooled, he applied a thin coat of clear satin polyurethane over his entire body. He knew this would prevent any skin cells or perspiration from being left at the scene. Then he dressed in a postman's uniform and placed a change of clothing in his mailbag. He ran down to the basement and added a bottle of wine, the GHB, an oral syringe and the treated certified letter with the green return receipt attached to it, all of which he kept in a zip lock bag. He also added several pair of fresh surgical gloves and a box of Trojan brand condoms. Finally, he filled a travel mug with day old coffee and headed out the door. His private war would now begin.

In the garage, Thomas bypassed his BMW and jumped in a black 1972 Volkswagen bug. He pulled out of the garage and headed to Charlottesville, VA to deliver a letter... and a death sentence to his first chosen victim.

At 5 a.m. Sunday morning the black ragtop 1972 Volkswagen bug was speeding down route 29 towards Charlottesville, VA. Thomas' vanity license plates greeted any onlookers with '*D8 WTH F8*' written in blue across the white background.
Thomas had purchased the car on the Internet. It was in superb shape considering its age.

At 6:30a.m., Thomas sat just outside of town in an empty parking lot. There, he applied actor's glue under his nose and above his eyes. Carefully, he pulled the pre-shaped hair from his bag and pressed it into place forming eyebrows and a mustache. He then pulled a pair of the rubber gloves from his bag, put them on and took the treated letter from its zipper bag. He ran his hand over the address,

Lynda Goodwin
429 Summer Grove Pl
Charlottesville, VA 23456

Lynda had graduated from UVA with an honors degree in Architecture. Two years after leaving a male dominated firm, she'd built an all female firm that was second to none in the state. The more successful her firm became, the more her marriage deteriorated. She felt her husband of six years began to hold her back in her professional life. Without a further discussion, he became her ex. She wasn't sure if guilt or a need to bond with people with similar experiences drove her to St. Ann's support group, but that's where she'd met Thomas.

During his one and only visit to the support group, Thomas remembered Lynda referring to her ex as 'the wimp.' He knew she was type 8 even before he gave the group the Enneagram test; it only served to confirm his conviction. Today, her animosity towards men would prove fatal.

Thomas became aroused thinking of his plans for Lynda, so much so that he found it hard to concentrate on the road. The rain pounded so hard against the little car that the windshield wipers feverishly worked to keep pace with the falling rain. He began to beat his hands against the steering wheel with a sound that complemented the beating wipers. The rhythm carried him to a near-euphoric state; he started to sing Elton John's *"The Bitch is Back."* When he reached the chorus he used his own words. *The bitch, the bitch, the bitch is back. Stone cold dead as a matter of fact.* He reached the climatic end of the song at the same time he reached the turn to Lynda's house.

He stopped singing— it was time for him to get serious. Thomas looked in the mirror to make sure his disguise was still in place. Driving down the long driveway, he stopped in the circular area just in front of Lynda's hand carved front door. In its center was a Yin-Yang supported by two dragons sitting on top of twin Mountains. Thomas opened the car door, unfurled his umbrella, then placed the mailbag across his shoulder and reached for the plastic zipper bag containing the letter.

On the way to the front door, Thomas pulled the letter from the bag and held it down away from his face to prevent breathing in the organophosphates and LSD. He pushed the doorbell and the Westminster chimes rang out. Lynda did not come to the door as quickly as he thought she should. Impatiently, he rang the doorbell again.

An intercom above the door came on. "Alright, alright! I'm coming." A few seconds later Lynda reached the door and opened it, she stood there in a white satin robe loosely tied around her waist. Her hair was wet as was her skin, which seemed to glisten when her breast moved up and down as she breathed.

Thomas was surprised to find Lynda ready for action. He found people in this area of the state much too trusting for his taste. She should have at least looked to see who was at the door before opening it. Nevertheless, he couldn't wait to untie her robe and run his hands across her breasts, squeezing her nipples until they hardened between his fingers. Licking them would be fun too, but he couldn't risk leaving anything behind that could be used to identify him later. Then he remembered, the hot water would wash away all traces of saliva. He was going to have his

ANTHONY P. JONES   D8 WITH F8

fun.

"Good morning. I'm sorry to have gotten you out of the shower, but I have a letter you need to sign for, return receipt requested."

"Who's it from, my ass-hole ex-husband?" She held her hand out for the letter. "Where do you need me to sign?"

"Right on this green card, on this line." Thomas pointed to the line, and then handed the letter to Lynda.

She reached out almost snatching the letter from his hand. Immediately, the drugs did their job and her unconscious body was rushing to meet the floor.

Quickly, Thomas reached out and grabbed Lynda. He didn't want any bruises on his victim. Gently, he eased her to the floor and reached in his bag for the GHB.

"That's it, drink it down. You'll feel better in the morning. Oh, I'm sorry, how could I be so callous? You won't be here in the morning." Thomas rocked his head back releasing a silent laugh.

Lynda didn't fight, she couldn't. She was still held captive by the lingering effects of the organophosphates and LSD as well as the rapidly acting effects of the GHB.

Thomas lifted Lynda from the floor and carried her to the master bedroom. There he took off her robe and laid her on the bed. He began slowly rolling her exposed nipples between his gloved fingers. In what seemed to be a predetermined rhythm he stopped and squeezed making Lynda's nipples rise between his fingers. Desperately, he flicked his tongue back and forth over her hard nipples and sucked them into his mouth. In the background he could hear Janet Jackson and Carly Simon singing, *Son of a Gun*— Janet's take on Carly's *You're so Vain*. He couldn't help but listen to the words, which he found most appropriate given the moment, *"I bet you think this song is about you."*

Lynda's eyes fluttered indicating that she was regaining consciousness. She started to laugh uncontrollably. Thomas knew it was a side effect of the LSD. She started to moan, and writhe. The LSD and GHB greatly heightened her level of sensitivity and right now she wanted to be touched.

Thomas spread her legs and slid her to the edge of the bed. Fully clothed, he started to grind against her. Lynda pushed her hips forward to meet him as he continued to roll her nipples with his fingers.

"I knew you were a little slut!" He said.

Lynda didn't try to push away. "Where did you come from?"

"You nasty bitch. You're going to be my whore. I bet you like giving blow jobs don't you?"

Lynda was laughing so hard her face hurt. "I've never been so horny in my life. I'll do whatever you want as long as you do something to put this fire out between my legs."

Thomas grabbed her hand and placed it between her legs. "Here, rub this and keep it hot for me while I get us some wine."

Lynda opened her eyes for the first time since she'd seen Thomas at the door. While she aggressively rubbed her crotch she looked at him. "I've always wanted to do it with a Black guy. I had the chance at UVA, but I chickened out. I just want to know if it's any different."

Thomas returned with the wine. "You won't have to worry about it after today, you'll have firsthand knowledge. Here, drink up."

Lynda drank the wine laced with GHB straight down then held her glass out for another. After finishing it she slid off the bed still laughing and let the empty glass fall where it may. "Let's see what you have in here." She unbuckled Thomas's belt and opened his pants. She reached in and pulled him out. "You won't need this on for me." She grabbed the condom to pull it off, but Thomas stopped her.

"It's not for you, it's for my protection." He reached down and grabbed the back of Lynda's head and shoved it forward. Without protest, she began to perform.

When she finished she crawled back onto the bed. "Now it's my turn."

Thomas went into the bathroom and removed his clothes, careful to place everything into empty zip-lock bags. He tucked the bags into his mailbag and rejoined Lynda in the bedroom.

The GHB was at full effect. All fear and inhibitions were long gone, replaced by Lynda's desire. "I want all you've got. Every thick square inch."

"You shall have it and more. But first let us toast our tryst, have another drink." Again, Thomas gave her the wine laced with GHB.

"Are you trying to get me drunk and take advantage of me?" Lynda moved back and forth in the bed.

"Let's just say I want you relaxed. Drink up then roll over."

Lynda came up on her knees and took the glass of wine, which she promptly drank. She handed the empty glass to Thomas, turned around and fell to her hands. She wiggled her butt in his direction and slapped one cheek. "I want it hard and fast."

He jumped on the bed and charged forward like a madman. He grabbed either side of her hips and inserted himself with one quick thrust.

He pushed her face down into the pillow. "It's not about what you want. I'm in control." Lynda tightly grabbed the sheets in an attempt to keep up with Thomas's wild thrashing. When he was finished he jumped from the bed as if he were going to run.

Out of breath, Lynda rolled to her back. "I hope you plan to control me some more. I feel as if I could do this all day."

"I'm just getting warmed up. Wait five minutes and meet me in the bathroom." Thomas went into the bathroom, turned the hot water on and plugged the tub so that it would fill. The steam from the hot water fogged the mirror. With his hands, still in the surgical gloves, he made a 'V' and the number '8' on the mirror. He reached in the mailbag for his cell phone and dialed. While the phone rang he retraced the '8.' Voice mail picked up. After the beep, Thomas left a message. "Dr. Gerard, I just took the first step towards recovery." He turned the water off in the tub and returned to the bedroom.

Lynda had fallen asleep, partly from exhaustion and partly from the wine and GHB. Thomas picked up the bottle of wine and the empty glass and took them to the bathroom. He returned for Lynda, but first he reached into his mailbag and pulled out another vial of GHB.

Thomas had Lynda drink the GHB using the oral syringe, and then he carried her to the bathroom placing her in the tub. Gently, he pushed her head beneath the surface of the water. The GHB took away all the fight; all he had to do now was to wait for her lungs to fill. After five minutes, he placed the empty glass into her right hand. Next, he put the practically empty bottle of Naked Mountain Chardonnay on the side of the tub near the cold-water faucet. Finally, he draped her left hand over the side of the tub and then placed an unopened can of V-8 juice just out of reach on the floor.

Thomas retraced all his steps in the house collecting his things. He made sure to pick up the glass he drank out of and placed it into a large plastic evidence bag. He used Lynda's vacuum cleaner to vacuum the bedroom and foyer rugs. He removed the vacuum cleaner bag, placed it in a zip-lock bag and took it with him. Then he walked naked, except for his socks, into the garage and pulled out a fresh set of lab greens from his mailbag, dressing as if he was going to work. Careful not to re-enter the house after changing clothes, he took the garage door opener from Lynda's jeep. He opened the door walked out and closed it with the garage door opener. He tossed it into his mail-bag, which he then threw into the trunk of his VW.

Once in the car, he pealed the polyurethane from his skin letting it breathe for the first time in hours. Thomas never looked back as he drove away from Lynda's house. He was off as fast as he had come, on his way home, reborn, rejuvenated, and reassured— he had a new reason to live.

Chapter

8

Monday morning Schaffer was up at 5 a.m. He'd finished Douglas' book the night before and was filled with excitement as he was preparing to leave for Quantico. He was excited about the upcoming class on profiling to a small degree, but was mostly excited to see Renita again. She dominated his thoughts all weekend. He'd spent most of Sunday preparing for the upcoming weekend when Renita would come to Charlottesville.

Schaffer came the down stairs talking to Gretchen about Renita. For her part, Gretchen was not jealous, or interested; she just wanted to get outside, despite the falling rain. He obliged her and went in search of his morning papers.

He laid them on the kitchen table in the order he usually read them, *New York Times, Washington Post, Richmond Times, and Charlottesville Daily Progress*. Schaffer took a small amount of plastic wrap from the bottom of each paper and jerked like a magician would trying to pull a tablecloth from under a table full of dishes. Three of the plastic wrappers slid off easily, but the Charlottesville paper went airborne. It smacked the wall behind him and hit the floor.

He went to pick it up and found it open to the front page. On the bottom of the page a headline caught his attention, ***Local Architect Found Dead***. As he continued to read, Schaffer couldn't believe what he saw. Lynda Goodwin, the architect who handled his remodeling was dead. The article ended by saying, *Her drowning appeared to be accidental*.

"Shit. She drowned in her own bathtub. That's a bitch." Schaffer thought about his own kidney-shaped sunken tub that Lynda had picked out. "I could think of better ways to go." He looked at his watch and realized he had to get going to avoid being late for the first class at the FBI's Quantico headquarters.

He ran to the door called Gretchen back in the house and tossed the Charlottesville paper back on the table with the others and headed out for the week. "Don't worry, girl. Donna will be by to let you out this week. I'll see you later."

Lynda's death was firmly planted in his mind causing him to question his own mortality. Schaffer planned on calling her next week to begin the design for the pool he wanted to put in, in the spring. He decided to call the firm next week to proceed with the project even though he would not have Lynda's input.

Schaffer drove down the highway and his thoughts quickly turned to Renita. It caused him to feel quite upbeat despite the rain. He always found jazz inspirational since it could touch most human emotions. This morning he put a Thelonious Monk CD in the player. Monk's syncopated beats would help to keep his mood high; *Straight No Chaser* was his favorite song on the CD. Charlie Rouche, Schaffer's favorite sax player, aided Monk in exploding the rhythms to the airwaves. Schaffer drummed the steering wheel in time with the musicians. When Monk's CD ended, Dizzy Gillespie's Bee-Bop hits carried him through the balance of his trip. Two other CD's waited on the seat for the return trip home, Louie Armstrong and Charlie Parker.

♦

Renita was glad to see that Schaffer arrived half an hour early. She wanted to see him as badly as he did her. Her initial instinct was to rush over to greet him with a hug and kiss. But, today was about business and she was leading the session, decorum had to be maintained. She walked over to meet him near the table holding their continental breakfast. Renita extended her hand. "Good to see you again Mr. O'Grady."

Schaffer looked at her with disbelief. "I don't think so! This just won't do. Now you'd better get over here with a hug right now!"

Happy that no one else was in the room yet, Renita threw her arms around Schaffer and gave him a bear hug.

"That's better." Schaffer said looking into the face that dominated his mind all week. "I guess this means I'll have to be on my best behavior all week?"

"We wouldn't want anyone to think that the teacher has a pet, now would we?" Renita asked as she continued to hold Schaffer. She felt secure in his arms and hoped moments like this would never end.

"It's too late for that." Came a voice from the back of the room.

Renita turned abruptly in the direction of the voice and stepped back from Schaffer. "Jim. I didn't hear you come in."

"Well, your attention was somewhat diverted." Jim pointed to Schaffer with a completely serious look on his face.

Renita blushed. "Schaffer O'Grady, meet Jim Clemente."

The two men shook hands. "I could hug you too if you like."

Schaffer said to lighten the moment.

Jim smiled and offered his hand. "That's okay. A hand shake will do just fine."

Renita rested on the side of a table. "Jim's responsible for a lot of what's going on here this week, in a matter of speaking. He's one of the top profilers at the FBI."

Schaffer tossed a blueberry in his mouth and nodded in Jim's direction. "I recognize the name. I've seen some of the things he's worked on for television. Some of those characters are beyond shocking."

"I'm glad you enjoyed it, though I hope you never encounter anyone like I profiled in the show. Which police force are you representing?" Jim reached between Schaffer and Renita for a piece of fruit.

"Actually, I'm here on behalf of the *Washington Post*. We want to help spread your message and keep the people informed. If one person is saved as a result, then we've done our jobs." Schaffer handed Jim a napkin and continued eating blueberries.

Renita joined the men competing for fruit and reached for a piece of fresh pineapple. "I was able to coax Jim here today to deliver the introduction to the group."

"Renita, you never have to twist my arm. I'll always come back for one of my best students." Jim turned and pointed to Schaffer with a strawberry between his fingers. "She should be running this department for the Bureau. She would be if I had a say so."

Schaffer reached out for Renita. "I couldn't agree more." He squeezed her shoulder and abruptly changed the subject. "I hope you both will allow me to buy you dinner this evening."

"I don't want to intrude on you two." Jim looked at Schaffer and then Renita, mentally noting their facial expression.

Schaffer didn't give Jim a chance to say another word. "It won't be an intrusion, it would be an honor."

Jim looked at Renita for her response. "It's okay with me." She said pouring a cup of coffee.

"Then I assume it's a date." Schaffer quickly added.

"Sure. I'd love to eat with you guys. What time will you wrap things up this afternoon, Renita?" Jim cut his eyes towards the classroom and gave his head a quick jerk.

"The first day is rather intense as you know, so I planned to end around three or four. We could head out then." Renita sipped her coffee enjoying Schaffer's impromptu suggestion.

"There's a great little crab shack on Route 1 in Woodbridge. It's the perfect place to grab some food and conversation. That is, if you two don't mind picking at your dinner." Schaffer reached for a glass of juice from an adjacent table.

Jim was the first to answer. "That sounds great to me. How about you Renita?"

"That's good for me too. I'll call Nina and ask her to pick Tina up from after- school. That way we won't have to be rushed."

"Great. Then I'll call ahead and have a table reserved for three around 4:45 this afternoon." Schaffer left to get the number and make the call.

Jim waited for Schaffer to leave the room. "Where did you run into him?"

"He's a reporter for Joe DeApuzzo at the *Washington Post*. He's also a good friend of Joe and Nina. What do you think so far?" Renita made no attempt to hide her excitement.

Jim frowned, concerned for the moment. "He seems like a nice enough guy. Can he deal with the demands of your job?"

"Jim, we just met last Friday. There's no commitment from either of us yet." Renita hid behind her coffee cup hoping she looked as innocent as she tried to sound.

"You could have fooled me." His facial expression softened. "You two seem as if you've been together a while, although, you both have that 'new love' look and smell."

"I know. I don't want to let my emotions get in the way of good judgment. But, he feels like an old pair of jeans, he's touching all the right places." Renita couldn't stop the smile that crossed her face.

"Just take your time girl." Jim's face took on a father-like quality. "I guess it's possible you've found your soul mate. I'll know more about him after dinner. I'm going to open him up like a can of worms, after I get through shaking the dirt off, only the worm will be left. If there's something there, I'll find it."

"You sound just like Joe DeApuzzo. I'm lucky to have you both looking out for me. Thanks, Jim." Renita took his arm and they walked into the lecture room.

"I'd be careful with the interrogation, he'll know what you're up to, he's former Secret Service."

"Really?" Jim's eyebrows shot up. "I guess I'll have to use the super secret technique on him."

Thirty minutes later, Renita introduced Jim to twenty-eight

ANTHONY P. JONES   D8 WITH F8

policemen from around the country. For a few minutes Jim's talk lifted information straight from the pages of Douglas' book and added more detail that would benefit the officers in attendance.

Schaffer had read every page of Douglas' first book, but still found himself clinging onto every word that left Jim's mouth during the presentation. Rather than feverishly taking notes, Schaffer used his digital pocket recorder after receiving permission from the Bureau. During breaks, he would download the recordings to his laptop. In his briefcase he had enough batteries to last two weeks. He would spend at least that amount of time reviewing the recordings from this week's class before delivering an article that first had to be approved by the FBI and Joe DeApuzzo. After both approved it, the article would be published in Schaffer's column in the *Post*.

Renita's lectures and exercises went straight through lunch but, an occasional break was thrown in to give things a chance to sink in and nicotine to be absorbed by those in need. At 3 p.m. Renita began wrapping things up for the day. The notebooks that were handed to each officer earlier were already beginning to swell with new information. To everyone's surprise, Renita handed out a fifty-page article that was to be reviewed before morning. The officers let out a collective moan. Before they had a chance to complain further they were reminded that they were there to learn how to catch the bad guys not just to listen to people talking for a week while they took it easy.

Everyone began filtering to their rooms to settle in before the evening. Jim was still surrounded by the most curious of the group asking questions, since he was not scheduled to return before the class ended.

Renita quietly exited the room closely followed by Schaffer. "You did a great job in there today. I'm impressed at how well you've maintained your sanity given the gruesome work you're involved in." Schaffer waved the notebook from the earlier class.

"Thank you, Mr. O'Grady." Renita reached for his arm. "Are you sure you can handle a relationship with someone involved in this type of work?"

Schaffer looked to the ground. "I don't know. From what I've heard today if you get tired of me I could disappear from this earth and no one would be the wiser. Does the position come with a built-in shrink?"

"Of course. All the resources of the Bureau are at your disposal." Renita smiled brightly and held on a little tighter to his arm.

"Disposal. I'm not sure I like your choice of words. For the record, Gretchen is the beneficiary on all my insurance policies. She gets everything, including the houses."

Renita shook her head. "Maybe I should have someone from the Bureau check you out so I know what I'm getting myself in to."

Schaffer scribbled a number on a piece of paper. "That won't be necessary. Just have them call the psych department at Walter Reed." He handed her the piece of paper. "They'll find my file to be quite illuminating."

Jim walked up to Renita and Schaffer. Both of them looked as if they had just been caught with their hands in the cookie jar. He looked at Renita first, then at Schaffer. "I'm afraid to ask." Jim turned and started out the door. "Let's get out of here before you two get me into trouble."

Schaffer shrugged his shoulders. "What's he talking about? We didn't do anything."

"What's this 'we' shit, crazy man? You're on your own." Renita let go of Schaffer and moved closer to Jim.

Schaffer shook his finger. "Rats deserting the ship."

Renita's jaw went slack. "Oh, so now I'm a rat?"

Jim rapidly shook his head from side to side. "What have I let you two get me into? I'm having dinner with a couple of Loons. There must be a full moon tonight."

◆

Before the Smooth Jazz station could complete their thirty-minute music set and interrupt the flow with commercials, three cars pulled into the parking lot of the Crab Shack. Renita, Jim and Schaffer were all much more relaxed than when they had been on base. They were looking forward to their first drink to cap off a stressful workday leaving behind the people with a lust for death.

Inside, their table was waiting. They were very politely greeted and seated in an area all to themselves. A waiter stood by to provide them with practically personal service.

Renita was impressed with their treatment at the restaurant. "Are you guys sure this is Northern Virginia. This place acts as if we're the only ones here."

"I think I may be able to explain that." Shaffer sheepishly raised his hand. "When I called earlier I told the owner that I was with the *Post* and that I would be bringing in two food critics with me this evening." Renita seemed embarrassed, so Shaffer reassured her. "Make sure you guys act critical."

Jim laughed and shook his finger at Schaffer. "At least it got us seated right away. I'm starved."

Renita was shocked and quickly turned her head towards Jim. "Would you consider that to be a character flaw, or does he just have weak morals?"

Jim tossed a pretzel into his mouth. "I'd say he's smart. He didn't want you to have to wait any longer than necessary. So, act like a critic."

"I knew I was going to like this guy. I can't wait to tell my analysts." Schaffer rubbed his hands together and hunched his shoulders forward looking like the preverbal mad scientist.

Renita kicked Schaffer beneath the table. "Behave."

"Okay, mom." Schaffer sat back and put his hands in his lap.

Jim watched their interaction and physically began to relax. He could already tell that Schaffer was a good person. "It took me a while today, but I remember where I know you from." He looked directly in Schaffer's eyes. "You found Harold Cosby's body a few years ago." His eyes dropped to the pretzels. "I was brought in as an expert on the case."

Schaffer leaned forward and rested his elbows on the table. Tension coursed through his body as he remembered Harold's death as if it had just happened. "What service did you perform?"

Looking more seriously, Jim slowly raised his head, meeting Schaffer's gaze. "I profiled you, to see if it were possible that you killed the Secretary. It wasn't the type of hit a former Secret Service guy would have pulled off. You guys don't typically deal with death, it wasn't messy enough for an amateur. Of course, you finally found the guy who did it on your own." Jim tossed another pretzel in his mouth. "That was impressive." Slowly he made eye contact with Schaffer.

"Thanks. We Secret Service guys are known for our investigative skills." Schaffer's voice conveyed his irritation. "Who were you working for when you profiled me?"

"You know damn well I won't tell you that. However, they were glad that I concluded that it could not have been you." Jim maintained direct eye contact with Schaffer and bit another pretzel, watching for any adverse reaction.

"What else did you tell them about me?" Schaffer demanded rather than asked.

Jim waited a moment before answering. He took a sip of water and let his eyes follow the glass to the table. "As I remember it, I told them that you were idealistic, you were on a quest for justice, and that you were stubborn. Did I miss anything?"

Schaffer understood that Jim was just doing his job, but he felt violated by the intrusion. "Just that I am good looking and that I love kids and puppies. Oh yeah, and that I'm husband material."

Renita was grateful that Schaffer broke through the wall of ice that was forming between the two men. "I think you guys need a drink, God knows, I do. You boys were beginning to turn blue."

"Sorry guys. I guess I still haven't gotten over what happened to Harold Cosby." Schaffer offered a weak grin then held out his hand to Jim.

Jim accepted it shaking firmly. "Hey, don't worry about it. None of us likes having our lives poked and prodded. Just be glad there's someone like Renita or me out there when the bad guys surface. Our poking and prodding can mean the difference between life and death, more than anyone wants to count."

The balance of the evening Schaffer was given a bird's eye view of what really went on in the Behavioral Analysis Unit at the FBI. Renita got to see that the man across from her was genuine and trustworthy. Jim's concurrence was evident by his comfortable and unrestrained interaction with Schaffer. Renita's body tingled inside with excitement and anticipation for her upcoming weekend at Schaffer's house. She sensed the beginning of a meaningful relationship.

Chapter

9

Thomas spent all of Sunday letting Jack Black wash away any speck of guilt that may have remained about killing Lynda. He rationalized that he was celebrating the elimination of a plague from the world. His first kill was simply a surgical procedure designed to bring healing. He drank just enough Sunday and Monday to remain slightly buzzed in case he had to move quickly.

By Monday evening, he was ready to resume his *eight-ectomies*. But first, he had to eliminate the evidence bags from Lynda's procedure that were in his trunk. Opposite the lab in his basement was an empty game room. There, he could use an Italian marble fireplace as an incinerator. The fireplace, which was five feet high and four feet wide, was one of three in the house.

Thomas retrieved the evidence bags from his trunk and threw them into the fireplace. He covered them with lighter fluid and bent down with a cigarette lighter to start the flame.

"Burn baby burn. Just leave me a pile of ashes."

The garage door opener would be the hardest to reduce to ashes so he continued to spray lighter fluid over it. Watching the flames Thomas freed himself from his pants and began to masturbate as he reflected on his first kill. The more the thoughts pulsed his brain the more violently he worked his arm. Shortly, he collapsed to the floor, spent but still aroused, watching the flames. Intermittently, he squeezed the can of lighter fluid streaming the igniter onto the fire, stopping only long enough for the can to gurgle as it took a breath.

After practically empting the lighter fluid can he lifted his arm to look at his watch. It was time for the news, which meant the weather would not be far behind. He felt so good that he wanted to kill again; nothing before had ever given him such a sense of satisfaction. With the rain falling at a steady pace, the weather was making it even easier to kill anonymously.

Upstairs, the weatherman provided Thomas with additional euphoria. "More rain all week as a second front passes through."

Thomas laughed and rocked in his chair. "Shit! I get to kill all week. Let's see who's next on the list." He pulled a list from the

Enneagram book next to his chair. Seven women's names were there. One was lined out and two of the remaining six were in the same city. Only two on the list were African-American. Lynda Goodwin was an expression of hate directed towards his mother; Gloria Stegal would be the first surrogate for his ex.

Other decisions had to be made since he decided not to kill more than one person in any one city. He pulled a coin from his pocket. Looking at the two ladies in the same city he put an 'H by one and a 'T' by the other. Then he flipped the coin into the air. It bounced once on the carpet and came to rest on tails.

"Lucky bitch." Thomas crossed out the name with the 'T' beside it. Next he had to decide what other cities he would visit to choose more victims. There he would seek out support groups to find his prey. On Wednesday he would be speaking to a forensics class at Virginia Tech. There were plenty of towns and cities nearby that he could choose from. He decided to arrive in the area early Tuesday afternoon to investigate. On an earlier trip he had gotten one name in Lynchburg. Thomas was careful to choose women from the four different autopsy regions of the state. That left one immediate concern, how fast could he get to Gloria in Hampton, VA, after the class was over.

Thomas read through his notes on Gloria and revised them. He listed her as a divorce lawyer adept at getting unusually large settlements for her all-female clientele. She refused to represent men no matter how much they offered her to take the case. Thomas recalled immediately hating her. He believed that she used the support group as a recruiting ground. All of her conversations centered on how much she had been awarded for her cases. It was a direct attempt to appeal to the greed of her potential clients. If anyone tried to get her to mention anything about her failed relationship she chilled like polar ice, her coldness cut to the bone. The only reason Thomas did not kill her first was out of disrespect for his mom, who like Lynda was white and needed to die for her part in his pain. But, Gloria was black like his wife and just like his wife; he wanted her to die as painfully as possible.

Gloria recently purchased a sixty-foot sail boat and waterfront home in Hampton just outside of Norfolk. Thomas questioned her when they met about sailboats and she pled total ignorance. She simply thought having one looked good on her personal resume, especially to her clients. When she wanted to take clients out she would pay a crew to sail the boat for her.

Her response only infuriated Thomas. His contempt grew every time Gloria opened her mouth. He fanaticized about how much fun it would be to take her out on the boat and drag her behind it while sharks tore away at her flesh, bite-by-bite. Anything that caused severe pain was what she deserved. But, that would break his pattern. As an organized serial killer he had to maintain consistency, there would be no deviation in the methods of their deaths.

Thomas wondered what the police would call him once they realized he was a serial killer. He knew it would take them a long time to connect the deaths and realize that a serial killer was at work. That's why he would kill the women in different cities, different autopsy regions and he would kill women of two different races. This was something most serial killers did not do according to John Douglas. As a forensic specialist Thomas knew how to cover his tracks, he also knew the lack of evidence would drive the police crazy. He thought it would be a hoot that the only thing that he would leave behind was the hair samples he collected from autopsies in Dr. Gerard's lab.

Thomas stumbled back over to the wet bar to refill his glass. The moment he sat down he took a long drink. His eyes closed and his head fell back on the chair. It was time to dream of the vile acts he had in store for Gloria.

Around 5:30 p.m., the Jack Black released Thomas from its grasp. He sat up in his chair and wondered when he had taken off his clothes. The blanket he took from the morgue felt rough against his skin, which caused him to scratch his legs and chest.

Thomas began to feel more alert and could feel the adrenalin flowing into his veins. He stood and walked to a window. Staring out into the darkness, he could hear the rain drumming against the windowpane. The smile that grew on his face was impossible to hide. "I love the rain!"

Thomas ran upstairs to take a shower. He turned the light on in his bedroom and looked around. There, the lingering indentions where the furniture once stood pocked the carpet. He walked to the bathroom, just outside of the shower stood a pile of dirty towels. Each one wore a large black stamp on the middle that read 'Property of the Virginia State Morgue.' Thomas found it perplexing that dead people could possibly need blankets, warming them was a useless effort. Then he made it a point to remember to take the blankets and towels in to the office so that they could be cleaned next week when he returned.

Every time he entered the bedroom, Thomas was infuriated. Its emptiness reminded him of everything Victoria took from the house, even the toilet paper including the half used rolls on the spools. He wished he could vacuum every grain of dirt from the floors and ship it to her. He even knew the note he would include with it. *Here bitch, you forgot this*! But, sending anything to her was impossible. She was nowhere to be found. There wasn't even enough of a trail for a well-trained bloodhound to follow.

Hate rose in Thomas's heart like mercury in a thermometer descending into hell. He began to concentrate on Gloria—with her he could exact his revenge. He wanted to cause her as much pain as possible without leaving anything that could be traced back to him. Therein lay his challenge, but after all he was the *master*.

By 6:00 p.m., Thomas was dressed in his postman's uniform and in route to Hampton, Virginia. Driving down I-95 in the heavy rain proved pleasurable. For once the highway was not overrun with eighteen-wheelers nearly kissing car bumpers in an attempt to make a deadline, driver safety be damned. I-64, which would take him from Richmond to Hampton typically, presented identical traffic concerns.

Less than an hour later, Thomas took exit 89, Lewistown Road and pulled into a truck stop just off the highway. There he looked for a real estate flyer to see if he could find any land for sale. He only moved to Fredericksburg as a compromise since Victoria hated Richmond. Living in Hanover County could cut his travel time to Richmond in half. He thumbed through the flyer and then tossed it into the mailbag and got back on the interstate.

The rain was falling harder in Hampton than it was when Thomas left the truck stop. He popped his umbrella open and stepped from the car, walked to the front door and rang the bell. Thomas listened intently at the door since the rain made it hard to hear.

"Who is it?" Came a voice from behind the door.

"Hi, Mrs. Stegal. I have a letter here you need to sign for." Thomas had to work to stay in control of his emotions; he could feel rage and excitement growing.

She opened the door. "Shit! What does that bastard want now, more money?"

"Excuse me." Thomas' face wrinkled puzzled by the outburst and its intended target.

"I'm sorry. I was speaking about my ex-husband. I didn't realize you guys delivered so late." Gloria looked past Thomas out into the darkness.

"The rain slowed the trucks earlier, so I'm running a couple of hours behind, usually we're finished around 7 p.m." Thomas stood there looking at Gloria. She was wearing a completely sheer pair of black pajamas with two darker pockets that barely covered her small breasts. Behind her stood a hundred and twenty pound Rottweiler Thomas had not planned for.

"Wow. I guess you shop at Victoria's Secret. Where does your friend there shop?" Thomas pointed to the dog.

"Sorry. I left my robe upstairs. Bruits here, makes sure that no one enters unless I want them to. Come in out of the rain and let me see what the bastard sent. Where do I sign?"

"Just sign here on the back." Thomas handed the letter to her.

Gloria took the letter and fell to the floor. Thomas stepped closer to make sure she was ready. Bruits moved forward and started to growl. Thomas saw the hairs on the dog's back stand up and the huge teeth that Bruits bared. The show of power caused Thomas to cautiously step back.

"Easy big guy. I just want to make sure she's okay."

Thomas slowly stood up and eased his hand into his bag. He reached the spray bottle containing the organophosphates and LSD. Bruits moved between Gloria and Thomas. He continued showing his teeth in an attempt to get Thomas to leave. Thomas sprayed the organophosphates and LSD in his face and Bruits fell to the floor beside Gloria. Thomas dragged the dog to the kitchen and closed the door, then returned to Gloria and injected the GHB down her throat. Before she woke, he carried her to the bedroom.

When she came to, Thomas already had her clothes off and was fondling her breasts.

"That feels good." Gloria said in a throaty voice. "But, I don't recall giving you permission to do that."

"I don't need your permission." Thomas squeezed harder. "It's going to feel better before it's over."

Gloria saw her face in the mirror on the ceiling. She started laughing hard at her reflection. Thomas knew the LSD was working.

"Get on your hands and knees and come over to the edge of the bed." Thomas demanded. He knew in another minute or so she would be begging him for stimulation.

Gloria rolled over and arched her back like a cat. She walked over to the edge of the bed and rubbed her cheek along Thomas's zipper. "What's behind door number one?"

"Why don't you open it and find out for yourself." Thomas grabbed a handful of hair and jerked her head back. With both hands he pushed her face forward.

Thomas was straining against his pants begging to be set free. She unzipped his pants with her teeth and he sprung out. Unprompted, Gloria moved in.

After a few seconds Thomas stopped her. "Turn around and move up on the bed further."

Gloria laughed. "You want to jump right in." She arched her back again and spread her legs waiting for him. Thomas climbed on the bed behind her.

"That's the wrong oh…ooh!" Gloria suppressed her scream.

"I know what I'm doing. Just shut up and take it." Thomas was as rough as possible.

Gloria grabbed two rungs on the brass headboard tightly, while Thomas thrust back and forth wildly.

"Shit! I've wanted to try this before but I thought it would hurt too much. It does hurt a little, but damn it feels good." Gloria clutched the bars tighter with each inward thrust.

Thomas started to move faster. He wanted it to hurt. He wanted to cause pain. Gloria buried her head in a pillow to mute her screams, but he could see he was achieving the desired effect.

"By the time I'm finished you'll have an out of body experience."

"I think I'm about to have one now." Gloria pushed to meet him and screamed loudly.

Thomas withdrew and collapsed into a heap on the bed. Her body quivered while Thomas watched.

"I've never done it like that before. If you have some other tricks like that I'd like to keep you around till death do us part." Gloria tried to kiss Thomas.

He turned away and got up from the bed. "I can promise you I'll be around until then. And yes, I do know other 'tricks' as you call them. I learned more in medical school than how to heal. One of my gross anatomy instructors was a freak. She liked to tell us how to get women off. Here, have some wine. I'll see what else I can whip up."

Gloria drank the GHB laced wine. She drank another glass between each round of their lust making. Within ninety minutes, she was dead, just as Lynda died, down to the exact detail.

Now Thomas had to deal with Bruits and let the dog out of the kitchen before leaving. He couldn't risk an investigator suspecting that anyone other than Gloria was in the house at the time of her death.

Thomas retrieved his organophosphates and LSD spray and went to the kitchen door. Bruits started growling and barking louder as Thomas approached the door. Instinctively, Bruits could tell that something was wrong. Thomas cracked the door slightly with the intention of spraying the dog. Bruits already had a running start and hit the door with all his weight. The door slammed into Thomas, knocking him backwards across a chair. He hit the floor with a loud thud. The vial containing the organophosphates and LSD flew from his hand and landed on the floor.

Bruits wasted no time assailing his prone target. Before Thomas hit the floor, Bruits was moving in for the kill. Thomas threw his left arm up as Bruits went for his throat. Bruits clamped down on it with his powerful jaws. Thomas could see the vial just out of reach to his right. Still, he put his hand out hoping to reach the spray.

Bruits shook violently as if he were trying to rip Thomas's arm off. Thomas helplessly bounced from side to side like a rag doll. Through the intense pain, he reached for anything he could find to get the dog off of him. His hand fell into his mailbag and he grabbed the tainted letter. Thomas shoved the letter at the dog. Bruits let go of Thomas's arm and went for the hand. Before he had the chance to bite down, Bruits collapsed on Thomas' chest.

Thomas pushed the dog off of him and used both feet to kick him in the head before he stood up. "Goddamned stupid dog! I think you broke my fucking arm!"

He was careful not to let any of the blood escaping his arm hit the floor. Thomas sat up keeping his arm pinned to his chest. He pulled his mailbag close and took out an extra shirt, which he wrapped around his damaged arm. Then using his good arm, he reached down, took the envelope from the dog's mouth and put it back in his mailbag. He crawled over and got the vial then sprayed several blasts into the dog's mouth.

"I hope it fucking kills you!" Thomas wanted to spit on the dog, but restrained himself. He went into the kitchen and found a can of Raid bug killer, shook it violently and put it in the dog's mouth before kicking his bottom jaw. The dog's teeth pierced the can and the insect killer sprayed out of the can into his mouth. When the investigators found the dog his death would appear suspicious. With any luck, they would consider it coincidental, or assume Gloria killed him before killing herself. Thomas gathered the rest of his things and left the house. During his struggle with the dog, the real estate flyer from Hanover flew from his bag and lodged itself under a rug beneath Gloria's dining room table. Thomas never noticed it missing.

In the car Thomas removed his extra shirt to examine the wound. He knew it needed attention, but he didn't want to stop in the immediate area. Closer to home would be better, preferably in a small unassuming town. Traveling across I-64 his arm hurt so badly that he almost blacked out at the wheel. He exited the interstate at Toano and began looking for a drug store.

A short time later he spotted a CVS. He pulled into the parking lot and reached in his glove box for a prescription pad. Several of the first pages of the pad had yellowed from non-use. A medical examiner seldom needed to write prescriptions, but he kept a pad around just for emergencies. He flipped to a clean page and wrote two prescriptions, one for augmentin and one for Percocet. To avoid any ethical issues of self-medicating, he made the prescriptions to Bob Smith.

The CVS had a drive-in window, which suited Thomas. This allowed him to stay in the car with his injured arm hidden, avoiding any nagging questions.

"Hello, sir. Are you picking up a prescription?" An overly pleasant attendant asked.

"No. I have to get these two filled for a friend of mine. I'd like to wait for them."

"Okay. Does Mr. Smith have an insurance card?"

"No. He sent cash."

"I'll need his address for the prescription."

"I don't have a clue what it is, I'm not from here. I came in town to check on him after a neighbor called me. Bob doesn't have a phone. He's in bad shape; I hope this won't delay filling his prescriptions."

"I think I can take care of it for you. Do you have a cell phone?" Thomas nodded. "When you get back to his house would you please give me a call with the address?"

"Sure. I'll do it the minute I get there." Thomas thought this was a stupid exchange, but he would tell her whatever he needed to, to stop the pain.

The pharmacist delivered the medication and was careful to explain exactly how Bob was to take it. Thomas wanted her to shut up so that he could get the percocet into his system for some relief. He left the pharmacist window in a hurry. Before getting back on the interstate he pulled into a service station and bought a drink so that he could take the pills. He was about ninety minutes from his house, so by the time the percocet reached full force he would be home.

When Thomas reached his front door the pain was gone. The three percocet he took made him feel almost as good as his Jack Black. Thomas stumbled to his basement lab. There he washed the wounds inflicted by

Bruits. The cleaned wounds were a clear indication of Bruits' intentions. Now Thomas needed to stitch several of the lacerations. He didn't have any suture material available, so dental floss would have to do.

Thomas ran upstairs and poured a large glass of Jack Black. Back downstairs he poured a little on the wound and the rest into his mouth. He hadn't practiced one-handed stitching since his surgical rotation, which felt as if it were twenty years ago. The effects of the alcohol and percocet made the stitches even more challenging but painless. Forty minutes later, he completed the ten-minute job and headed upstairs to get some sleep before leaving for Blacksburg, VA at 4:30 a.m.

Chapter

10

Along his route to Blacksburg Thomas would make a short stop in Lynchburg. There, his third victim, Sandy Nanney would be waiting because she would be getting home just before he arrived. Sandy worked the night shift.

◆

Thomas thought back to their first meeting. He thought that Sandy was the perfect mate. She ran the medical lab at the local hospital and did cancer research on the side. The fact that she had flirted with him all evening only increased his interest. They had met at Virginia Baptist Hospital's conference room, where interdenominational divorce recovery meetings were held. The night Thomas attended, everyone was eager to learn about the Enneagrams and Thomas was happy to oblige them.

They finished taking the test and Sandy stood behind him placing her hands on Thomas' shoulders. She let her hair gently brush against his neck while he interpreted her test.

"You're an 8." Thomas said trying to hide his disappointment.

"Is that good or bad?" Sandy slid her hair behind her ears.

"The Enneagrams don't work that way. They don't presume that anyone is good or bad, you simply are what you are. Good or bad only comes into play when you consider who to have a relationship with." Thomas picked up a 'quick view' Enneagram chart and put it in front of Sandy. "As an 8, there are two relationships that absolutely will not work no matter what you do. They are relationships with either a 2 or a 5. Your ideal relationship is with a 4."

"So, are you a 4?" Sandy smiled waiting for him to answer.

"Unfortunately no, I'm a 2." Thomas turned his attention to another test he'd just picked up.

"Well, maybe we can break the stereotype. You've got to admit that there is a strong magnetic attraction between us." Her eyes held a wanton look.

"That's a natural reaction. People always gravitate to their opposite. But, before long you would tire of me, then where would we be?" Thomas asked sternly as he looked up from the papers he was holding.

"Why don't we cross that bridge when we come to it?" Sandy suggested and winked before turning to leave for her seat.

"I can promise that you will see me again. It may not be tonight or tomorrow, but you will see me again." He stated definitively and then lowered his eyes to the test to complete his analysis.

"I can't wait." She smiled again, took her test and left for the evening.

"Me either." Thomas took her address and phone number and put them in his Palm Pilot.

◆

Tomorrow morning around 7:30 a.m., Sandy would see him. This time, she would not live to regret her wish to see him again. Thomas didn't feel an overt need to cause her pain, but she did need to die to make his world safer. He knew that she would metamorphose into his enemy if given enough time. She was just a bitch in camouflage waiting to ambush him at the first opportunity. For that reason, her time on the earth was about to come to an abrupt end.

Thomas got another drink and attempted to force his heart to harden to hate. His effort was useless. He was attracted to Sandy despite knowing she wasn't good for him. Regardless of his feelings, her fate was sealed.

◆

Tuesday morning Thomas arrived early at Sandy's house. When she answered the door she didn't recognize him because of his mailman's disguise. Thomas felt it was unnecessary to give Sandy the letter if she knew who he was, but he wanted to remain consistent. He handed the letter to her, five minutes after his arrival they were in Sandy's bedroom actively pursuing the end of her pent up sexual frustration and his sexual rage.

Sandy requested, through a semi-cognizant state, that Thomas tie her to the bed. He eagerly complied, but quickly realized that she was exhibiting control over his will. He was in charge not her. So he quickly took over, forcing her to do his will.

It proved difficult for Thomas to maintain the upper hand because

Sandy was so willing to comply especially after he revealed his identity.

"I knew you would come back to see me." Sandy told Thomas.

"Here, have some wine. I don't want to talk, I want to fuck." Thomas answered as he rudely dumped the wine into her mouth.

Sandy talked incoherently between shit-eating grins and laughter.

"Please stop talking. Have some more wine." Thomas lifted her head and poured more wine and GHB into her mouth. He shoved pillows under her so that he would not have to lie on top of her to perform. He didn't have to worry about her trying to embrace him since she was tied to the four-poster bed.

Sandy moaned and tried to move her hips to meet him. "Damn, you're making me crazy.

Thomas soon tired of her persistent coaxing and reached into his bag for the organophosphates and LSD spray, which he liberally applied to her chest and face. "Now you're just like one of my clients, no complaining and no unnecessary conversation."

He finished then took Sandy to the bathtub for his final ritual. He watched as the bubbles rose rapidly from her mouth and nose. The bubbles slowed until they struggled to rise from her face. When there was no air left to exchange with the water, Thomas moved from the room— Sandy's lungs were full of water.

"Finally, total silence." Thomas left the house as quickly as he had come. The rain stopped by early afternoon and was not scheduled to return until sometime next week. He would use the time off to replenish his list of victims since it was currently dwindling. He would spend the next few days collecting names in Western and Northern Virginia. Three women down and seven more to go. This was the wildest vacation he'd ever been on so he decided to extend it until he was finished, no matter how long it took.

ANTHONY P. JONES   D8 WITH F8

Chapter
11

4:45 p.m., Thursday afternoon Renita finished the last presentation for the week. The officers from around the country were armed with new information that would allow them to identify and pursue serial killers more successfully in their respective cities and towns.

Schaffer, on the other hand, had gathered enough information to write a series of articles for the *Post*. He planned to write a weeklong column that would help his readers understand that most serial killers are seductive and manipulative. They perpetuate their will with brutal ease.

With the hour late and the traffic impossible, the officers were given the option to spend another night at Quantico. Two thirds of them passed on the offer and left to fight the relentless Northern Virginia traffic. Those who stayed were treated to a tour of the FBI facilities and a rare chance to test their shooting skills with paintball guns in *Hogan's Alley*. They jumped at the once-in-a-lifetime opportunity.

Renita and Schaffer went to the F.A.T.S. interactive shooting classroom. Their laser pistols eliminated any noise that could prove distracting. When they completed the course, she glanced over and noticed the smirk on his face. "That was an impressive display of marksmanship mister."

Schaffer shrugged one shoulder. "I'm a bit rusty, but I guess I did alright."

"Go ahead and let the cockiness shine, you've earned the right. When they set these things up, no two people get the same scenario, so it's not like you could have watched anyone else to gain an upper hand." Renita sat her gun down and leaned on the counter. "The instructor pulled me aside after we came out. You're the only person who shot the grandmother-looking hostage with a gun to her head. As a matter of fact, you shot both of them, grandma and the guy with the gun to her head."

"I guess I screwed up."

"That's the point, you didn't. They were both bad guys working as a team. How'd you figure that out?"

"Well," Schaffer couldn't hide his grin. "Grandma had the hairiest legs I've ever seen on a woman and she had her hand in her pocket. I figured she had to be holding a gun."

Renita's head moved side to side. "Not many of the experts that shoot here get that one right."

"That's because they're FBI. In the Secret Service, we're used to guarding the President. We have to make split second decisions about people or someone could kill the man in our charge."

"Yeah, but you haven't been in the Service for quite a while."

"What can I say; our training must just be better."

Renita popped him on the arm and left for the playback session. "I hope you found the presentations interesting." Renita said as they walked into the video area of the classroom where an instructor would let them watch the playback while critiquing the session.

"That's the understatement of the year. I've got so much material it's going to take weeks to sort it all out." Schaffer held up his digital recorder. "I found myself wanting to help you guys track down the bastards that prey on people."

"Be careful what you wish for. You may get your chance yet; even though we don't typically allow you Secret Service types to cross over to a better agency." They stepped through Renita's office door. She walked straight to her desk and shuffled a couple of memos.

"I don't know, I'm above the cut off age to join the Bureau. Besides, we sign an oath not to degrade the Service by stepping down a level. Even if I weren't too old, I don't feel up to the training." Schaffer sighed and sat in a chair in front of Renita's desk.

"Bull shit! You're former Marine re-con and you're in great shape. The training would be a cakewalk for you. I've read your records. You're an expert marksman with multiple weapons and you received several commendations and medals both in the Corps and the Secret Service. Not to mention, your profile lists you as a skilled Martial Artist. You were an instructor for God's sake. You'd more than likely show up some of the instructors if you went through the academy."

"I was trying to be modest. But, since you brought it up, I would be great wouldn't I?" Schaffer straightened his tie and stood at attention.

Renita shook her head and rolled her eyes. "Too bad you couldn't pass the mental evaluation."

Schaffer squinted and shook his finger at Renita. "You'd better be nice to me. I'm doing some of the cooking this weekend."

"In that case, I'll have to see if I can have you appointed as a deputized U.S. Marshal." Renita sat on the edge of her desk and crossed her arms.

"Can you really do that? I've got the background." Schaffer's eyebrows raised and he relaxed his shoulders.

"Maybe, it's usually reserved for retired law enforcement officers without mental issues. Renita grabbed Schaffer's arm and they started towards the door.

Schaffer touched her hand. "So, are we doing dinner again tonight?" He looked down to her face for an answer.

Renita stopped and answered apagogically. "Thanks, Schaffer. I'd love to, but I've spent too much time away from Tina this week. As quiet as it's been, I don't think she's missed me as much as I have her. She's having too much fun with Nina and Joe."

"Not a problem. I've got twenty-eight papers waiting for me when I get home. I only read the *Post* here this week; there wasn't time for any of the rest." Schaffer rubbed both eyes with his hands. "Gretchen may have moved in with my neighbor by now too. I usually try not to be away from her this long." They stopped walking when they reached the door to the parking lot. Cars were lined up waiting to leave one parking lot for another, I-95. "I think I'll have a glass of scotch while I'm waiting for traffic to die down."

"Don't have too many. I want you to get home safely." Renita turned to face him and for the first time kissed Schaffer on the lips.

"Who needs a drink after a kiss like that? Let me walk you to your car, I'm going to go ahead and get on the road as well." Schaffer pulled Renita close again. "You realize that you're not going to be able to get rid of me now?" He inched his face closer to hers without apprehension.

"I hope not." Renita put one finger across his lips as if to say, *that's all for now*. Then she lowered her head and hugged him tightly.

Schaffer kissed the top of her head. "Are you trying to drive me crazy?"

"No, just keep you interested. Renita released her grip of his waist.

"Come on; let me get you to your car. You don't want to be in this traffic any longer than you have to." Schaffer put his arm around Renita as they strolled across the parking lot.

Chapter

12

Schaffer drove in silence towards Highway 3 near Fredericksburg. Thinking about everything he'd heard this week, Lynda came back to mind. He lifted his IPhone and called an old friend. When the answer came, he responded happily. "Bacchus Jones!"

Schaffer and Bacchus had met when they'd worked a case together involving a drug dealer, who was also counterfeiting US currency faster than the Mint could make it.

Bacchus got his name because his mother said he arrived after a night filled with wine drinking. And since the original Bacchus was the god of wine, the name just seemed to fit. Most people who knew him just called him Tree because his arms were often described as tree trunks.

Bacchus was a private investigator, specializing in cases involving abused women and children. He decided to dedicate himself to this cause after losing his wife and kids. A case he was working for the DEA had him tracking a Mexican drug lord. When Bacchus got too close, the drug lord found Bacchus' family; raped his wife and killed her and the kids.

Bacchus came home to the bloody scene. He buried his family and boarded a plane to Mexico. It took him two weeks to locate the drug lord. When he found him, Bacchus took the man out into the desert. There he staked him out in the hot sun. Bacchus used a pair of pliers to individually break the man's fingers and toes. When the pain would begin to subside, Bacchus let an agitated scorpion sting the man.

Bacchus kept him alive for three days. By then, he had used a ball peen hammer to break the man's arms and legs. The drug lord was praying for death, so Bacchus shoved a quarter-stick of dynamite up the man's rectum. He used a blowtorch to set the man's hair on fire and finally lit a fifty foot fuse. The explosion eased his pain and he promised to bring pain to anyone who purposefully hurt women or children. He resigned from the DEA the next day.

"Mr. O'Grady; Black man with the Irish name."

"At least it's my last name. I can't say much for a Black man with a Greek first name."

Bacchus smiled. "Okay, little man, what's on your mind? I'm busy getting sleaze-balls off the street."

"Tree, there's something I want you to look into for me. A friend of mine died in Charlottesville a few days ago. Her name was Lynda Goodwin. The paper said it was an accidental death."

"But you don't think that's the case."

"It could be." Schaffer paused, deciding whether to share his next thought. "I just left the FBI's National Academy…"

"Oh, God, Schaffer, didn't you listen to them at the end. Not every death is the result of a serial killer."

"Yeah, yeah, I know. I'm just looking for some peace of mind."

Bacchus' eyes fell on a picture of his wife and kids. "I'll see what I can find."

"Great, I'll be back home later tonight. I'll call you tomorrow." As he turned onto Highway 3 he flipped through the CDs in the seat next to him. He popped Louis Armstrong in and relaxed. Louie started to sing in the gravelly voice he was known for, *A Kiss to Build a Dream On*. The lighthearted melody and words made Schaffer smile; they were the perfect expression of what he was feeling. The kiss Renita gave him twenty minutes ago was the kiss described in the song. He wanted to close his eyes, listen to the words and think of that moment over and over again. The road however demanded his attention. He knew he would listen to the song several more times before the night ended, giving it his full attention.

When the garage door went up Gretchen began barking and whining, she knew Schaffer was home. She pounced on him the minute the door opened. Her tail wagged furiously showing her happiness at having him back.

"I'm glad to see you too girl." Schaffer patted Gretchen on the head. She refused to move from his leg. "Are you going to let me come in? Come on. We'll go running in a few minutes."

Gretchen dashed into the house and Schaffer followed. Inside he found all the weeks papers neatly stacked on the breakfast table. His mail was in neat piles above the papers.

"Wow. Donna is more obsessive than I am, huh girl? She stacked each paper by name and date." More than once Donna asked Schaffer how and why he read so many papers a day. He always told her he needed to stay informed. So she prepared the papers in eight neat piles, *New York Times, Washington Post, Richmond Times Dispatch, Charlottesville Daily Progress, USA Today, Miami Herald, Chicago Tribune, and the LA Times*.

Schaffer picked up the *Charlottesville Daily Progress* to see if there was any additional news about Lynda Goodwin. Not finding anything additional in the *Daily Progress* he turned to the Richmond

Times. There was nothing in Monday's, nothing in Tuesday's. And Wednesday's paper contained nothing on Lynda.

Schaffer threw the paper back on the table and went into his study. There he turned on his desktop PC and waited for it to boot up. From the start up page he clicked his Internet service, and instantly it appeared. For the past two weeks, each time he logged onto the Net, Schaffer wondered why he'd waited so long to install a high-speed connection. He typed in several parameters for a search, death by drowning + Virginia obituaries. Almost fifty matches jumped on the screen. Schaffer narrowed the search, death by drowning + bathtub + Virginia obituaries. This time only five matches appeared on the screen, two of them were children the other three were women.

Lynda Goodwin of Charlottesville, Gloria Stegal of Hampton, and Sandy Nanney of Lynchburg all had died from drowning in their bathtubs. The first and last were ruled accidental and Gloria's had been ruled a suicide. They all died within a four-day period. Schaffer's mind began racing with the possibilities, despite what he was told during the class.

Jim Clemente and Renita warned the class to be aware that they were more sensitive to the possibility of a serial killer just after the class. It never failed, after officers attended the National Academy, calls to the FBI's BAU increased. The training made each officer suspect that every murder in their jurisdiction could be the work of a serial killer. Especially, one in which they had no suspects. Jim compared it to second year medical students who began to exhibit symptoms of the diseases they were studying.

Schaffer sat back calmly in his chair and took a deep breath. "Okay let's look at this rationally, Gretchen. Each of these women died in the bathtub, that's a check in the serial killer's column. From the obituary pictures we can see that two of them were White and one was Black, that's a check in the random column. They died in three different parts of the state, another check for the random column." Schaffer looked for other similarities, but there were none. The most obvious fact should have been that none of these deaths were considered murder. Still, Schaffer wanted to break everything down. He looked at his watch, 7:25 p.m. The Chief of Police for the city of Norfolk was in class with him all week. Schaffer was willing to bet that the first thing the chief would do when he returned home was go to the office.

Schaffer got his notebook from the class and opened it to the page that contained all the names and numbers of the officers attending that session. He slid his finger down until he found the Chief's name and number, then he picked up the phone and dialed. To Schaffer's surprise, the Chief gave them his direct dial number, so he answered the phone himself, bypassing all underlings.

"Hey, Chief. This is Schaffer O'Grady. From the profiling class."

"Yeah, O'Grady. That was one hell of a class wasn't it?" The chief sat back and thumbed through several files.

"You can say that again. Say, Chief. I was wondering if you could help me." Schaffer moved the pointer to Gloria's name and clicked. The obituary came up. "There was a young lady who drowned down that way on Monday." Schaffer listened for any reaction from the chief.

"Yeah. Gloria Stegal. A lot of men will rest easier with her gone." The chief pulled a file from the group in his hand. "She had a hell of a reputation of skinning them alive in divorce court. She also refused to represent men; she's a man-eater. That probably led to her breakup about a year ago."

Schaffer listened impatiently, drumming his fingers on his desk. "That's the one, Chief. Do you think you could get me a copy of the police report?"

The chief set down the stack of files and opened the one he pulled out. "That shouldn't be too hard, even though she lived in Hampton. I'll have to put in a call over there. Give me your fax number. If they'll send it I'll get it off as soon as possible. If not you'll have to come down here in person."

"Thanks, Chief." Schaffer gave him the number, hung up and immediately called the Charlottesville police central office. He was told that he could pick up the police report on Lynda Goodwin on Monday. At the Lynchburg police department he was advised that he would have to speak directly with the Chief, who was gone for the day, to obtain that information.

Schaffer went upstairs to shower away the grime of his travel. He emerged a few minutes later wearing a purple silk Tai Chi uniform and a pair of Kung Fu slippers. Gretchen ran to the door leading to the basement and started down.

"Not tonight girl. My workout will have to wait until tomorrow." Schaffer looked at his outfit then realized that Gretchen couldn't tell the difference between black and purple, silk or cotton. His purple Tai Chi uniform was for relaxing.

Gretchen came back to the top step and barked urging Schaffer to come with her. But, he was already pouring a glass of his favorite scotch, Balvenie. Then he walked to his office to see if the fax had come while he was in the shower.

Schaffer felt a sense of rejuvenation every time he entered his office. Lynda told him that the color red charged the creative mind and gave him power. But, waiting for the police report to come made him feel neither creative nor powerful. Schaffer only felt sadness thinking about the woman who designed his home, now lying in the morgue.

The printer came to life spitting out information. Schaffer lifted the first page and began to read. Subject found in tub of master bedroom. Empty bottle of wine on side suggest subject was drinking before death. There was no sign of forced entry into home. Employee who found subject says all doors were locked. Death appears to be suicide. Autopsy ordered. Video of home and scene of death on file in the evidence room. On the bottom of the page was a short note.

"I'm sharing this with you as a favor to our friend in Norfolk. The full report will only be available if you come here in person. I understand your reasons for wanting to know, but, I have to be comfortable with you before releasing any additional information." It was signed W. Winston Wellington III.

Schaffer propped one foot in his chair and exhaled. "Why would anyone want to kill themselves?" Gretchen came into the office whining. "I'm coming girl. Let me grab an Hemmingway Masterpiece then we'll go to the deck so that I can smoke my cigar." Schaffer threw the report on the desk and dialed Tree once again.

"Damn, you again? I know I'm good, but even I can't solve a case that fast."

Schaffer lifted an Hemmingway Masterpiece from his humidor. "I just had a question. How hard is it for a person to drown themselves in a bathtub?"

"Yeah, I saw that in the report. Accidental, they say, well, she'd been drinking. So if she'd had too many, it wouldn't be that hard."

"I wasn't speaking about Lynda. I found a couple of other drownings in the state and one was ruled a suicide. I just thought that'd be a bit difficult." Schaffer pinched the end of the cigar and placed it in his mouth.

Tree thought for a second. "If they had some help, say alcohol or drugs, it still wouldn't be that hard. What are you up to? I hope you remembered what I said earlier and you're not chasing wild geese."

"I'm preparing a story about my week at the National Academy. I doubt these cases are related. I'm just starting my research. I'll catch you later; the little woman is waiting for me on the deck."

"Damn dog. You'd better get yourself a real woman before you're too damned old to remember what to do."

"We'll just have to see about that." Schaffer hung up and followed Gretchen to the deck. He lit his Hemmingway, walked to the rail and looked up into the sky. All the clouds were gone and the air had cooled considerably. The smoke that left Schaffer's mouth was part tobacco smoke and part vapor. He walked over to the antique *Coke- Cola* outside thermometer, forty-eight degrees. "Now that's my type of nighttime temperature. Gretchen, we're coming to the best part of the year." She walked over and put her front paws on the rail next to him.

Schaffer scratched behind her ears and continued to puff on his cigar. "We've got to get ready for company tomorrow girl. We'd better turn in early."

Sleep was approaching rapidly when the phone rang. Schaffer wanted to let it ring, but he thought it might be one of the police departments calling back so he answered it.

"Hello." Sleep was obvious in Schaffer's voice.

"I'm sorry. Did I wake you?" Renita asked.

Schaffer softened immediately recognizing Renita's voice. "No, not at all. It's good to hear from you."

"Thank you." Renita busied her hands arranging and rearranging items on her nightstand. "I thought about only working half a day and heading out, but I don't want to disturb your plans if I arrive early."

Schaffer picked up on her tentativeness. "The earlier the better; I can't wait to see you."

Renita sat still and her breathing relaxed. "I can't wait to see you either. I've got to do a little paperwork, but I should be finished around ten."

"Great. Then you and Tina should be here around noon. I'll have lunch ready." Schaffer turned the clock to see the time.

"I hope you don't mind. I'm coming alone." Renita's words were part apology and part warning. "Tina will be coming with Joe and Nina later."

Schaffer paused trying to think through the fog in his head. His heart raced and he couldn't think what to say for a moment. "Okay, then it's lunch for two."

"Thanks Schaffer." He could feel the weight of her burden lifted. When she began speaking again, her confident tone returned. "I'll see you at noon." Renita hung up the phone.

Chapter
13

Schaffer woke early Friday morning filled with excitement anticipating Renita's arrival. The police reports would have to wait until Monday when he could resume his detective work.

Right now, however his attention was on lunch. But, before he could fix lunch he needed to run to the Kroger to pick up a few items. He called Gretchen, who ran in soaked from her morning romp, so he made her wait in the garage until he returned.

Less than thirty minutes after leaving, Schaffer was back home. As the garage door went up Gretchen moved forward, just out of reach of the rain, which seemed to want to taper off. She barked, informing him that she was now dry and wanted to return to the inside of the house.

Schaffer got out of the car, leaving the groceries for the moment and gave Gretchen a good spray of doggie deodorant. He brushed it through her coat then she ran down the corridor to the door that led to the kitchen.

"Just a minute girl, I have to get the groceries." Her tail pounded furiously from side to side as she patiently waited for him to arrive and open the door. "Let's go in and fix lunch."

Gretchen didn't move more than two feet away from him. "I take it you want to eat as well?" She looked up and wagged her stubby tail. "Today I have something special for you." Schaffer reached in the bag and quickly pulled out a can. "Ta-da! Canned food. Maybe this will help your gas problem. You'd better be on your best behavior. There will be no farting in the house this weekend!"

There was an immediate lack of acknowledgement for his statement. The vet said that it was very common for high protein food to cause gas, but Gretchen's was intense. Schaffer knew that one fart could asphyxiate anything within a one-mile radius. What made it worse was the fact that she didn't have the common decency to fart loudly. She let them slip out silently only to be detected by the olfactory gland. By then, it was too late for anyone to take cover. Gretchen made short work of her food. Since it was still raining, Schaffer let her go to the solarium with some of her toys. His attention turned to the kitchen where he was fixing lunch for Renita.

Schaffer decided on a recipe that was in his head even though he

ANTHONY P. JONES   D8 WITH F8

only made it a time or two. One cup of cottage cheese one cup of ricotta, forced through a sieve. Then add fresh chopped basil, salt, pepper and jumbo crabmeat. He mixed it all together and put it into the fridge until after he made the fresh pasta. Schaffer had raised hell with the clerk at Williams-Sonoma when she told him a pasta machine cost $100. As it turned out it was one of his best investments. He could make pasta from scratch before a pot of water on the stove could come to a boil.

Before finishing the pasta Schaffer needed to make a sauce. He often said that the sauce is the most important part of any pasta dish. The Sauce needs to complement the ravioli filling without overpowering the pasta flavor. Heating a pot, he added a splash of extra virgin olive oil and then chopped garlic, onions and tomatoes. While their flavors blended in the hot oil Schaffer pureed several other tomatoes, eventually adding them to the pot along with the fresh basil, oregano, parsley and just a touch of rosemary. All of the herbs he had gathered earlier from the herb beds in his backyard. Schaffer considered fresh herbs a must to give food the best possible taste. The sauce needed at least an hour to simmer before it was ready, so he used the free time to join Gretchen and smoke an Hemmingway Masterpiece.

Nearly an hour later, Schaffer moved to the kitchen with Gretchen in tow. Within moments of her arrival, she had that *I hope you drop something* look on her face. Schaffer was a sucker for that look and he gave her a petrified pig ear to chew on. They were effective at satisfying her so that she didn't beg, which kept the peace.

Schaffer left one bay door up in the garage anticipating Renita's arrival. A chime from the alarm system beeped twice letting Schaffer know that someone had just entered the garage. It also caused Gretchen to drop the pig ear and run to the door leading to the garage and begin barking.

"Hush, girl. We have company." Immediately, she quieted and Schaffer opened the door and started down the corridor to meet Renita. Gretchen ran past him and arrived at Renita's car first. As the car door opened Gretchen sniffed to see if it was friend or foe. Dogs always seemed to know the difference. Renita got out and Gretchen jumped up to greet her.

"Gretchen, get down!" Schaffer shouted and tugged at the dog's collar.

Renita rubbed Gretchen's head. "She's okay. She's just protecting her man. Aren't you girl? What a good-looking dog. Where'd you get her?"

Schaffer eased his grip on the collar and pet Gretchen as well. "In Winchester, from Longacre kennel. Janet breeds German Short-Hairs and Irish Wolfhounds there. She even guarantees their personalities, if you can believe that."

"She's a real sweetie." Renita shook Gretchen's head from side to side between her hands.

"Don't let her fool you. Come on Gretchen let Renita come in." Schaffer peaked inside Renita's car. "Do you have any bags?"

"Yeah, just a couple." Renita pointed to the trunk. "The FBI teaches you to travel light."

"That's refreshing. A woman who travels light." Schaffer moved to get the bags.

"Watch it or I'll have to arrest you for sexual harassment." Renita slid the handcuffs from a pouch on her belt.

Schaffer put his hands in the air. "Do you promise to use your handcuffs and slap me with the handle of your Mag light if I'm bad?"

"Oh shut up you dirty old man." Renita walked over and gave him a big hug and kiss.

"Welcome to my humble abode." Schaffer started down the hall with one bag on his shoulder and pulled the other behind him.

"Abode yes, humble, I don't think so, at least not from what I've seen so far. It's beautiful! I can't wait to see the inside." She walked beside Schaffer noticing every detail of her surroundings.

"I'll show you around as soon as we're inside." Schaffer put his arm around Renita and they walked down the corridor that connected the garage to the house. He opened the door that led to the kitchen and showed her in.

"It smells wonderful in here." Renita inhaled deeply and looked around the room. "Where did you order from?"

"Please! I'm the best chef in the area." Schaffer pointed to the wizard on his chef's jacket. "I wouldn't dream of ordering out on a first date. Are you hungry?"

"Starved!" Renita had to fight to keep from drooling.

"Then let's eat first and I'll show you around later." Schaffer set the bags in the family room.

Renita looked around the kitchen. "Wow! How many houses did you put together to build this kitchen?"

"Hey, I don't like working in confined spaces. I think the kitchen is the heart of any home, so I designed it with that in mind." Schaffer slid out a chair and patted the cushion. "Have a seat here at the breakfast bar while I finish the pasta. Would you like a glass of wine?"

"Sure." Renita sat down and watched him move about the kitchen.

"Red or white?" Schaffer held up the bottle of red wine and pointed to the refrigerator for the white.

"I'll leave that up to you." Renita answered cautiously since she didn't know if Schaffer was a traditionalist or not; some would insist on a red wine with the red sauce she could smell simmering on the stove.

"Then, why don't we start out with a white? I have this lovely, crisp Sauvignon Blanc chilled." Schaffer set the bottle of red wine on the breakfast bar and moved to the refrigerator for the white.

"I'll have to trust your judgment."

"A cop trusting a reporter's judgment. That's a first." Schaffer handed Renita a glass and popped the cork using a 'rabbit' corkscrew. He poured just a little in her glass. "Have a taste and let me know what you think."

She swirled the wine and drank what was in her glass. "It's fine, sir." Renita set her glass on the bar to be filled.

Schaffer filled her glass and his. Then he added water to the bowl of the Kitchen Aid mixer, which contained the pasta flour. While the ball of dough was forming he pulled fresh spinach from an ice bath. "I'll make the ravioli while the spinach is steaming. Then we can begin with our mixed greens salad just before I boil the ravioli."

"You'd better watch yourself. A girl could get used to this treatment, fresh pasta, mixed greens salad and wine. If you set your hook too deeply you won't be able to throw me back." Renita looked over the top of her glass for his reaction and took a sip of wine.

"In that case, you'd better not have desert." Schaffer rubbed his stomach and then reached for his glass.

"Did you make that too?" She asked and looked around to see what it could be.

"I did. But I'm not telling you what it is." He walked to the pasta machine.

"That's not fair." Renita protested and slightly pouted her lips.

"My lips are sealed." Schaffer moved his fingers across his lips as if zipping them. Then he ran the dough through the pasta machine. The second time through, he added the cheese and crab mixture in between the two layers of pasta and perfect little raviolis popped out."

"I'm impressed." Renita said watching his skill as a chef. Her appetite grew each time a perfectly formed ravioli fell from the pasta machine.

"How about going over there and putting on some music while I set the table?" Schaffer had all types of music in his CD case. He wondered if Joe told Renita that Jazz was his favorite.

Renita walked to the stereo and Schaffer went into the solarium to light the candles. The rain playfully splashed the glass ceiling and danced down the ten-foot glass sides of the room. A warm orange glow crossed the table in waves moving with the flicker of the candles.

Through the speakers in the family room and the solarium Wynton Marsalis began blowing *The Very Thought of You*. Schaffer slid the lighter back into his pocket and walked into the family room with Renita. She turned to him with a soul piercing stare. He took the glass from her hand and placed it on a table next to his. Renita melted into his arms and they danced to Wynton's melodies. The music said everything that needed to be said. Schaffer could feel Renita's heart beating against his chest as she did his.

When the song ended neither of them wanted to let go. They stood in the middle of the floor and held each other tightly, not daring to move.

Schaffer stopped rocking as the music ended. He laid his cheek on the top of her head. "Should I play it again?"

Renita looked up, smiled and lightly kissed him. "I'm afraid if you do I'll never be able to let go. Let's go eat, I'm starved."

Half way through the salads Schaffer got up to cook the ravioli. In three minutes, he returned with two pasta bowls. "Here you are, crab ravioli on a bed of steamed spinach topped with a basil red sauce."

Renita looked at the red sauce lightly covering the butter colored ravioli. The steam rising from the bowl filled the air with aroma that she could taste, even before taking a bite of the food. "You went to a lot of trouble for lunch."

"Well, to tell you the truth I'm trying to impress this young lady I recently met. So, I thought it best if I tested this dish out on you first. If you don't like it I'll know not to serve it to her." Renita slid off her shoe and kicked him under the table.

She cut the ravioli and slid a piece into her mouth. "This is wonderful." She held another piece in the air and waved it in front of his face. "You've got talent."

"So, will you keep me around?" Schaffer playfully tilted his head and batted his eyes. Renita stopped chewing and looked at him. His heart stopped, waiting for her to say something.

She looked down at her plate and cut another bite of food. "I promised myself that I wouldn't rush into a relationship again. They never seem to work out when I do and they're just too hard on Tina when they don't. I can't do that to her again."

"I don't want to rush you or Tina." Schaffer could feel the lump growing in his throat, making it difficult to speak. "I knew the moment I saw you that you were a very special lady. And Tina is adorable."

Renita looked up, fearful of the pain Tina would feel if he left. "You've already swept her off her feet."

"How am I doing with her mom?" Schaffer asked more seriously and looked into Renita's eyes.

"Honestly, I was gone before I met you. Nina painted a picture that no one could resist. If you listen to her, you're about as perfect as they come. As a profiler I'm trained to look beneath the surface, so I have to wonder why no one has plucked you from the garden yet." Renita gave Schaffer a melancholy smile. "Then, Nina told me about Doran."

Schaffer's face dropped in complete shock at the mention of Doran's name. All the color left his face. The statement caught him completely off guard and he was unable to speak.

Renita broke the awkward silence. "I've also learned to trust my gut."

Schaffer looked at Renita through their silence. Breathing again, the muscles in his neck relaxed. "What does your gut tell you?"

Renita slightly chuckled and began running her finger around the rim of her wine glass. "It's kind of like that old song, *It's Too Late to Turn Back Now.* I know what I feel and it scares me to death. I also know that I have a tremendous obstacle to overcome. Doran still owns your heart."

Schaffer nearly choked on his food. "God, what did Nina tell you? I completely understand your feelings of fear. I have them too. However, we can't ignore the more powerful feelings at hand. Don't worry; I'll never push you. Let's just let things develop." He looked down at his food and aimlessly pushed it around. "It's true that Doran has had a tremendous grip over me even though I haven't seen her in eighteen years. Until I met you, no one ever made me want to let go of the past, not initially, not even after time passed."

"I'm not sure I can compete with the greatest love of your life." Renita let her eyes drift back and forth from Schaffer's gaze.

Schaffer held his palms open towards her. "You already have. Hell, if you listen to Nina and Joe, we're practically married." They both laughed.

"Just yesterday, Nina said that she could see a new light surrounding me. Of course, I denied it. Then this morning Tina told me you were the one. She's never said that about anyone I've dated before." Renita toyed with a ravioli before lancing it with her fork and bringing it to her mouth.

"She's a smart girl. You should listen to her. There's no need to hide our feelings, at least they're honest." Schaffer reached for his wine.

"Are they really?" Renita sat her fork down and folded her hands in front of her face. "Or are they manifestations of what we would like them to be? Are you sure you're ready for what they mean if true?" Her question rolled from her mouth sounding like an interrogation.

"We just have to trust ourselves." Schaffer answered calmly and placed his hand over his heart. "I know what's here."

"I guess you're right. I've felt the same thing. It's just hard for me to trust. I've been burned too many times in the past."

"That's because until now, you've never met the right man." Schaffer beat his chest like Tarzan and grunted.

They finished eating, moved to a love seat near one of the windows and continued talking for what seemed like hours. The rain, which had been falling so hard earlier, stopped suddenly and the clouds gave way to the sun's intermittent peaking.

"This is stunning." Renita said looking out of the window at the rays of sunlight jutting from the clouds.

"What's that?" Schaffer turned to look in the same direction.

"That is one of the most beautiful rainbows I've ever seen." She walked to the window and pointed to a clear patch of sky.

"I think this calls for an investigation. Did you bring your jeans and hiking boots?" Schaffer asked, while looking at the rainbow.

"They're in my bag." Renita turned and started towards the family room.

"Great. Then I'll take your bags up to your room and you can change. Then we'll go search for our pot of gold."

"That sounds good." Renita followed him upstairs.

Renita changed and came downstairs. They headed out across the deck to start their walk. Gretchen made sure that she was also involved. No sooner had their feet hit the ground before Gretchen wedged herself between them. Her favorite covey of quail and her desire to run soon proved too tempting. Gretchen gave in and took off across the field in search of the quail.

Schaffer watched Gretchen run through an area of the field where he had sewn seed-bearing plants for the birds. "Now that our chaperone has fled I guess it would be okay if I held your hand."

Renita slid her hand in Schaffer's and they continued on their tour. They had not gone five hundred feet before Renita noticed Gretchen. "Look at her; she's so graceful holding that point. Not much can get your blood flowing as fast as watching a good bird dog find a covey of quail. Even though you know that the quail are in front of the dog you still jump when they take to the air."

Schaffer raised the eyebrows in surprise. "It sounds like you have personal experience in this matter. Did you hunt much in Louisiana?"

"My dad taught me at an early age. We looked forward to the time together every autumn. It was our bonding time."

Schaffer watched Gretchen as he reminisced about his hunting time. "Back in Kenbridge I used to go every afternoon. After I trained my first dog, I lived in the woods. The first time she held point I almost peed on myself. I was so excited I missed all the birds. Shana was so excited she didn't care."

"Was she a German Short Hair too?" Renita asked.

"No. She was an Irish Setter."

Renita stopped walking and looked at him intently. "What's with you and dogs' names? Isn't Rover and Spot good enough anymore?"

"They're okay, but I believe you give an Irish dog an Irish name and a German dog a German name."

"I see. Everything in your life has its place. So," she raised one eyebrow and gave him a devilish smile, "how did you get the name Schaffer O'Grady? Schaffer is German, I believe and O'Grady is Irish."

"Schaffer was my grandfather's name. His grandfather set his father free and gave him three thousand acres in Amelia County Virginia because they looked so much alike. In return, my great grandfather was required to choose a different last name. A local priest, Father Sean O'Grady had a hand in great grandpa's freedom, so he took the priest's last name. Like the priest, great-great grandpa was Irish. By the way not everything has a place, just clothes, CD's and dog's names. I'm not a 'tight ass,' but I am compulsive about a few things."

"What's the difference?"

"Simple. Tight asses only see things in black and white. People like me believe there's a lot of gray in the world, except when it comes to my clothes, CD's and dog's names. I guess that really makes me obsessive. Of course you already knew all this. After all you're the profiler." Schaffer smiled wickedly at his evident sniping.

"Guilty as charged. I can see now, not much gets by you. I'll have to stay on my toes." Renita started walking towards Gretchen.

"Maybe I should be a profiler." Schaffer said and followed her.

"Honey, you already are. That's one of the first things I noticed about you. You have the ability to sum up a crowd in a matter of seconds. That's a good quality to have."

"I take it you've already summed me up. How about us?" Schaffer stopped and turned her to face him.

Renita blushed and looked in his eyes. "I know what I'm feeling, I can't explain. We've known each other for a week and already I feel as if I've known you all my life. I'm totally comfortable with you and that goes against everything I've learned at the Bureau."

He held her shoulders. "Hasn't the FBI taught you to trust your instincts?"

"Sure they have. They've also taught me to consider all the possible angles before making a decision. I'm not sure I know all of them yet." She looked down at her feet.

Schaffer gently lifted her chin. "Trust yourself. Trust your heart, it won't lie." They walked in silence for a few seconds. He stopped and turned to face Renita. Reaching out, he brushed the hair from her eyes and held her face in his hands. "I'll never let you down, even if we simply remain just friends."

Renita stepped closer and laid her head on his chest and hugged him tightly. Schaffer rocked her in his arms and kissed her on the forehead. "Schaffer, I'd be lying if I didn't tell you that our situation scares me a bit."

"I know what you mean. It seems too good to be true. The early stages of any relationship are both euphoric and frightening. But, unless we are willing to let go and jump in we'll never know if the water feels good." He held her a little tighter then eased away.

Renita laughed at his choice of words. "It looks like we're going to get wet."

She looked up and they kissed. Neither of them ever wanted it to end. Passion and desire covered them from head to toe. They dove right in, never looking back. When they came up for air they both began to laugh.

Schaffer's euphoria was evident by his facial expression. "Wow, when you decide to take the plunge, you go off the high board."

"I don't do anything half way. You need to know that right now." Renita's face was humorless and her eyes searched for understanding from Schaffer.

"I hear you loud and clear." He held Renita close. They both

ANTHONY P. JONES   D8 WITH F8

jumped when Gretchen frightened the nervous birds to the air.

No other words were needed. They both understood what they were doing. Their lives could never return from where they had come in such a short time. Though they were involved in love relationships before, they were now in the virgin territory of a new relationship, full of promise, possibility and uncertainty.

They walked down near the edge of the brook and carelessly tossed in rocks as if throwing pennies into a wishing well. Gretchen came to the brook for a drink. Renita and Schaffer waited for her to finish so that they could resume their rock tossing.

Inadvertently, Schaffer looked down at his watch. "It's almost four. We'd better get back to the house. We have guests coming,"

He hadn't realized his inference to them as a couple. Renita didn't miss it. "*WE* have guests coming."

"Yeah. Joe said they were leaving DC around two to get ahead of the traffic. They should be here in a few minutes."

"Then I guess *WE'D* better get ready for them." Renita smiled and stood to leave.

That's when it hit him; Schaffer knew there was no turning back. His mother always said that he wasted no time falling in love. He managed to be very cautious over the past few years, but it was hopeless to fight his heart when it came to Renita. He stood up and followed her. Out of the blue a question escaped his lips. "What makes you happy?"

Renita's brow furrowed. "That's an interesting question. There are so many answers. Without a doubt, seeing Tina smile tops the list. Feeling secure isn't far behind."

"Security?" He pondered her answer.

"Yeah. It makes me comfortable. When I'm comfortable I'm happy. What about you?" Renita eased her hand into his.

"I'm living my happiness. The only thing I had been missing was a committed, comfortable relationship. Now that I've found you and Tina I don't think there's anything else I need." Schaffer's face held a look of contentment.

"How can you be so sure we're what you need?" Renita started swinging his hand.

"I've only had this feeling once before. It's really hard to explain, but I know that we have a special connection. You said earlier that you felt like you have known me all your life. To me, it feels like I've found something I've been searching for all my life. What I feel inside is what the Knights of the Round Table would have felt like if they had found the

Holy Grail."

Renita stopped swinging his hand and stood still. "Did you feel this way with Doran as well?"

"Everything happens for a reason. I know that I was in love with her, but our relationship really frightened her. She couldn't commit completely. Some strange force kept her just out of my reach. I've spent many unproductive years wondering why. I don't feel the same type of negative force between us, we're a natural fit."

"Where is she now?" Renita continued to pry, still in need of convincing.

"I have no idea."

Renita pursed her lips and looked at Schaffer apagogically. "So, if she shows up tomorrow, her feelings haven't diminished and the force holding you two apart is gone. What then? The two of you have a history. We've only shared a couple of kisses."

He sighed and crossed his arms. "Doran is a part of my past. She was a special part of my youth. It's also true that I haven't let anyone else get as close to me as she was eighteen years ago. I can never forget what we had and if she showed up I'm sure we would still be friends. However, the same force that kept us apart pushed me in a different direction. I wasn't looking for a relationship when I found you. As a matter of fact, I conceded the possibility of ever having a serious relationship. Then, in walks this FBI agent." Schaffer reached out and held her. "From the moment I laid eyes on you I knew you were what I have been looking for all these years. Short of Jesus walking up to me and telling me you're not the one, nothing and no one can change what I believe or what I feel."

Renita raised her hands and rested them on his arms. "So what makes me different?"

Schaffer's face softened. "As strange as it sounds, I don't feel butterflies when I'm around you. I don't feel as if my head is in the clouds. What I do feel is peacefulness. When I'm around you, I feel calm and content. I was very anxious waiting for you to arrive today. The minute you got here a sense of tranquility surrounded me. Tina plays into my feelings as well. When I was around her I could feel a sense of renewed life. She brings happiness to everyone she's around."

"You can tell a lot after just one meeting." Renita grabbed the sleeves of Schaffer's shirt and pulled him closer.

Schaffer didn't resist. "Call it ESP if you want. I can just tell. I can also tell that she has a great teacher. But of course, I should expect nothing less, just look at her mom."

"You're too kind." She hugged him with one arm and they started walking to the house. "Are you sure it doesn't bother you that she came to me out of wedlock?"

Schaffer stopped walking and held her with both arms. "As I said before, everything happens for a reason. You wouldn't be the person you are if she had not come to you. Your ability to carry on and not be deterred speaks volumes. You didn't drop her off at your mom and dad's and hit the streets. Many of your counterparts would have been out partying and hanging out in the streets."

"I couldn't be separated from her. She's too important to me. I didn't know how I was going to make it when I went to the Academy for training. Tina encouraged me by phone daily even though she was too young to talk, hearing her coo kept me going. Being apart from her was the hardest thing I've ever done."

"You've done an excellent job. Not many people could have accomplished what you did under the circumstances." Schaffer put one arm behind her back and they resumed their walk.

They came to the back portion of the vineyard and Gretchen stopped and looked towards the house. This time she wasn't holding point; she perked her ears and looked intently.

"What is it girl?" Schaffer asked and moved closer to her.

Before he got another word out, she bolted towards the house barking.

"That bark means someone has just arrived at the house. Joe, Nina and Tina must be here."

Chapter
14

Before they reached the side of the house they could hear Joe fussing with Gretchen.

"Shut the hell up you mangy mutt! We know you're here." Joe yelled

"Joseph! Why do you insist on yelling at the dog?" Nina hissed, "You're setting a terrible example for Tina. Come here Gretchen. Just ignore that rude old man." Gretchen stopped barking and whined as she went over to Nina for a friendly pat on the head.

"Tina, meet Gretchen." Nina waved Tina closer.

Tina patted her too. "What kind of dog is she? She's pretty."

"She's a German Short Haired Pointer. And she's a sweet dog, aren't you girl?" Nina hugged and rubbed Gretchen over and over.

Renita and Schaffer came around the side of the house. "I see you've met the lady of the house." Schaffer watched Tina playing with the dog. "So Tina, what do you think?"

"She's great. Does she know any good tricks?" Tina asked hopefully, never taking her eyes off the dog.

"I'm still working on that." Schaffer looked at his other guests. "How was your trip Nina? Did the old man drive you crazy?" He moved his index finger in circles next to his head and cut his eyes in Joe's direction.

Nina took his arm. "Schaffer, you know how Joe drives. Once we got to the mountains everything was fine. It's so beautiful up here. It had a calming effect on Joe and he stopped yelling at everyone in front of him."

Tina ran to Renita. "Hi mommy, did you miss me?"

"Always sweetie." Renita wrapped Tina in her arms and kissed her. "Did you behave for Uncle Joe and Aunt Nina?"

Joe didn't give Tina a chance to answer. "She's never a problem." Joe cocked his head towards Schaffer. "Speaking of problems, how's your day been?"

"Wonderful." Renita eased back into Schaffer's arms. "A girl could get used to this kind of treatment." Renita's face lit up.

Nina punched Joe's arm and leaned close. "I told you they would be good together. You shouldn't have taken so long to introduce them. I was beginning to wonder if you were trying to keep Renita for yourself."

"Hush up woman. You know there's no one else out there for me. Just the same, I like to keep my options open. You never know what can happen." Joe ducked expecting Nina's right hook to answer his comment.

"He's impossible." Schaffer shook his head. "Nina I don't know why you put up with him, it's not like he's that great of a catch. I've got a list of much more exciting eligible bachelors if you're interested."

Joe interrupted. "Nina, did I tell you that we're short one reporter? This young boy got so uppity that I had to fire him. I wonder how he's going to pay for that big house in the country with the vine-yard." Joe pronounced it as if it were two words.

"That's vineyard. Speaking of wine, why don't we go in for a glass? My 1997 Hendry Cab just arrived this week." Schaffer held his hand towards the door.

Joe needled him. "Does it have a screw cap like your usual week-old vintage?"

Schaffer remained undeterred, speaking to Nina and Renita. "Actually, Renita, you tried this one at the hotel. After tasting it, I called George at the vineyard and had him send a case. Thank God, he had one left." He turned his attention back to Joe. "Joe, I've got you a bottle of Hog Head premium peach wine. It's fresh too they made it this morning. I couldn't believe how much it had gone up in price. It's over a dollar now."

They began moving towards the entrance to the house. Tina tugged on Renita's hand to get her to stop. When they were just a little ways from everyone else she stuck out her finger and curled it motioning for Renita to come closer. Her whisper was like most little kids, loud enough for everyone to hear. "Why do they fight all the time?"

Renita frowned at Joe and Schaffer. "They're not fighting sweetheart. They're men. So they just don't know any other way to express their love for each other. We'll just have to set a good example for them today, okay?"

"Okay." Tina giggled, covering her mouth.

Nina smacked Joe and Schaffer on the back of their heads at the same time. "You two should be ashamed."

Schaffer put his arm around Joe. "Truce?" Schaffer puckered up as if he were going to give Joe a kiss.

"Let go of me! I ain't no gay, faggot, lesbian, homosexual." Joe struggled to get free.

"Hey! Discrimination is a federal crime." Renita shot back with no sign of humor.

Tina was between Nina and Renita. She sighed, shook her head, and looked up at them. "They're going to need a lot of work."

In the kitchen Renita grabbed the glasses and Schaffer got the wine. He opened the bottle and poured a little into a glass. George had never disappointed him in the past, and this proved to be no different. "I think the George has out done himself with this one. Prepare your taste buds to be dazzled." Schaffer poured the adults a full glass and Tina got a teaspoon full in her glass. "Here's to lasting friendships." He said raising his glass.

"Wow, this is good!" Tina exclaimed. Everyone laughed at her.

Renita pulled the handcuffs from her belt and grabbed Schaffer's arm. "You know of course, that I have to arrest you now?"

"Have you got an extra set of those?" Joe asked immediately looking like a mischievous child. "I want to try them on Nina."

The smack was heard before Nina spoke. "Joseph!"

"On that note, I'm moving to the porch. Come on Tina help me pick out a cigar." Schaffer took her hand.

"Okay Schaffer." Tina grinned looking pleased.

"Hey, you know better young lady! You don't call adults by their first names." Renita warned, pointing her finger in Tina's direction.

"Sorry mommy. I meant Mr. Schaffer."

"Schaffer is fine. Mr. makes me feel as old as Joe. I'll see to it that it's okay with your mom." Schaffer didn't look back, fearful that Renita's 'mommy look' was waiting for him too.

"Don't you start young man." Renita yelled to Schaffer.

In his best kid's voice he answered. "Yes, mommy." Then he turned to Joe. "Would you like one too?"

"Sure." Joe leaned down to Tina. "Tina, find me one with H-a-v-a-n-a on it." Joe smiled widely at her.

"Okay." Tina tugged Schaffer's hand. "Let's go Schaffer."

Schaffer looked down at Tina. "What uncle Joe isn't smart enough to realize is that my Hemmingway Masterpiece cigars are better than most of what he requested. They even come in a box shaped like a book, but we'll get him a Cuban, they're cheaper.

Joe's mouth went slack and he blinked several times as if looking for the right words, yet nothing made its way to his mouth.

Renita followed them down the hallway. "Since we're doing New Orleans cuisine tomorrow night, is there something I can fix for tonight?"

"Usually Fridays I go with S.O.S." Schaffer said looking over his shoulder.

"What?" Renita scrunched her face looking confused.

Schaffer grinned. "Same old—"

Renita put her hand in the air. "Never mind, I get the idea, leftovers."

"Exactly, but, since I wasn't here all week I made pizza sauce and dough. If you don't mind you can take the balls of dough from the fridge to warm and rise. Everyone can make the pizza of their choice."

"Oh boy! Homemade pizza. I can't wait till dinner." Tina rubbed her stomach. "Will you help me with mine, Schaffer?"

"Sure Tina." He leaned down close to her face. "I like veggie supreme, with pineapples. What about you?"

"That sounds good, but what are you going to make for mommy?" She asked and turned to Renita.

Schaffer looked directly at Renita when he answered. "What ever her heart desires."

Renita looked at him seductively with her eyes half open. "That's a tall order mister; I hope you're up to it."

Schaffer put his hand under his shirt and pretended to make his heart beat, through his clothing. "I'm up to the challenge, however; I may need a bit of coaching."

"I'll be glad to assist." Tina answered proudly. Schaffer and Renita both laughed.

"Here, Tina." Schaffer handed her a cigar. "Take this to Uncle Joe. Tell him I brought it back from Cuba two years ago and we'll meet him on the porch in a few minutes."

Tina took off from the den running back to the family room. "Uncle Joe. I've got your cigar. Schaffer and mommy will meet you on the porch."

Schaffer took Renita in his arms and held her close. "You know, I think you'll have to be my prisoner here in Charlottesville."

Renita looked up and touched her chest. "Me the prisoner? If you steal any more of my heart I'm going to put you away for life."

They kissed deeply and held each other. There was no hesitation or indecision in either of their actions. "You know we're perfect for each other." Schaffer ran his fingers through her hair.

"You've been saying that all day. You seem perfectly sure of it. How is that?" Renita pulled on the bottom of his shirt.

"One can never be completely sure. On the other hand, I've never been so sure about anything in my life. How's that for a contradiction?"

He kissed her forehead.

"I don't know if you've cast some type of spell over me, but I feel just as you do. And, Tina is completely entangled in your web. She keeps telling me that you're the one." Renita rests her head on his chest.

Schaffer stroked her hair. "What great faith. If only we could believe as the little children do. I think you should listen to her."

"She's never steered me wrong before. Her intuition is amazing at her age."

"Then I guess we'd better pick out a date?" Schaffer put his cheek on her head.

"Slow down big fellah. We still have a lot to talk about." Renita hated putting the brakes on, but she wanted Schaffer to be sure.

Schaffer snapped his fingers. "Damn! And I invited a priest over for dinner tomorrow."

Renita was grateful he had lightened the conversation. She stepped away from his grasp. "What? You haven't even talked to my dad yet."

"An old fashion girl, I like that." He pulled an Hemmingway Masterpiece from the humidor and pinched off the end. "However, at almost forty I'm capable of deciding what I want without permission."

"You most certainly are. But, I'll warn you." Renita looked up with a faint smile.

"Warn me about what?" Schaffer slid the cigar between his teeth

"Dad won't be your problem." Renita said dropping her smile.

Schaffer furrowed his brow. "Then, who should I be concerned about?"

"Megan." Renita's face was completely serious.

"Who's she?"

"My cousin and self proclaimed protector. She's the sister I never had."

Schaffer looked unfazed. He slipped his hand into his pocket and pulled out his lighter. "I take it she's the older?"

Renita held up one finger. "By one year."

"Okay, then when do I win her over?" He asked, holding the lighter nearer to the cigar.

"You seem very sure of yourself."

"I'm not trying to be cocky. I just have a way with women. She won't last ten minutes in my hands." Schaffer moved his fingers back and forth as if molding clay.

"We'll see about that. She lives in Woodbridge, so it won't be long before she finds out about you." Renita patted his chest.

Schaffer kept one hand on her shoulder and put the other on his hip, striking a Superman pose. "Bring her on. Did she attend Xavier too?"

"Yes she did. And before you ask, we don't look just alike. She's got short hair and green eyes. Our personalities are like night and day. I go with the flow and she creates the flow. I once accused her of planning her entire life thirty minutes after she was born. Now she's just living out her plan." Renita shook her head half serious about her comment.

"Is she in law enforcement too?"

"No. She started a Medical Internet firm. I always knew she would have to be her own boss."

Schaffer watched the changing expression on Renita's face. "Is she married?"

"Not any more. Not many men know how to cope with a woman that rules. They can't accept playing second fiddle. Her first husband and I are very much alike, but blood keeps Megan and me together. Chuck wasn't so lucky. Megan walked all over him." She angrily shook her head. "They both deserved better. Divorce was the best thing that could have happened to them."

Schaffer raised one eyebrow. "If I were him I would have left the area. I hope they didn't have kids."

"Thank God, they don't have any kids." Renita cut her eyes to the sky. "I think he's a glutton for punishment though because he works for her. The Internet Company was his idea, but Megan made it a reality. They seem to have a co-dependent relationship; they need each other to survive, although they claim to hate each other. I guess that's why the company is so successful. Their relationship is also what has frightened me about us." Renita looked down.

"We'll never be in that type of relationship. If you were like her I'd move to another state." He laughed and hugged her.

"Are you talking about my cousin?" Renita now took the Superman pose.

"She is who she is." Schaffer lit the flame on the lighter and brought it close to his Hemmingway Masterpiece. Before it touched the end, he pulled it away. "I'll not judge her and I'll ask her to do the same."

Renita shook her head. "I don't think you will have a problem. As a matter of fact, I'll have to watch her around you. She likes her boy-toys."

Schaffer lit the flame again, holding it out in front of him. "We'll be fine. I'll just turn on the charm and she'll be putty in my hands."

"Come on Don Juan before the people in the other room send out a search party."

Schaffer pulled the flame to the cigar and lit the end. Several clouds of blue smoke rose from his head. He slid the lighter back into his pocket and put one arm behind Renita. They joined Joe, Nina and Tina, who were already on the porch.

"Nice of you two to join us." Joe spun around facing them. "I was beginning to think we needed to take Tina for a walk."

"You don't have to worry about me, Uncle Joe. I already saw them kissing." Tina walked over and hugged Renita and Schaffer.

Chapter

15

The rain held out long enough for Thomas to get to Warrenton, VA. As good as killing made him feel, he knew that he needed to take a break. He played each kill over and over in his mind, planning every minute detail. He knew each plan was foolproof, but killing with such rapid momentum made one overconfident and could cause mistakes. Today however, would be the first kill in the Northern Virginia Autopsy District and he decided it would be the last for a few weeks. As of this moment, no one even suspected a serial killer was at work. Thomas wanted to give them a chance to figure it out. He knew that realization would cause fear in the hearts of women around the state.

Driving down Route 17, Thomas took a moment to review his first three victims. Lynda Goodwin's autopsy, performed by Dirk's chief assistant, confirmed the police conclusion that her death had been accidental. Speculation was that she used GHB before sex, blacked out in the tub and slipped below the surface of the water. There was no sign of forced entry into her home and no sign of a struggle in her bedroom, or anywhere else. These facts aided the police in reaching their conclusion, effectively closing their case.

Gloria Stegal's death was ruled a suicide. The police remarked about the determination she displayed by forcibly keeping her head below the surface of the water with sheer will. Her success in achieving death matched her accomplishments in the courtroom. *Success on steroids.* One of the policemen commented. The M.E. even suggested that Gloria used GHB to increase the sensation of the water as it traveled into her lungs. Not only did she want to die, she wanted to feel death as it slowly crept over every inch of her body. The only question that remained for the police was why the dog bit down on a can of Raid, causing the massive dog to kill himself as well.

Just as with Lynda's death, there was no sign of forced entry or struggle in Gloria's house. Interviews with her friends revealed her despondency regarding her recent divorce. She handled numerous clients with ease, walking them through the process of divorce and suggesting that they never look back. But, dealing with her own failed marriage was beyond the scope of her expertise and proved to be more than her emotions could handle. Calling her death a suicide made it easy for the police to solve their case. Her case file was marked *CLOSED* in big red letters.

Thomas hadn't read Sandy's police file, but he knew what it would say. He'd written many medical opinions describing causes of death. When there was no sign of foul play and everything appeared to be accidental the case was judged accordingly and the file closed. This was routine and easier for all involved, especially the police. Her death would raise no more suspicion than the others had, Thomas was confident of that.

Kenesha Williams was the first prospect that Thomas hadn't met. Nevertheless, he knew her well. She was responsible, in many ways, for the birth of the killer within him.

Kenesha would be his last kill until Thomas was sure the trail had gone completely cold. Every day lost in an investigation made it harder to find anything useful that could tie a suspect to a crime. Thanks to the police and ME's, there were no suspects, because there had been no crimes committed.

For the past ten years Kenesha practiced psychology in Warrenton. Her clients, particularly those of influence, appreciated the anonymity her office provided being far removed from the Washington, DC metro area. For those in 'society' having an analyst is as common as owning a toothbrush. Even though many hold this view, there are some who prefer to hide the fact that they are in therapy. Such was the case with Victoria.

Victoria kept her visits with Kenesha secret from Thomas until her enthusiasm about the Enneagrams caused her to blurt out the analyst's name. In an instant, nine months of secrecy was erased and the truth rose to the surface like a nuclear submarine conducting an emergency surfacing drill.

Victoria proudly pronounced herself a number 8, just like Kenesha. Thomas remembered exactly how the conversation proceeded from there.

"Who's Kenesha?" Thomas asked initially interested in Victoria's comments.

Victoria looked away, apprehensive about answering him. "Kenesha Williams is the analyst I've been seeing for the past nine months."

"Analyst?" Thomas' interest turned to anger.

"Yeah, Thomas. I had to do something. You're always at work. When you're here we avoid one another. I don't have any friends here yet. I was at the end of my rope."

"So, things are that bad?" Thomas stood and began violently

swinging his arms in the air. "I moved to this area because you burned bridges with any friends we had in Richmond. You find this big-ass house in the middle of nowhere and then you say you have no friends. And to top it all off this, just like every other event that doesn't go your way, it's my fault. I guess I'm the worst husband a girl could have."

Victoria's face dropped and then she snapped at Thomas. "I didn't say that. But, when I found myself praying you wouldn't make it home ever again, I took some action and started seeing Kenesha. I thought maybe it would make things better."

Thomas' anger sharpened. "You should tell that bitch she's wasting my money! I don't see anything she's done for you except make you more repugnant and distant."

Victoria stood, facing Thomas and crossed her arms. "I think my treatment is coming along just fine. Kenesha says that I'm making great strides."

"She could have fucking fooled me." Thomas slammed his fist into his hand and went to the wet bar for a drink. Three months later, Victoria was gone, leaving no trace of where she'd gone.

♦

Thomas fantasized that when he arrived at Kenesha's he'd find Victoria. Then he could eliminate all of his problems, mind-fucker and mind-fuckee. Thomas was ready to do some mind fucking of his own as he pulled in front of Kenesha's home-office.

Thomas hardly needed his disguise since Kenesha didn't have a clue who he was. Even so, he kept it in place to leave behind his forensic countermeasures. After one last quick glance in Kenesha's glass door to make sure his disguise was in place Thomas pressed the doorbell.

Kenesha answered the door wearing sweats that were spattered with several colors of paint. Her shoulder length dreadlocks, strong jaw line and glasses made her look like Angela Davis. Even beneath the sweats, he could tell that her skin was taut and her muscles firm, almost as firm as he was against his pants.

"I'm sorry. Did I interrupt you from painting your house?" Thomas said as his eyes moved up and down continuing to admire her body.

"I wasn't painting the house. I am working on piece of art. I find it relaxing." Kenesha answered in an even-tone soft voice. There was a slight smile on her face; she found Thomas' roving eyes amusing.

"Do you sell your paintings professionally or are they just for you?" Thomas tried to look past her to see her work.

Kenesha smiled reassuringly and moved slightly, so that Thomas could see her work. "I have an agent. I'll be happy to get you her card, but I don't think that's why you came here today."

"Oh. No ma'am. I have a letter you need to sign for." Thomas's hand rose with the letter between his fingers. He flipped it and showed Kenesha where to sign.

"Thank you." As she reached out she said, "Who could this be from?" As soon as her fingers touched the letter her world went dark.

Thomas grabbed Kenesha just before she hit the floor. "It's from me bitch, the doctor of death." He began his ritual GHB cocktail and trip to the bedroom.

Thomas was glad to see that Kenesha owned no *killer* dogs. He wondered why Black people felt the need to have such vicious dogs for pets. Black folks bought whichever breed possessed the worst reputation at the time, Dobermans, Pit Bulls, Rottweilers, it didn't matter as long as they were killers. Thomas believed they would buy wolves if they could find a place to get one without raising suspicion. He considered asking Kenesha for her professional opinion on the subject before killing her.

With Kenesha out and full of GHB, Thomas took a moment to walk to her office and check her calendar. He didn't want any patients with appointments showing up in the middle of his fun. He lifted the book from her desk. "Good. No appointments until 2 p.m. That gives us about five hours."

He returned to the bedroom and Kenesha began to stir. Thomas rolled her onto her stomach and started to massage her perfectly round, firm buttocks. The motion alone, made him want to release his first load.

Kenesha placed her hands beneath her head and lay quietly enjoying the moment. Almost in a whisper she suggested. "Why don't you go over and light some incense."

Thomas looked around the room and saw a table in front of a statute of Buddha that contained incense, a small mallet and bell. He walked over and lit the incense placing it in the holder. The smoke rose filling the room with the sent of Patchouli.

On the bed, Kenesha rolled onto her back. Her hand lazily danced across her breasts, which were perfectly round and firm, but not as large as Thomas liked.

Thomas stopped and watched her for a while. Her motions were hypnotic. He broke their silence. "Are you a Buddhist?"

114   ANTHONY P. JONES   D8 WITH F8

Her chocolate brown lips parted exposing a brilliant white smile. "It helps me stay calm and balanced."

"I take that as a yes." Thomas reached for her breast and started to rub. He squeezed her nipples and she closed her eyes. In a few minutes her breath deepened and her motions became quicker and more deliberate as did Thomas's. Without warning, her body stiffened and then jerked uncontrollably.

Kenesha rolled from the bed into Thomas's arms. Hesitantly, he held her. But, this was not what he wanted to feel. Passion would destroy his moment. Kenesha subtly gained control over him and the realization caused Thomas to blister with hatred.

"It's my turn bitch!" He said with no hint of warmth and dropped Kenesha to the bed.

"What would you like me to do?" Kenesha looked in Thomas's eyes, which were wild, teetering on the edge of maniacal lust.

He stood and began ripping his clothes off. "I'll make it up as I go along. Before we get started would you like a glass of wine?"

"Don't you think it's a bit early for wine? Besides, I told you I'm a Buddhist. We don't drink."

"You're going to need something sweetheart. What can I get you?" Thomas slipped himself out of his pants.

"Just let me have a little wine, very little. I really do try to abstain." She looked at the size of the hardness between Thomas' legs. "Go ahead and fill the glass, but I'll only have one."

Thomas poured a glass of wine and watched Kenesha drink it down like a pro. "There's more where that came from when you need a refill."

"That made my chest warm and the feeling is moving all over." Kenesha looked up at Thomas between the dreadlocks that fell into her face.

Thomas was having a hard time summoning up the anger he felt when he first arrived. In order to regain his edge, he told Kenesha to get on her hands and knees and face the headboard. "We're going to play a game. If you answer correctly I'll fuck you the traditional way." Thomas inserted himself. "But, if you answer incorrectly you'll get butt-fucked." Kenesha tightened her 'glutes attempting to deny him access. Her reluctance excited Thomas even more and he eased himself slightly into her anus.

"Why do you feel it necessary to fuck with people's minds? My life and marriage were going along fine until you entered the picture."

In her mind, Kenesha knew she should feel panic, but the effects of the GHB only allowed her to desire Thomas' advances. Unable to clearly formulate a response she said, "Why would I want to disturb my patients?"

Kenesha's question infuriated him. "Wrong answer." Thomas jammed himself past her tightened gluts, inserting his full length.

Kenesha almost screamed as she grabbed the sheets. "I'm sorry. I'll answer, please just pull it out." Thomas never slowed his rocking motion, despite her whining. "Okay, it's how I earn a living."

Thomas withdrew. "At least you finally answered honestly." He positioned himself against her tightened muscles and asked the second question. "You've been seeing a woman from Fredericksburg, Victoria—"

Kenesha didn't let him finish. "Victoria Richards. Yes, she suddenly stopped keeping her appointments a few weeks ago. I've called, but the number no longer works."

Thomas slid himself in effortlessly, this time into the vaginal cavity. "That's better. You anticipated my question and answered truthfully. Let's try another. When did the bitch go back to using her maiden name?"

Kenesha was tentative. "I didn't know Richards was her maiden name, it's the only one she ever used with me."

Thomas continued to move rhythmically, slightly increasing his speed. He felt Kenesha relaxing and he decided to let her relax even more before resuming his questions.

Kenesha started laughing and rocking back and forth in unison with Thomas. He knew the LSD was reaching its peak. "You made my wife leave. You couldn't leave well enough alone could you?" His strokes became more violent.

Laughing and grinning made it hard for Kenesha to answer. She gained a little control and then answered. "Victoria hated your ass. She said you ruined her life. There was nothing left to save. I tried. She said the only thing left to save was her life."

"Wrong answer." Thomas jerked himself out and redirected his aim higher.

Kenesha fell to her elbows still laughing. "Oh shit, here we go again, back in the butt hole." She couldn't resist, her muscles were not under her control, but the GHB's. All she could do was laugh in her drug-induced state.

"Now bitch, you're going to pay for what you did!" Thomas appeared to be trying to drive a nail rather than please a woman.

Fear was not an emotion GHB allowed. If kept alive, Kenesha

would not even remember the conversation, or her actions. Thomas felt it was a shame to waste such a beautiful specimen of human perfection. Nevertheless, letting her live was out of the question.

Thomas believed every human was born to do one thing…die. Anyone who chooses life is required to choose death as the ultimate reality. This is the ultimate irony of living. Death is a cruel, often impatient master. It waits until you believe its promise is forgotten, and then it creeps in to collect its reward.

Victoria promised to love Thomas until death arrived demanding payment. But, she broke her vow and reduced herself to hiding. Thomas knew he would find her eventually. Until then, he would give death a hand, delivering retribution for the sins of tainted love, even if it meant applying its sting to a surrogate.

Twenty minutes later, Kenesha joined the other three members crossed off of Thomas's list, into the realm of death. He left Kenesha's house and headed home. For the next two months he decided to remain dormant. The time off from killing would allow him to complete his list of prospects for vengeance. As soon as he was home, Thomas looked through Kenesha's date planner, which he'd placed in his mailbag on the way out of the door. There, he hoped to find clues to where Victoria was currently hiding.

Chapter
16

Renita was up early on Saturday morning to fix breakfast before everyone else got out of bed. She remembered as a young girl the smells that woke her up on the weekends. Her mother made the temptation too much to resist, bacon, eggs, cheese grits, and hot biscuits summoned everyone to the breakfast table drooling for food.

When Renita arrived downstairs Gretchen was nowhere to be found. She noticed the basement door cracked open a little. Renita approached the door and saw light coming from the basement. The sounds of slapping and chains jingling rhythmically trickled up stairs. She walked to the source of the noise and there found Schaffer in an old pair of tattered sweat pants, no shoes or shirt with a pair of Kempo gloves on his hands.

"Good morning." He said without turning around.

Renita opened the door little wider and walked into the workout room. "Good morning." She looked around. "How did you know I was here?"

Schaffer remained focused on the heavy bag striking it every few seconds. "Ahhh, my little Grasshopper, even silent feet can be heard when one is in harmony with his environment."

She stepped further into the room. In the corner on top of a stack of mats sat Gretchen. "You were tipped off by your partner." Renita pointed towards the dog.

"Environment includes everything surrounding you." Schaffer answered and stepped back from the bag.

"You cheated." Renita walked to the heavy bag shaking her finger. "What Martial Arts system are you practicing?"

"Kempo, with a little Shaolin thrown in for good measure, are you a student of the Arts?" He threw several more punches at the bag.

"Dad wanted to make sure I could take care of myself so he sent me to a school in New Orleans. It was at the end of Carrolton Ave just before the streetcar made the turn to St. Charles Ave."

Schaffer stopped punching and grabbed the chains above the bag before turning to face her. "I know it well. That's where I got my start. As I remember it Master Po was balding, but his hair was long and stringy. He also had his index fingernails sharpened to a point; one was painted red and the other black. The man never spoke above a whisper, which made me wonder how he practiced law. Can you imagine going against him in court?"

"You remember him well. He's a real nice guy, always in control. Did you know that he studied at the temples in China? I guess that's why he was so good." Renita walked closer to Schaffer.

"Is he still in New Orleans?" Schaffer wiped the sweat from his brow.

"I don't know. The last time I was home I didn't have the time to go by. I'd love to see him again." Renita leaned on the bag grabbing the chains for support.

"I remember when I first started. He was working with me on a technique one-on-one. He instructed me to get out of a hold, which I did. The final move required me to do a spin kick to the head." Schaffer started acting out the move. "I spun with all my force. Master Po caught my foot just as it reached his head. Then he asked me if I thought I should exhibit more control when working with the Master. I was so scared I could barely breathe. I answered, yes, sir. He simply released my foot." Schaffer let out a short laugh and shook his head.

Renita moved her hand from the chain and lightly patted him on the cheek twice. "So you're the one he was talking about when I started class. In your defense he did say that he told you to kick him in the head, but he didn't think you would be able to reach him so quickly. He said that should be an example to never underestimate your opponent and to always be ready for anything."

"I never reached him that quickly again." They both laughed. "Did you bring your workout clothes?"

Renita folded her arms across her chest. "No. I didn't expect any Kempo lessons this weekend."

"Look in my room. There are several extra pairs of sweats in my closet on the shelf. Put on a pair and come back down."

Renita put her hands in the pockets of her robe and rocked back and forth a couple of times as if she were contemplating Schaffer's offer. "Okay, I'll be right back."

He watched her leave the room. "She's quite a woman, Gretchen." No sooner had the words left his mouth than Doran clawed her way to the front of his brain. Schaffer moved from the heavy bag to the speed bag. He punched and kicked harder and faster in an attempt to clear his head of Doran, yet his thoughts persisted.

Gretchen, like any good psychoanalyst listened as he talked. "I'm here in the presence of a beautiful woman that has feelings for me as I do her and I can't get Doran off my mind. If I plan on having a successful relationship I know that I have to find Doran and put an end to that chapter of my life. I haven't found her in eighteen years and I don't know how I'll find her now. I just know that I have to, or her memory will not leave me alone. I needed absolute closure." Just as Schaffer landed a spin kick he heard clapping in the background.

"That's impressive." Renita leapt into the air and landed a chicken kick to the speed bag followed by a series of strikes and punches.

"Look who's talking." Schaffer felt like a cartoon character having to pick his jaw up from the floor. "I don't think I even saw half of those punches. I might have bitten off more than I can chew. Why don't you loosen up while I slide the mats out?"

"That sounds like a good idea." Renita dropped into a full split on the floor. "I'll only need a few minutes."

Schaffer slid several mats out and watched Renita do several more full splits while placing her chest flat on the ground in front of her. He immediately knew that he was in trouble. Schaffer put the last mat in place and stood up.

"Okay, I'm ready." Renita jumped up. "Where are your extra gloves and footpads?"

"Come over here I'll give you a hand." Schaffer slid back a part of the wall that revealed all types of Martial Arts equipment. He took down a pair of Kempo gloves and footpads. "Slide these on and I'll lace them up for you."

Renita's hands slid easily into the gloves. Standing so close, Schaffer could smell the sweetness of her perfume. He moved in closer to inhale deeper. "I don't think I've ever gotten an ass kicking from anyone who smelled quite as good as you do."

"That comment won't save you once we hit the mats mister." Renita threw a series of punches and blocks. "I'll show you no mercy."

"Yes, ma'am." Schaffer bowed and stepped back.

She finished getting her footpads on and they moved to the mats. Renita and Schaffer both shook their arms along their sides and rotated their necks counterclockwise. Simultaneously, they dropped into cat stances. They circled the mats sizing each other up. Finally, Schaffer threw the first punch, which Renita blocked easily.

"Surely you can do better than that." Renita said taunting him to try again.

"So, the lady talks trash while she fights." Schaffer wiped a drop of sweat from his nose with his thumb.

Renita slipped a punch through his hands, and caught him in the chest. Schaffer shut up and started to concentrate. The next few minutes they really went at it. They were making so much noise that an audience had gathered near the door of the workout room.

"Kick his butt mom!" Tina shouted and threw several punches of her own.

Schaffer's eyes momentarily glanced towards Tina. It proved to be a mistake. Renita's fist connected with his right eye. Then, a hook kick behind his ankles swept his feet from under him. Schaffer went down hard, but was able to roll into a crouch and throw a sweep kick. Renita fell to the mat beside him. They both howled with laughter above the gasp of their audience. Then, Schaffer's hand went instinctively to his eye.

"Girl, you hit hard." He said rubbing his sore face.

When his hand came down everyone could see the blood trickling down the side of his face. They also saw the swelling around the eye.

"Are you okay? Let me see." Renita placed both her hands on his face. "God, I didn't mean to hurt you. Nina, will you get some ice please?"

Joe laughed. "The only thing you hurt was his pride. He needed to be brought down a notch or two."

"Hush, Joe. I could have put his eye out." Renita said concerned.

Schaffer shook his head. "I'm okay. This is what I get for looking away."

Nina arrived with the ice in a zip-lock bag and a kitchen towel. Schaffer took it, placed it on his eye and fell back on the mats. "Anyone see the phone? I need to call my lawyer. I've been assaulted by a cop." He waved his free hand in the air. "Rodney King, Rodney King."

"Oh hush." Renita slapped his chest. "You'll live."

She helped him up and they headed upstairs to the showers. Schaffer put his arm around Renita and walked as if he had been mortally wounded, moaning for effect. "It's good to know that you can beat me up and carry me away too."

"You're a silly man." She said wincing as she looked at his eye.

Renita held Schaffer a little tighter and he put the bag of ice on the back of her neck. She screamed and punched him again. "Alright, I'm going to let you fall." Renita lifted his arm from her shoulder and held it as if she were about to flip him.

When they got upstairs they both headed for the showers. A few minutes later there was a knock on Schaffer's door. "It's open, come in."

Renita walked in the room dressed in a loose fitting sweater and a pair of fitted jeans. "Hi. Let me see that eye."

"My lawyer has instructed me to have it photographed first. Can you help me with the camera?"

"Oh shut up and come over here." Renita winced harder than before when she got close to Schaffer. "Ouch! That's going to be quite a shiner." She put her hand over her mouth, but couldn't hide the smile behind it.

"It already is. I see the bad guys don't stand a chance against you. Are you as accurate with that big Glock you carry?" He looked to see if she had it on.

"Hey mister, I'm an FBI agent."

"Excuse me! How could I have overlooked that fact?" Schaffer hugged Renita. "Okay Ms. FBI agent, let's go fix these people some breakfast."

About thirty minutes later cheese grits, eggs, bacon and biscuits were passed around liberally. Joe couldn't wait to needle Schaffer on his choice of bacon.

"They call that stuff bacon? Try a piece of the real thing." He handed Schaffer the platter holding the bacon. "You need to leave that bean-bacon alone."

Schaffer looked at the grease-soaked paper towel. "Thanks anyway, Joe. My arteries prefer this one." Schaffer said as he took a bite of his Morning Star Farms bacon.

Joe ate another slice of bacon. "Have you got any butter for these biscuits?" He looked at Nina. "According to you, the wine we're going to drink later will take care of your arteries." Joe insisted.

"Why work so hard? Start out clean, end up cleaner." Schaffer took another bite of food.

Joe shoved a whole piece of bacon in his mouth. "Umm, umm good." He licked the grease from each of his fingers savoring the greasy taste.

Schaffer leaned close. "Nina. Is his insurance policy paid up? He's ten years older than me and people usually think he's my grandfather."

Nina attempted to cover for Joe. "I've been encouraging him to exercise more. He just doesn't seem to have time, with work."

"You mean he doesn't take the time." Renita looked over at Joe.

"Renita, you took the words right out of my mouth. I told Joe years ago that I would teach him some stretching techniques that would help him limber and tone at the same time." Schaffer put his arms up flexing his muscles.

Joe bristled. "I don't need your chop Suey stuff. I know how to hang on my own. Thank you very much."

Schaffer looked directly at Joe. "I'll make you a deal." He took a drink of his coffee. "If you can go down stairs and workout on the heavy bag for one minute straight I'll leave you alone."

"You got it." Joe said as he shoved another piece of bacon in his mouth.

Schaffer put up one finger. "Give me a second to finish first. During that minute you have to throw at least twenty punches and three kicks."

"Piece of cake." Joe said confidently and reached for something else to eat. "When do we start?"

Schaffer shook his head side to side. "Let's give your food a chance to digest first."

Joe pulled out his wallet. "Should we include a wager, say one-hundred dollars?"

Nina didn't hesitate before reaching for the money. "I'll make it double or nothing."

The look on Joe's face was priceless. For the first time all weekend, he had nothing to say.

Renita was the first to finish breakfast. She left the table and walked into the family room. Intently, she scanned Schaffer's CDs. She slid one from the shelf and popped it in the player.

When the music began Schaffer looked in her direction. "Abbey Lincoln. The lady has musical taste."

Renita smiled. "Thank you. Are the speakers on in the solarium?" Silently, she wiggled her finger for him to follow.

Schaffer stood taking his plate from the table. "Press the button that says A+B. That will turn them on." He lifted his coffee mug from the table. "I'm going to refill my coffee. Would you like some more?"

"Sure."

Tina started to snicker. "Ooh, ooh. Mommy and Schaffer are getting mushy."

Joe pretended to gag by putting his finger down his throat. "I know baby. Kind of makes you sick doesn't it?"

Nina put her hand up. "Alright you two. I'm going to have to separate you." She shook her finger in Joe's face. "Joseph, you're a bad influence on Tina."

Joe threw his hands in the air. "What'd I do?"

Nina turned and watched Renita and Schaffer walk into the solarium. "This is going better than I had expected."

"What is?" Tina asked. Her face brightened expecting Nina to fill her in.

"Nothing dear. Now finish your breakfast then Uncle Joe and I will take you and Gretchen out for a walk."

Gretchen's ears perked up hearing her name. Tina patted her leg and Gretchen came over to her. "You want to go for a walk girl?" Gretchen wagged her tail.

In the solarium, Schaffer approached from behind and wrapped one arm around Renita's waist. Renita laid her head back resting it on Schaffer's chest. She swayed with the music gently rocking to the beat.

"I love this song." Renita started to sing with Abbey. *I'm so lucky to be me.*

Schaffer kissed the back of Renita's head. She turned and took the coffee cup from his hand and placed both of them on a table. She put both arms around Schaffer and they started to dance. Renita continued singing the words.

The words of the song stopped and a piano solo took over. Renita and Schaffer looked into each other's eyes. They stopped dancing and slowly moved their faces closer. Just as their lips met a yell from the kitchen broke their mood.

"Oh, God!" Joe yelled and quickly walked towards the solarium.

Nina pinched her nose in disgust and followed Joe. "Gretchen!"

Schaffer looked at Renita. "We'd better go check on them."

Tina met them at the door holding her nose. "What was that?"

Joe was rapidly moving towards the door. "That damn dog farted!"

Schaffer laughed uncontrollably and pushed Renita back in the solarium. "Get back. Her farts are lethal."

Renita started laughing watching everyone running from the kitchen. "Is it that bad?"

"Trust me. You don't want to find out." Schaffer couldn't stop laughing. "We'd better go outside for a walk. We could all use it after that breakfast."

"You should keep that stupid dog outside." Joe insisted. "I'll bet you don't even need a gun when you take her hunting. She just farts and the birds fall from the sky."

"I'm with you on that one, Joseph." Nina quickly added fanning the air.

In the safety of the solarium everyone looked back at Gretchen, who looked at them as if to say, *what's the big deal?*

"You guys go on out. I'll let Gretchen out." Schaffer held his nose and reached for the door. Everyone else scrambled for the fresh air.

Chapter

17

Everyone was so full after lunch on Saturday that Schaffer and Renita moved the New Orleans dinner to Sunday after the game. They were both up early Sunday morning preparing everything for later in the day; authentic food from the 'Big Easy' was better if it slow cooked all day.

Whenever Washington and Dallas played festivities surrounding the game were high, as was the sense of competition. This however, would be the first time internal opposition would be felt within the walls of Schaffer's house, Renita liked the Cowboys. In the past she tried rooting for the Saints only to be left like a bride waiting at the altar for a groom that never came. New Orleans Finally won a Superbowl, but Renita was too wrapped up in the Cowboys to fully change teams now. Schaffer proudly donned his Washington jersey. Though somewhat worn, it was in good shape considering the name on the back above the number 17 was 'Williams.'

Renita looked at the name and faded shirt with her face wrinkled. "Williams?"

"Of course." Schaffer pushed out his chest and looked at her as if she should know the name. "As in, Doug. The first Black quarterback to win the Superbowl."

"Yeah. And some might say the last decent quarterback your team has seen. We all know that he came from—" Renita cleared her throat and rubbed her nails across her chest. "Louisiana."

Schaffer stopped chopping onions and raised his head. "I can see that even you rooted for the Skins at one time."

Renita cocked her mouth to one side and pointed to Schaffer with the knife in her hand. "I rooted for Doug, not for your team. I don't see how you can root for a team that possesses a racist name. Especially since you're part Native American yourself."

"What are you talking about? They have always been the Redskins. I've never heard very much complaining from the Indian community."

"Schaffer O'Grady! You need to quit." Renita stopped cooking and put both hands on her hips before shaking the knife in his direction more forcefully this time. "You know damn good and well that the Natives have complained. Let me ask you a question, if your team was called the Blackskins how long would it take you to get up in arms against the team name in your column?" She waited a second for a response, even though she never expected one. "I'll tell you, zero seconds! As a matter of fact, you would lead the charge to have them thrown out of the league. But, as long as they're exploiting some other minority it's okay. And let us not forget, their reasoning for keeping the name is said to be out of respect to Native Americans, bullshit!" She threw the onions in a pot and slammed it on the stove. "What you should be doing is joining forces with the Natives demanding a name change. Until we're all treated equally, none of us is free!"

Schaffer set his knife down and looked at Renita, but kept his distance. "I must admit I never looked at it that way. I've always been a fan; I didn't view their name as a form of discrimination." He resumed cutting. "Boy, do I feel stupid."

Still seething, Renita flung the other vegetables in the pot and began again. "Not only is it discrimination, it's discrimination in the city that is the seat of our country's government. Did you ever stop to think how outsiders view something as blatant as that? If it's okay to discriminate in DC then it's okay everywhere in the US. If all the minorities in this country joined forces we could end discrimination, as it currently exists at the drop of a hat. But, no! We have to corridor off each group, Blacks here, Latinos there, Asians on this corner, Whites on the hill and God bless the Natives who once owned this country— you stay on reservations."

Schaffer waited a moment and let the gravity of Renita's statement linger. Then, as usual, he attempted to lighten things. "Are you planning on running for office?"

Initially she snapped. "What?" Renita threw a dishtowel at Schaffer. "Oh shut up. I just care about people." She crossed her arms and leaned back on the cabinets. "When this country is willing to grow up and is willing to view what's inside a person rather than what they look like on the outside, I'll get off my soapbox."

"Good for you." Schaffer swiped his fist through the air. "God help anybody that's opposing you while you're on it. If I promise to do some articles expressing your viewpoint can we kiss and make up now?"

Renita walked over to his arms. "I'm going to hold you to that." She kissed him on the cheek. "I'll expect nothing short of your best. Is that understood?"

Schaffer tucked his head like a scolded dog. "Yes, ma'am."

Renita stepped back and grabbed a handful of his jersey. "Are you planning on wearing that to church?"

Schaffer looked at his jersey. "I didn't realize we were—" He stopped abruptly.

"You didn't realize we were going to church? Joe told me you're Catholic. I've taken the liberty to call around and get times for Mass." She stopped and looked at the expression on his face. "Don't tell me you're one of those 'fallen' Catholics."

"Not exactly, I go once in a while." He turned away from Renita. "I just get tired of seeing people attend church parading around talking about what they have and who doesn't have the same. God is in my heart and He knows what I feel."

Renita started looking around the kitchen. "Where did I put my soapbox?" Then, looking at him sternly, she put her hands back on her hips. "You don't go to church for other people, you go for yourself and to give thanks for your blessings. It's what gets you through the tough times."

Schaffer put both hands up by his sides with his palms facing her. "I'm sorry. What time did you say Mass was? I want to be ready on time."

"It's at 11 a.m. at St. Thomas. Today they have a real treat, St. Joseph's choir from Alexandria is singing. It should be quite a moving experience; they're a gospel choir like we had at Xavier."

Schaffer saluted Renita. "Then I guess we'd better go wake the rest of the troops."

◆

Mass ended with a rousing rendition of *Every Time I Feel the Spirit*. St. Joseph's choir stirred the spirit of the entire congregation. Joe was feeling particularly upbeat. "That song could wake the dead. Nina, when we get home we're going to have to look into St. Joseph, especially if they sing like this every week."

Nina looked skyward. "It's a miracle."

Renita looked over at Schaffer, who was unusually quiet. "I see someone else was moved by the service."

Schaffer was finding it difficult to speak. Looking down, as if trying to find the words, he got past the lump in his throat. "The song after communion was beautiful. I've heard a different version, but it wasn't called *Know My Heart*. I've never heard it sung that beautifully. It really touched something deep inside me. No matter what form I've heard it sung it always reminds me of a friend from Xavier. The first time I heard it, she was singing it"

Joe frowned. "She! Here we go again. How many other skeletons are in your closet?"

Schaffer's face never changed. "She was a good friend, a good person. The last time I saw her she was headed to the convent. I never got the chance to tell her good bye. We used to have the best conversations." A weak smile came to his face. "That song always reminds me of Roselyn. I've made it a policy to get in touch with anyone from my past that pops into my head. Ever since a friend from the past popped in my head and I didn't get in touch, two weeks later, Oscar was dead." He swallowed hard. "I don't know where to start looking for Roselyn; I don't remember what order she joined. I guess if Sister Nathalee Bryant is still at Xavier I may be able to locate Roselyn, they were close friends."

Renita took his arm. "Why don't you let me see what I can do on Monday? I'm still in touch with the powers that be at Xavier."

♦

Schaffer's somber mood after church was replaced with anxious anticipation. He put on his jersey and headed downstairs ready for the pre-game countdown. Joe, Tina, Nina and Renita quickly joined him in front of the fifty-two inch flat screen television mounted on the wall.

The house was filled with the smells of New Orleans. Even though everything was ready, they would not eat until halftime. Until then, snacks and drinks would serve as a temporary substitute, no one moved from their seats.

The second quarter wound down with the score tied 10 to 10. Renita and Nina grabbed the bowls and plates down from the cabinet while Joe and Schaffer set up the TV trays between their cheers and yelling as Washington made their way down the field. With two seconds left till half-time, Washington's quarterback called timeout to allow the field goal unit to come on and attempt a thirty-five yard field goal, they had already missed two shorter ones.

Joe and Schaffer watched the ball go into the air. They were unable to move, the trays in their hands remained unopened. Neither of them took a breath waiting for the ball to go through the goalposts. The game clock ticked to zero just as the ball hit the goalpost and bounced outside the area of play.

Nina shook her head and turned to Renita. "You would think their paychecks were tied to this silly game."

"I can't believe he missed that kick." Joe yanked the TV tray open and slammed it in place. "I could have made it in my sleep."

"Yeah, Uncle Joe. They should be looking for a new kicker tomorrow. That guy sucks." Tina crossed her arms and slammed them to her chest in agreement.

"Watch your language young lady." Renita shot a look in Tina's direction that only a mother can deliver. Then she gave Schaffer and Joe a similar look.

"Sorry, mom." Tina bowed her head. "How come Uncle Joe and Schaffer can say things like that?"

Renita now looked at the two men again. They turned and began putting the trays up trying to avoid scrutiny. Nina walked over and grabbed Joe and Schaffer by their ears. "I've warned you boys to behave, if you can't set a good example I'll have to teach you both a lesson."

Joe and Schaffer answered in unison. "We'll be good, honest."

Tina put her hand over her mouth and snickered watching the men struggle against Nina's ear twisting.

"That's not funny young lady. Keep it up and you'll be next." Renita turned her back to prevent Tina from seeing her laughing at the sight of Schaffer and Joe.

Yes, ma'am." Tina got up and went over to help Renita.

♦

Crawfish shells lay in piles on the five TV trays. Empty bowls and glasses had not moved since the last morsel of food was eaten from them. The game was close. The fourth quarter was ending much like the second quarter did. The score was tied 16 to 16, and Washington had driven the ball down the field. With seven seconds left on the clock it was third down for Washington. The coach sent in the field goal team. The kicker had made two field goals since his mishaps during the first half. This one was forty-five yards out. The ball went into the air, floating towards the goal and it went just outside of the left upright.

The Dallas players cheered and sent their offense onto the field. With two seconds on the clock, they planned on taking a knee and going into overtime. The referee interrupted Dallas' jubilee when he announced, "off sides, Dallas."

The kicker knew his job was on the line with one more chance to kick the winning field goal. The stadium was silent watching the ball flip through the air. This time it split the uprights and Washington won the game. Tina, Joe and Schaffer hugged in the middle of the floor and sang, *Hail to the Redskins*.

Nina and Renita shook their heads and took the empty dishes to the kitchen. Renita sat the dishes in the sink and turned to face the jubilant singers. "I hate to break up this party, but you three get to wash and dry the dishes."

Tina looked over at her mom, then up at Joe and Schaffer. "She's got her hands on her hips. That means she's serious."

Chapter
18

Monday morning Schaffer was out of his house by 8 a.m. He had three stops to make. If things went as planned, he should be back at home by 6 p.m. His first stop was police headquarters in Charlottesville.

Chief of Police, Fred Logan stepped from his office and waved for Schaffer to come in. The two men went into the office and closed the door.

"That was some class last week wasn't it?" Fred popped a stick of gum into his mouth and offered Schaffer one.

"Thanks." Schaffer took the gum and joined the chief chewing. "It sure was. I'm really thankful the FBI and the officers there didn't mind me tagging along."

"Most of us are a little shy of the press, but you added a lot to the conversation. Maybe we all learned something." Fred winked and sat back in his chair. "So, you have some interest in the Goodwin case?"

"I guess you could say that. I'm really more interested in following up on last week's class." Schaffer pulled a memo from his jacket and handed it to Chief Logan. "This will explain the project I'm working on for the *Washington Post*. We're trying to educate the public about serial killers in general."

"I don't see how this case could be involved." The Chief looked over the memo and scratched his head. "Remember what they told us at the academy? We shouldn't rush out thinking every unsolved case is the work of a serial killer."

Schaffer put his hand in the air and politely interrupted. "I have no reason to believe this case is tied to a serial killer. I just want you to walk me through the procedures you follow when investigating an equivocal death case like this."

"Well now, that shouldn't be too much of a problem." Chief Logan picked the file up from his desk. "I'll consider that oath of confidentially we took at the academy to be binding here as well." He looked at Schaffer, but didn't release the file from his grasp. "Do we have an understanding?"

"Absolutely, Chief. I won't even use your name in the article as a source of information unless you give your permission." Schaffer sat back in his chair to prevent himself from appearing too anxious.

"A little positive press can be a good thing. I'll wait until you submit your article before I make any further assessment." Chief Logan handed Schaffer the file. "Did you want to go out to the actual scene, or should I just tell you what we do?"

Schaffer sat the file down, unopened. "I don't think we need to go to the actual scene. You're a professional; your verbal walk-through will be just fine."

Chief Logan propped his feet on the desk and knitted his fingers, letting his hands fall to the buckle of his gun belt. "Of course, we don't see this type of thing up here too often. Charlottesville is a quiet little town, and I like it that way. But, accidents can happen anywhere, just as they did with Ms. Goodwin." Chief Logan shook his head and motioned for Schaffer to open the file. "Whenever we arrive on a scene like this," he pointed the picture, "the first thing we do is to tape it off. Death is always a cause for extra care."

Schaffer looked at Lynda's naked body submerged beneath the water in the tub. Her foot and hand dangled over the side as if they were futilely trying to breath for her. He noticed the empty wine bottle leaning towards the inside of the tub. "She must have fallen asleep after drinking too much wine."

"Seems you and the Doc think alike." Chief Logan slipped on a pair of reading glasses and took the file from Schaffer. He took the glasses off and used them to point to the doctor's line in the report.

Schaffer read the line and continued reading until he reached the bottom of the report. "Case closed?"

"Yeah." Chief Logan carelessly tossed his reading glasses back on his desk. "If the Doc says it's accidental and there's no evidence indicating otherwise, we close the case. There's no need to beat a dead horse."

Schaffer couldn't hide the distress on his face. "Was an autopsy performed?"

"Sop." Chief Logan said and crossed his legs, which were still on the desk.

Schaffer's face wrinkled with confusion, he wasn't sure if the chief said slop or sop. "Did you say S.O.P.?"

"You got it, standard operating procedure. Whenever there is a death that is ruled an accident, or homicide an autopsy is mandated by Virginia law. We haven't gotten the results from the autopsy yet, but we don't expect any surprises. This one is pretty cut and dry." Chief Logan let his feet fall to the floor and spit his gum into the wastebasket beside his desk. "Damn stuff doesn't hold its flavor like the old gum."

Schaffer held the file, looking over the limited contents. "Is this the only picture you shot at the scene, Chief?"

"No. We've gone hi-tech, we shoot digital video of all crime scenes now. Since we had no way of knowing what to expect when we arrived, it was videoed. Chief Logan picked up a remote from his desk and pressed a button. A nineteen-inch television-DVD combo near Schaffer's head came on. "Put this DVD in will you?"

Schaffer put the DVD in and watched as it came on. Editing work was performed on this copy, a catalogue number, date and scene title appeared before pictures of the actual scene. The first picture was filmed just outside Lynda's house. The policeman who filmed the scene took great care to show the locks, door jams, and windows to prove that none of them were tampered with. He was silent except when moving to a new area of the house. Then, he announced what room he was entering, or what they were viewing.

Schaffer paid close attention to everything he saw, especially when the film showed the bathroom. It looked very much like the digital picture and ended at nearly the exact same position. Then the screen went blue. "Thanks for sharing that with me Chief." Schaffer stood to leave. "I'll get back to you when I have the story together. If you don't mind, I may need to call on you with some further questions."

Chief Logan stood up as well. "Any time." He extended his hand. "If I'm not here, just leave me a number where I can reach you and I'll call you back.

The two men shook hands and Schaffer left for his second stop, police headquarters in Hampton, VA.

Schaffer's IPhone rang and he was surprised to see Tree's number. "Hey, Tree, what have you got for me?"

"This is some weird shit. Your girl was loaded with GHB. That's probably what made her pass out."

"Okay, that's unusual, but why did you say weird."

Bacchus looked at the report in his hands. "GHB is considered a 'date rape' drug. So you would expect that someone gave it to her. The autopsy report says that she had indeed had sex."

Schaffer interrupted. "Wait, how'd you get the autopsy report?"

"Didn't you hire me to find out what happened here?"

"Yeah."

"Then shut up and let me tell you." Bacchus shuffled the papers in his hand. "There's no way she came home with the concentration that was in her blood, so we have to assume that she was at home when the GHB entered her system. And this is where it gets weird. There's no sign of anyone else being in the house."

What about the bottle of wine?" Schaffer asked quickly.

Bacchus scratched his head. "That's a bit weird too. The bottle was empty, except for a small amount of water. But the lab tests indicate that she didn't drink more than a glass or two."

"So, there's no trace of GHB in the bottle, yet she's loaded with the stuff, so much so that she couldn't have been anywhere but home when she consumed it." Schaffer took a sharp breath and held it a few seconds. "The bottle of wine is empty, but she'd only had a glass or two. And there's no hint of another person ever being in the house. Tree, did they find anything that may have contained the GHB, say a vial or something like that?"

"Not a thing." Bacchus glanced at the report looking for something he'd not seen before. "We know that GHB spikes the libido and that she had sex. The amount that she had in her body would have made her pass out, so when did she get the last dose and where's the person that gave it to her?"

"Too bad the police don't see it like we do, they've closed the case."

"Maybe they'll reopen it if we dig something else up. I'll see what else I can find. I'll catch you later." Bacchus disconnected.

Chapter
19

Two and a half hours after leaving Charlottesville Schaffer arrived in Hampton. At police headquarters he was escorted to the Chief's office. On the door in bold lettering was W. Winston Wellington III, Chief of Police. The lettering was as intimidating as was the Chief himself.

Chief Wellington rose to greet Schaffer as he walked in. Schaffer tilted his head upward to reach the chief's eyes. Schaffer could tell that no one gave this chief any bullshit. At six feet seven inches tall, three hundred and fifty pounds and a voice that boomed like James Earl Jones' not many people would cross him.

Chief Wellington's beefy hands swallowed Schaffer's. Instead of saying hello, Schaffer said the first thing that came to his mind. "How come you're not playing football for the NFL?"

Chief Wellington held Schaffer's hand firmly and shook it enthusiastically. "Damn knees blew out on me during my first year at Tampa Bay. Luckily, my coach at Hampton made the college insure me as long as I finished school, which I'm proud to say I did. I kept the insurance policy in good standing when I was drafted as part of my contract. When I got hurt the insurance company settled for enough that I didn't have to worry about anything. With nothing better to do, I decided to give back to the community and here I am."

"Now I remember reading about you." Schaffer was happy to have his hand back in one piece. "You were odds on favorite to be rookie of the year until your leg got caught in a pileup. I always wondered where you ended up after that."

"I don't dwell on it too much. It gave me the opportunity to come here and try to do some good." Chief Wellington offered Schaffer a seat. "I got a call from Special Agent Duplechain this morning saying to expect you. What I want to know is how a reporter got in good with the FBI?"

Schaffer blushed, embarrassed that he had asked a favor of Renita. "She's a good friend. Since you didn't make it to the workshop at the National Academy last week I thought her call might help assure you that I'm on your side. The last thing I want is for you to feel that I'm snooping around in your business."

"I appreciate that. Too many times reporters try to barge in demanding information while yelling 'freedom of information act.' In those cases, I refer them to our public relations officer. He keeps them tied up in red tape until I'm ready to part with any info." Chief Wellington put his hands behind his head and leaned back in his chair. "So, why are you so interested in a lawyer's suicide?"

Schaffer looked reflectively at the chief. "It's not so much a lawyer's suicide. It's more process of how your office investigates a case such as this one and the methodology of how you eliminate other possible manners of death." Schaffer sat up in his chair and brought his hands together as if he were praying. "I would like to educate our readers about serial killers and how thoroughly the police investigate each crime, especially if they suspect a pattern."

Chief Wellington brought his arms down, rested one elbow on his desk and leaned towards Schaffer. "Why do you suspect a pattern with Mrs. Stegal's death?"

Schaffer put one hand across his chest. "I don't. When I talked to Agent Duplechain about the story I wanted to do, she suggested I search one type of death, shootings, stabbings, hit and runs, you know, that type of thing and see why they aren't similar. It was raining when I began my Internet search, so I typed in drowning in bathtub. There weren't that many in the state, which made my research easier."

"That's interesting." Chief Wellington raised one eyebrow. "You picked a suicide, the one type of crime that doesn't get logged into the National Crime Bank at FBI Headquarters."

"Why's that?" Schaffer raised his eyebrows as if he wanted to see where this would go.

The chief grunted. "Well, it's not like they can do it again. So why log it into an over-burdened system. It's less trouble for everyone."

Schaffer hit himself on the side of his head. "Duh, that makes sense. That's the exact kind of information I'm looking for, for this story."

Chief Wellington raised the file from his desk and held it in front of Schaffer. "I believe in networking. I'm going to help you with your story, one day I may call you for some help with your friends at the FBI." He handed the file to Schaffer, but kept holding it until he finished talking. "What you see is all there is."

Schaffer took the file and opened it. Several digital prints were in the inside jacket pocket. He pulled them out and looked through them. The last one stopped him from breathing. Gloria Stegal lay in a tub in the exact same position as Lynda Godwin. On the side of the tub in the same position was an empty bottle of Naked Mountain Chardonnay. Schaffer took a deep breath before speaking. "Chief, by any chance do you digitally record your crime scenes?"

"Sure. Everybody does these days, if for nothing else just to cover our asses. Give me a second and I'll have an officer set up the video for you in a viewing room." Chief Wellington lifted the phone and arranged for Schaffer to see the recording, then walked him to the room. "Let the officer outside know if you need anything else. I'll be in touch with you soon."

"Thanks for the help, Chief. I'll be expecting your call." Schaffer sat down and pressed play on the remote control. As the screen lit up, Chief Wellington closed the door and left the room for his office.

Chapter
20

Schaffer bolted from the Hampton police station. His heart rate soared the minute the police videographer entered the bathroom where Gloria Stegal's body was found. The only difference in the two scenes was one woman was White and the other was Black. He felt he knew what to expect at his next stop, but Lynchburg, VA was more than two hours away.

Schaffer's mind raced thinking about what he should do next. He lifted his IPhone and punched in Renita's number.

This is Special Agent Duplechain. I can't take your call right now. Please leave your number and I will call you at my earliest opportunity.

Schaffer hung up before the beep sounded. He recalled the warning they received at the National Academy and was glad Renita had not picked up. He wanted to wait until he confirmed his suspicions in Lynchburg before talking to her.

Schaffer found it difficult to calm himself during the drive. He wished his Vette were a plane so that he could cut his travel time in half. Although he was anxious, he knew a ticket would only slow him down more. He reached for a Dexter Gordon CD, *Ballads* and put it in the CD player. Dexter kept him calm enough to drive faster than the speed limit, but slow enough to avoid a ticket.

Schaffer knew he had to talk to Tree; he had to know what he was working with.

Bacchus looked at the incoming number before answering. "Look, this is starting to be pathological. What's up?"

Schaffer held a copy of the picture of the crime scene. "Tree, we're really going to have to do some digging to find out what's going on here. The crime scenes are identical, I mean down to the position of the feet hanging over the tub."

"Maybe it's time to call in the FBI."

"Not yet, I'm on my way to Lynchburg. That's where the last death occurred."

Bacchus tapped a pen against a pad on his dashboard. "You want me to look into the second scene?"

Schaffer though before answering. "I don't think so. If my hunch is right, I'll call in the FBI."

"You'd better make it quick. Most possible leads are already ice cold."

"I'll talk to you soon." Schaffer hung up and looked at the phone thinking about calling Renita.

♦

Schaffer pulled into police headquarters around 3 p.m. By 3:30 p.m. he knew all he needed to know, a serial killer was at work in Virginia. The evidence was overwhelming, even though this was not the textbook variety. Serial killers usually killed within their race and they usually operated in one location unless the police were getting close. The identical crime scenes let Schaffer know that the perpetrator was an organized killer. He probably planned each of the crimes well in advance. From what Schaffer learned at the National Academy he didn't know if the submerged face of each victim suggested remorse, or some other underlying theme. Generally, remorseful killers covered their victim's faces after their deaths.

His mind raced trying to cover the points that he learned from Renita and Jim. Anxious about his discovery, Schaffer dialed Renita's cell phone.

She answered after the second ring. "Hello, Mr. O'Grady. What's up?"

Schaffer dismissed any pleasantries and went straight to his point. "Can you meet me in Charlottesville?"

Renita didn't immediately pick up on the seriousness in his voice. "Is this official business?" She asked in a flirtatious tone.

Schaffer's inflection firmed. "It's deadly serious. I was doing some research for my article as a follow up to your class. I found something you need to see, but I want to share it only with you at this point." He tried to slow his breathing, which raced despite his effort. "Ever since I collected the evidence, I haven't been able to slow my heart rate."

Renita rested her head in her hand. She smiled, still feeling lighthearted about the call. "I hope you're not going to be one of those guys who becomes a statistic after attending my class. You remember the type I warned you about, the guy who starts finding serial killers everywhere after learning about them in class."

Schaffer gripped the phone tightly, frowning as he sighed. He resumed speaking with no hint of amusement in his voice. "If I am, then you explain how three different crime scenes had three different women placed in identical positions with the exact same items positioned around their bodies."

Schaffer's words sobered Renita. The smile left her face and her FBI persona took over. "We haven't heard from any police force concerning these deaths. They should have noticed the pattern by now and alerted us, or at least downloaded the data to the national crime computer."

Schaffer relaxed slightly since he could tell Renita was taking him seriously. "It would have been difficult for them to notice the pattern. These women were killed in three different cities. I've been driving all day crisscrossing the state to view the evidence. Renita, what I saw sent a chill through my body. I've got copies of all the reports. Two of the deaths were ruled accidental and one a suicide. I requested copies of the videos, but you may have to get them."

"Who else did you tell about what you found?" Renita asked quickly conveying a sense of urgency.

"No one. I called you just as I left the last police headquarters. I thought you should be the first to know." Schaffer looked at his speedometer, which was approaching eighty. He eased his foot from the pedal and pushed himself back in the seat.

Renita looked at her watch and grabbed her keys. "It's 3:45. I'll be at your house in an hour and a half. Sit on this info until I have a chance to figure it out." Renita was already leaving her office. She stopped long enough to yell over her shoulder. "I'm going to be out the rest of the day. I'll check in later." Her fellow agents waved and returned to the work on their desks, oblivious to the tension in her voice.

Schaffer could hear the excitement in Renita's voice and rapid breathing. "I know this is important, but don't drive recklessly getting here. I want you in one piece. You might want to call Nina to pick up Tina, you may end up being here a while."

"I'll do that as soon as I hang up with you. Make sure you calm down enough to drive safely too. I'll see you in ninety minutes." Renita blew a kiss into the phone.

Schaffer blew out an extended sigh, emptying his lungs and followed it with a deep breath. Talking to Renita helped to lighten his burden. "Do you need to stop by your house for anything?"

Renita smiled and unlocked her car door. "Are you flirting with me mister?" "No, I just thought—"

Renita's laugh cut his comment short. "I have a change of clothes in the car. I'll see you soon." She hung up her phone and pulled out of the parking lot.

Chapter
21

Schaffer arrived home with just enough time to uncork a bottle of wine before Renita pulled into the garage. In his study, the three reports were laid out by date with a photocopy of each of the digital prints above each folder.

Gretchen bolted from the house to meet Renita at her car. "Hi girl, are you the official greeting party?" Gretchen wagged her tail and led the way back into the house.

Schaffer met Renita at the door and traded a glass of wine for her overnight bag. They kissed briefly and then started towards the study. "I've got everything set up in here. I only got here a few minutes before you so I haven't started anything for dinner yet."

Renita patted him on the back. "I knew it couldn't last. That's okay. If what you have is real we may have to order out."

"It's as real as it gets." Schaffer pointed to the three pictures on his desk and placed the first one in her hand. "See what you think."

Renita set the pictures side-by-side. It only took a couple of seconds for her to see the commonality between them. "Oh, shit, they're identical." She turned facing Schaffer. "How did you stumble onto all three of these deaths?"

He hunched his shoulders. "I had heard that a friend of mine, my architect, died recently and I wanted to find out what happened to her. All I did was Google 'Virginia + deaths + drownings,' and out popped a list. I narrowed the search by adding '+ tub' and these three were all that were left." He lifted the first picture and stared at it.

Renita gently took the pictures from his hand and looked at each of them more closely. "This is good work mister. Is your computer on?"

"Yeah, I turned it on just in case we needed to take some notes." Schaffer sat in front of his computer and stroked a key to stop the screen saver.

"Good. Sign on to your Internet service and type in the same thing you did when you found these three." Renita's face never left the pictures or reports. She made a list of each of the police stations and telephone numbers.

"It shouldn't take but a second. My high-speed connection is never disconnected." Schaffer's fingers sped across the keyboard. "Here they are now. Wait. There's a new one on the list."

"I was afraid of that." Renita turned and looked at the list. "This guy is working fast. Which one is new?" Schaffer pointed to the name. "Pull it up so we can take a closer look."

Schaffer read as fast as he could. "Shit! Look at this; she died in her bathtub," he turned to view Renita's reaction, "accidentally."

Renita pulled out her cell phone. "Schaffer, get on your phone and call police headquarters in Warrenton. Speak directly to the Chief and tell him it is an FBI emergency." Renita turned her attention back to her call when she heard the voice on the other end. "Chief Logan, please. This is Special Agent Duplechain with the FBI."

Schaffer quietly interrupted Renita. "They just went to get him. What do you want me to say if he gets here before you're finished?"

"Ask him about the crime scene and have him e-mail a copy of the report. Oh yeah, if they have a copy—" Renita spoke into her phone. "I'm sorry. I'm trying to carry on two conversations at once. Chief Logan, this is Special Agent Duplechain with the FBI's Behavioral Analysis Unit. Earlier today you met with Schaffer O'Grady about a death in your jurisdiction."

Chief Logan paused. "Yes. That's correct. He said he was doing a follow up for a story. I hope I did the right thing giving him the information."

"You did just fine, sir. I'm at Mr. O'Grady's home as we speak. Could you bring over a copy of your crime scene video?"

Chief Logan paused and his face contorted. "Is there something I should know about?"

Renita wanted to put him at ease and at the same time get him in gear. "I assure you, Chief there's nothing for you to worry about. I'll fill you in when you arrive. Do you need directions?"

"No ma'am. He left his address earlier. I'll be there in fifteen minutes." The chief leaned over his desk to retrieve the tape.

Schaffer tapped Renita on the shoulder and pointed to the phone. He needed her to take the call. "Thanks, Chief. I'll see you shortly. Chief, don't speak to anyone about this. We're dealing with a sensitive situation here. The fewer people involved the better."

"I understand." He hung up the phone and left his office.

Renita took the next call while Schaffer called Chief Wellington in Hampton on her cell phone. He got up, covered the mouthpiece and whispered, "I'm going to put on some coffee. I can see it's going to be a long night.

◆

Two hours later Schaffer's house resembled a mini command center. Renita dispatched Evidence Response Teams to Charlottesville and the three other crime scenes to begin gathering evidence, while Schaffer downloaded all the video clips onto a CD. Renita's team brought sophisticated computer equipment that allowed them to split the screens of two laptops so that they could view the four crime scenes frame-by-frame.

Renita connected her phone to re-charge because of the volume of calls she and Schaffer made consecutively. She was currently on the house phone requesting autopsy reports and exhumation orders for the remains of the four victims. Gloria Stegal's remains would be of no help since she had been cremated just after her death. The other three remains would be at the FBI Lab in the morning, as would the team.

Schaffer looked around the family room where they had moved for the extra space. One FBI agent was busy looking for other similar crimes in surrounding states. Two others were electronically labeling each item they could see in each of the four photos. Schaffer and Renita were looking over the video footage along with Chief Logan.

Renita raised her head from the computer screen. "Has everyone completed their initial work?" Heads nodded in unison. "Then let's brainstorm on what we have. I want to get a line on this sick son of a bitch as soon as possible."

The other agents looked in Schaffer's direction and waited for Renita to excuse him. Schaffer felt like a stranger in his own house. "Why don't I check the coffee?" He stood to leave.

Renita stopped him by raising her hand. "Boys, if it was not for Mr. O'Grady we wouldn't even know about this sick-o. He's earned the right to be here. Besides, he's former Secret Service, I can vouch for his integrity and discretion."

One of the agents spoke up. "That's a switch. A discrete reporter, isn't that an oxymoron or something?"

Renita bristled. "He's in the perfect position to help us implement our media strategy. Considering how little we have to go on at this point some media coverage may be just the thing we need to pull this guy out into the open. Most serial killers, as you know, crave attention. Schaffer was planning to run an article in the paper about his experience at the National Academy. Let's have him release just enough info to raise our killer's interest."

"Shit." Another agent said. "That just might work if we craft it just right."

Renita pointed to another agent. "Set the board up. Let's list what we have so far."

The computer in Schaffer's office chimed. "You've got mail." Schaffer went to the office to see what came in. He yelled back to the family room. "Renita, it's the first of the autopsy reports. I'll print it out and bring it in."

"Great. Maybe that will give us a little more insight to our UNSUB makeup. Schaffer, can you put all of the files on CD and bring them in here?" Renita walked over to the board and opened a marker.

"Yeah, it'll be just a minute." Schaffer started transferring the files.

Renita wrote 'UNSUB' at the top of the page. Beneath that she wrote two columns, 'Victimology, Certainties' and 'Probabilities.'

Schaffer came back and joined the group holding the CD. Renita pointed to one of the agents and Schaffer handed him the disk. On the board, they began making the list.

Victimology
-all victims mid thirties
-women all driven, highly motivated, successful, in positions of power
-all know UNSUB, no sign of struggle, all killed at home
-all divorced, or going through divorce
-no evidence of children in home
-interviews reveal all exhibited extreme control, 'my way or the highway'
-all have something to do with the number 8
Certainties
-classic serial killer
-organized
-leaves calling cards (V-8 juice, Naked Mountain Chardonnay)
-Broad geographic footprint (statewide killer)
Probabilities
-male, late thirties early forties
-bed wetter, abusive to animals, arsonist?
-possibly two killers, (victims represent two different races)

The agent who was handed the CD read the autopsy report as the group was brainstorming. "Just a minute guys. We may have to wait for the other reports to conclusively add these things, but Lynda Goodwin had sex just before she died. The wine also seems to be a cover. A large amount of GHB was found in her system. That suggests the sex may not have been consensual."

Renita pointed the marker in her hand towards the agent. "Get on the horn with the other M.E.s and see if they found the same thing. We need to know now."

Chapter
22

Late Tuesday afternoon the FBI gave their okay to have Schaffer begin running a series of articles in the *Washington Post*. In the first column entitled, ***The Killer in Your Neighborhood***, Schaffer wrote about serial killers that no one suspected— the person next door. He painted a picture based on profiles Renita and Jim Clemente used in the class at the National Academy. The classic examples included someone who was a bed wetter, who was cruel to animals and who liked to start fires.

Near the end of the article Schaffer promised to examine two sets of data. One set focused on an actual serial killer and the other involved the recent deaths of four women found drowned in their bathtubs. He ended by asking, "Has the world spawned a new type of killer?" He promised to reveal the answer the following day.

♦

Wednesday Renita was in the office by 5:30 a.m. Her team began drifting in around 6:30. Renita arranged for the *Washington Post* to have all inquiries about the article sent to her team at the FBI's Washington Field Office. Four separate phone lines were set up just for calls coming into the FBI from the *Post*. In addition, all e-mails were forwarded. The separate lines would help prevent any mistakes when the agents answered the incoming calls.

At 8:30 the first call came in. An older lady called to say how afraid the article made her feel and that in the future she hoped the *Post* would refrain from printing such alarming trash. They received the usual spectrum of calls ranging from people saying they had information on a serial killer, to questions about how they could learn to become a serial killer. The FBI didn't find any of the calls amusing and promptly dispatched teams to check out the leads and quacks. After four or five hours of FBI and police interrogation, the pranksters no longer felt their comments were amusing.

Renita's team spent an exhausting day listening to people on the other end of their phones and reading all emails that came in about the article. Renita hung up on her last call for the day and sat back in her chair and loosened up her tired muscles by spinning her upper and lower body in opposite directions as far around as they would go. As she did this she looked at the other members of the team. "If today is any indication of what's to come, this is going to be a long and strenuous week."

The agents agreed completely. By the end of the day twenty-five kids were pulled from class because of their prank calls and another eighty-three leads were checked out with negative results.

Renita called Schaffer on her way home. "How was your day? Did anyone make contact with you?"

Schaffer was glad to hear from her. "Hey. I didn't get any calls until yours. It's good to hear your voice. What do you think of tomorrow's piece?"

Renita blew a laden sigh. "I think today's paper will certainly increase sales tomorrow. That means we have to listen to even more crazies that call in tomorrow. That's something I could sure do without. But, wading through the shit is a necessary part of tracking down a monster."

"I know what you mean. The paper gets enough of those calls on a normal day and that's when I write mundane stuff." Schaffer picked up the paper and looked at the article.

"Have you ever been threatened before?" Renita asked. Her question sounded more like a 'mother hen's' than it did a cop's.

"It happens a lot to all kinds of reporters. The 'food lady' got a death threat the other day because she didn't include someone's favorite spice in a dish." Schaffer blew into the phone as if he were cold. "I'm so scared. What am I going to do?"

"Alright, you. Don't start crying wolf. You might need me one day." Her face straightened and she asked more seriously. "Do you have protection at home?"

Schaffer laughed. "Please. I'm former re-con, Devil Dog, Marine Corps, ooh-rah. If I don't have a weapon, I become a weapon. Improvise, adapt, overcome, if God doesn't control it, I do."

Renita looked up as if she were trying to see inside her brain. "What was I thinking? I forgot I was calling the Marine recruiting station." She loved the fact that he always tried to put her at ease. "Just be careful. I'm not so worried about our UNSUB killer. I worried about the other crazies out there. Someone's always trying to make a name for themselves and they could decide you'd be their best target."

Schaffer eased back in his chair. He used her concern to redirect the conversation. "If you're that worried about me maybe you should come over and be my bodyguard."

"I'll be happy to send one of the boys over. I'm protecting a certain young lady tonight, but thanks for the offer." Renita heard his audible pout. She tilted her head down and lowered her voice. "You can wait until this weekend, can't you?"

"I hope the boogey man doesn't get me before then." He looked at the dog sitting on the floor without a care in the world. "Gretchen will protect me." Schaffer changed the tone of the conversation without missing a beat. "What time are you going home?"

"I'm on my way out the door now." Renita looked at her watch.

Schaffer sat in front of his computer screen aimlessly staring at part two of his column. "Make sure you get enough rest tonight. Tomorrow is going to be an interesting day. I'll give you a call when I get into town."

"I'll be waiting." Renita hung up and turned the lights out in her office.

Chapter
23

Thomas stopped at Starbucks on his way into the office Thursday morning. He ordered a triple shot of espresso and added five packs of sugar to the small cup. The young lady at the coffee bar watched him curiously. "I've never seen anyone do that before."

"Strong and sweet, that's the way the Cubans and Egyptians drink it. You should try it sometime, it's a real eye-opener." Thomas took a sip, picked up the Washington Post and took a seat in one of the big cushy chairs near the back of the store.

He opened the paper, went directly to Schaffer's column and quickly scanned it. "That bastard! He left out the best part. I took great care in making sure each of them was laid perfectly in the tub." He frantically ran his hand back and forth across his hair. "Shit, he didn't even mention how well fucked each of them was before they died."

Thomas gulped down the rest of his coffee, folded the paper tucking it under his arm and hurriedly left Starbucks. In his car, he dialed his cell phone. While it was ringing, he pulled down his visor and flipped open the mirror to fix his disheveled toupee. Putting his hair back into place he began to talk into the phone. "Dr. Gerard, this is Thomas. I decided to take you up on your offer. I'll be out for a few weeks. Sorry I had to leave this message on your voice mail, but your cell number was busy. I'll check in, in a couple of weeks, just in case."

Thomas drove home and took the laptop computer from the trunk of his car. Law enforcement remained well behind technologically, which allowed him to purchase a program that kept the origin of an e-mail undetected. Even if the FBI was cleaver enough to trace the e-mail they would find it came from Morocco, not Fredericksburg. It would take months to break the code, which protected his identity, but even if they did it would be traced back to Kenesha Williams... and Thomas knew she couldn't talk.

Kenesha paid her Internet subscription service three years in advance to take advantage of a pay for two get one free deal offered by her service. Thomas had lifted the file and software from Kenesha's desk. She had carelessly written her password on the inside back cover of her service provider's manual next to their eight hundred service number. He knew the ISP wasn't going to attempt to contact the survivors of a client who paid in advance.

Thomas downloaded his encoding program, then went to washingtonpost.com and located Schaffer's name. Sending him e-mail was as simple as clicking his name. Thomas filled in the subject field, "RE: drinking in the bathtub." Then he completed the message.

"Why are you playing games in your column? Today you indirectly compared a conservationist to some whacked out kid who began killing prostitutes to get his rocks off. Frankly, that's an insult. I am on a mission. I'm just a girl providing the world a service, thinning out the herd to maintain a proper balance. If it weren't for my preserving the environment, pathetic assholes like you would be eaten alive." Thomas stopped typing for a moment to think of the best way to authenticate his message.

"By the way, yes I do know what I'm talking about. You neglected to mention finding the bodies of Lynda, Gloria, Sandy and Kenesha positioned in their tubs in exactly the same manner. Nor did you tell your readers about the Naked Mountain Chardonnay (nice touch don't you think?), or the juice just out of reach on the floor (if they could have reached it, it would have saved them).

He's Gr8

P.S. Don't bother trying to trace this back to me or sending a return message. I may be doing the work you don't have the guts to do, but I'm not, by any means, stupid. In addition, you might as well go ahead and tell the world about me, they're going to find out soon enough anyway."

Thomas read over his message, and then sent it to Schaffer.

Chapter
24

Schaffer arrived at his Georgetown duplex around 9:30 a.m. He went in, turned on the computer and logged on. Twenty-seven messages were waiting in his e-mail. One-by-one they began popping onto the screen. One item moving at about the same speed as a snail running a one-foot dash clogged the flow of the remaining messages. Schaffer knew his high-speed service in Charlottesville would have prevented this snag downloading such a large file.

While he waited, he called Renita. "Hi. I just got here."

"Have you had the chance to look at your messages yet?" Renita's tone was all business this morning.

"My drive here was just fine. No I didn't encounter any difficulty navigating the traffic I left this city to escape." Schaffer paused for half a beat. "And how was your morning?"

"I'm sorry. The calls have already started this morning. None of these callers are worth talking to." Renita softened her tone in an attempt to recover. "Are you dealing with 'freaks' as well?"

Schaffer turned around and looked at the screen. "I've got twenty-seven new messages coming over the wires right now. One of them is clogging the pipes. It's probably an obscene picture someone felt compelled to share." He turned and lifted his briefcase from the floor and took out a pad.

Renita looked back at her team as they busily answered calls. "Let me know if you see anything interesting. I'd better get back and help the guys."

The balance of Schaffer's messages jumped onto the page. The computer chimed letting him know the emails were complete. Schaffer scanned down the list. Trying to talk and read at the same time. "Okay... I'll let...you—" He fell completely silent when his eyes fell on one subject line. "Hang on a second. Here's one that looks interesting." Schaffer doubled clicked the line. When it came up there was nothing in the message area, only an attachment.

Renita strained, pushing the receiver closer to her ear. "What is it?"

Schaffer double clicked the attachment and a 'Word' document began forming on the page. Schaffer scrolled down to see how long it was. When he reached the bottom his breath almost left his body. "Oh, shit. Renita, you'd better get over here as soon as possible."

"What is it?" She nearly yelled. Her heart pounded hard against her chest.

Schaffer stared at the letter, completely dumbfounded. "I've got a Word document, and on the bottom of the page are four thumbnail pics of the victims in their tubs. It's signed, 'He's Gr8'"

Renita leapt from her chair. "I'm on the way. Don't close that file; don't make a copy, as a matter of fact, just move away from the computer until we get there." She yelled for two other members of the team, who jumped up and ran behind her.

Sirens blistered the air on their way from the Washington field office enroute to Georgetown. Renita barely slowed down for traffic to move out of her way. She was talking out loud to the traffic and then to herself. "Oh, God."

"What's wrong?" One of the agents asked.

"I hope Schaffer's not on AOL." Renita's eyes were wide with fear.

"Why not?"

Renita briefly looked at the agent. "Because I told him not to touch the computer until we got there. I don't want them to bump him off before we try to establish a link."

Schaffer heard the howling of a siren approaching his door. He picked up the copy he printed and went to let Renita in. "I see you brought company."

Renita seemed ready to pounce. "Where's the computer? Hurry before you get bumped."

"AOL doesn't do that to its corporate customers. Everything's still there. Here's a copy for you." He handed it to Renita and led the team to the computer.

Renita sat down and read the letter. "Well gentlemen, that's our boy. Now let's find this son of a bitch." Renita stood and the IT specialist on the team took the chair.

He keyed in several commands and every hop, or routing station the message went through appeared on the screen. The agent traced the hops back to their origin, and then looked up at Renita. "If this is our boy, he's on vacation."

Renita moved her face closer to the screen. "Where do you put him?"

The agent put his finger on the end point. "Morocco." The agent stroked several more keys. "I take that back. This is a smart son of a bitch; he's used masking software to hide his real location."

Schaffer looked at the screen. "How can you tell?"

"I tried to send him an e-mail a second ago. A message has already been returned that no such address exists. He's covering his tracks and doing a damn good job of it."

Schaffer looked around the room. "Where's your equipment? You should be able to break the code in no time."

Renita shook her head. "Unfortunately, the laws haven't caught up to the technology. Breaking these codes could take longer than any of us will live. They're constantly changing and shifting so that you can't break them. We're going to have to find him the old fashion way, through good police work. He'll make a mistake soon."

Schaffer exhaled and looked at the screen. "Until then let's hope he takes some time off."

Renita flipped back to the e-mail and stared at it. "He may take a short break, but he'll be back. He told you in the letter he was on a mission. These dead women are just battles along the way."

Schaffer wrinkled his brow. "Whoever this is said, 'a girl providing a service,' in the letter. Are you using 'he' generically?"

"No, although we can't be certain, the highest probability, based on the types of murders, is that the UNSUB is a male. Using the female pronouns was done to throw us off." Renita looked up at Schaffer.

"So what do we do next?" Schaffer nodded his head towards the computer.

"I want you to complete your stories in the paper and we'll see if they generate any more contact from this creep. We're going back to each crime scene and dissecting them piece-by-piece. Organized Serial Criminals always think they commit perfect crimes. But, no matter how good they are, they always leave some trace evidence behind." Renita turned to the other two agents. "Come on boys, we've got a lot of work to do."

On the way to their car Renita barked out orders as if she was reading from a list. "I want to know everything about our victims' lifestyles, where they ate, how they got their rocks off, and with whom. I want to know who found the bodies and when. I want to talk to all of the Medical Examiners who performed autopsies on these women. I want a list of the friends, associates and relatives of each of the victims in the area. Get started gentlemen, because I want it all within the next forty-eight hours.

Schaffer followed Renita and the agents at a modest distance. He listened to Renita's list and decided he too would begin to look into the backgrounds of the dead women. Since he had known Lynda he figured he'd be viewed as less obtrusive than the police, so she was the most logical one to start with.

As he watched tail lights leaving his driveway, Schaffer pressed the quick dial number for Tree. "We've got a problem; these deaths are not mere coincidence. We're dealing with a serial killer."

"I hate to tell you, but it only gets worse. I was at Lynda's house; crime scenes aren't this cold in Antarctica."

"Has someone cleaned the house?"

Bacchus scratched his five o'clock shadow scanning the house in his mind. "I doubt it. The bed wasn't even made. It doesn't appear that anyone has been in the house since the coroner."

"We're going to have to rework our strategy because the FBI is all over this thing now. We won't be able to get anywhere near the crime scenes. I guess we'll have to concentrate on the victims' backgrounds and look for commonality there." Schaffer sat at his computer and stared at the pictures of the four dead women again.

"I'm on it. I'll call when I have something." Bacchus flipped his phone closed, raised his monocular and resumed his surveillance of the evidence response team at work at Gloria Stegal's house.

Chapter
25

Friday morning Schaffer was back in Charlottesville and up early ready to begin his investigation. He planned to be at Lynda Goodwin's firm by 9:00 to meet with some of her employees. The phone rang just as he entered the corridor that lead to the garage. He decided to answer the call on the garage phone. "Hello."

"I was just about to hang up and try your cell phone." Renita sat on the passenger side of the Range Rover bringing her team to Charlottesville.

Schaffer leaned on his car. "Where's the investigation leading you today?"

"Funny you should ask." Renita looked out the car window at a mile marker. "I'm about fifteen minutes from your house on my way to Lynda Goodwin's residence." She paused. "Would you like to see how we get it done?"

"Sure. Should I head over there now? Or do you guys have some preliminary things you need to do first?"

"Come on now. You'll be fine." Renita couldn't prevent the smile that crept across her face.

Schaffer walked to the phone's cradle and rested his hand on the wall. "I'll meet you there." He hung up and put the phone back, jumped in the Vette and roared out of his driveway.

In the Range Rover the forensic specialists in the back seat watched Renita talking on the phone. "Hey guys, in my professional opinion I would say that phone call was more than just professional cooperation. Did you guys see the tilt in her head and the playful way she grabbed her hair. Something's brewing here." All the agents laughed.

Renita's face glowed red. "Hush. You don't know what you're talking about." Renita looked out the window, the corner of her mouth lifting in a barely discernable smile.

The agent continued. "See guys, it's just like she taught us, even the highest trained professional can't hide guilt when it's there."

This time Renita laughed with the rest of the agents. "Bastards!"

The other agent in the back seat reached forward and touched Renita's shoulder. "What can I say? We were trained by the best."

Renita flipped them off by extending her middle finger. "You guys make it impossible for me to be a lady."

The agent driving looked in the rearview mirror. "Guys, when we get there, Agent Duplechain and the reporter are not to be left alone. We want to protect the integrity of the crime scene."

Renita laughed with her team. She looked over at the agent driving and touched his leg. "Might I remind you gentlemen, that payback's a bitch. So enjoy yourselves while you can."

The other agents looked at each other. Renita had a reputation for pulling off spectacular practical jokes. Their guard would be up for the next few days expecting her to take retaliatory action.

Schaffer was waiting for the team when they arrived. He was on the hood of the Vette enjoying the tail end of his Hemmingway Masterpiece. As the Range Rover came up the driveway he tossed the cigar and popped in a piece of gum.

Renita and her team got out of the car. When Schaffer saw their faces he knew he was the only one in the dark about what appeared to be a joke. "Good to see you again, Agent Duplechain."

Renita walked over to him, grabbed his head and kissed him deeply. She stepped back wiped her lipstick from his lips and patted him on the chest twice. "Good to see you too. By the way, are you trying to become a suspect? Pick up that cigar butt, your DNA is all over it." She looked back at the team. "Can we get started now boys?"

They all looked at Schaffer and saluted. "Yes, ma'am." They answered in unison and started to laugh.

Schaffer was frozen in place. "Are you coming?" She called back.

Schaffer shook his head and caught up to the group. "I'm almost afraid to ask, but what just happened back there?"

The forensic specialists turned to him. "Standard FBI greeting."

"Okay, I knew I should have kept my mouth shut." Schaffer looked down and kept walking.

Renita didn't break stride or turn. "What fun would that have been?"

The team chuckled heartily. When they reached the door a few seconds later, all the laughter ceased. The hunt for evidence began before they opened the door. One agent used an alternative light source on the doorknob hoping to find fingerprints and the others looked around the steps and flowers for anything that might give a clue as to who was at Lynda's house the day she was killed.

Renita called Schaffer over. She pointed to the agents combing the area. "People leave all kinds of evidence when they go to someone's house. In a case like this, the killer may have tried to be cautious. Even so, there are things no one thinks about, like Schaffer's DNA-loaded cigar butt. That's what were looking for today."

Schaffer listened, but still had questions about Renita's greeting. "Are you going to explain what happened when you arrived?"

"We'll talk about that later. Let's focus on the task at hand." Renita examined each of the windows around the house. "If I came here to kill someone, I wouldn't want anyone to see me and be able to place me at the scene of the crime."

Schaffer moved closer to the window, looking at it from different angles. "That makes sense." He pointed to the upper corner of the window. "Wouldn't a criminal have noticed the alarms on these windows?"

Renita examined the windows closely. "Most likely he would have, but let's say he decided to look in one of the windows to make sure no one else was here. He could have left a fingerprint, an eyelash, an eyebrow, or even skin cells."

Schaffer stopped looking at the window for a second. "According to the autopsy report, Lynda died on Sunday. It was raining like hell that day. I remember because it was the night before I started your class. It was still raining Monday morning when I left for Quantico. Wouldn't that have washed away everything you're looking for here?"

"Most likely, except for fingerprints or a head smudge. Those are oil based and could hang around until they were wiped off." Renita walked to the front door. "Okay, let's take the search inside. Mr. O'Grady informed me that it was raining like hell the night our victim was killed. Unless anyone found prints, it's likely the rain washed away anything else we could have used here on the outside."

Inside the house Renita and the other agents used the grid method to search for evidence. Each person was responsible for covering every square inch of their grid. After a close physical examination of the grid, where even the most minute trace material was collected, each agent would vacuum their area. Separate vacuum bags were used for each grid and labeled accordingly. The same process was repeated in each room of the house.

Lynda insisted on hardwood flooring throughout the house, making the agents' job a bit easier. The Oriental carpets strategically placed in the foyer, dining room and bedrooms were enough to hold any fibers or hairs that may have touched them. The shorter pile of the rugs also made evidence easier to see.

Renita and Schaffer were working the rug in the foyer. Down on all fours, each of them held a pair of tweezers to lift any evidence they found. "What have we here?" Schaffer pulled a hair from the rug.

Renita was careful to remain in place as she looked in his direction. "Bag it. It's pretty long. It probably belongs to the victim. We'll know soon enough." She continued looking over the rug, tediously examining every inch. "This is what I've been looking for." Renita held up her tweezers.

"What have you got?" Schaffer never looked up, afraid he might loose his place.

"This, my friend, is a cloth fiber belonging to someone who was in this house. This little speck of cloth will allow us to determine exactly what this person was wearing and where they originally purchased the item. There's a ton of information in such a tiny artifact." Renita bagged the fiber and labeled it with the exact location she found it on the rug.

When the team reached the master bathroom they removed the traps from the sink placing them and any remaining water was put into an evidence bag. If the killer stopped to wash his hands, skin cells would still be in the drain. DNA typing would then allow the FBI to narrow their search.

Five hours after they began, Lynda's house had been completely swept for evidence. So Renita and her fellow agents began the trip back to Washington, where the bodies of the victims should be waiting at the forensics lab. Schaffer watched the Range Rover leave the driveway. He had a new appreciation for the amount of work and effort the FBI put into solving a case. He felt certain the obsessive attention to detail each of the teams employed, would quickly bring an end to the killer's freedom.

Schaffer arrived home and turned the computer on to see if any new emails came in while he'd been out. He found fifteen new emails in his in-box. He scanned down the list for anything interesting. About midway down his list one subject line simply read, "Guess Who?" He double clicked to open the file.

"My Dear Mr. O'Grady,

Haven't you been able to come up with a clever name for me as of yet? I've waited to see what you would put in the paper. But alas, nothing has come forth. Maybe what you need is more victims. Perhaps then you will become inspired.

Of course by now you understand why they must die. I left you a clue. You should be bright enough to see the pattern. Let me know that you understand and give me my name. I'll check the paper on Monday. If you haven't figured it out I'll force feed it to you too.

He's Gr8

Schaffer called Renita to read her the e-mail. He looked it over while waiting for her to answer and involuntarily mouthed. *This son of a bitch is crazy.*"

"Special Agent Duplechain."

"This guy is a real basket case." Schaffer thumped the computer. "He's sent another e-mail. He wants me to give him a name in the paper by Monday. He also said that if I didn't get it right, he would leave more clues, in the form of victims."

Renita sighed and looked down at her knees. "Forward the e-mail to me. I told you these guys like attention. They'll do anything to get it even though it raises the risk of them getting caught. You shouldn't feel under any pressure, he's already planning on killing again, or he wouldn't be talking to you. Let me know what you come up with. I'll work on it from my end as well."

Schaffer pulled out a pad to write down possible names. "He always signs the emails 'He's Gr8' and of course, he leaves a can of V-8 near his victims. But something just doesn't seem right. He even said he left a clue and plans on leaving more if we get the name wrong."

"I believe he's just searching for more attention. We'll have to play along for the moment. Maybe he'll show his hand. Let's see what the evidence shows. I'll give you a call later. Are you going to be home?" Renita looked out the window.

Yeah, I'm not going anywhere. Give me a call when you're free."

Renita disconnected the phone and it rang again before her finger left the button. "Special Agent Duplechain."

The voice on the other end of the phone was compassionless, and just barely north of cruel. "This is Governor Phillips of Virginia."

She was anticipating a call from the state, but was surprised the Governor, rather than the state police initiated it. "Hello, Governor, What can I do for you this afternoon?"

"You can tell me how four teams of FBI Agents can be deployed in my state without receiving permission from me or the state police. This is not a federal case." He tapped a pen on his desk waiting for an answer.

Renita stood and snapped her fingers in the direction of another agent. When she had his attention she directed him to listen in on the call. "Sir, I can assure you the FBI has no intention of stealing a case from the state of Virginia. We were following leads given directly to this office. It was our objective to first confirm that a serial killer was operating before we involved the Virginia State Police. There's no need for two agencies to duplicate efforts."

"Indeed." Governor Phillips coughed giving himself time to think of a response. "Excuse me. Surely, you're acquainted with the reputation of the State's most successful M.E., Dr. Dirk Gerard."

"Of course." Renita pursed her lips.

"Good. Then you won't mind his assistance on this case." The Governor waved an aid to place a call to Dr. Gerard. "I've contacted him and asked that he join you to review the collected evidence."

"We would be happy to have the assistance of such a noted professional. I will personally make the necessary arrangements for Dr. Gerard's arrival. Would you prefer we deliver our findings directly to your office, or to the state police?" Renita rolled her eyes in a mock gesture to the other agent listening to the call.

Governor Phillips sounded pleased having successfully exerted his authority. "The state police should be your main contact. However, inform my office as well."

"Very well, sir. Will you also be sending a representative from the state police?" Renita placed her pen on the pad to write any additional names.

The Governor was silent as if he had not considered sending the state police. "Why don't we wait to see what you find first? I'll make a decision after that."

Renita scribbled as he spoke, and then showed the other agent her note. *That's an original thought.* "Is there anything else we can do for you, Governor Phillips?"

"No. That will be all for now. I'll expect your call." He hung up before she could respond.

Renita pointed the receiver in the direction of the agent listening in. "Find out all you can about Dr. Gerard. If he was dispatched from Richmond he'll be here in about two hours. I want the info in forty-five minutes." She cradled the receiver and started walking out of the room. At the door, she turned before walking out. "I'll be down in the lab. Bring the info there."

♦

Thirty minutes after leaving her office, Renita was checking on a lab tech completing his analysis of fibers found at the four crime scenes.

The agent researching Dr. Gerard came over to Renita's microscope station. "This is all we could find." He held out the papers.

She never looked up from the microscope. "Let's hear what you've got."

The agent pulled the papers back and read his findings. "Dr. Gerard was born in Orange County, Virginia in 1960. He attended college at Virginia Union University and medical school at Tulane. He completed his internship at the Medical College of Virginia, where he's been an M.E. ever since. He rose to fame quickly, solving complicated cases. He was named Chief M.E. in 1995. Since then, he has a one hundred percent solve rate on his cases."

Renita rose from the microscope and took the papers. "So, we're dealing with Mr. Perfect. Did you find out if he's ever worked a serial killer case before?"

The agent shook his head. "Not that I could find."

Renita handed him the papers back. "Well, let's see how he does on this one."

Chapter
27

Dr. Dirk Gerard strode into the basement of the FBI Academy in Quantico as if he owned it. He walked up to Renita completely free of humility. "I'm here to offer my expertise on this case."

Dirk watched as the FBI Forensics Specialist examined the bodies of three of the victims. One of the agents was drawing vitreous fluid from just behind the eye of Lynda Goodwin.

Renita held up her gloved hands and refrained from shaking. "Welcome, Dr. Gerard. I'm sure you know your way around a lab. Just let me know where you would like to start and I'll show you around."

Dirk leaned over the body watching the forensics agent work. "I see you're drawing vitreous fluid. You must suspect some type of drug use that wasn't found in the blood upon initial examination of the bodies." He nodded his approval and turned to Renita. "Why don't you fill me in on what you have so far. After that, I'll fit in wherever you need me."

"O...kay." Renita was surprised at the seeming one-eighty degree turn that Dirk's personality took, now he wanted to be a team player. "Why don't I get you a lab coat and show you where you can put your things. I'll fill you in along the way."

Dirk walked beside Renita. "How did you stumble across this case? Given what I've read it seems very unlikely anyone would have picked up on such an abstract pattern."

"A reporter from the *Washington Post* came up with the theory. It takes an abstract mind to find an abstract pattern." She smiled, amused at her joke at Schaffer's expense.

Dirk frowned. "I know what you mean. Reporters are the hyenas of our society, preying on other's misfortune."

Despite feeling insulted, Renita remained upbeat. "In most cases, I agree. In this instance however, Mr. O'Grady broke the case. We're farther ahead of the curve than we would have been if he hadn't clued us in."

"He got lucky, blind dumb luck." Dirk scratched his bald head. "Even blind pigs find acorns once in a while."

"Actually, he had just completed our week-long Serial Homicide In-service, Dr. Gerard." Renita stopped walking, put her hands behind her back and looked at him. "I venture to guess, luck had very little to do with it."

Renita started walking towards the office she set up for Dirk. "Here's what we have so far. Fibers from four different mail carriers' uniforms were found at the scenes. We also found three different sets of hairs at each scene, the victim's and two unidentified. Tests are being run as we speak to attempt to determine their origin. The unidentified hairs appear to be the same at each crime scene. Each of the women had sex before death, but the killer left nothing behind. Not a single pubic hair. And each of the women was posed in the same position in their bathtubs with the same items present at the scene. All of which were placed in the exact same locations around the bodies. It's almost as if the killer measured distances for consistency."

Dirk never moved his eyes from the floor. "The autopsy reports I've read indicated trace amounts of drugs present at the time of death. Is that consistent with your findings here?"

"That's why we were collecting the vitreous fluid. These women were all embalmed so we have no blood to draw. We're still waiting on the blood samples from the state labs, so that we can retest them. As you know, the vitreous fluid is more reliable anyway." Renita tilted her head and held out her hand in Dirk's direction. "You stated as much earlier."

"So I did. I guess I'm just trying to cover all the bases." Dirk raised his head and smiled at Renita.

They arrived at a temporary office for Dirk. Inside were four lab coats and a box of surgical gloves. Renita opened the door and they both walked in. She lifted two card keys and a temporary ID badge from the desk, which also served as a card key. She held up another card key. "This is the key to your hotel room. The room number is on the sleeve for the card. This ID badge is for entry into this office, treat it as your own. The ID badge is also what you will need to get in and out of this building, so you won't need an escort every time. Should you need anything else please don't hesitate to ask anyone in this area."

Dirk took the items, hung the ID badge around his neck and the cards in his pocket. "Thank you. I'll just get my lab coat and return with you now. I'd like to see the hair and fiber samples if you don't mind."

♦

The team worked until just after seven. With no startling revelations, everyone agreed a dinner break was in order. Dirk requested Renita join him for dinner, but she declined in favor of Tina's company.

Dirk managed a pleasant look and turned to face Renita. "It's a pity I can't convince you to join me for dinner. I so hate dining alone."

Renita looked at the rest of the team for help. "I'm sorry, Dr. Gerard. I don't get to spend enough time with my daughter. This case has kept me away too much lately, maybe another time."

"That's the right thing to do. Too bad there aren't more mothers with your devotion." Dirk looked at the other members of the team. "Gentlemen, do I have any takers?"

A sense of duty propelled the youngest and only unmarried member of the team to accept Dirk's offer. The others left for home.

During her drive home, Renita called Schaffer. "Hi, anything new on your end?"

"I was just thinking about you." Schaffer sat down in front of his fireplace. "I've just made my first fire of the fall. I wish you were here to enjoy it with me."

"Me too. I've had a long day, I just left the office." She stopped at a red light and took a moment to breathe deeply. "The governor sent one of his people to help us, or watch us, I'm not sure which. He sounded as if we were totally incapable without Dr. Dirk Gerard." She rolled her eyes and said his name with as much contempt as possible.

Schaffer took a sip of wine. "Sounds as if it hasn't been too pleasant of a day for you. After you tuck Tina in for the night draw yourself a hot bath and fill it with bubbles. Of course, I'd do it for you, if I were there."

"That sounds divine." Daydreaming about his suggestion, she didn't notice the light change. The blowing horn behind her quickly brought her back to reality. "The only thing you left out was a glass of champagne to complement the bubbles in the tub. Unfortunately, I'm fresh out of both at the moment."

Gretchen moved her head to Schaffer's lap and he stroked it. "My, my we do think alike. Don't forget to put on Miles Davis to drown out the problems you had today."

"I was thinking, John Coltrane's *A Love Supreme*. That should just about do it. Unless…you're in the area." Renita loved the way Schaffer made her feel. She didn't want to consider what it would be like without him.

Schaffer stood and walked to his CD collection. He pulled out a John Coltrane CD and put it on. "What's your dad's number?"

Renita smiled and frowned at the same time. "Why?"

"Because, I'm calling him right now. I've got to let him know that

I'm taking his prized possession. If he's available this weekend I'll bring him up to witness our union."

"Damn!" Renita's voice strained.

"What's wrong? Are you okay?" Schaffer spun around looking as if he were about to run to the door.

"Yeah, I'm fine. I just saw a pig flying over the car." Renita laughed.

Schaffer's muscles relaxed and he gulped a mouthful of wine. "Oh, so you doubt my intentions? Give me the number and you'll see I'm serious."

Renita adjusted her sitting position and continued her game. "Talk is cheap mister. One day you're going to have to put up or shut up."

"Let's see how you react when the shoe is on the other foot." He patted his leg for Gretchen to jump up.

"(504) 555-4417." Renita cocked her head waiting to see what he would say next.

Schaffer's face wrinkled and he looked down at Gretchen. "What's that?"

"See, I knew you weren't serious. You don't even recognize a phone number when you hear it. I just got to Nina and Joe's. I'll call you when I get in." Renita walked to the house and closed her cell phone.

♦

Tina was peeking out of the window when Renita arrived to get her. She opened the door with an 'I'm up to something' look on her face. "Come in mommy. We've been waiting."

"I'm glad to see you too." Renita's face held a happy, yet confused frown. "What are you up to young lady?"

"Nothing, I'm just glad to see you." Tina hugged her then held the door open wide.

"Hi Nina. Hi Joe." Her eyes fell to a table in the foyer. "Wow, that's a beautiful basket. Did Joe give you that?"

Nina looked at her trying to prevent her eyes from giving away the secret. "I'm glad you like it, because it belongs to you." Nina folded her hands in front of her face like she was praying.

Renita walked over to the basket. Inside was a bottle of Champagne surrounded by bath salts, bubble bath and a dozen roses. The card read, *Service for one. Love, Schaffer.* Her smile lit the entire room. "How did he do this so fast? We were just on the phone."

Nina reached out and hugged Renita. "They've been here all afternoon."

"But, how could he have known how my day would go?" Renita sent Tina in with Joe. Renita's tears flowed the minute Tina was out of sight.

Nina held Renita's hands. "What's wrong?"

Renita tried to slow her tears. Nina, I don't know what I'm going to do if things don't work out between Schaffer and me. No one has ever made me feel this way. I've become so attached in such a short time. He's like a drug." She lifted the basket. "He feels my needs even when he's not around. The thought of losing him scares me to death."

"Let's not write the obituary just yet. You have to think positively, it keeps your karma positive." Nina patted Renita's arm. "Schaffer's a good man. He's been waiting for you as long as you've been waiting for him."

"Then, why didn't you introduce us earlier?" Renita dabbed her eyes with the tissue Nina handed her.

Nina looked off in the distance. "To everything there is a time and place. I know that sounds cliché. You have to believe that you met him the very moment you were supposed to, now accept it. Always remember that someone is watching out for you." Nina gently touched the side of Renita's face. "Let that thought carry you forward."

Renita let her head fall touching Nina's. "What would I do without you? Thank you." She kissed Nina on the cheek and hugged her. "Tina, get your things. We've got to get home. It's a school night."

Chapter

28

For nearly two weeks things had been quiet; contact with the killer had tapered off completely. The crime scenes had been turned inside out and they were no closer to a suspect than when they'd started. Frustration was setting in fast. If they didn't make any progress soon, everyone knew there would be more carnage. As bad as that sounded, the investigating team almost wished the killer would resume so that they could catch a break. With the killer this quiet, they didn't stand a chance.

Schaffer and Bacchus met in Richmond, VA at the Starbucks near Parham and Brook Roads. It seemed like neutral territory, half way for each of them, though no one, not even Schaffer knew where Bacchus really lived. Since losing his wife and children, Bacchus had cut all ties that could link him to any permanent place. He canceled bank accounts, credit cards, land phone lines and anything else that required an address. He lived on cash and paid-up Visa cards that could be purchased at any convenience store.

Schaffer stood near the front of the coffee shop watching as cars pulled into the parking lot. Tree never got out of any of them, but right on time, he walked through the front door.

"How in the hell do you do that?" Schaffer asked truly puzzled by Tree's arrival.

Bacchus shrugged. "It's a gift; what can I say?"

"It's one I'd like to learn." Schaffer looked around the store for a quiet spot. There weren't many secluded seats. "I don't see any good place for us to talk."

Bacchus pointed toward the back of the shop. "We can sit in that alcove near the back. It's busy as hell in here so we won't have to worry about the workers listening in. Besides, who's going to bother two rough-neck-looking brothers that appear as if they'll start shooting up the place if someone says the wrong thing? You are packing aren't you?"

"You're starting to sound like Renita." Schaffer patted the side of his purple Land's End jacket.

"Who?"

Schaffer had to smile. "Special Agent Duplechain, the lady who's in charge of this investigation."

"Boy, don't you know better than to mess with a woman who can shoot you and get away with it? There ain't no use in denying it, your face has already given away the whole story." Bacchus was actually pleased for Schaffer but refused to let his face show it.

Schaffer reached for his espresso. "Can we stay on task here? So what if I've found someone that I could settle down with?"

Bacchus slapped his 'bear paw' of a hand across Schaffer's forehead. "You must have a fever. *'There ain't but one girl for me… Doran.'* I know you're sick if you're talking about some new woman."

"Damn, Tree. Your hand has to weigh as much as, I don't know, a side of beef? You damn near snapped my neck slapping that big thing against my head." Schaffer rubbed the back of his neck.

"Stop being a pussy. You got hit harder by Renita the truck." Bacchus pulled his notes from his jacket. "I've never seen anything like this case before. There's no evidence, no witnesses and the friends of the victims I talked to didn't have anything to say worth hearing. Are you doing any better?"

Schaffer waited a second until he was sure all ears were otherwise occupied. "He contacted me."

"You're shitting me."

"He did it via e-mail. He knows his shit too; he's covered the hell out of his tracks. He's using some type of encryption program that hides the origin of his signal so well; it might as well be coming from Mars."

Bacchus took a big swig of coffee. "I thought that deep down, all serial killers wanted to be captured."

"Yeah, it seems that way, but what they really want is to show how much smarter they are than the law enforcement personal trying to catch them. He's killed four people that we know of and we're no closer to him than he wants us to be. I'll give it to him; he's a smart motherfucker."

"Even smart motherfuckers fuck up before too long."

Schaffer finished his espresso. "Let's hope he does before someone else has to die. I expect he'll start to get bolder now that he's made contact. It's as if he's throwing it in our faces, *here I am and you guys are too dumb to find me.*"

Bacchus' face visibly hardened. "If I catch him before you guys do, I'm going to reach down his throat and rip his balls off."

"I have no doubt you will." Schaffer answered knowing Bacchus was capable of making good on his threat.

"What do you suggest we do next? You've got nothing to go on; I haven't found anything worthwhile and you're expecting this maniac to start killing again."

"The FBI teams have finished re-processing the four crime scenes. I know that they're hard to beat when it comes to gathering evidence, but why don't you take another look. I can't help but believe whatever we're missing is staring us right in the face."

"Okay boss." Bacchus leaned back in his chair. "Did you happen to remember the newspaper I asked for?"

Schaffer pulled a folded USA Today, laden with money, from his briefcase and handed it to Bacchus. "This always makes me feel like we're doing a drug deal."

Bacchus took the paper. "Chasing down those scum bags for fifteen years taught me something; if you look suspicious and scary at the same time, people will leave you the fuck alone."

Chapter
29

November arrived with a sharp crispness in the air, leaving little doubt of what was to come. It was a marked contrast at the J. Edgar Hoover Building in DC where nothing was certain. All leads about the serial killer went cold and dead. Schaffer ran more stories in his series, *Body Count* in the *Post* trying to draw the killer out. His efforts proved fruitless; still he was not ready to give up.

Renita's team suspected that the killer may have been picked up on some other charge and was therefore out of circulation, at least for the moment. With dwindling coverage came dwindling interest and the leads they received in conjunction with Schaffer's stories were minimal and worthless.

Resolution of the case evading him, Dirk returned to Richmond. He wished the killer would strike again so that they could get back on his trail. After all, his reputation was at stake. The week before Thanksgiving seemed more quiet than usual. While shaving, Dirk's phone rang.

"Hello, Dr. Gerard. Did you miss me?"

Dirk held the phone on the shaven side of his face. "Where the hell have you been? I told you to take some time off. I didn't tell you to drop off the face of the Earth."

"Sorry about that. I've been recovering from my loss. It's amazing how good you feel being proactive with problems. Shit, it's like washing your problems down the drain." Thomas' laugh was guttural; not at all what Dirk was used to. "Did you realize that water is used to cleanse our bodies, but it can also cleanse our souls?"

Dirk lifted his razor and started shaving the other side of his face. "Thomas, what the hell are you talking about?"

"Victoria! If I can submerge her in the tub it will cleanse her and free me."

Dirk felt a chill run through his body. He sat the razor down. "Thomas, are you trying to tell me you had something to do with those women's deaths?"

"I don't know what you're talking about. Besides, you're the great M.E., what does the evidence tell you?" Thomas paused. "I'll tell you. It doesn't tell you shit. If it did you would already have someone in custody. Maybe I should come back and give you a hand."

"That won't be necessary. We have everything under control." Dirk washed away the remaining shaving cream.

"Are you firing me Dr. Gerard? You told me to take some time off. I was just following your instructions."

"Thomas, it's been over two months. What do you expect?" Dirk ran his hand across his shaven head and face.

Thomas slammed the receiver down hard on the side of the table. "Fuck you Dr. Gerard. I thought you cared, but all you want to do is butt-fuck me just like everyone else in my life. Not this time. It's my turn to do the butt fucking." Thomas pumped his body simulating his suggested action. "Bend over and spread your cheeks. What you will feel won't be my finger." He slammed the phone against the wall, disconnecting the call.

Dirk went into his room and sat on the side of the bed. For a long time he held the phone in his hand contemplating calling Renita. Finally, he decided against it. If Thomas was involved, he now knew who he was looking for and that gave him alone a decided advantage. Thomas often said that one day he would have Dirk's job. It always irritated Dirk when Thomas would use a line from the old Yogi Bear cartoon; *I'm smarter than the average bear.* What pissed Dirk off the most was Thomas' poor job of imitating the voice of the character. Now, Dirk would have the last laugh. He would let Thomas kill again and this time, he would be waiting to catch him. It wasn't luck, it was Dirk's skill as an investigator that solved cases… or so he thought.

♦

Thomas logged onto his computer and signed in using Kenesha's stolen IP address. A program automatically attached itself to the mail system masking his true location. "Where do I want to be today? Australia's a great location." Thomas typed a message to Schaffer.

Mr. O'Grady,

We haven't had a decent conversation in some time. I've read your attempts to contact me in the *Post*, but I was much too busy. Thank you, by the way; 'Tony the Tiger' seems like a great name for me. I assume you selected it because of the way I signed my e-mails to you. Good thinking, you're very close, just not quite formal enough. But, that's okay since everyone is already using it. We wouldn't want to confuse them, at least until I'm ready to change it.

Since the holiday is fast approaching I've written you a poem.

It's the Christmas season and Santa has to live up to his fame.
Of course this means the naughty girls will get fucked again.
I've checked my list, and then checked it twice.
I alone know who's naughty, not nice.
Check your list; you've checked it you say?
Girl number five is on it today.
Run, run and grab your shoe.
Six and seven are on it too.
Feeling sluggish because of all you ate?
It'll be better tomorrow when you see number 8.
Come one come all and pay Santa's fee.
Try as you might, you can't stop me.
Merry Fucking Christmas,
He's Gr8, a.k.a. Tony the Tiger.

P.S. Sorry this arrived too late for you to prevent my fun. Maybe I should have sent it by Fed/Ex. Tough shit! You wouldn't have arrived in time anyway. You had no way of knowing where to look. Let me know when you find number 8, I h8 that fucking number, there's a clue there, if you know where to look. You'll finally understand why they had to die after seeing it. Any of you can stop me from killing if you only give me what I want. Don't make me wait. I've tasted death and it's delicious.

Thomas set the e-mail to be sent on delay so it would arrive on Schaffer's computer the day after Thanksgiving. After sending the e-mail, Thomas pulled a list from its hiding place in the basement. With only three days before Thanksgiving Thomas needed to begin his road trip. He was prepared with a magnetic car logo that read, FED/EX. He also had a uniform to match the sign.

Richmond was the first stop on his current tour of death. It would be a night strike. The Tiger was back. Unlike most predators, he wasn't looking for the weakest in the herd. He wanted the strongest, the leader, or as Helen Palmer called them in the title to her book, number 8, 'The Boss.'

A fifty-year-old CEO of a regional banking empire was the perfect next target. Emily Purcell gained power by biting off the heads, or stepping on the necks, of anyone that got in her way. This included her husband who had occupied the next rung up the ladder she was climbing. Not only did she step on him to get higher, she kicked him off altogether after she got there. For her efforts she received the nickname, Black Widow. She knew everyone called her that, but she didn't care since it demonstrated their fear of her.

Emily was so rigid, nothing in her routine ever changed. At 5 a.m. she got up and headed to 'SEAL Team Training' down on the James River. By 7:30 a.m., she was in the office. She worked late every night except Tuesdays when she attended a divorce recovery workshop at First Baptist on Monument Avenue. Tonight, Thomas would be waiting for her when she returned home; he had attended the workshop at an earlier date.

Thomas waited in the Starbucks on Huguenot Road less that a quarter mile from Emily's home. When she arrived home she would find three sticky notes on the door, each one saying the same thing. "Sorry we missed you. We have a package that we are required to deliver tonight; will try back in one hour." Thomas left all three notes at the same time to make it appear as though he had been there several times. In fifteen minutes he would return, he knew Emily would be waiting, the workshop let out half an hour ago.

Emily arrived home right on schedule and went into the house through the garage. She never even saw the notes on the front door.

Thomas arrived and saw the notes on the door. Things worked just the way he planned. Now he would substitute the notes he left earlier with an official one he had in his pocket. Once in place, he rang the doorbell and stood there waiting for her to answer the door. The clipboard holding the signature page also held the organophosphate and LSD cocktail that would render Emily helpless.

She arrived at the door holding a glass filled with amber liquid. She used her free hand to slightly pull back the curtains covering the glass side panels of the door. "What do you need?" She asked through the closed door.

"Fed/Ex, ma'am, I've got a package for you. I left a message earlier." Thomas pulled the official message, complete with tracking number, from the door and showed it to her.

She looked at her watch. "I've never received anything this late before. What kind of scam are you trying to pull?"

Thomas looked down and reached for his wallet, which contained his fake ID. He held it in front of her face. "It's a new service we offer to meet the needs of clients that don't keep regular business hours. Would you please take this so I can go home?" With each second Emily kept him waiting; he became more and more excited.

"Set the package on the porch—"

He cut her off. "Can't do that ma'am. You've got to sign for it." Thomas was on fire. He wanted to rub his crotch, but he knew it would scare her from the door.

Emily tossed the remaining scotch into her mouth and swallowed. She opened the door. "Give me the goddamned thing!" She reached out rudely grabbing the clipboard. It was her last conscious memory.

Thomas gave Emily the GHB. Normally, he would wait for her to begin to regain consciousness, but he was too stimulated. He took her clothes off on the foyer rug and went to work. A short time later he got off of her. During the act she did not move, moan, or ask for anything.

Emily's eyes fluttered, opening slightly. "Well, look who's awake. You know, I like you older bitches; you don't mess around. You fuck hard, fall asleep and wake up ready to fuck again."

Emily fanned her hand near her face. "God, it's hot in here; I must be having a hot flash."

"I'd say. And I guess it's time for me to take measures to heat it up again." Thomas didn't give her time to respond. He rolled her over and pulled her to her knees, inserting his will.

Emily never complained even though she was fuzzy as to how she'd gotten into this predicament. Rocking to meet his thrusts, she began to revert to a business-like stance. "When did I let you in here?"

"Why are you asking such silly questions? That can wait until we're finished."

"I guess it could. It's not unpleasant, but I usually like to know who I'm fucking. What's your name?"

"Why must you women have to try to control everything? You can't just shut up and enjoy the moment; you've got to fuck it up by talking." Thomas sprayed the organophosphate solution directly in Emily's face. Once she lost consciousness, Thomas injected another vial of GHB down her throat and took her to the tub. He gleefully looked on until the bubbles from her nose and mouth ceased rising through the water.

♦

Thomas knew arriving in Franklin, VA before dawn would raise suspicion among the local police. He didn't want to check into a hotel, where someone might remember him. Driving aimlessly around Richmond, he remembered Dirk always took off Thanksgiving week and the week after to visit friends, so he knew just where to go.

He drove to Seminary Avenue and pulled into Dirk's driveway. There were no lights on in the house, so he pulled up to the garage with his car lights out. He got out of the car, walked to the keyless entry pad, and punched several numbers. The door rose and the lights inside the garage came on; Dirk's car was gone.

Thomas walked over to a tool cabinet and ran his hand down behind the right side. The key was still there. Dirk was as predictable as ever. He never changed his codes or hiding places. House sitting for Dirk when he was out of town on business proved to be invaluable; Thomas was now in the house making himself at home.

Before going to bed, Thomas wrote Dirk a note.

"For someone who has investigated so many murders you're very careless. Over the years how many students have you let stay in your home? How many of them still know the entry codes as I do? By the way, you're out of town and forgot to put the alarm on. You're asking for trouble. I started to mark my territory around the house, but we can't leave any bodily fluids can we? Fuck it! I'm going to have to pee in the morning, I'll put it somewhere. You're going to be very busy when you get back; I've made sure of it. Happy evidence hunting, maybe I'll take some of your stuff to my next stop, talk about fucking up your day. I guess by now you realize you can't say anything to your friends about me. If you do, I'll make sure their investigation points to you.

Blackmail? No, I like to think of it as your nuts roasting on an open fire. Kind of goes with the season don't you think?

Happy Holidays
Tony the Tiger

Chapter
30

Renita wanted to take the entire week of Thanksgiving off, but Tina didn't get out of school until noon on Wednesday. There didn't seem to be enough time to do all the things she planned if she had to wait till then, but there was nothing she could do to remedy the situation. Her dad would be in from New Orleans at 2 p.m. Everything was packed for the trip to Schaffer's. She would get Tina, then head straight to Dulles to pick up her dad. After that they would rush on to Charlottesville.

She felt as if she was in a cage looking at a key that was just out of reach, completely helpless. She wanted everything to be perfect when her dad met Schaffer for the first time, but she wasn't in Charlottesville to oversee the preparations.

The phone summoned Schaffer at 10 a.m. for the fifth time since Tuesday night. He lifted the receiver and spoke first. "Why don't you relax? It's just your dad coming. You've known him all your life."

Renita paced the floor and nodded, listening to Schaffer. "Yeah, I know you're right. I just want everything to be perfect."

"It already is. The only thing that could make it better is for you to calm down and be yourself." Schaffer opened the door for Gretchen, who was returning from her morning romp.

"He's going to be here in a few hours and I haven't even been to your house to help make sure everything is ready." She looked at her nails and contemplated biting one or two of them.

"Believe it or not, I do a pretty good job of making sure things are ready on my own. We'll be just fine." Schaffer took a puff of his Hemmingway Masterpiece and looked out at the mountains in the distance. "We're going to have a perfect weekend, you'll see."

The strained tone in Renita's voice lessened. "I'll have to trust you. I can't do anything about it anyway."

"That's my girl. Now you sound like the levelheaded FBI agent I fell in love with." Schaffer's first statement compelled Gretchen to come over to his side. He scratched behind her ear.

"So." Renita's voice was full of mischief. "Are you going to tell me what the surprise is you have planned for Friday?"

"Surprise? I thought you knew." Schaffer slapped the side of his face as if he forgot something. "How could you not know? Everyone else does."

Renita put her hand on her hip and took a defiant stance. "Everyone else like who? You better not have told Nina and Joe and not told me."

Schaffer chuckled. "Nina, Joe, Tina…your dad. Everyone knows. I was sure it would have slipped by now." He looked as if he would pop keeping the secret from her. He enjoyed making Renita squirm. "It's nothing to worry about. As long as—"

"As long as what?" Renita hated surprises, especially if she was the only one left out of the loop.

Schaffer walked over and put a Wynton Marsalis CD on. "Never mind. I'll tell you when you get here. It'll have to hold until then."

Renita backed off from her questioning. She heard the first few notes of the song. "The party's over, huh?"

Schaffer wrinkled his nose and brow. "What?"

"The song you just put on. *The Party's Over*, by Wynton Marsalis." She waited for her words to sink in. "Are you trying to tell me something?"

Schaffer became defensive. "No. I…I just like Wynton. It's the first song on the CD." He tried to recover. "You've got a good ear."

"Don't try to change the subject." Renita put one fist on her hip, assuming a position of power. "First you won't let me in on what you've apparently told everyone else in the world. Then you send me a negative message through the music you chose to play. I guess I know where I stand. And I can tell you it's a long way from home-cooked, candlelight lunches for two."

Schaffer hung his head in defeat. "I guess I'd better have two surprises for you when you get here. Do you like milk chocolate or dark?"

"Dark, of course. But, if you think that's going to make up for being slighted, you'd better think again." The laughter in her voice was obvious. "So, mister, I'm waiting."

"I don't guess getting down on my knees and begging your forgiveness would work?" Schaffer grunted and went down on his knees. "Okay, I'm down here. You know how much I love you."

Renita's heart began to race. "Go on." She urged him and tried to find something else to do with the hand that was on her hip.

"Well, you're still going to have to wait until you get here to find out your surprise." He started to laugh. "If you try to pry it out of your passengers on the way here all bets are off. I'll come up with something they don't even know about."

"Schaffer Zechariah O'Grady!" She stomped one foot knowing he'd won this round. "This had better be one hell of a surprise, or you'll pay dearly. Do I make myself clear?"

"Yes, ma'am." Schaffer looked at the kitchen clock. "You'd better get it in gear. Look at the time. Don't you have to be at Tina's Thanksgiving play?"

Renita looked at her watch shocked that so much time had elapsed. "See what messing around with you does to me? I get all off kilter. I've got to run. I'll see you around five."

"Drive safely. I don't know what I'd do without my girls."

"We'll be just fine. I'll have dad, remember? He makes me do things by the book, especially the speed limit."

Schaffer sat in his easy chair. "I'm glad he'll be watching out for you. Since I know you'll be in such good hands, I think I'll take a nap."

Renita sounded stressed again. "Don't you have something you need to do?"

Schaffer pushed the chair back into a reclining position. "Yeah, sleep."

CHAPTER
31

Thomas watched bubbles flow more rapidly from Deborah's nose and mouth than he remembered in any of his other kills. Deborah Lewis had been a high school English teacher, loved by her students and desired by her colleagues. She had a reputation for being hard but fair with her students, and for collecting hearts from the local townsfolk.

Her slender five foot ten inch frame was covered by smooth, blemish-free reddish-brown skin. The jet-black hair that flowed freely to the middle of her back was hers and natural. Both her skin and hair was said to be a blessing from a Native/African-American ancestry.

Thomas spent more time with her than he had intended. Now he would have to cut breakfast at the Virginia Diner short to stay on schedule for a prompt arrival at his next victim's house.

Thomas looked around the restaurant wondering how many of the people were tourists and how many were regulars. Some of them may have even been colleagues of Deborah's. He wondered whether they would be sad because they missed her or because they missed the chance to fuck her.

A woman, who felt compelled to open up to Thomas at a 'Singles Again' group meeting in Franklin had told him everything he needed to know about Deborah. She suggested that Deborah didn't care how many people she hurt in town, not even if it meant destroying families. Men kissed and she told, even about the married ones.

Thomas knew she would never tell anyone about him. He figured she liked to tell because it gave her power and control. Even though everyone knew she freely bragged about the men she slept with, they were helpless to resist her.

From the very moment she woke from Thomas' initial drug induced stupor, Deborah had wanted to be in charge. Thomas filled her mouth so that he didn't have to listen and looked though her copy of the Karma Sutra while she performed. She had hi-lighted all the positions she had tried. Thomas found one that looked to be the most uncomfortable and hi-lighted it. Then he folded her legs back along her chest and her feet beside her head. He held them in place and entered her. The combination of drugs eased her strain, but she still found it difficult to breathe as Thomas had pumped away.

♦

Breakfast was over and Thomas stood to leave. He had two more stops to make today. He arrived in South Hill, VA before 8 a.m.

Cindy Garrison was out at her construction site around 6 a.m. She returned home at 7:30 a.m. The rain prevented her crew from doing any outside work today. So she gave them the day off and left the subcontractors to fend for themselves, working on the interior of a building her men had recently completed.

Cindy was glad to see the rain. She could use the extra time to extend her stay in Philadelphia with her mom and dad. This would be her first time home in over a year. It would also be the first time there since her rocky two-year marriage had ended.

Her husband never officially became her ex. One careless moment on top of a thirty-foot scaffolding sent him plunging to the ground and into the arms of his maker. She'd avoided court, lawyer's fees and having to fight anyone for his estate. They'd only been separated a week at the time of his death. Neither of them had taken the time to see a lawyer, so all of his things were still at her house.

Cindy's crew became her unofficial protectors. She was one of the guys and at the same time, their little sister. She was so comfortable with them that she would change her shirt in front of the guys if she needed to look presentable for an on-site meeting. Her men may have found the sight of Cindy standing in front of them partially clothed appealing, however nothing was ever said. If anyone couldn't control themselves the foreman sent them packing. She was flattered by their 'mother henning,' but thought it was unnecessary. She could bench press as much as most of them and knew how to handle herself with unruly men.

However, her strength and knowledge of self-defense were no match for Thomas, or his organophosphates and LSD. Thirty minutes after his arrival, Thomas was preparing to leave. For fifteen minutes he used her body and fifteen more he spent watching Cindy expire in the tub.

Cindy seemed more of a notch on the belt rather than anything else. She was needed to fill a space on the list of ten that had to die. She did not resist or excite Thomas. He quickly grew bored and ended their session earlier than he had originally planned.

Thomas had to wait several hours before he could kill again. This was his record day, three kills within a twelve-hour period. The last one for the day was special; she was the eighth number 8. What made her even more special was Thomas knew her well. They had dated until his junior year in college, when Victoria announced that he was not right for her best friend, Ava. Two months later, Victoria took him for herself.

Thomas consistently promised Ava that one day he would stop by for a quick fuck. Today he planned to keep his promise. Ava Hayes owned an artist management firm. Her clients included some of the country's most successful sculptors, painters and visual artists. She operated the firm from Roanoke, VA, but had offices in LA, New York, and Miami. She was an aggressively shrewd businesswoman who didn't take no for an answer and got everything she ever wanted, except Thomas.

He called her the night before last and she was anxious to see him again. She even delayed her departure for her Thanksgiving destination to collect on Thomas' promise. Competition between Victoria and Ava was always fierce, but the battle for Thomas had strained their friendship. Other than Christmas, they rarely even exchanged greetings.

At 8 p.m. Thomas rang her doorbell. Waiting for Ava to answer, he reminisced about the taste and softness of her lips. Victoria had been a lousy kisser. Now, standing on the front porch, Thomas couldn't wait to have Ava try to suck the life from his body, while passionately kissing him.

Ava answered the door wearing only a silk teddy and a smile. "Come on in. I see you haven't had time to get out of your work clothes. Do you need to shower or something?"

Thomas looked around at the vast collection of artwork on the walls and sculptures displayed throughout the house. "Nice place. You've done well for yourself."

She walked to the bar to fix him a drink. "Thanks. Does it make you regret not ending up with me?"

"Shit, yeah. The only thing Victoria ever wanted to do was spend my money and complain." Thomas inhaled the smells coming from the kitchen. "It smells good in there. Whatcha cookin?"

Ava returned with the drinks and handed him a glass. "Here's to what should have always been." Their glasses clinked. "For dinner we've got prime rib roast, mashed potatoes and garlic string beans. And for desert I'm going to fuck your brains out." She kissed him and could feel him rise against her.

"I'm feeling like I may need an appetizer." Thomas took her glass and walked to the bar. "I'll freshen these up a little first." He drained his glass.

Ava walked to the kitchen to turn off the roast. At the bar, Thomas filled her glass with GHB and tequila. They met back in the dining room. Thomas handed her the glass. "I bet I can still finish before you can."

Ava took the glass shaking her head. "You could never beat me drinking. Ready, set, go." They turned the glasses up and Ava drained hers first. She set the empty glass on the table and slid one of the high-back leather chairs from the table. In what seemed like one swift motion, she jerked Thomas' pants off and pushed him in the chair. She noticed he already had a condom on. "I see you came ready for action."

Ava stood over Thomas and he unsnapped her teddy. "That's right baby. You got to wrap Willie so he won't get chilly." Ava lowered herself down hard on Thomas. She grabbed the back of the chair for support and aggressively rode up and down taking out twelve years of frustration with each thrust.

They both started to sweat trying to match each other's pace. Ava momentarily placed one hand under Thomas' chin. "See what you've been missing all these years? We could have been great together."

Thomas didn't answer. He grabbed her hips and pulled her harder towards him. Their lovemaking seemed almost violent until they both lost control. Thomas whispered each time he drew close enough to kiss her ears. "It's a shame I have to— It's a shame I have to—"

She listened, but took time to savor their union before responding. "It's a shame you have to what?"

He looked down at her legs on either side of him. "It's a shame I have to go so soon. I could get used to this. Let's go up stairs, I want to shower before dinner."

Ava led the way. She never noticed Thomas slipping the organophosphate and LSD spray from his bag. He sprayed her in the crotch as she walked ahead of him on the stairs. And she joined the other seven women in a watery grave. Unlike the others, he laid her face-down in the tub with her arm draped out holding the glass in a backwards position. He knew this would give the FBI a moment of pause. Lastly, he crossed her off his list.

After finishing the dinner Ava prepared, Thomas left a copy of the Enneagrams on the floor just beneath Ava's bed. He knew the FBI needed all the help they could get. He cut out Schaffer's smiling picture from his column in the *Post* and used it as a bookmark for section "8".

Chapter
32

Schaffer and Gretchen continued to doze in front of the fireplace waiting for their guests. Schaffer was sleeping so deeply that he didn't hear the chime letting him know someone had pulled into the garage. Gretchen didn't miss it though; she rose and looked at her master who was resting back against the arm of the sofa. When he didn't move to get off the sofa she headed down the corridor to greet their guests on her own.

Tina saw her first and clapped her hands. Gretchen went right to her. "Hey, girl. Where's Schaffer?" Gretchen wagged her tail and waited for everyone to follow.

Renita's dad looked around. "This is some place. I'll be glad to see it when the sun's out."

Renita hugged her dad. "You're going to love him dad. He's a good man."

"So you've told me. Where's this good man? Doesn't he come to greet his guests himself?" He patted Gretchen's head.

"Come on. Let's go in." Renita stopped her dad from going to the car. "Just leave that stuff, dad. We'll get it in a few minutes. Let's go see what's keeping our host."

They walked through the door laughing and talking. Schaffer never budged. Tina walked over and sat in his lap and hugged his neck. Schaffer's arms instinctively held her gently. Slowly, one eye opened and caught a glimpse of her eye to eye. He hugged her tighter. "Hey there baby girl. Did you have a good trip?" Schaffer yawned trying to wake up.

"Mommy and Papa are here. You'd better wake up." Tina tapped the sides of his face.

Schaffer stood up and stretched. "There's nothing like a fire to put a person into a coma." He turned towards Renita's dad. "Please excuse my rudeness, sir. My trusty sidekick neglected to wake me." He extended his hand. "Schaffer O'Grady."

"Gavin Duplechain." The two men shook hands.

Schaffer turned to Renita and kissed her on the lips. "Hey, baby. I guess you guys are hungry? What took you so long?"

Renita rolled her eyes. "The traffic was horrible at the airport and for thirty miles down the I-95 corridor. Everyone in DC must be leaving to visit someone this weekend." She threw one arm around him.

"I had dinner ready two hours ago." Schaffer nodded towards the stove. "It shouldn't take too long to reheat it." He motioned to the dining room. "Gavin, there's a decanter of wine on the dining room table. Would you be kind enough to pour three glasses, I'd like to make a toast."

Gavin went into the room and poured the wine. He returned handing a glass to Renita and Schaffer. "To what shall we toast?"

Schaffer reached for a mini wine glass from the counter and poured a couple of drops in it and handed it to Tina. He held his glass high. "To two beautiful women and to the first man in their lives, Papa Gavin."

They all took a drink. "That's better than the last one." Tina said licking her lips.

Renita shook her head. "What am I going to do with her?" She turned to her father. "You see dad, he's a bad influence."

Gavin looked at Schaffer. "I'll decide how bad he really is. What's for dinner? I'm starved. Someone wouldn't let us stop for a burger." He cut his eyes to Renita.

"Yeah, I thought I was going to faint." Tina added as she posed with the back of her hand against her forehead.

"All I did was throw something together. It'll only take about three minutes to reheat. It's red snapper baked in cream of shrimp soup. I steamed some asparagus tips and we're going to toss that over fresh linguini with olive oil and roasted red peppers."

Renita looked at her dad. "See. What did I tell you?"

"Renita, the water should still be hot, dunk the linguini for a few seconds and I'll heat the fish and asparagus." He leaned down to Tina. "Why don't you show papa where the bathroom is so that he can freshen up?"

Tina waved her hand. "Come on Papa. I know where EVERYTHING is."

Schaffer and Renita watched as they walked away. He hugged and kissed her again. "I'm so glad to see you."

"I'm glad to see you too." She took the linguini to the stove. "Have you heard from Nina and Joe?"

As soon as she asked the garage chime came on. "There they are now."

Gavin and Tina walked back to the kitchen. Everyone could hear Joe through the door. "Every idiot in this country must have been on the road tonight. Damn fools almost killed us several times. Stupid bastards!"

Renita ran into the dining room and poured Nina a glass of wine and ran back to the kitchen. When the door opened and Nina stepped through Renita handed her the glass. "Here, it sounds like you need this."

"Thanks. I believe Joseph thinks the roads were created just for him." Nina kissed Renita, Tina and Schaffer.

"Nina, this is my dad, Gavin Duplechain."

"Pleased to meet you." They shook hands. Nina pointed to Joe. "That old sourpuss over there is my husband, Joe."

Joe stopped fussing and extended his hand. "Well, I finally get to meet the Judge." They shook heartily. Joe leaned close to Gavin. "I tried to keep her away from that guy, but she wouldn't listen."

"She's a smart girl; she knows where to place her trust." Gavin looked at Joe then at Renita. "I think she's done alright this time. She's going to be just fine."

Joe shook his head. "You sound just like her. How can you tell that after thirty minutes? He could be some crazed serial killer. Just like the ones he writes about."

The smack was heard before it was seen. "Joseph! That's enough." Nina's face was red with embarrassment.

Schaffer wanted to put her at ease. "On that note, and boy, what a note, whack, I think it's time to eat." He looked at Joe's head. "Would you like some ice for that?" He touched the spot on the back of his head that Nina just hit.

Gavin found it hard to stop chuckling. "Talk about swift justice. I could use you in my courtroom." He said to Nina, imitating her smacking motion.

She was still seething. "I don't know what gets into him at times. He can be the sweetest man and then he can screw it all up by saying the first thing that comes to mind."

"It's not that bad Nina." Schaffer touched her shoulder.

Nina shook her finger at him. "You stop right there. You bring out the worst in him."

Schaffer did an abrupt one-eighty. "I'll get the things from the kitchen now."

♦

Dinner was over and everyone gravitated toward the family room. Schaffer added a couple of logs to the fire. Renita walked to the CD collection looking for something to play. Nina was calm again and snuggled with Joe on the sofa. Gavin and Tina stood near Schaffer watching him stoke the fire.

Billie Holiday's soulful voice cut through the silence. Renita sang along with Billie, *Some One To Watch Over Me*. She walked out to the dark solitude of the solarium. For the first time she noticed that the fireplace opened to this room as well.

Gavin noticed the look on Renita's face and followed her to the solarium. For a moment he just watched and listened to her sing. Slowly, he approached her from behind. He hugged her, showing his support, and waited for her to speak.

Renita swayed in his arms. "Daddy, you ever notice how the sadness in Billie's voice always comes out even when she's singing a happy song?"

He kissed her on the top of her head and gazed at her reflection in the glass. "She had to deal with an awful lot of sorrow in her life. Even the best actor can't hide what's buried deep inside. Some tell-tale signs always seem to seep through."

"I wish mom were here to share this evening with us. She really would have liked Schaffer." A single tear escaped Renita's eye and slowly carved a wet crease down her face. "Having her here would be about the only thing that could possibly make this night more perfect."

"She knows that. She's right here with us baby. Hell, I bet she even had a part in bringing you two together." Gavin hugged her tightly. "I miss her too, but I know she's always looking out for us."

"Nina reminds me of her. I guess that's why we've gotten so close." Renita rubbed her arms as a chill shot through her.

Gavin spun Renita around, kissed her on her forehead and pulled her close. "You're going to be just fine. See that man peaking through the fire." He pointed to Schaffer who tried to make it appear as though he was tending to the fire. "He makes you happy, even Ray Charles could see that."

"Oh, daddy stop."

"Look at him. He wants to be in here with us." Renita and Gavin started to laugh while pointing in Schaffer's direction. Gavin did most of the talking. "See, he's about to go crazy just trying to figure out what we're saying. Do you think we should put him out of his misery?"

Renita laughed. "Thanks daddy." She kissed him on the cheek and turned to look at Schaffer through the fire. Playfully, she put her finger out and wiggled it for him to come join her.

Schaffer took his time standing. He brushed his pants using his hands and then carefully placed the poker back in its stand. Leisurely, he walked towards the solarium, determined to show no anxiety. "You need me?"

Gavin and Renita looked at each other and laughed. He took Renita's hand and held it out to Schaffer. "Boy, I hope you know what you're getting yourself into." He put her hand in Schaffer's. "Take care of her as if your life depends on it, because it most certainly does. By the way, that's not a threat, it's a promise."

Schaffer took her hand. "Sir, you will never have to question my sincerity or intentions where your daughter or granddaughter is concerned. I want nothing but the best for both of them, if they'll have me."

"If they'll have you? Didn't you notice the shackles connecting your ankles to hers?" Gavin pretended to bang his gavel. "I hereby sentence all three of you to life, a life of happiness together."

Tina, Nina and Joe walked in just as Gavin was pronouncing his sentence. Schaffer saw them enter. He held his arms open. "Group hug."

Chapter
33

Thursday morning at 8 a.m. Schaffer's house was filling with the unmistakable aromas of Thanksgiving. Renita and Schaffer were busy in the kitchen putting together their feast for the evening. Nina came in to join them and to lend a hand.

"Good morning." Nina let her nose guide her to the freshly brewed coffee. She poured a cup and sat at the breakfast bar, savoring the fullness of its taste.

"Good morning." They answered in unison. "Did you sleep well?" Schaffer asked.

"Perfectly. Joe snored all night." Nina took a sip of her coffee. "What do you need help with?"

Schaffer looked around. "Just enjoy your coffee first. There'll be plenty of work to do when you're done. I assure you we won't waste your talents."

Renita was putting the finishing touch on several pies before putting them in the oven. "What's your Thanksgiving specialty?" She asked Nina.

Nina looked at the ceiling. "Let's see, I love making my own cranberry sauce and I'm not bad at the stuffing either."

Schaffer pointed to the bags of cranberries. "I've got five bags of cranberries over here. We can do one with oranges, one with raspberries, one plain and one strained for anyone who might not like the whole berries. The extra bag can be split between the orange and raspberry."

It was all Nina could do to keep from jumping up and diving into those cranberries, but she heeded Schaffer's advice and sipped her coffee instead.

One by one, everyone else made their way down to the kitchen invited by the smells of the season. No one ate more than a small bowl of cereal, or a grapefruit for fear that they might be too full to gorge on dinner when it was finally ready.

Joe walked into the family room. "You know the games are going to be on soon."

"You've got another two hours before they come on, Joe." Schaffer said after glancing at the clock.

Joe picked up the remote and pointed it at the television. "Yeah, well how about the pre game shows?"

Schaffer never raised his knife from the cutting board. "That's at least an hour away. If you don't mind we could do without the TV on right now. Music stimulates creativity. That's why I always try to listen to it while I cook. If you feel compelled to watch TV, there's one in the study."

Joe left for the study without another word. Nina shook her head. "He's worse than a kid sometimes."

Renita gathered the extra crust and rolled it into a ball. "He's just set in his ways, Nina. When he doesn't get his way, he stomps around the cave like an old teddy bear."

Gavin came in next. "Good morning everyone. What time do the games come on?"

Renita, Nina and Schaffer all threw their hands into the air. "I give." Schaffer said.

"Did I say something wrong?" Gavin pulled back from the breakfast bar as quickly as he would from a hornet's nest.

"No, daddy. We were just listening to the music. The games don't come on until noon. You may want to join Joe in the study. He's watching the Macy's parade."

Gavin grabbed a handful of grapes and a banana. "That's okay. I'd rather listen to the music. It's great to listen to when you cook. It helps your creativity."

Nina and Renita looked at each other and started laughing. Schaffer smiled. "Thanks for understanding." Schaffer said between chops of his knife.

Gavin nodded his head toward the women and asked. "What's wrong with those two now?"

Schaffer hunched his shoulders. "I couldn't even begin to imagine." But he couldn't drop the smile from his face.

Gavin cautiously moved back to the breakfast bar for a coffee mug. He let his hand fall on Schaffer's shoulder. "Son, don't you know you should never lie to a judge."

Schaffer nodded. "Yes, Your Honor, I throw myself on the mercy of the court." He looked over at Renita and Nina. They started him laughing again. "Well, sir, the truth is, I really don't know why they're laughing. It could be that I just finished telling Joe that music stimulates creativity."

"Oh, I see." Gavin hooked both thumbs on his belt. "They're laughing at the similarities between you and me. Well son, you could do a hell of a lot worse." He walked over to Schaffer's recliner and sat down.

Nina put her hand on top of Renita's. "That should just about seal the deal. It couldn't have been scripted any better than that."

Schaffer took off his chef's jacket. "I need a break. Would you like to join me for a cigar, Gavin?"

"Don't mind if I do." He stood from the chair.

Schaffer patted him on the back. "Renita said you wanted to see the grounds. Let's get a couple of Hemmingway Masterpieces and I'll show you around the place."

Schaffer and Gavin walked outside with Gretchen in tow. They each lit their cigars, puffing out clouds of thick blue smoke.

Gavin pulled the cigar from his lips. "The first thing most future Father-in-laws would want to know is how you are going to provide for my daughter. That question is obviously not necessary in this case. If the two of you were much younger I would also be concerned with the fact that you have only known each other a few months. That too is something that needs no further discussion." He took another puff from his cigar and let the smoke slowly drift out of his mouth. "There are, however, two items that merit discussion. First, why have you waited until you're damn near forty to get married? Second, do you fully understand that Renita and Tina are a package deal? Are you going to be able to love her as your own blood?"

Schaffer blew out a stream of smoke. "If I were you, I would have asked the very same questions. So I have answers for both. I spent almost twenty years of my adult life waiting for a woman I was destined not to be with. I didn't even know how to reach her for most of that time. Eventually I came to my senses. I was incomplete, until I met Renita. I knew the minute I saw her that we were going to have a special bond. About two hours later I met Tina. You'd have to be deranged not to love her. The three of us have already become close, family almost. I wouldn't want it any other way."

Gavin put his hands behind his back. The smoke escaped his mouth effortlessly. "I couldn't help but notice how she went straight to your arms when we got here. She trusts you with her life. Make sure she always has reason to."

Gretchen stopped running long enough to point her favorite covey of quail. Most days she went in search of them. It had become as much a game for the quail as it had Gretchen.

Gavin watched her. "How long will she hold point?"

"I'm not sure. Usually it depends on whether the birds move

before I tell her to get them."

"You should shoot one once in a while so that she stays sharp." Gavin watched the birds take to the air.

"Not here." Schaffer called Gretchen over. "I don't want to scare her playmates. They know they're safe in this area. Renita told me you taught her to hunt."

Gavin smiled. "She's pretty good too, even better since her FBI training. That was our special time together." He walked over and leaned on the railing. "They grow up so fast."

Schaffer let the older man's words pass. They remained outside until their cigars were finished. When they got inside the first football game was about to begin. Joe was now in the family room waiting for their return.

"What took you guys so long? You almost missed the kickoff." Joe barked through a mouthful of chips.

"I was just showing Gavin around the place. Where are the ladies?" Schaffer walked to the kitchen and looked in the ovens, checking on the food.

"I think they're in your study. Joe motioned to Gavin. "Come on Judge, let's have a seat in here and watch the game."

◆

Nina demanded the television be turned off during dinner. After stifling all protests, she won. Schaffer put a Dave Grusin CD on and suggested to set the mood instead.

Just as the last song was ending, Schaffer began to speak. "I have an announcement to make. Most of you at the table are already aware of our plans for tomorrow. It's time we clue in the last member of our party."

Renita looked up from her wine glass. "Oh, so finally I get to find out what's going on. It's about time."

"Drum roll please." Schaffer pointed to Tina, who obliged. "We are spending the next two days in New York City. Tomorrow night the six of us will be the guests of Wynton Marsalis at the Lincoln Center's Kick Off to Jazzy Christmas concert." He turned to Joe and Gavin. "Gentlemen, I trust you have your tuxedoes?"

They each gave a thumb's up. Nina and Tina said that they were ready too. Renita looked at Schaffer horrified. "Why didn't you tell me? I didn't bring anything formal to wear. I can't believe you did this to me."

Schaffer put his hand in the air. "Not to worry, everything is taken care of. Tina, if you please."

Tina jumped up from the table and sprinted out of the room. "I'll be right back."

"What is going on?" Renita looked to be on the edge of tears.

Tina came running back in the room with a big box. "Here mommy, open it."

Renita took the box and tore off the wrapping. She pulled out a black full-length evening gown. "Oh... my... God! It's beautiful." Her eyes bore directly into Schaffer's as she mouthed. "Thank you."

"It's from all of us. We heard a certain FBI agent seldom dresses up." Schaffer slipped his hand into his pocket.

Renita looked around the table, finally finding her voice. "Thank you. All of you."

Schaffer cleared his throat and pulled his hand from his pocket. "This is from me." He passed a long thin box down to Renita.

"What's this?" She took the box and ran her hand over the outside.

"Open it and see." Schaffer put his hands out to his sides.

Tears filled Renita's eyes. She reached in the open box. "Pearls."

Now Schaffer stood and walked behind Renita taking the pearls from her hand and securing them around her neck. "I knew this would be the perfect accessory for you in this dress."

Renita stood up and kissed Schaffer. "You'll never get rid of me now."

He gazed into her eyes. "No, I never will." They hugged.

"It's time for dessert. I can't wait to sample all three of your pies." Schaffer started walking to the kitchen and stopped abruptly, spinning on his heels. "Oh, I almost forgot. I have a surprise for each of you all as well. We also have matinee tickets to see Disney's *Lion King* on Saturday."

Tina clapped and jerked her hand through the air like Tiger Woods. "Alright!"

Chapter
34

One of the two cell phones hooked on Dirk's belt started ringing. He knew it had to be work. Otherwise he would have heard *The Music Box Dancer* instead of the ring. "This is Dr. Gerard."

"Yes, I know. Have you been enjoying your time off?" Thomas tilted his rearview mirror to make sure none of the glue from his fake mustache was visible.

"I was, until I heard from you." Dirk wanted to hang up, but knew that by staying on he increased his chances of getting a clue that could lead him to Thomas.

In a singsong voice Thomas said as if teasing. "You're going to get called back in early."

"What makes you think that?" Dirk listened intently, knowing any tidbit might help.

"Didn't you get my message? I stayed at your house the other night. I even thought about bringing one of my girls over for a little fun, but she was all wet." Thomas' laughter was deep and throaty.

Dirk realized Thomas had killed again. He had to work hard to maintain control over his emotions. "Thomas, you're sick. Why don't you come in so that I can get you some help?"

"Listen to yourself. The great doctor wants to help poor lil'ole Thomas. Fuck it." Thomas' eye started twitching. "Look you ball-less twit, I'm out here busting my ass so guys like you have a safe place to date. Shit, you won't stand up for yourself. I bet Viagra can't even make your dick stand up. You're pathetic."

Thomas' voice sounded far away, as if he wasn't holding the phone next to his face. He was still voicing his disgust for Dirk when the phone line went dead.

Dirk pulled the phone from his ear and looked at it. "I'm coming to get you Thomas, man to man. You will be the jewel in my crown."

♦

Thomas drove to a shelter in Richmond and went in to help serve meals to the homeless. He stood right next to policemen and firemen from the city's force who volunteered every Thanksgiving. This was his first time. He knew there was no dinner, or family waiting for him at his house. This was a way to get a free meal and interesting conversation as well.

When all the meals were served, Thomas sat at a table by himself. One of the men he served earlier came over to join him.

"No one should have to eat alone on Thanksgiving."

Thomas looked across the table at the man. "Thanks. It's really not that bad. I've grown accustomed to it."

"It sounds like there's a story behind that comment." The man stroked his beard.

Thomas shook his head. "It's a tale too often told, wife leaves with family, man has to eat alone."

"I can relate. I used to be a successful psychologist. My wife drained all of the bank accounts, including the business account, and left. I went into depression and eventually had a breakdown. I lost everything. Now I'm on the streets just trying to survive."

Thomas' face reddened. "You should find that bitch and cut her heart out, if she's got one."

The man sat back and looked at Thomas. "I see you're still dealing with a lot of anger. I take it; it hasn't been very long since she left."

"It's been a few months. But, I'm not taking it lying down; I'm actively looking for her." Thomas tore at his food like a wild animal.

"What will you do if you find her?" The psychologist eyes began blinking with an exaggerated force, clearly disturbed by Thomas' anger.

"I'd cut that bitch's heart out and eat it while it was still beating. Then I'd fuck her in the ass." Thomas' face lit up, excited by his fantasy. He looked over at the man who was now rocking back and forth making a primal sound. "Maybe you should open an office again Doc, I feel better already."

The psychologist wildly shook his head back and forth, still rocking and moaning. "Don't talk to people. People are crazy." He repeated the words over and over again.

Thomas stood up and winked at the man. "Yeah Doc, the story fucked me up at first too. Find your ex, Doc. They'll rule it justifiable homicide."

The man repeatedly slammed his hands over his ears. Thomas left the table and walked out of the building, leaving the man rocking and howling in a fit of terrified rage.

Chapter

35

Bacchus didn't consider Thanksgiving a holiday, especially one used for giving thanks. It was just one more reminder that he no longer had a family to share the holidays with.

He used the time to dig a little deeper into the case. He had a hell of a time convincing the sheriff to let him into Gloria's house, but his persistence had paid off. He stood in the living room alone after promising to lock up and leave the place exactly as he'd found it. Other than the FBI team, Gloria's house had not seen another human being. Dust covered everything, otherwise things were just as they were when she'd died.

Bacchus walked into the dining room, pulled out a chair, and sat down. He reached into his coat pocket and pulled out a pint of scotch, unscrewed the cap and took a slug. He knew he would find nothing new in the house, but he still felt he had to try.

He turned in the chair and his foot scratched across something under the table. He reached down and picked up a real estate flyer for the Richmond, VA area. He found it interesting that Gloria was looking at real estate in Richmond. Maybe she was looking to expand her practice to that area.

Bacchus took a note pad from his jacket and flipped to the notes he'd taken on Gloria. The only person he had listed on the pad was Gloria's niece, Sharon Johnson. Beside her name was a cell phone number. He thought twice about disturbing Sharon's holiday evening but figured it could be important, so he dialed her number.

It took several rings before Sharon answered. The noise in the background suggested she was with family enjoying the festivities. "Hello."

Bacchus hesitated. "Hi, Miss Johnson, this is Special Investigator, Bacchus Jones." He couldn't think of a more official sounding title, so he kept the conversation flowing. "I'm sorry to disturb your holiday, but I'm investigating your Aunt Gloria's death and I had a question I needed answered."

Sharon looked around at her relatives and moved to a quieter room. "This couldn't wait?"

"As I said, I'm sorry for any inconvenience. I only have one question, though. Do you know if your aunt was planning on purchasing any real estate in the Richmond, VA area recently?"

Sharon looked puzzled. "Why would you want to know something like that?"

Bacchus fingered his bottle of scotch. "I just need to know if she discussed any purchases of real estate in Richmond— it's part of the case."

"She never said anything to me about it and I really believe that's the type of thing she would have mentioned. She always told me about any of her business plans. But I don't see what this has to do with anything."

"Thank you. I'm sorry to have disturbed you." Bacchus hung up and took a second hit from the bottle of scotch. He slid the flyer into his jacket pocket and put the top back on the scotch.

Bacchus took a look around the house and left, making sure he secured the door. As soon as he got home he planned to treat the flyer with ninhydrin for prints after he used an alternate light source to search for any traces of DNA. If he found any, he'd get it processed and run it against the data bank. As soon as he had any results, he would call Schaffer.

◆

Bacchus' examination of the flyer revealed what he believed to be two distinct sets of prints. The first was one thumb print on the center of the front page and the other was a set of four fingers along one edge of the back of the page. Attached to his computer, he had an inferred print scanner that allowed him to send the prints to the FBI's data bank for comparison. Within minutes, the thumb print came back with an exact match. It belonged to a guy who had been convicted of leaving his graffiti tag on several buildings in the Richmond area. Bacchus crossed referenced a few other data bases and found that the guy was on supervised release and worked for the company that had distributed the flyers around the city.

Bacchus made a note of the guy's last known address and the address of his employer. Tomorrow, he planned a visit to have a discussion with the man.

The other prints came back a few minutes later. As he suspected, they belonged to another person. She was a truck driver and her prints were in the data bank as a result of her being bonded by the trucking company she worked for. Bacchus jotted down her name, address and employer's information. She too was from the Richmond, VA area. He hoped she had taken the holiday off and would be home tomorrow when he came to town. If he got lucky, he could catch them both on one sweep.

The following day, Bacchus got an early start beginning with the truck driver. She was easy enough to talk to and he determined that at Gloria's time of death, the truck driver was in Mississippi making a delivery. Her story checked out with her company's log. So that was the end of that.

The graffiti artist was a bit more difficult to locate. Bacchus had to wait in his employer's office for him to arrive for his pick up. As with many employees the day after Thanksgiving, he was late. Bacchus' presence seemed to disturb to the people who had arrived on time, but he was far too imposing for any of them to ask him to wait outside.

When the young man walked in, he was frozen by the stares of his fellow workers. "Sorry, I'm late. I guess I was still sleeping off Thanksgiving dinner."

His boss walked over. "There's a gentleman here that needs to ask you a few questions." He leaned closer. "You've kept your promise to me and not gotten into any more trouble, right?"

The young man nodded and looked towards Bacchus. His first inclination was to run. But despite Bacchus' size, he could tell the large man was agile; he definitely recognized the budge beneath Bacchus' left arm as serious hardware.

Bacchus moved slowly towards the frightened delivery boy. He could see fear in the boy's eyes. His massive hand firmly gripped the boy's shoulder. "Your face has lost three shades of color since you walked in here. You're not in any trouble, I just want to know a little about your delivery routes, you know, these flyers." Bacchus held one of them in the air.

The boy could hardly speak. "I...I cover the Richmond area out as far as Hanover county."

Bacchus nodded. "That wasn't so bad now was it? Do you deliver south of the city?"

The boy's head shook side to side. "No, sir, someone else handles south of the city. I don't think we go that far south." He looked to his boss for reassurance.

"That's right, we don't go any father than New Kent and there're only a few boxes there.

Bacchus knew the boy wasn't involved in the killings. With his long hair and scraggly beard, he would have left evidence all over the crime scene. He slid the flyer from his jacket and handed it to the boy. "Is there any way of telling where you placed this one?"

The boy's face contorted. "How do you know I left it anywhere?"

Bacchus' face came as close to a smile as it ever did while he was working a case. "Your thumb print is on it. I ran it and that's how I found you."

The boy examined the numbers on the back of the flyer. "This lot would have been at the truck stop just off Lewistown Road in Hanover County."

Bacchus raised one eyebrow. "You seem pretty sure of that."

"That's because I always leave the same lot number at the same location. If someone calls a realtor about a house listed in here the realtor asks them for the number on the cover. That's how they track which box locations are providing them with the most leads."

Bacchus took the flyer from the boy's hand. "Thanks for your help." He left the office without another word.

Chapter
36

Schaffer woke everyone early Friday morning. They had to catch the train from Charlottesville to New York in two hours. As everyone scrambled to get ready, Schaffer went to his study and turned on the computer. One click later, he was on the Internet. He downloaded his e-mail and clicked on the icon so he could review them quickly. One subject line caused his blood to run cold. "A Gr8 Poem."

Schaffer read the e-mail, and then quickly scanned the list to see if there were any more. Another one caught his attention. "H2O48." He clicked it and the music from *The Brady Bunch* television show came on. One by one the pictures of eight dead women came onto the screen, four he had already seen; the other four were new. Schaffer pounded his fist on the desk.

Coming down the hall, Renita heard the noise. "Is something wrong?"

Schaffer quickly turned off the computer. "No, I just bumped my knee." He was rubbing it when she walked through the door.

"Let me see." Renita approached him like she would Tina.

"That's okay." Schaffer stopped rubbing. "It'll be just fine."

Renita sat on the edge of his desk. "Everyone's just about ready." She looked at her watch. "I don't think we'll have time for breakfast though."

"Why don't we eat on the train?" Schaffer stood and hugged Renita.

"That sounds like fun. It'll make Tina feel important."

Schaffer rubbed Renita's back. "Then it's settled. But, I am stopping to get my espresso on the way to the train station."

Renita looked up and kissed him on the chin. "Can I have one too?"

"I'll have to think about it." Schaffer crossed his arms and tapped his foot on the floor. "Okay."

Renita took his hand and they walked to the kitchen. "Who's going to let Gretchen out tomorrow?"

"I've arranged for one of my neighbors to do that. We'll be back late Saturday. She'll be just fine. He poured Gretchen a bowl of food and put it on the rug where she happily wolfed it down.

The doorbell rang. Schaffer opened the back door for Gretchen and then went to answer the front door. He turned and called for Renita. "The van's here. Let's get moving."

While everyone went to the van, Schaffer returned to his office and placed two calls; first to the senior member of Renita's team and the other to Tree. Tree didn't answer so he left a message.

♦

The train pulled into the New York's Pennsylvania station just below Madison Square Garden. Schaffer looked out the window. "We can catch the shuttle to the hotel right upstairs. I booked a suite that sleeps six."

Joe didn't give anyone else a chance to ask. "What are the room assignments?"

"Well, Joe. I thought I would let Nina stay with the Judge, you with Tina and Renita with me. How does that sound?"

Joe bristled as he turned to exit the train. Renita patted him on the back. "Don't worry Joe; you get to stay with Nina."

"Yeah, well. That still leaves you four." Joe scowled looking at Schaffer. "If you wear that silly hat outside, one of those funny boys is going to pick you up. That's the only kind of man who would wear a hat like that."

Nina turned to Joe. "Only a man who knows exactly who he is can wear a dark purple beret. Schaffer is very secure, unlike others who won't even wear a hat when his head is cold."

Mimicking a character from a *Batman* movie Schaffer said. "Rats, foiled again by Nina Woman."

Renita elbowed him in the stomach. "Watch it, or you're next buster."

♦

The five-block walk from the restaurant to Lincoln Center served as the perfect aid to stimulate digestion and refresh everyone after dinner and before the concert. Renita and Schaffer silently walked hand-in-hand for most of the way.

Renita could see that something was troubling Schaffer, but she waited until Lincoln Center was in sight before asking. "Something's been eating at you all evening. Would you like to talk about it?"

Schaffer looked over and attempted a weak smile. "I'm okay. I've just had a lot on my mind. We can talk about it later."

She reached over with her free hand and rubbed his arm. "Okay."

Tina pointed towards the Lincoln Center. "Look mommy, limos. I wonder who is in them."

Joe bent near Tina. "You would think somebody would have gotten us a limo instead of having us walk from the restaurant."

"It's not very cool out tonight, Joe. The walk did you some good." Schaffer peaked over his shoulder. "We're going to walk home too."

♦

Wynton Marsalis was introduced to a thundering crowd, clapping and cheering. The mesmerizing tones of his trumpet quieted them when he began playing *Sleigh Ride,* as only the jazz master can. He played for ninety minutes, stopping only to introduce the songs. After playing *Walking in a Winter Wonder Land,* he stopped to talk to the audience.

"I got a call from a friend of mine last week. He asked that I play a special song tonight. Now, it's not a Christmas song, but I suspect it will make someone's Christmas a bit brighter."

Wynton stopped and looked out over the crowd. The spotlights dashed across the people helping him search. The light finally stopped over Schaffer and Renita in the front row. "There he is right there." Wynton pointed Schaffer out. "Man, this cat's got it bad. Stand up so everybody can see you."

Schaffer stood and waved. "Thanks for playing my song."

"I haven't played it yet." Wynton put the trumpet to his lips, as if he was about to blow. Then, he pulled it down. "Aren't you supposed to fall down on one knee before you ask that woman to marry you?"

The applause drowned everything out as Schaffer went down on one knee. He reached in his pocket and pulled out the ring. Renita's hands were over her face and the tears were already flowing. A stagehand ran over with a microphone and held it to Schaffer's mouth. "Renita, I would appreciate it very much if you would consider becoming my wife."

Renita's hands were still in front of her face and she sat there motionless. Schaffer held the ring for what seemed like an eternity, waiting for her answer. Wynton intervened. "Shay, either you've sent that woman into a state of shock, or she doesn't want to give you an answer in front of several thousand people."

Renita's head nodded. "Yes. My answer is yes." She held out her hand. The crowd sent up another thunderous applause. Renita jumped from her chair and hugged Schaffer just as Wynton began playing *The Very Thought of You.*

Backstage after the concert, Wynton waited for the newly engaged couple and their family. He walked up to Renita and gave her a hug and kiss. "At last, somebody is bringing this guy to the alter. I heard it was the Crawfish Etouffe." He turned to Schaffer. "I told you about my homegirls, one bite of their food and you're hooked."

"It started way before the Etouffe. But, after her daughter took me out for ice cream, it was all over." Schaffer pulled Tina close with a hug.

"Come on everybody. I believe there's some champagne on ice back here." Wynton took everyone to a room he had set up for a small reception in Renita and Schaffer's honor.

♦

Back at the hotel, Renita was sitting in Schaffer's arms in front of the fireplace in their suite. Everyone else had gone to their rooms to give the couple some quiet time alone.

Schaffer poured two snifters of cognac. Renita took the glass and slid back into his arms. He held her without a word, enjoying their closeness. He stared into the fire. "Gas fireplaces are convenient, but I miss the crackle of the fire."

"Why don't you be the guy who invents crackle sounds that come from gas fireplaces?" Renita took a sip from her snifter.

Schaffer stroked her hair. "That sounds like a good idea. Maybe we should start on it when we get back."

Renita sat up and put her snifter on the hearth. "I almost forgot. I've got something for you. I'll be right back." She went into her room and came back out with a folded piece of paper in her hand. "You know that I want to marry you worse than anything in this world, but first you have to do something for me." She handed Schaffer the paper.

"What's this?" He took it and unfolded it. When he read it, his face lost all color.

"She was living less than twenty miles from you all the time you were in Georgetown." Renita smiled, but her heart was heavy.

"Where did you get this?" Schaffer found it difficult to speak.

"Did you forget I'm an FBI agent? All I needed was her name and where she went to college. The rest was easy. Schaffer, go and see Doran. Make certain it's me that you really want."

Schaffer looked confused. "Why would you do something like this? Especially, the night I give you a ring and ask you to marry me."

"Because, I love you." She reached for his hand. "I know that you love me. Believe me I'm not questioning your intentions." She moved one hand to the side of his face. "This is for you, because it's something you need to do. If you don't, you may question yourself for the rest of your life. I can't be responsible for something like that."

"I don't know what to say." Schaffer dropped back down to his place on the floor. Renita sat with him, only this time she held him. He lifted the note and looked at it again. "You know, a man never would have done something like this."

She ran her hand across his hair. "You would have. When you love a person as much as we love each other, it's the only reasonable thing to do. I just have to have faith that things will turn out the way I hope they do."

Chapter
37

Saturday night fresh from an action packed two days in New York, they arrived back in Charlottesville. Tina fell asleep during the van ride from the train station. Schaffer carried her inside and tucked her into bed. Renita waited downstairs with Nina, Joe, and Gavin.

Nina walked to the kitchen. "I'm going to fix some coffee. Would anyone else like any?"

"Count me in." Renita said. "Schaffer's probably going to want some too."

"I'll make a pot." Nina filled it with water.

Joe sat next to Renita on the sofa. "Let's see that finger." Renita held out her hand. "He did good."

Renita pulled the ring closer to her eyes. "Yes he did."

"What's behind the look in those eyes?" Gavin asked.

"There you go again, daddy. You always could tell when something was on my mind." She looked at the ring again. "I gave Schaffer Doran's address and phone number."

Nina hung her head and put both hands on the counter. She knew what would come next. Joe spun towards Renita. "Why in the hell would you give him a way to contact a woman he's pined over for almost twenty years?"

Gavin looked shocked. "Baby, a man would never do that type of thing. Why did you feel it was necessary?"

"Daddy, I think you and Schaffer share the same brain. You guys have responded the same way time and time again." She walked over to the breakfast bar.

Nina raised her head and looked at Joe and Gavin. "She knew exactly what she was doing. I would have done the same thing. Stop to think how much love and courage was required to do what she did." Nina took the coffee mugs down from the shelf. "No woman wants to be a consolation prize, even if she is treated like a queen."

Schaffer stood in the stairwell leading to the kitchen listening to their conversation. He stepped into the room with them. Everyone looked away silently as if they were preoccupied. "I was as shocked as you were when Renita suggested I contact Doran. But finally, I understand. Too many things were left unresolved the last time Doran and I were together.

I need to bring closure to that chapter in my life so that Renita and I can begin our lives together unencumbered." He walked to Renita and massaged her shoulders.

"Thank you." She turned and hugged him.

"What I find most amazing is the fact that Renita and Doran will probably turn out to be good friends." Schaffer kissed her forehead.

"Don't count on it." Joe said.

"I don't know, Joe. We do have something in common; we've been loved by the same man." Renita rested her head on Schaffer's chest.

Gavin walked over and touched Schaffer's arm. "Son, I hope you truly understand what you have here."

Schaffer looked into his eyes. "I told you, I've known since the moment I laid eyes on her."

"Good. Then if it's all the same to you, I think I'll have one of your cigars."

"Please, help yourself." Schaffer turned towards Joe. "Would you like one too?"

Joe stood to join Gavin and Schaffer. "That sounds like a good idea." He slapped Schaffer on the back. "By the way, that was one hell of an impressive feat you pulled off in New York. I'm real proud of you. They'll be talking about that for a long time to come. I'm happy for you both."

Renita hugged Joe. "Thanks."

Nina put her hand over her heart. "Joseph, that's the nicest thing I think I've ever heard you say to anyone, let alone Schaffer."

"Don't go getting mushy on me woman. I only said it for Renita's benefit. Nina threw up her hands and rolled her eyes towards the ceiling. Schaffer reached out and hugged Joe. He whispered in Joe's ear. "Thanks old man.

Renita and Schaffer walked to the study with Joe and Gavin. Schaffer opened the humidor and let them each get an Hemmingway Masterpiece.

Renita watched him close the top. "Aren't you going to have one too?"

"Not yet. We've got something to do in here first." He turned on the computer and sat down.

Joe and Gavin left for the porch. Renita sat in Schaffer's lap. "So, what's up?"

"I've got a confession to make. What I'm about to pull up came in on Friday before we left. Instead of telling you, I called your team." He clicked on Gr8 Poem.

Renita knew who sent it as soon as she saw the subject line. She read the note. "Oh, My God! Why didn't you tell me Friday?"

I just couldn't ruin our weekend. It was too late to do anything anyway. Besides, I'm sure your team handled it well enough."

Renita turned back to the computer screen. "How do you know that?"

"Because, you trained them." He paused a second. "It gets worse. This one came in Friday too." Schaffer opened H2O48.

Renita watched as the music came on and the pictures came up. She pointed to one of the pictures. "This woman is facedown in the tub; I'd bet he knows her. This is one sick bastard. I've got to call the rest of the team to see what they've found out." She lifted the receiver and placed the call. It was answered on the first ring. "Okay, so I heard you guys kept me in the dark about what was going on, so now you better have something good to report."

We're working on it. Did you want me to call Dr. Gerard too?" The agent asked.

Renita paused a few seconds. "I guess you'd better. I'll meet everybody at CIRG at the Academy tomorrow at 3 p.m." She hung up the phone and leaned back. "Do you feel up to a drive to DC?"

Schaffer wrapped his arms around her. "Sure. What do you need me to do?"

"Catching this bastard tops my list, but I need a favor from you while we try to find him. Dad has a 2 p.m. flight out of Dulles tomorrow. Can you take him to the airport?"

"Of course. Tina and I will see him off."

Renita looked at the pictures again. "I want you at CIRG as soon as you can get there after that. We've got to map out a strategy. You're the only person he's communicated with. We need to draw him out. You can help with that."

Schaffer pulled up a document he was working on. "I don't know if this will do the trick, but it's worth a try."

Renita read it. "You've written a profile on the people hunting for this psycho?" She slid back on his lap. "That's a good idea. He may try to contact one of us as well."

"He's going to make a mistake soon. When he does you'll have him." Schaffer ran another database search for drowning deaths. Only one was reported, Cindy Garrison.

"That looks like one of ours." Renita pointed to the screen.

Schaffer got up and pulled out a bulletin board with the map of Virginia attached to it. It was smaller than the one the FBI used at the Hoover Building, but identically marked. Four pins were placed in the cities where the previous bodies had been found. Black pins marked the cities of the Black victims and white pins marked the cities of the White victims. He pushed a white pin into South Hill, and then stepped back to take a look.

"Why do you guys use string to tie together the murder locations?" Schaffer moved his finger as if he were connecting the dots.

"We're looking for a pattern, just as you are now. Also, sometimes there can be a connection between the distances separating the murders. One pattern is confirmed, he's alternating the races of these women, White—Black. Until we get them in the lab we won't know which of these two White women died first. We only know that Cindy was the first body discovered."

Schaffer turned his head, first to one side and then the other. "I think there's a pattern here; we just can't see it yet. I hope we can figure it out once we get the others up here."

"Me too. Do you have any theories?" Renita shifted her head as well.

Schaffer continued looking at the map from different perspectives. "Only one, it has something to do with the number 8. The killer said he left a clue at the house of the eighth victim. We might have to wait until then to figure out what he's up to."

Renita lifted the phone again and dialed her office. "I forgot to mention it earlier, get those pictures out to all the police precincts in the state."

"I assumed you wanted that done, so I sent them when we began calling, but we haven't heard anything yet. The agent waited for further instructions.

"You're on top of things, as always. I'll see you tomorrow." Renita hung up and turned her attention back to Schaffer. "It's a shame reality couldn't have waited till Monday."

"Yeah, I hope you don't mind that I waited to tell you about all this. If you would have found out about the acceleration in his attacks, you wouldn't have been around for me to propose to."

"Under any other set of circumstances I'd be furious. But after all was said and done, I'm glad you waited too." Renita looked at her ring and then to Schaffer. "This type of thing will probably constantly interfere with our life together. Are you sure you want to put up with it?"

ANTHONY P. JONES   D8 WITH F8

Dirk's cell phone rang during his drive to DC. He pressed the hands free button and answered.

"Hello Dr. Gerard." Thomas' haunting voice pierced the silence. Have you been home since our last conversation?"

Dirk looked in his rearview mirror at the car behind him. Then, at the cars on either side, he didn't see Thomas. "Where are you?"

"Come now. You don't think that I'm that stupid. If I told you, then you would put an end to all of my fun. More women still have to die. Maybe I'll tell you when I'm done." Thomas laughed like a madman.

"Why are you doing this? What can you possibly gain by killing these women?" Dirk found it hard to concentrate on the road with his eyes darting back and forth scanning every vehicle within sight.

"Given our past history I would think you'd understand. Victoria has to pay for what she put me through. Since I can't find her, the blood of the women I've killed is on her hands. It's not like they didn't need to die anyway. If I had let them live they would have continued sucking the life out of guys like us." The anger in Thomas' voice grew. "Shit, I did you a favor."

"Then do me another favor." Dirk demanded. Come in so that I can get you some help. I can send you somewhere that no one else has to know about."

Thomas made a sucking sound through his teeth. "We both know you don't have anything on me. If you did, you would have already come after me. You don't even have any circumstantial evidence."

"You've confessed to me on the phone. What would you call that?"

"I would call you an accessory to murder. Think about it, you haven't told the police. Everybody's looking for me and no one knows who I am. You've kept it nice and quiet, just the way I knew you would. So now if they find me, they find you as well. You tell them who I am and I'll sing like a bird." Thomas laughed harder than before.

Dirk heard the phone line go dead. "Fuck you Thomas, fuck you."

◆

Schaffer and Dirk arrived at the underground parking deck of the Hoover Building at about the same time. Schaffer got out of his car just as Dirk was walking to the automatic sliding glass doors to the elevators. "Hello, Dr. Gerard. Hang on; I'll walk in with you."

Dirk waved his hand. "Hurry up. We're late."

Schaffer could see Dirk was agitated and ran to catch up to him. "It's a damn shame 'Tony the Tiger' is taking away even our Sundays now."

"We do what we have to do to catch the bad guys, Mr. O'Grady. If that means living at the lab twenty four-seven, then that's what we must do."

"That's true. It's still a damn shame." Schaffer followed Dirk through the doors and they walked into CIRG.

When they exited the elevator on the main level an officer manning the security desk sent them to a conference room where the team was working. Schaffer was last through the door and the team members began clapping when he stepped in.

Dirk looked at them with mild irritation. "What's going on here?"

One of the agents addressed Dirk. "Agent Duplechain got engaged Friday to the guy walking in behind you."

"Yeah, well congratulations." His voice was filled with equal parts of insincerity and doubt. "Let's hope you guys will remain happy." Dirk pulled out his seat and sat down with a heavy flop.

Renita stood and scanned her team. "On that note, I guess we should get started." She walked over to the map containing the pushpins marking the sites of the murders. We have identified the four new victims, Cindy Garrison from South Hill, Emily Purcell from Richmond, Deborah Lewis from Franklin, and Ava Hayes from Roanoke. The local Medical Examiners have gone to retrieve the bodies. Our Evidence Response teams are on their way out to each site to collect further evidence."

Schaffer jumped from his chair. "I've got it." He walked over to the map. "We've been looking at this thing wrong. May I?" Schaffer began taking the string from the pins.

"Wait a minute." Dirk demanded. "We're not even sure the order these last four women died in. Why would you rearrange our connections?"

Schaffer continued removing the string. "Because, the order doesn't matter at all." He rearranged the string. "It was right in front of us all the time. It's the locations of the kills. He's killing in a distinct pattern, 'V-8.'"

"Oh shit." One of the agents said when Schaffer moved from in front of the map. The pattern was obvious.

Renita focused on the map. "Based on the pattern we should be able to extrapolate the next possible points of attack."

Dirk let his hand fall to the table, causing a loud noise. "This could be a phenomenal waste of time. Instead of concentrating where he might strike next we should be collecting evidence at the scenes. We need to listen to the evidence to guide us in the right direction."

"This bastard hasn't left us any evidence other than fibers from a postman's uniform and hairs that were obviously cut from someone else's head. He's smart; forensically sophisticated. He knows exactly what we're looking for and leaves us what he wants us to find." The agent looked down at the notes he'd made since the case began.

Renita stepped away from the map. "He's more than forensically intelligent; I'd say his IQ is off the charts. He thinks this gives him the upper hand."

The agent sat his notes down listening to Renita. "When you examine all the evidence, this guy could work for any crime lab in the surrounding area."

Dirk gulped thinking of Thomas. He decided to add his insight. "That's highly possible, but I'd guess he's not at the assistant level. He exhibits knowledge that you'd only find in a seasoned professional."

"That's even more evident by his staging of the crime scenes. He's planted evidence that he knows won't stand up." Renita quickly glanced at the other faces in the room. "It's his way of calling us stupid."

The agent stabbed his notes with his finger. "Yeah, we're so stupid that we know that he's gotten into the victims' houses by posing as a mail man or delivery personnel."

"I want to know what kind of woman would have a drink with a mail man. If all these women knew the UNSUB, why the uniform? And then there's the wine, GHB and traces of LSD and organophosphate all these women have in common; how could he force it on them? There's no sign of struggle, no bruising." Renita paused as if another thought was forming.

"Well, he was dressed as a mail man; maybe he gave them some type of package." Dirk offered.

"I guess it's possible." Renita frowned. "Damn water always screws up evidence. I'm sure that was planned as well."

There was a knock on the door; another agent stepped into the room. "I may have something that could help. We've been working on decoding the e-mail messages sent to Mr. O'Grady. We still haven't gotten a lock on a location, but we've identified the ISP client." He looked at the team members who were hungry for the information. "It's registered to Dr. Kenesha Williams. I'll go back and try to track her down now."

"Don't bother." Renita said. "She's on a slab back there." She pointed to the lab. "She was one of his first four victims."

"I told you he was a smart fucker." One of the team members said. "He's using the identity of one of the women he's killed."

Maybe this article will help to draw him out." Schaffer passed around a copy of the article he was preparing for the *Post* after the FBI team mapped out a strategy for the article designed to enlist a response from the UNSUB. "I still need to get some personal background info from each of you to complete it."

Before they began reading, Renita passed out the location assignments. "After each of you meets with Schaffer, head out to supervise the search at the crime scene I've given you. Be back here tomorrow at 11 a.m. for a full debriefing. The autopsies should be finished by then."

Dirk walked over to the other members assigned to his team. "I don't have time for an interview. I'll meet you at the crime scene in Richmond." With that he abruptly left the conference room; fifteen minutes later he was flying down I-395 on his way to Richmond.

Chapter

39

Schaffer moved to an area where he could be alone. Even though Tree couldn't get to the crime scenes yet, Schaffer needed to know about the latest vics. As he was dialing, Schaffer realized that he was going to catch it since he'd not returned Tree's earlier call.

"Oh, so you finally dragged your ass out from under whatever rock is was under. I thought this case was a priority? I thought you wanted to catch this bastard before he killed somebody else. Good luck with that effort."

Schaffer knew it was time to stop Tree, even though he deserved his moment of ranting. "It's too late to stop him; the bastard killed four more women over the past couple of days."

"Shit! Were any kids involved?" Bacchus held his breath.

"No kids have been involved at any of the scenes, thank God. But, he's accelerating his attacks. He's bound to get sloppy. God help us if he doesn't." Schaffer looked over his shoulder to make sure his privacy had been maintained. "We may have a small break. He said that he left us a clue at the scene of the eighth killing. We're just hearing about them, so which one was the eighth hasn't been determined yet."

Bacchus felt his muscles tighten as his anger grew. "I need to check out the film from the scenes as soon as possible."

"That's a good idea. I'll forward the e-mail to you along with a list of the crime scenes. I haven't seen any of them yet, so I don't think I can help at this point."

"How about your girlfriend?"

"I haven't told her about you yet. If you find anything then I'll spring you on her."

Bacchus let out a half grunt-half laugh. "I've got to earn my keep before you're willing to talk to her about me. I love you too. And just to prove it, I found something that her people missed at Gloria Stegal's house."

The pause lasted longer than Schaffer was comfortable with. "So are you going to tell me or are you going to make me beg?"

"A little groveling would do you good, but it would be a waste of time." Bacchus took the flyer from his jacket. "It's possible the killer is considering a purchase of real estate in the Richmond, VA area. I found a real estate flyer under the dining room table at Gloria's house."

"That can't be all you have, I know you too well. What are you holding back?"

"Give me half a fucking chance, damn!" Bacchus tapped the flyer against his leg. The flyer had two sets of prints on it, but they checked out. However, there were surface traces of organophosphates, LSD, GHB and fibers from a mail bag; all of which you guys have found at each scene."

"Renita is going to be pissed that someone overlooked that piece of evidence." Schaffer wondered who'd made that mistake.

"Well, I'm not defending whoever fucked up, but the flyer was placed under one foot of the table as if it was being used to stabilize it. I spoke with Gloria's niece. She said that Gloria wasn't looking at any real estate in Richmond. If Gloria had picked up the flyer, her prints would likely have been on it as well."

"I was just about to ask you about her prints, but after hearing about the chemicals, I assumed it was our boy and I didn't expect that you would have found any usable prints." Schaffer looked at the ceiling and sighed heavily. "Maybe I should get the flyer for the lab. I don't want to burn your time scanning each individual page and looking for other clues page-by-page."

"I guess that means you have to break your silence about our relationship. What's your girlfriend going to think about your two-timing?"

"I think she'll be grateful we found additional evidence and pissed her people missed it."

"Can I make a suggestion?"

"Sure. I think they could use the help."

Bacchus tucked the flyer, which was protected by a zip lock bag back into his jacket and patted his pocket. "Why don't you bring your girlfriend when I give this to you? Then, I suggest that she has someone totally outside the current team run the test. What if it wasn't so much overlooked as intentionally left behind?"

"Stranger things have happened. I'll pass on your suggestion, even though I can't imagine any one on the team would be involved."

"Who put the team together?"

Schaffer swallowed hard. "Renita; all except for Dr. Gerard, who was sent by the Governor."

"Well, if this was intentionally left behind, that's your suspect list." Bacchus braced himself for what he knew was coming.

"I can assure you, one of those people doesn't belong on that list." Schaffer bristled.

"I expected you'd say that. Then you know what you have to do."

Schaffer allowed his defensive posture to fade. "We'll get it done. Thanks, Tree."

"Hey, I'm just collecting a paycheck." A grunt was as close as he could come to a laugh. "For what it's worth, I don't think your girlfriend's involved. These killings are the work of a very pissed off dude."

"That's my take. We should get together as soon as possible so we can get the flyer to the lab."

"Just say the word."

Schaffer exhaled, thinking about visiting another crime scene. "I'll call you in a day or so. Thanks again."

Chapter
40

Schaffer rode with Renita and the other team members to Roanoke. He sat with her in the back seat, where they discussed the case. "How did you find the other three so quickly?"

"We sent out alerts to all the police departments in the state and told them to pay special attention to any missing person reports. It took them no time to get back to us with all three."

"That's probably a good thing; the crime scenes should be well preserved."

"Let's hope so." Renita looked over the notes. "The most glaring similarities these women share are success and divorce. That is, all except Ava, she was never even married."

"The question that stays on my mind is how he selected his victims." Schaffer unfolded a map of Virginia. He circled the cities where murders occurred. "He crisscrossed the state hunting for prey. Now we know that they were not just random killings, these women were selected. Divorce, success and the number 8 seem to piss him off."

"There has to be something else that ties these women together." The agent driving said. "Other than divorce, success and the number 8."

"It's not like we can warn every divorced woman in the areas we suspect he will hit next, to avoid postmen." The other agent added.

"I'm sure our UNSUB is not a postman. The fibers we found were left intentionally. Nothing he's done has been accidental or random." Renita flipped a page. "He must be as bald as a newborn rat since we haven't found a single hair sample with a follicle except for the ones he planted."

"He must also wear a body condom since we haven't found any skin cells other than the victims'." The agent driving laughed.

"That may not be as far fetched as it sounds." Schaffer edged forward in his seat. "I saw a program on TV where people covered their bodies in latex for kicks. To them, it was some kind of freaky sexual turn-on."

"What the hell were you watching?" Renita slid over, increasing the distance between them.

"It came on after boxing one night. I woke up just as they were airing the story." Schaffer's face reddened.

The agent riding in the front seat turned around. "Maybe we should check this guy out a little closer before you say, I do."

"That's okay, boys. I sleep with my gun on." Renita patted her side.

When the laughter died down Schaffer redirected the conversation. "Something that has bothered me for the longest is Gloria Stegal's dog. A Black woman doesn't have a hundred and twenty pound Rottweiler around the house for decoration."

Renita flipped back to her notes on Gloria. "It's more than just a little strange that the dog would bite down on a can of Raid." She read through the notes. "Dirk's notes from the scene said that the dog was cremated along with Gloria."

"Winston didn't mention that to me. Of course, at the time we didn't know we were dealing with a serial killer." Schaffer lifted his IPhone and dialed. "Winston, it's Schaffer O'Grady. I've got another question about the Gloria Stegal case. Our notes say that the dog was cremated with Gloria. Is that what you show?"

Chief Wellington didn't answer right away. "That's not entirely true. It was supposed to be cremated with her, but her niece showed up at the crematorium. She was handling the arrangements and at the last minute she ordered the dog to be removed."

"Why would she do that?"

"Because, she's in Vet-school at Virginia Tech, they use dogs for dissection during their freshman year anatomy class. She wanted to work on this dog." Winston paused again. "Should I call the school?"

"No, I'll take care of it, if you have the number handy." Schaffer wrote the number down. "Thanks, Winston. We'll talk to you later."

Renita tapped her pad, waiting for Schaffer to hang up. "What did he say?"

The dog was sent to the Vet-school at Virginia Tech. Here's the number." Schaffer handed it to her.

Renita dialed it immediately. "This is Special Agent Duplechain with the FBI. I need to speak with the person in charge of your gross anatomy lab."

"That would be Dr. Pritchard. I'll connect you."

"Hello, Dr. Pritchard. This is Special Agent Duplechain with the FBI. About three months ago a dog was donated to your lab by—" Renita looked at Schaffer. "What's the niece's name?"

"Sharon Johnson."

"Sorry, Dr. Pritchard. The dog was donated by one of your

students, Sharon Johnson."

"Yes. I remember. It was a very large Rottweiler. Sharon began dissection of the dog when it came in. She and her lab partners were lucky to have such a beautiful specimen."

"Dr. Pritchard." Renita cut him off. "What is the condition of the dog now?"

"The students spend several months with dissection. They begin with the torso of the dog and work to the tail, saving the head for last."

"Dr. Pritchard, I need for you to prevent any further dissection of that dog. Quarantine the animal and keep everyone away from it."

"Is there something we should be concerned about?" Dr. Prichard's head jerked with a nervous twitch.

"You don't have to worry about a thing as long as you keep everyone away from that dog." Renita issued a final warning. "It's a federal matter. My team and I are on our way to the school as we speak. We should be there within the hour." She hung up the phone and tapped the agent driving the car. "Hit the blue lights and get this car moving."

He flipped down the visor emergency lights and flipped the activation switch. The high frequency blue strobe flashed a warning to anyone in their way. The speedometer jumped from seventy-five to ninety-five, occasionally surpassing one hundred as they flew down I-81.

◆

Dr. Pritchard began walking to the lab. "Agent Duplechain, do we need to administer any vaccines to the students?"

Renita realized she had needlessly caused him to worry. "No. The dog had no disease that we know of. Although hopefully, his body still retains evidence we can use. Tell me how you prepare the dogs for dissection."

"We wash and embalm them. Then, we put them on ice, I mean, in the freezer. They are taken out only when we need them for class."

Schaffer stepped beside Renita. "Dr. Pritchard, is anything done to clean out the inside of the dog?"

He looked at Schaffer. "No, but I'm afraid it's too late to find anything inside the dog. The digestive track has already been covered in class, it's already been removed from the dog."

"Does that include the mouth?"

"No. We save the head and brain as the last part of the dissection."

Schaffer looked at Renita. "That's exactly what we need if my thinking is correct."

◆

While Renita continued to speak with Dr. Pritchard, Schaffer stepped away from the group to contact Bacchus. "Hey, Tree. We've found Gloria Stegal's dog, it was never cremated."

"Really, I've got a feeling that's where you'll get your first break. Dogs are instinctive about poison they don't bite down on cans containing something that can harm them."

"Yeah, I always had a problem with that one too." Schaffer noticed the team moving to meet Renita. "I've got to run, I'll call back as soon as I can."

◆

Bruits had been dead for three months. The only part of him left intact was the head and a small section of the neck. Dr. Pritchard handed each of the team members a pair of latex gloves.

Schaffer slid his on with the skill of a surgeon. "Dr. Pritchard, is there any chance water was put into the mouth?"

"There would have been no reason to. We like to leave the mouth untouched so that the students can confirm what the animal had as its last meal. In some cases, fragments of that meal can be found in the mouth and esophagus."

Schaffer nodded. "That's exactly what I hope to find, his last meal, so to speak." He carefully lifted the dog's upper lip.

Renita used a magnifying glass to look for any foreign matter. She used a cotton swab to sweep the gums for particles. She slid the swab out. "This is what we're looking for gentlemen." She held up the swab, which was covered in small brown particles of about the same size and consistency as fine sand.

"Dried blood." Schaffer said and moved in for a closer look inside the dog's mouth. "Pass me the tweezers. There's something caught between his teeth." He pulled it out and Renita handed him an evidence collection tube.

Renita held up the tube and looked at the evidence. "If this is what I think it is, we'll begin to know more about our UNSUB as soon as we get this back to the lab."

The other agents pulled out yellow crime scene tape and prepared to section off the dog's table.

Renita looked around the lab. "Dr. Pritchard, is there a more secure location we can place this animal?"

"Sure. We can put him in the freezer where we store all incoming animals. It has very limited access."

Renita placed the vials in a cool storage bag. "We're going to need blood and hair samples from everyone who worked on this dog. We want to be sure we didn't find their blood or skin samples in his mouth."

Dr. Pritchard looked at his watch. "The students should be here in twenty minutes, or I can take you to their current classes."

"We'll wait." Renita walked back over to the table. "Don't seal it just yet, guys. Let's get a tissue sample from the dog as well." She signaled for Dr. Pritchard. "In your expert opinion, would a dog bite down on a can containing poison?"

He studied the dog. "I found that quite odd when I was told how he had died. Dogs can be quite destructive, but they instinctively avoid poisons, unless they are hidden inside their food."

"We can rule food out. Could something like this happen playing fetch?" Renita knew she was reaching, but wanted to cover all possibilities.

"Not likely. Even though a dog this size is capable of crushing human bones, when playing, they are very gentle. If he were angry he could have done it. But, even then I would suspect he would avoid poison. They have an incredible sense of smell."

Schaffer looked over Renita's notes. "It says here that the can in his mouth was dented from the top teeth and punctured by the bottom teeth."

Dr. Pritchard wrinkled his brow. "That's odd too, because the top jaw is stationary and the bottom jaw moves. One would expect the top teeth to puncture the can and the bottom should have been crushed, unless—"

Schaffer finished his sentence. "Unless someone placed the can in his mouth and used force to make his jaw move."

"Exactly." Dr. Pritchard examined the dog's mouth.

Renita looked at the area beneath the jaw. "Who's you best cutter, Dr. Pritchard?"

"Sharon, the young lady who's responsible for the dog being here."

"Get her and bring a new set of dissection instruments. You do have them available don't you?" Renita looked up.

"Yes. I'll bring them back with the student." Dr. Pritchard left the lab.

Renita looked at one of the agents. "Go to the truck and bring the camera and tools." To the other agent she said. "Find a clean place to work and begin typing the blood on the swab. Give Schaffer the results so that he can log it in and forward it to headquarters. This should be helpful to everyone collecting evidence."

Thirty minutes later, Renita and Sharon completed removing the skin from Bruits' bottom jaw. The agent assisting Renita measured and photographed the remnants of a bruise. "From the shape of the bruise I would say the toe of a shoe made the mark. Knowing that the very tip of the shoe takes most of the impact, we can find the center by looking for the darkest part of the bruise.

The other agent walked over. "Then this should really narrow our search. The guy has type AB negative blood, the second rarest type."

"Get that on the wire as fast as possible Schaffer. The troops can begin a search of rapists with that blood type and they can do a search of the blood banks in the state for anyone who donates with that blood type. We're going to catch this bastard. He screwed up by pissing off the dog."

Schaffer walked away from the group using a quiet corner to call Bacchus. "I've got a bit more to go on. We think the UNSUB has AB negative blood type."

Bacchus scribbled the information on a pad. "Now you're talking; it's about time we caught a break."

Schaffer looked over his shoulder to make sure his call was still private. "I assume you still have access to a national data bank."

"I might have a way to check on things."

"Remember your conclusion earlier about who could be involved; why don't you check him against the data we just collected."

Bacchus' pause was notable. "Don't you think I should run both of them?"

Schaffer gripped his IPhone tighter. "I can assure you, Renita doesn't wear the size shoe that could make a bruise like the one we found. She's not a suspect."

"Okay, I'll just run the good doctor. I'll get back to you." Bacchus disconnected.

Chapter
41

Each team of agents routinely used Blackberry handheld devices to communicate with headquarters. They are the most efficient means of disseminating and receiving pertinent information on an active case from a remote location. Around noon each team's blackberry beeped indicating there was new information.

As the leader of his team, Dirk pulled out his Blackberry to see what came in. Flashing in red on the screen was the memo from Renita.

-Gloria Stegal's dog was not destroyed. Blood and tissue samples collected.

–Suspect's blood type AB negative.

Dirk knew that the walls would quickly close in on Thomas now. If he could help him, he needed to find him soon. He called the other members of the team together. "There's been a break in the case." He showed them the note.

"Gentlemen, I've got to leave, I feel as if I'm coming down with something."

Dirk certainly appeared ill. His face was flushed and perspiration covered his forehead and upper lip. "Would you like one of us to drive you home?"

"No, you need to stay here and finish the sweep of the house. I don't live far from here. I'll be fine." Dirk left the house. He briskly walked to his car parked at the curb. Once there, he walked around to the far side, bent over and threw up several times.

Dirk got in the car and flipped down his visor. In the mirror he could see his face covered with sweat. He used his sleeve to wipe it away. Then, his phone rang.

"Hello, Dr. Gerard."

"Thomas. You're in a lot of trouble. It won't be long before we have you in custody." Dirk looked in the mirror and mopped his face again.

"I've told you before; you don't have shit on me." Thomas' voice tightened with anger.

"I'm afraid we do." Dirk started the car and drove down the driveway. "You forgot about the dog at Gloria Stegal's house. We just got blood and tissue samples from him."

"That's bullshit! That dog was cremated with that bitch. That happened long before anyone even knew she was killed." Thomas slammed his fist hard against the wall.

"How could you possibly have known that? We never released that information." Dirk gasped several times trying to regulate his breath.

Thomas laughed. "See, I knew you were fucking with me. I know because I snuck into your office late one night and read the report on your desk. Did you forget you gave me a key?"

Dirk's head drifted downward. "Shit." He wiped his face again. "That's where you're wrong. The dog was not cremated. It ended up at Virginia Tech's Vet-school."

Thomas rubbed the spot on his arm where Bruits attacked him. He started screaming wildly. "You fucking bastards aren't playing the game fairly. Fuck you! Fuck all of you." Thomas slammed his fist repeatedly against the wall. Then, as if someone flicked a switch in his brain, he came back on the phone calm, cool, and collected. "Well then Dr. Gerard, I guess there's only one thing for me to do. I'll just have to accept your help."

"That's the first smart thing you've said so far. Where can I meet you?" Dirk looked at his watch.

Thomas grunted several times trying to remain in control. "Come to Fredericksburg. Get off at the Massaponax exit and park at the McDonalds. When I'm sure that you have come alone I'll give you further instructions. Dr. Gerard, if you fuck me, I'll kill you where you sit." He disconnected the phone.

Dirk got on I-95 north and headed up to Fredericksburg.

♦

At 11 a.m. the following day the teams reassembled at the Hoover Building in Washington. The tissue and blood samples were already in the lab undergoing analysis. All of the Virginia Tech students were ruled out because none of them had type AB blood. By week's end the priority rushed DNA profile would be complete and the focus of the investigation narrowed.

Renita stood at the head of the table. She projected their findings directly on the wall. "Where is Dr. Gerard?"

"He went home sick." One of the agents from the Richmond detail said.

"I hope it's nothing serious." Renita answered.

"He was sweating like a pig. When he got outside to his car he puked his insides out." The agent squirmed telling Renita about what had happened. "I can deal with blood, but puke makes me sick."

"Thanks for the graphic details." Renita turned back to the projected notes. The guys in the lab will add their findings as soon as they are ready. This is what we have so far." She used a laser pointer attached to the projector's remote control to draw their attention to the notes.

-A review of Dr. Williams' patients shows no connection between her and the other victims.

-Tony the Tiger has alternated the race of his victims with each kill.

-All of these women were in positions of power, or climbing in their chosen fields.

-All of the victims were divorced, except Ava Hayes, who had never married.

-Fibers found at the first set of crime scenes were from a postman's uniform.

-Hair samples found at these scenes were cut from several unidentified women's heads.

-Fibers collected at three of the second set of crime scenes match, but their origin is still unknown.

-Fibers found at Ava Hayes' house are different. Why?

-Ava Hayes was drowned facedown, suggesting he knew the victim.

-Only known contact by UNSUB has been with Mr. O'Grady. Why?

-Suspect had sex with all victims, anal sex with Black victims, except Hayes. Why?

-There are no signs of struggle at any scenes. Why?

"This is quite a list gentlemen. Based on a V-8 pattern, where have the Geographical Profilers projected our next possible points of attack?" Renita looked at the agent handling those calculations.

"Five cities come up as the most likely targets. They are Alexandria, Woodbridge, Martinsville, Danville, and South Boston. Once we have the order of death of the most recent women, we should be able to narrow it to one area, either Northern or Southwestern Virginia."

Schaffer sat up. "Wait a minute. Renita, bring up that last e-mail I got from him."

Renita pulled it up from her files and projected it onto the wall. The first four women came up in the order that they had died. "I'll be damned. He sent them in order. He's an organized killer, it stands to reason; Ava Hayes must have been the last to die."

"In that case, expect his next victim to be White, living in the Northern Virginia area." The agent circled the area on his map.

Renita looked at the calendar. "It's less than two weeks till Christmas and we've got to warn divorced White women in the heaviest populated region of the state. This is going to be a nightmare."

One of the agents interjected. "They also have to be successful divorced women."

"I'll get something in the paper right away. Even though I'm not sure anyone will turn away a mail carrier with gifts from grandma." Schaffer shook his head. "Hopefully the DNA profile will narrow things down quickly. The blood type narrows him to one in one hundred and sixty-seven people. The population of the area you suggest in Northern Virginia is what, two or three million people? That still makes things difficult. If we can narrow things down by locating successful divorced white women, we may be able to reach them."

"One thing's for sure, we can't do anything inside here. Let's see what the lab comes up with by tomorrow morning. Then we can get out and shake the bushes." Renita looked at the clock. "It's almost nine, guys. We've all had a busy day. I'll hit you on your Blackberries tonight if there are any updates. Otherwise, get a good night's sleep and I'll see everyone tomorrow morning.

♦

Dirk waited in his car for seven hours. He made occasional trips into McDonalds for food and to use the bathroom. On one trip he explained to the manager he was working a sensitive case so that they would stop having the police cruise by every few minutes.

At 9:05 p.m. Thomas called. "Have you been waiting long Dr. Gerard?"

Dirk sighed. "What do you want me to do, Thomas?"

"Start your car."

Dirk started the car and looked up to adjust his rearview mirror. "There's no need to look in there Dr. Gerard. I'm not behind you. Looking to either side is useless as well, because I'm nowhere and everywhere. Just follow my instructions and you'll arrive at your destination." Thomas took a sip of his drink. "Make a right on Rt.1 and drive until you come to Rt.3. There you will head West. Then follow the signs for Raven's Wood Homes. When you reach the entrance wait there stop until you hear from me again."

Dirk followed the instructions. The last five miles of his trip were in total darkness, except for his headlights. He reached the front entrance. No houses could be seen from the road. The developers designed the subdivision to maximize privacy. A couple of times Dirk actually thought of lifting the phone and calling Renita. But, the feeling soon passed.

Dirk's phone rang again. "Okay, I did what you asked. What now?" His patience was wearing thin.

"You've been such a good sport. Try to remain patient a while longer." Thomas' tone was firm. Drive about a mile and a quarter further. You will see a golf course sign about half way to your destination. Point six-five miles from the sign there is a turn to your left. Take that turn and drive until you see the house. Are my directions clear enough?"

"I think I can handle it." Dirk answered rudely.

"Just in case you didn't remember my warning, if more that one set of headlights comes down the driveway, you're dying first. Nothing cute, you and only you better come up this driveway."

"I understand." Dirk answered.

As he pulled up the driveway, spotlights hit his car from the front of the house and from the trees on either side of the path.

Thomas was still on the phone. "Stop right there and get out of the car."

Dirk got out and put his hand up to shield his eyes from some of the glaring light. "Thomas where are you?"

"Walk to the house. The door is open."

Dirk walked into the house. The door slammed behind him and his world went totally black.

Chapter
42

Snow started falling around 2 p.m. on Christmas Eve. Fire crackled and popped spreading warmth and light across the family room. Renita sat on the floor wearing a baggy sweatshirt, sweatpants and fuzzy 'bear feet' slippers. She typed on a laptop cross-referencing the National databank with the evidence they had, trying to narrow the profile of any possible suspects.

Schaffer was at the breakfast bar composing another article aimed at bringing 'Tony the Tiger' out of hiding. He had written three articles over the past week and a half with no success. Schaffer stopped typing and spun around in his chair. "How about some popcorn?" He got up and started to prepare it even before she answered him.

"That sounds good. Of course you realize the smell will rouse the natives. Tina can smell popcorn a mile away." Renita stretched, reaching high in the air and pointed the bear feet as far as they could reach.

Schaffer yawned after seeing Renita do it first. "Stop that. It's catching." He added the popcorn to the hot oil. "Have you checked on your partner lately?"

Renita's head rose from the computer. "Who are you talking about?"

"The great, Dr. Dirk Gerard. He probably got sick just to start his Christmas vacation early."

Renita got off the floor and walked to the kitchen. "Things are just fine with him out of our hair. He must be catching heat from the governor. This case is more difficult than anything he's faced in the past. Not being able to solve it quickly has been a blow to his ego, as well as the governor's."

"His ego, what about mine? I'm the only person a serial killer wants to talk to. What does that say about me?" Schaffer shook the pot as the popcorn kernels ricocheted off the sides.

"You're the best person for him to be in touch with. You can maximize his exposure. These guys crave attention. You were the first to recognize his work and acknowledge it." Renita sat at the breakfast bar awaiting the popcorn.

"I'd just as soon not hear from him again. Every time I do the UNSUB has killed again." Schaffer took a handful of the popcorn and placed the rest in a bowl on the bar. "I've got to go pull up my e-mails. Joe and Nina said they would send a note to let us know what time their plane lands tonight."

"I wish we could have gone with them." Renita wolfed down a handful of popcorn.

"Me too. Then I could have seen you in a bikini for three days." He pinched Renita's bottom as he walked by.

"You couldn't handle it mister." Renita stood and posed, as a model would have. "This package is lethal."

Schaffer grabbed his heart. "Kill me already then!" They both laughed and he went to the study.

He pulled up his emails and opened the one from Joe. They would be in from the Bahamas at 9 p.m. Joe didn't mention whether they would come straight to Charlottesville or wait until the morning. The computer chimed, indicating the receipt of another e-mail.

Renita walked down the hall. "What did they say?"

"They'll land tonight at—" His eyes fell on the new e-mail. "You'd better get over here."

She walked through the door. "What's wrong?"

Schaffer maneuvered the mouse bringing the pointer over the subject line. 'Merry Christmas from The Gr8 One.' He looked at Renita and clicked the mouse. Their hearts pounded waiting for the words to appear.

What would Christmas be without gifts? There's one for you at the bottom of this page. Remember, it's the thought that counts. I've read the profile that you all have developed on the FBI's intranet page. It's quite interesting.

The bullet points Renita listed the day before were on the computer screen. "How in the hell did he get this?" Renita recognized the memo.

DNA findings
-Mixed race
-Male
-Eye color, (hazel)?
Evidence at scene
-AB blood type
-Naked Mountain Chardonnay empty
-V-8 juice, unopened
-GHB in high doses
-Rain the day of murders
Profile

-Bed wetter

-Early arsons

-Late 30s to mid 40s

-Hate for mother, White women killed slightly older.

-Hate for another female, probably wife, younger Black females

-Females in his life were domineering & controlling.

-Need for attention & revenge

Schaffer read the list out loud. "Oh shit, this guy knows every move we make. He's found a way to tap into our intranet site. I thought it was secure."

Renita looked over the list again. "He didn't tap into our site. I don't know how he got this info, but it wasn't by breaking in."

"Are you suggesting that he's one of us?"

"That would seem logical. However, I don't think he's from inside our group." She pointed to the bottom of the page. "Click on the flashing gift box. Let's see what he sent."

Schaffer moved the pointer and clicked. A small picture of a disheveled man holding a newspaper came up. "I'll make it larger." The picture covered the screen. Dr. Dirk Gerard holding a Christmas Eve addition of the *Washington Post* starred back at them.

Words eerily crawled across the bottom of the screen. "I've got a suspect in custody. Give me what I want for Christmas if you want to see him alive again. I'll send a few reminders soon. The Gr8 One. P.S. His Blackberry is here too. Love your intranet site."

"Shit!" Renita hit the desk. "I wonder how long he's had Dr. Gerard?" She lifted the phone and pointed the receiver at Schaffer. "I want this bastard real bad."

"Schaffer looked at Renita's side. "I think you'd better keep your gun handy. If he could find Gerard, he could find us too."

Renita dialed the phone. "He won't disturb you. You're his only means of glorification. But, I've got to warn everyone else on the team. There will be no more messages posted on our intranet site. Our personal e-mail addresses were not posted on the site, so we're switching to them now."

Renita delivered her message to the other team members and to headquarters. The intranet site was wiped clean and the agents were put on high alert. Renita told them to carry their guns everywhere, including the bathroom. This was going to be an uneasy Christmas.

Renita set the phone down. "Schaffer, get your gun out right now.

From now on I want it with you at all times."

"Ooh-rah, yes ma'am. Schaffer saluted. "He keeps telling us to give him what he wants. What do you think he wants?"

"No doubt about it, he wants a person and he thinks we can help him find her."

Schaffer frowned. "So, he wants us to figure out who he is and who he's looking for. Then, lead him to this person. I suppose that will make him stop killing other Women."

Renita nodded. "At least that's what he wants us to believe. Once guys like him have tasted blood they won't stop killing until we catch them. Sometime I've seen them lay low for months or years, but they all start killing again eventually."

◆

Schaffer sat by the fireplace reading a copy of *The Enneagrams* that he bought after seeing the one at Ava's house. Ava's copy was still in the FBI lab along with everything else collected at the scene, waiting to be reviewed. He heard Renita coming down the hall and called to her. "You should check this out."

"What's that?" She asked.

"The Enneagrams; remember the book we found at Ava Hayes' house. It's a personality typing system that dates back to ancient China. A nine pointed star represents the points of the Enneagram." He showed a page to Renita. "They're numbered."

"Let me see that." Renita reached for the book.

"Okay, but I think you need to see this part back here too." Schaffer used a finger to hold the book open at a second spot. "This is the section on point number eight. It's called 'The Boss.' What I've read so far sounds a lot like our dead women."

Renita almost jerked the book from him and read at a furious pace. "Hand me the phone, please."

Tina walked over with the phone in hand. "But you said no work tonight. It's Christmas Eve."

Schaffer reached out for her. "Come over here. This is real important. It would have to be. There's no one else your mom would rather spend time with other than you."

Tina sat in Schaffer's lap. "She likes spending time with you too."

Renita blew Tina a kiss waiting for the headquarters Duty Agent to answer. "Hi. I need you to look something up on the Tony the Tiger case."

"Here I thought working Christmas Eve would be quiet. What are you looking for?" The agent asked.

"We brought in a box from the Ava Hayes crime scene. Has everything been processed?"

"Let's see." He pulled up the list on the computer. "Everything in the box was checked for fingerprints. They were all hers. No outside prints of value were found."

"Were there any other tests done on the book?"

"No. Is there something specific you're looking for?"

"Go get the book. I'll hold." Renita looked down at the copy she had, reading about Point Eight. The agent returned with the book. "Does it look like she read the book? Are there any marks in the book?"

He flipped through it. "It naturally opened up to page 306, Point Eight. And there's a picture of Schaffer marking the page. Shit— the whole damn chapter is hi-lited."

"Bingo. You might want to start reading the beginning of the book and the section on Point Eight. It will answer some of the questions about what 'Tony the Tiger' is looking for, women who are eights. Schaffer's picture identifies the book as the clue 'Tony the Tiger' referred to earlier."

Chapter
43

Gretchen lazily lifted her head when Schaffer and Renita walked into the family room. She watched as they walked past to play Santa in the solarium. The fire proved to be more inviting than a pat on the head. Suddenly she jumped up and ran through the pet door that led to the garage.

"What's wrong with her?" Renita asked Schaffer as she pulled her Sig from its holster.

"Someone's here that's what the beep was." Schaffer looked at the clock, 1:30 a.m. "It's probably Nina and Joe."

"Let's check to make sure." Renita walked to the kitchen with the gun in ready position.

Schaffer stopped her at the door. "I'll check. You stay here. If something was wrong Gretchen would be barking."

"Get back you mangy mutt." Joe's voice rolled down the hallway.

Renita relaxed as she re-holstered the gun, then followed Schaffer down the hallway.

"Damn. We've been met by the Calvary." Joe looked at Renita and Schaffer, who were both wearing sidearms.

Nina pulled gifts from the trunk. When she heard Joe, she sat them down and looked at Renita. "What's going on? Why are both of you wearing guns?"

"It's a long story. Let's get your things inside and we can talk about it over a drink." Schaffer lifted two of the bags and they walked to the kitchen in silence.

Nina took Renita's arm. Renita looked down as they walked. "He took one of our team members hostage. The guns are just a precaution." Nina didn't respond she just patted Renita's arm.

"It's Christmas guys. You shouldn't look so glum. Look at Joe; he's bright enough to make anyone smile." Schaffer slapped him on the back.

"Ouch! Keep your damn hands to yourself." Joe squirmed to get away from Schaffer.

"Mister, 'I never burn' decided to prove to everyone in the Bahamas that a pale White man could withstand the sun that browned all of them. He wouldn't even consider using sun screen." Nina was still

234   ANTHONY P. JONES   D8 WITH F8

angry.

"I'll get you some Neosporin. It will start to heal your skin; scotch will help with the pain." Schaffer held the door for everyone to walk in.

Gretchen assumed her place in front of the fireplace. Nina and Renita joined her sitting on the sofa. "I think it's an overreaction, but I want to be safe. This guy is an organized killer. None of us fits his victim profile; I was shocked when he took Dr. Gerard hostage. It's a sign that he's desperate. We're getting too close and he wants us to back off." Renita looked into the fire. She appeared lost between the flames.

Joe walked over to the fireplace. Then he backed off; he opted for a cooler spot away from the direct heat of the fire. "It seems to me that he singled out the weakest one in the herd. Dr. Gerard is the only person in the group that's not an agent, other than 'bone head' over there." He nodded in Schaffer's direction. "All you guys carry guns. Gerard probably doesn't even own one. He was the safest person to take hostage."

Schaffer walked over to join them with four glasses and a bottle of scotch. "I don't see how he's going to let Dr. Gerard live. He's the only one who can identify 'Tony the Tiger.' Besides, we have no way of knowing who he really wants. It's for damn sure not the women he's killed, or Dr. Gerard."

"I agree." Renita held out her hand for the glass of scotch and turned to Joe. "Did I tell you Schaffer solved the mystery of the eights?"

Schaffer picked up the copy of *The Enneagrams* and handed it to Joe. "Eight is the personality type of the women he is killing."

Joe took the book. "Then 'V' is probably the initial of the person he's looking for, the lover who jilted him."

"God Damn! You may have something there." Schaffer blurted, clearly surprised at his boss' keen insight.

Renita looked at Schaffer. "There's your next article. Talk about the Enneagrams and concentrate on the eighth point. Tell the readers that he's looking for someone whose name begins with 'V.' Maybe we can draw out the person he's looking for and they can identify him."

"It's worth a shot." Nina took a drink. "I want to see him off the street and those guns back in hiding."

Gretchen jumped from the floor and ran to the front stairs. Renita and Schaffer quickly followed. Renita's hand rested on the butt of her Sig.

"What are you guys doing?" Tina asked rubbing her eyes.

Renita held her arms open. "Come on baby. We're just talking to Nina and Joe." She hugged Tina tightly.

Tina returned the hug and took Schaffer's hand. They walked into the family room. Tina climbed onto Schaffer's lap and rested her head on his chest. She sat up and looked at Joe. "Uncle Joe, you look like a crawfish that's been cooked. You must have been out in the sun too long. What were you braining?"

Schaffer, Renita and Nina laughed at Tina's comment. "She meant what were you thinking?" Renita said trying to stop laughing.

"You tell him, Tina." Nina added.

Tina leaned back on Schaffer. Just as she got comfortable, she sat straight up and looked in the solarium. "Santa's been here!"

Chapter

44

Schaffer called Bacchus first thing Christmas morning. "Things are coming together fast now. The killer has been using a book, *The Enneagrams* to select his victims. We found a copy at the house of his eighth victim."

Bacchus was working his way out of an alcohol induced fog. He still had a hard time with holidays. "Slow down. What the hell are you talking about?"

Schaffer exercised patience knowing that Bacchus sounded a bit under the weather. "The killer uses a book called *The Enneagrams* to pick his victims. The book is a personality typing system that places people in one of nine categories. Our killer is eliminating women categorized as eights."

Bacchus rubbed his beefy hand across his face trying to bring himself back to life. "Why eights? What does he dislike about them?"

"We're not sure just yet, but they seem to have a very dominant personality. My guess is he feels threatened by them for some reason. If I had to guess further, I'd say some woman in his past exhibited these traits and he's trying to get back at her. I've got some more reading to do before I can be certain."

Bacchus yawned bringing a rush of oxygen to his brain, shuddering at the end as if it would speed his recovery. "By the way, the doc's blood matches the blood type you found in the dog. What's he been up to since you found the information?"

"I don't think we have to worry about him. The killer is holding him hostage; I received an e-mail last night with his picture. He didn't look so good."

Bacchus was beginning to feel alive. "Are you sure the e-mail came from the UNSUB?"

"Yeah, he made sure we knew it was him. I guess this puts us back at square one."

"Anything's possible. But what I keep coming back to is the fact that you guys haven't found anything useful at the scenes. Only someone that knew what you were looking for would be astute enough to know how to keep those things hidden."

Schaffer looked out over the snow that had fallen over night. "I told you he was a smart fucker. When you think about it, it does make sense that he has a working knowledge of forensics; he's consistently covered his tracks."

"Which leads me back to someone within the system; who else would think to cover his skin and remove all hairs, including the nose and ear hairs since they are the most commonly found at a crime scene?"

Schaffer considered what Bacchus had to say. "When you ran your profiles using the blood type did you come up with anyone else that works in the forensic sciences area?"

Bacchus ran his hand over his head as if he were preventing slippage back into his foggy state. "One name popped up, but then it gets strange. The guy seems to have disappeared from the face of the earth. His name is Thomas Brothers. That's where it dead ends."

Schaffer felt his excitement grow. "Where does he work?"

"That's the thing, he was a student at Virginia Union University and he seems to have vanished shortly after becoming a lab assistant for the state forensics office. Either this guy is a magician or he's an apparition." Bacchus scratched his face. "This whole thing is some really strange shit."

"'Tony the Tiger' has gone to a lot of trouble to kill incognito. The only mistake he's made is to get the dog pissed off. Look how long it took us to find that out. Given his escalation in killing and meticulous planning, the worst could be yet to come."

"You know, I could never figure out how these super-smart motherfuckers can be pushed so easily to the dark side. Something as insignificant as a dog pissing on their car tires can send them into a rage and they'll kill the whole neighborhood."

Schaffer thought about Tree killing a drug lord in his past. But that was a one shot deal for him. Schaffer's eyebrows shot up. "Super-smart and madness are two sides of the same coin; when it's flipped in the air there's a fifty percent chance either side will land up."

Bacchus stretched and spoke through his yawn. "What's the chance of it landing on its edge and spinning so that we see both sides? That's what you're dealing with here."

"I'm afraid that the spinning has stopped and he's completely over the edge."

"Then, we'd best get him off the street quickly."

Chapter
45

"Merry Christmas, Dr. Gerard. One more week and this will all be over." Thomas looked out the large picture window at the new fallen snow.

Dirk, weak from exhaustion, slowly raised his head. "Why one week?"

"You see the snow out there? No two flakes are alike; each one falling from the sky is unique. Too bad people aren't like that. If they were, then my anger could be focused on only one person."

Dirk's head involuntarily fell to his chest. "I don't understand why you're so upset with Victoria. You two are much better off being apart. Just think of what your marriage was doing to your kids."

Thomas swung around; his face full of rage. "Shut the fuck up. Keep your goddamned opinions to yourself." He smacked Dirk on the side of his face and unzipped his pants. A bright yellow stream of urine flowed out of Thomas onto Dirk. Amused by the color he made a rhyme. "Vitamin B, vitamin B, the more you take the brighter your pee."

Dirk had no choice but to endure the humiliation and continue to press Thomas. "How come you didn't piss on any of your victims? You seem to enjoy marking your territory."

Thomas laughed. "Dr. Gerard, you're a funny bastard. I always was a better M.E. than you. I made cases for you time after time, but you got all the credit."

"Is that why you decided to kidnap me, because you're trying to prove you're better than me?"

"I don't have to prove a fucking thing. I know I'm better than you, and you know it too. That's why you want to send me to some institution where they'll try to mind-fuck me, poking, prodding and filling me full of their mind fucking drugs. Hell no! Fuck you and fuck them."

"Were you hospitalized before? You neglected to mention that on your medical school application." Dirk raised his head and tried to look Thomas in the eyes.

"Would you tell someone if you once were institutionalized?" Thomas lunged at Dirk. "The fucking judge did it because that motherfucker asked him to. The judge said I had violent tendencies. Shit, I had just gotten out of high school. Four years earlier I lost my parents.

I needed someone who cared. But my wicked step-grandfather stuck me away in a boarding school. So after graduation I blew the motherfucker's truck up." Thomas rubbed his crotch thinking about the explosion. "The fucking judge wouldn't let me out until I paid for that sick sonofabitch's truck."

"If you were in the hospital, how did you pay for his truck?"

"Dad left me in good shape when he died. By the time I graduated, I had three million in my trust account." Thomas rubbed two fingers together.

Dirk couldn't believe what he was hearing. "Why did you sit out of medical school under the guise of needing money?"

"Because, I needed to see who really cared. Other than my lawyer and the judge, you're the only person that knows about the trust. If Victoria had known how much money I really had she never would have left, stupid bitch. Now she's gone into hiding just like her mother did after her father died. She told Victoria she never trusted me and didn't want me to know where she lived. If I find her, I'll kill her too, just for the hell of it."

"Why don't you just disappear to some remote island where no one can find you? You've got enough money for several lifetimes."

"I'm having too much fun here. Why do you care what happens to me?" Thomas stood over Dirk.

Dirk looked reflective. "Before you started killing people you reminded me of myself. You were an eager go-getter out to prove to the world that you were the best at your job. I came here to try to save you from yourself." Dirk shook his head. "It's been painful watching you self-destruct."

"You know doc, it's a damn shame I have to kill you. We would have continued to be a hell of a great team in the lab." He stepped back from Dirk and turned around. "I promise you, it won't hurt."

Dirk laughed nervously. "In as much as you're going to kill me, can you tell me one more thing?"

Thomas sat next to Dirk. "Sure. Anything for you doc."

"I understand why you killed the Black women since Victoria is Black, but, why the White women?"

Thomas pulled his knees up and wrapped his arms around them and rocked for a few seconds before answering. "It was my thirteenth birthday. Dad had been out of town on business and wasn't going to be able to be home for another few days. He called to sing Happy Birthday to me with mom just before we cut the cake. I opened my gifts, then dad said goodbye. After he hung up, mom said she had a special present for me. I had already gotten just what I wanted, a brand new stingray bike, so I was surprised to find that mom had something else for me. She walked over and dropped to her knees." Thomas' head fell to his knees. "When she unzipped my pants, I thought I was going to pee on myself. She reached in my pants, looked up at me and said, 'you're my little man now. Mommy's going make you to feel like one.' That bitch took my innocence right there. She gave me a blowjob. When she was finished I ran to my room and cried all night."

Dirk wasn't sure what to say. "How long did it go on before you told your dad?"

"I never told him. It had been going on every time he was out of town for about a year when he found out. He immediately took me away and filed for divorce. I was so relieved. But the judge, in all his wisdom, awarded custody to mom. Since I was not allowed to testify, it was his word against hers. That decision destroyed dad, but he still had a plan. He offered mom a truce and invited her on a vacation in the Blue Ridge Mountains. Dad was a private pilot, so he was flying. He flew the plane into the side of one of the mountains. He killed them both." Thomas got up and walked to the kitchen to get Dirk a plate of food.

"Maybe it was an accident." Dirk reached out and took the food.

"No it wasn't. He gave grandma a note to give me on my twenty-first birthday. In the note, he explained what he did. I wish he could have just killed her. I needed him. My step-grandfather sent me to Fork Union Military Academy. He said he had raised his children and he didn't plan on rising any more. He barely let me come home for the summer. He insisted on summer school so that I wouldn't be around too much. I know dad did what he thought was right, but I really needed him. He was my best friend."

Dirk felt as if the breath was being sucked from his body, just listening to Thomas' story. Between bites of food he said. "That still doesn't explain why you killed White women."

Thomas patted Dirk on the back. "They remind me of Mom."

Chapter
46

The week after Christmas Renita and Schaffer returned to the BAU near Quantico. Joe was back at the *Post*. But, Nina and Tina were still in Charlottesville.

Schaffer's column ran four days after Christmas.

Tony the Tiger Seeks Specific Personality Types

Enneagrams are an ancient personality typing system that has its roots in China. For hundreds of years, this system was passed down in the oral tradition. In more recent history, many learned people have studied this system. They have written books dedicated to the understanding and dissemination of the Enneagrams.

When properly used, the Enneagrams are an effective tool, helping people interact more productively in all facets of their lives. Educators of the Enneagrams, such as Helen Palmer, use the system to predict the success, or failure, of interpersonal relationships.

Since his initial contact with the Post, Tony the Tiger has been obsessed with the number 8, going as far as saying that he hated the number. FBI sources have confirmed that his victims were indeed representatives of 'Point Eight' in the Enneagram system. This has lead to further speculation by the FBI, that their suspect is a representative of 'Point Two' in the system.

Point Eights are characterized as "The Boss," always in control and in charge of every situation. By contrast, Point Twos are "The Givers." They come across as people who want to be loved by everyone, giving in order to get. But most of all, they want to be someone's hero.

The FBI has released a statement warning women, especially highly successful divorced women, that the suspect is once again on the prowl for victims. To date, he has posed as a mailman to kill four women, as a FedEx deliveryman to kill three women, and as a physician to kill one woman.

Women that live alone should ask to see proper identification before opening the door for anyone. This is one serial killer who preys on the strong not the weak, proving him to be extremely dangerous.

The FBI has established a special hotline for any woman who has been approached by someone offering a free Enneagram typing test. Anyone who may have taken such a test in the past nine months is encouraged to contact the FBI. The hotline number is (888) 555-FBI8 (3248).

Every paper in Virginia, and several in adjoining states, ran Schaffer's column. Schaffer volunteered to help the team staff the phones at the Hoover Building. Calls came in nearly as fast as they could take them. Particular attention was paid to calls that came in from cities that the other victims were from. They also prioritized those that originated in cities where the FBI expected the suspect to strike next, an item purposefully left out of Schaffer's column.

Descriptions that were received varied widely. However, that wasn't the case with the descriptions from the cities the FBI focused on. The only variation in those descriptions was the race of the suspect. By early afternoon the calls had tapered off so only two agents were left to handle any additional reports.

Renita assembled the remainder of her team in the conference room. "Let's filter out the extremes and come up with a description of our UNSUB and get that bastard off the streets. She uploaded the descriptions into the computer and projected them onto the wall.

           -5-10 to 5-11 feet tall
           -190 to 200 pounds
           -Dark curly hair-natural looking
           -Straight auburn hair-wig, toupee
           -Mustache
           -Soft hands
           -Hazel eyes to brown eyes
           -First name, Thomas
           -Majority met at divorce recovery workshops
           -Victims of two different races, may indicate bi-racial
UNSUB

"Okay gentlemen." Renita leaned back from the computer. "I want the names and addresses of the women from the fourteen target cities who gave the best descriptions."

Renita typed the names and addresses as they were read. Each time she entered the individual data, the computer automatically positioned the name on the map. Twenty names into the list Schaffer took over to give Renita's hands a rest.

One of the agents flipped through his notes. "I must have missed this one on the first pass. He was very detailed with his description. Father Tom Moore runs a divorcée workshop in Alexandria. His address is 243 Church Street, Alexandria."

Renita almost jumped from her seat. "What was that address again?"

The agent repeated the address.

She looked at him in total disbelief. "Did you record the phone number from the caller ID?"

The agent looked at his paper. "He called from a pay phone. That was all that showed up on the caller ID."

Renita pointed her pen in the agent's direction. "Have the Operations Center pull the records of your incoming calls. Give them the exact time of the call; I want to know the exact location of the pay phone it came from. That bastard gave you my address, it had to be our UNSUB, 'Thomas,' not Tony the Tiger any more."

♦

Thomas sat at his computer altering the FBI ID Dirk received when he first arrived at the Hoover Building. In the background a song played over and over, *Crazy Love* by Scottish Rocker, Van Morrison.

When Thomas had called the FBI hotline pretending to be Father Tom Moore, the agent answering the call had provided him with all the necessary information to make his next kill, by saying. 'We'll send someone by to do a composite drawing in the next couple of days.' That also gave Thomas plenty of time to do what he needed. Special Agent Thomas Brothers would reach his appointments before the agents from the Hoover Building would have a chance to prevent his fun.

Thomas entered the room with Dirk. He was dressed in a custom made navy blue suit. The heavily starched white shirt and solid dark tie made Thomas appear to be one of the Bureau's more conservative agents.

"What do you think Dr. Gerard? I've even got the miniature handcuffs tie tack." Thomas walked over to a mirror and slid on a pair of dark glasses. "I am a G-man."

He walked over to Dirk with a sandwich and a glass of Kool-aid. He kicked Dirk's foot. "Wake up. You'd better eat now. I won't be coming back for quite a while."

Dirk drank the Kool-aid in one long gulp, and then started in on the sandwich. "You're going to kill again aren't you?"

"How'd you guess that, doc? Don't I look great for the job?" He spun around.

"Thomas they're going to catch you. There's no way you can

continue to hide." Dirk wolfed down the last bite of his sandwich.

"Would you like some more to drink?" Thomas reached for the glass.

"You're being generous tonight. Yes, thank you I would."

Thomas took the glass, refilled it and handed it back to Dirk. He watched him drink the Kool-aid and then left the room.

Thomas returned twenty minutes later wearing only his underwear. Dirk was sitting on the floor rocking back and forth. He jerked the chains Thomas used to restrain him. With each pull Thomas laughed harder and harder.

"I see the LSD is in full effect." Thomas looked down on Dirk.

Dirk continued rocking, and then he mumbled and laughed at Thomas. He pointed and between laughs spoke. "Look at you. I guess you're going to fuck me now." He laughed harder and leaned over to one side. The loud expulsion of gas made him laugh almost to the point of convulsing. "There, that fart cleaned the pipe line for you." He got on all fours. "Go ahead and cause a traffic jam on the Hershey highway." He fell to his elbows and laughed until he coughed.

Thomas grew angry. "Get out of those fucking nasty clothes." He freed himself and started to masturbate.

Dirk followed instructions. It wasn't hard because Thomas had only allowed him to keep his pants on. He looked at Thomas again. "I didn't know you liked boys."

"I don't, faggot, you do. Look at your dick, it's harder than mine."

Dirk looked down, his laughter began to rescind. "That's just the effects of the LSD. Why do you think some people call it the 'fuck all night' drug?"

Thomas handed Dirk a paper towel. "Wipe your ass."

Dirk took the paper towel and fell to the floor. Thomas carefully moved the paper with his gloved hands and looked down on Dirk. "You're going to be the first person to die with a sustained hard on." He dragged Dirk to the bathroom and dumped him in the tub. Finally, he arranged the bottle of Naked Mountain Chardonnay and V-8 juice. His camera's flash captured the watery death scene.

Thomas went back to his room, dressed, and left for Alexandria in Dirk's BMW.

Chapter
47

Ashley Warren was one of the first women to call the FBI hotline. She owned a small chain of women's boutiques in Tyson's Corner, Baltimore, and Philadelphia, which were opening at 7 a.m. to get the jump on the New Year's Eve traffic. Ashley suggested a meeting in one of her stores early the following morning.

Later that evening, she answered the door and was surprised to find an FBI agent standing opposite the locked storm door and holding up his credentials for inspection. She looked over the ID and then at the man holding it. "I wasn't expecting to see you until tomorrow morning."

"Yes ma'am. I understand that was the plan. However, we have reason to believe he'll attack in the next day or so. So, I'm sure you can understand why we would like to capture the suspect before he has the chance to kill again. Your assistance in coming up with a composite drawing should expedite his identification and apprehension."

Ashley looked to the ID and back to the agent's face. "What are you going to do a drawing on? I don't see any paper in your hands."

"I didn't want to be presumptuous I left the pad in the car." He reached into his pocket and pulled out several photograph sized cards and held them up. These help us to identify individual features such as eye shape or ear shape. Once identified, we put them to paper. There is also one photograph we have of a possible suspect." He reached into his pocket and pulled the picture from its plastic bag and held it out to her backwards.

Ashley opened the door and took the picture. Three seconds later, she was on the floor. Thomas rushed in and closed the door. "Sorry honey, I only have time for a quick fuck." He opened her mouth and gave her double the normal dose of GHB and took her straight to the bathroom.

"There's no need for a condom any more since the FBI found the dog. You'll just have to suck it up." Thomas slid himself into Ashley's mouth and pumped away, holding it closed by placing one hand behind her head and the other beneath her jaw.

Ashley never opened her eyes; the GHB held her in a comma-like state, but her mind was active. When Thomas slid her beneath the water, she wanted to scream. She tried everything in her power to will her arms and legs to move; yet they refused to respond. Ashley drowned, just as the other eight women had, fully aware of every drop of water entering her lungs.

Thomas left the house in a blur. He needed to get to South Boston, Virginia ahead of the truth and the FBI.

Judy Bell owned a racehorse farm where she also doubled as the head trainer. Her former husband, Hip Hop star, Badd D, provided Judy with the farm and stable of horses after winning his first Grammy. He'd earned 'ex' status by acquiring a stable of two legged fillies that provided him with ego support and any thing else he desired.

Although Judy's operation was only a few years old, after her prized stallion placed second in last year's Kentucky Derby, her business grew exponentially. There were still those who believe it might have been a fluke. In their minds, a short Black woman had no business participating in such a complicated endeavor she knew nothing about. However, Judy's horses came in 'in the money' during the current racing season time and again. Her horses knew how to win, and that's as complicated as Judy wanted it. Proving her skeptics wrong was just icing on the cake.

Thomas arrived at her farm by midnight. He turned off his headlights and slowly drove up the long driveway, careful not to disturb the horses and alert his prey. He was too restless to sleep; instead he pulled over under the cover of an old oak tree and kept vigil over Judy's house. At 4:30 a.m., the first lights appeared upstairs. Thirty minutes later, the main floor lit up as well.

Thomas eased the car back onto the driveway and pulled up in front of the farmhouse. Judy stepped out of the front door holding an 1894 Winchester octagon-barreled 30-30 rifle her grandfather had given her years before. She kept the rifle pointed forward, but not directly at Thomas. "How can I help you?"

"I'm Special Agent Thomas Brothers with the FBI." He put one hand in the air and showed her his Creds with the other. "I believe you spoke with one of our agents yesterday."

"Yes I did. And she said that she would be here around ten this morning." Judy lowered the rifle, letting the butt rest in the crook of her arm.

"That's absolutely correct ma'am. But we believe we've had a break in the case and we need to see if you can identify the suspect immediately." Thomas knew all the names of the agents involved with the case and there was only one female. "Agent Duplechain asked me to come over right away since I'm stationed close by. If you'll take a look at this picture, I'm sure we can clear this up and I can be on my way."

Judy indicated the front door with the rifle. "Come on in, I've got some coffee brewing." She walked through the door followed by Thomas.

Thomas started to dig for information. "I'm surprised you don't have a dog to help around the farm. They can be another pair of ears, not to mention additional protection."

"I had one. He was hit by an eighteen-wheeler and it tore me up emotionally. I may get another one day but I'm not ready to move on just yet. I usually have an exercise rider here by now anyway, but she had to go to court this morning." Judy poured two cups of coffee. "Let's have a look at that picture."

Thomas handed her the picture and watched her collapse to the floor. "Time for a GHB cocktail and a butt fucking you'll never remember." He poured the GHB down her throat and held her head, stroking her hair repeatedly. "You're very special to me; my final kill." Thomas looked out the window. "Well, at least in this state. To mark the occasion, I'm going to fuck you extra rough."

Thomas was with Judy for an hour and had just gotten her in the tub when he heard a car pull up the driveway. Hurriedly, he dressed and ran down stairs. He looked out the window at the Sheriff's car pulling up to the front door. Thomas grabbed Judy's octagon-barreled rifle and sat at the kitchen table facing the door. He held the gun under the table so it was concealed beneath the tablecloth.

The Sheriff knocked at the door. "Come on in, it's open." Thomas answered.

The Sheriff slid his gun from his holster, stood aside and slowly opened the door. "Identify yourself."

"It's okay Sheriff. I'm Special Agent Brothers with the FBI. Ms. Bell is just upstairs. She went to get some papers she received the night she met our suspect."

The Sheriff stepped through the door, still holding his gun. "Judy." He called out.

"My credentials are right there on the table Sheriff." Thomas pretended to be sketching on a pad unconcerned with the Sheriff's apprehension.

The Sheriff eased over to the side of the table and picked up Thomas' ID. He lowered his gun and placed it back in its holster. "I spoke with Agent Duplechain about ten minutes ago. She said Judy was the only person who fit the profile at the divorced meetings in our area the night the UNSUB attended and that I should get here until she could get an agent here. I was surprised you got here so quickly." He looked around the room. "The suspect you're looking for sounds like a real bastard."

"That he is Sheriff. Here's a fresh cup of coffee I just poured." Indicating the cup on the table. "Have a seat and I can tell you a little about this guy."

"Don't mind if I do." The Sheriff sat down and took a sip of the coffee.

As soon as the cup touched his lips, Thomas pulled the trigger, propelling the Sheriff backwards off his chair. Thomas stood and walked over to the Sheriff. He had a look of disbelief on his face, but was still clinging onto life. "You said it right Sheriff, I'm a real bastard." Thomas put the rifle to the Sheriff's temple and pulled the trigger again. He reached down gathering the Sheriff's keys and pistol and then sped away in the sheriff's car.

Chapter

48

Renita and Schaffer were up early on New Year's Eve. They had come back to Charlottesville with Joe in tow so they could spend some time with Tina and Nina. Thomas had proven to be anything but predictable, but Renita felt certain that they had nothing to fear at Schaffer's. Being there with him put her mind at ease.

Nina came down stairs when she smelled the coffee. "You two better be careful out there today."

"We'll be just fine, Nina. I put my re-con face on this morning." Schaffer knew his attempt to use humor to put her mind at ease was wasted, but he felt compelled to at least try.

"I hope we can get that bastard off the streets by the New Year." Renita said, as she took a sip of her coffee.

"I know you'll do your best." Nina got a coffee mug off the shelf. "I think everyone in the state will feel better after he's in custody."

Renita and Schaffer grabbed their coats and started out the door. "Gretchen, look after the family today." Schaffer patted her head and followed Renita.

"I'll drive." Renita said when they reached the car.

Schaffer looked at his watch. "It's one hundred and twenty miles to South Boston we should be there in about two hours."

Renita checked the extra magazines for her gun. "Did you put the laptop in the car?"

He looked in the back seat to be sure. "It's right here. I think it's amazing how modern technology has influenced police work today. You go to a witness' house and take a description of a suspect and a composite artist at headquarters builds the sketch and beams it right back to you at the site. With the way things are headed, soon you'll be able to just tell the computer and it will build the sketch on its own."

"That concept is already being tested. Templates already exist with every shape and variation of human features. We point and click and the computer does the rest. That program will make every field agent an expert sketch artist." Renita pulled onto the interstate.

"That sounds very efficient. But, I still don't see how you can replace the human touch."

"We're not trying to replace anyone. Hell, we need all the help we can get. In the Bureau, even our expert artists are field agents first. When we get a positive ID on a suspect, one click and we can transmit it worldwide. The more agents available, the more we have out there hunting down the bad guys."

Schaffer saw a State Trooper parked on the other side of a bridge. He pointed in his direction. "Will your new system transmit directly to the new onboard computers those guys have in their cars?"

"Renita looked over at the trooper. "Not only will it transmit to them, it will print out a picture of the suspect instantly giving us hundreds of additional eyes on the streets. There's even a site individual citizens can go to and see the drawings. Believe it or not, there are still some out there who care. With all that help, it will make it very difficult for a suspect to hide."

Schaffer looked at people in cars as they passed. "What's the incentive for a citizen to help? My experience is most of them don't want to get involved."

Renita glanced in his direction. "You're familiar with the 'Crime Stoppers' initiative in most communities. Their program offers up to one thousand dollars for information on criminals. The FBI takes millions of dollars of 'crime money' off the street each year. Some of it we use to get even more criminals off the street, we offer up to ten thousand dollars for information. The amount varies depending on how badly we want someone."

"Remind me never to become a criminal." Schaffer reached over and stroked Renita's hair.

An hour and thirty minutes into their trip Renita's cell phone rang. The agent assigned to Ashley Warren's interview was on the line. "Ms. Warren hasn't shown up for work today. Her employees say that this is highly usual, she's known for her punctuality. I sent a couple of squad cars to check out her house."

Renita's heart pounded. "Good work. I want to know the moment you hear from them."

"As soon as I get word I'll call—" He paused in mid sentence. "Hang on a second. I've got another call coming in." The agent took the call and returned to Renita. "The Alexandria police just found Ms. Warren—"

"Say again, you're breaking up." Renita yelled into the phone. "I said they found—"

"Shit, the phone is out of range. He was saying something I didn't catch."

"Do you think we should stop and call him back from somewhere else?" Schaffer looked at his phone. It had no signal either.

"We should be there in a few minutes. Maybe one of the phones will come back in before then." Renita pushed down harder on the gas pedal.

Schaffer checked the phones for a signal every few seconds. "I've got a signal. What's the number?"

"Look at my phone log. The number should be on the incoming calls list." Renita tried to drive and watch Schaffer at the same time.

"Got it." He dialed the phone. The agent picked up on the first ring. "This is Schaffer O'Grady; Agent Duplechain didn't hear the last part of your message."

"I said they found Ms. Warren in her tub, dead."

"Shit. Thanks." Schaffer sat the phone down. "He killed her."

Damn it, he beat us again. Call the Sheriff's office in South Boston. Have someone inform the Sheriff, he's at Judy Bell's house."

Schaffer lifted his phone. "My signal's out; yours too."

Renita activated the police light in the grill of the car. The engine hummed with a low growl and the speedometer jumped to the right. "If you're a nervous rider you best grab your Jesus strap."

"My what?" He looked at her.

"Jesus strap, the handle above your window."

"Why do you call it a Jesus strap?"

A crooked smile crossed Renita's face. "Because when you're going this fast and you hit a turn, nervous people grab the strap and yell, 'Jesus.'"

♦

Renita saw a road sign, South Boston 10 miles. "Judy's farm should be just ahead on the right."

"There's the beginning of the fence. Her driveway splits the two pastures." Schaffer watched the horses playfully gallop and prance inside the fences.

Renita turned the car up the drive and drove slowly. "The Sheriff should be here, but I still want to approach the house cautiously."

As they came around the bend they saw a pickup truck and a white BMW 750i. "That's Dr. Gerard's car. I remember it when we arrived at Hoover together." Schaffer looked at Renita. "What do you think that means?"

"It means take your gun out of its holster. We're not sure what we're going to find up there." Renita pulled her gun out as well.

They pulled the car behind Dirk's and got out. The front door of the house was open. "That's very odd. How many people leave their doors wide open when it's about forty degrees outside?"

Schaffer nodded his agreement. He whispered. "I'll check out the door, you cover me."

"I should be the one up front; I get paid to do that kind of work." Renita whispered back.

"Yeah, but you're the better shot. If someone shoots me, you shoot them."

"Go in low. I'll follow behind you high." Renita signaled for him to move.

They jumped through the door together and saw the sheriff lying on the floor in a pool of blood. Most of the left side of his face was scattered across the kitchen. They continued to move through the house cautiously, looking for any signs of life.

Upstairs an unmistakable sound, 'plop, plop, plop' greeted their ears. It was the sound of water droplets falling into a tub full of water.

"Can you hear that?" Renita's eyes darted in all directions searching for movement.

"Yeah. He's been here. I hope he's still here so I can end his reign, permanently."

"It's too late, he's gone." Renita reached the bathroom first. "He killed her first and the sheriff second."

Schaffer saw Judy lying in the tub. "How can you tell?"

"Because, the sheriff was lying on his back and his head pointed towards the door. If the assailant shot his way into the house the sheriff would be laying in the other direction." Renita looked at her cell phone, the signal strength was good. She called headquarters. "We were too late, she's dead. Let the director know Thomas the Tiger has graduated; he killed South Boston's Sheriff. Also tell the SAC he might want to call the governor. Since we found Dr. Gerard's car at the scene, he's probably dead too. Did anyone have any luck with a composite drawing?"

"Yes, but we're waiting for a couple of others to come in so that we can compare them. They should be on the wire soon."

"Get on the site and alert everyone that the suspect left Judy Bell's house in the Sheriff's car. Call South Boston and get as much info about the car as possible and get it out to the state police. He probably won't be in it long, so let's get them looking in a hurry."

"Do you want me to dispatch a team there?"

"You might as well. These folks aren't going anywhere. I'll talk to you later."

Renita and Schaffer waited until the team arrived. She handed them several evidence bags. "This is what we've collected so far. We're out of here."

Chapter
49

Thomas turned on the police lights to pull over a man driving a truck. The octagon-barreled rifle and sheriff's pistol convinced the man to surrender his truck and keys. A stalled and abandoned car on the side of the road provided a different set of license plates to slow anyone looking for him.

He arrived in Fredericksburg, Virginia, bypassed his house and drove straight to the high-speed train terminal. He left the keys in the truck and the door wide open. He didn't care who came to claim it, but he knew the temptation would be great for some to resist. They could take the fall for stealing the truck and plates.

During the ride to DC, Thomas placed a call. "Rachel, it's Thomas. I'm coming to DC. If you don't mind I'd like to stay with you."

"Thomas, I'm so glad you're coming up. I haven't seen you since September."

"I know. I've been very busy, but I've called you every week." Thomas looked out the window silently saying goodbye to Virginia. He planned on never returning.

Rachel began picking things up around the apartment. "I'm so excited you're coming. You'll be here for New Year's. This will be the perfect start to a new year for me."

"I want you to start thinking about a trip, I need a vacation. Let's get away for a week. Hell, we may like it so well we may never come back."

"Where do you want to go?" Rachel sat down thinking about the possibilities. No one had ever taken her on vacation before.

Thomas plugged his computer into the train's outlet. "I'm leaving that up to you. Wherever you decide is where we'll go. "I've got to finish some work. I'll see you when I get there."

◆

Renita was curled up in Schaffer's arms on the sofa. The fire in the fireplace had died down long ago. Only a few embers glowed among the ashes.

Schaffer heard a small set of feet approaching and opened one eye.

Tina was wearing Renita's bear feet slippers, which were too big, so they made a swish, swish sound as she crossed the hardwood floor. "Can I go on the internet?" She asked Schaffer.

Renita answered without opening her eyes. "Wait until morning. You're going to have to go to bed right after we toast in the New Year."

Schaffer's chest jumped with laughter. Renita opened her eyes and saw one glass of bubble-less Champagne on the table. "Happy New Year." He said and kissed her on the head.

Renita sat up and saw the sunshine filling the room. "You let me sleep through New Year's?"

"We tried to wake you, but you were having no part of it. I thought it was best to let you sleep." He turned to Tina. "Go ahead, but make sure you don't talk to anyone you don't know."

"Okay, I won't." Tina ran to the study, leaving the slippers behind.

Renita slid back on the sofa and let her head rest on the cushions. "You held me all night? Your back must be killing you."

"This is a very soft sofa and you have a very light head. I'm just fine." He reached over and stroked her hair. "What would you like to do today?"

Renita sighed. "I need to go in to work."

"No you don't. I called in already and told them you wouldn't be in today. We can go in and see what developed since yesterday, after breakfast."

Joe and Nina came down and fixed breakfast while Renita and Schaffer were in the shower. After eating, Schaffer went to the study to retrieve his emails.

He was not in the study two minutes before he called Renita. "You need to see this. I think it's our guy."

Renita ran down the hall to the study. She entered and closed the door behind her. "What's up?"

"It's him. He's sent another e-mail." Schaffer pointed to 8-e-ose. He clicked it and the e-mail came up.

"My work here is done, but I'm thinking about taking my show on the road. Sorry I can't invite you along. I've left you a little something to remind you of me. Check it out," they did.

Schaffer clicked the video link at the bottom of the page. Bob Hope's voice came up but the screen remained white. Bob was singing, *Thanks for the Memories*. A small dark circle appeared and began to grow. On the page was Dr. Dirk Gerard, submerged in a tub of water. The camera panned to the foot hanging out of the tub. Abruptly, the foot changed sizes, as the music changed to a different song. Harold Melvin and the Blue Notes were singing, *If You Don't Know Me By Now.* The camera panned back to the head and it was Ashley Warren's face. The camera went out of focus, when it refocused Judy Bell was in the tub. The circle began to close. Just as it narrowed, what looked like a little hand opened it back. The sound of a jet plane taking off could be heard in the distance. The next sound was steel drums pinging out a beat. The camera then showed the back view of a man wearing a straw hat sitting in a hammock. Without looking around, the man raised his arm and then the middle finger on his hand. Porky Pig ended the video clip in his usual stuttering manner, *th..th..th..that's all folks.*' The screen went dark.

Schaffer looked at Renita. "Don't tell me that sonofabitch got away."

"That's what he would have us believe." Renita pointed to a second e-mail. Pull this one up. Let's see what this bastard looks like."

When the picture came up, Renita and Schaffer looked at each other and said the same thing. "Holy shit!"

CHAPTER
50

"Thomas, you haven't been out of the house for more than two weeks are you sure you feel okay?" Rachel handed him a soda.

"I'm feeling fine. I'm just catching up on my sleep and mapping out a plan I need to implement." Thomas looked through a cruise brochure. The ship was sailing from Baltimore, Maryland to Bermuda on Thursday. He booked a trip using Thomas Brothers Inc.'s credit card. "I'm going to be heading out of town for a few days, beginning Thursday."

"Would you like me to come along?" Rachel asked.

"Not on this trip. There will be plenty of places to go together later on. I've got to do this one alone. Thomas flipped the brochure over and put it in his pocket. You've got a vacation to plan. Have you decided where you want to go?"

"Not yet. I thought I would select a destination after I got to the Travel Agent's office. They may be able to help with some ideas I haven't even dreamed about." She showed Thomas the information she received so far.

Thomas walked over to a small mirror. He ran his hand across his beard, which he had grown over the past two weeks. "When you look in the mirror how can you ever be sure what you're seeing is real?"

Rachel looked at him, wondering if he'd asked a trick question. "Because, you can ask the person with you if they see the same thing."

He continued to rub his beard. "You ever want to totally make yourself over? You know, giving yourself a fresh start."

"I did that when I met you. You saved me and gave me a makeover. In the past four months I've gotten a nice place to live. I start college in the summer and I've been able to spend my days reading, preparing for school. None of that would have been possible without a total makeover. You've made a huge difference in my life." Rachel walked over and kissed Thomas.

He held her with one arm. "I like to make people happy, you in particular. You've brought a lot of happiness into my life. Don't ever leave me."

"I don't plan on it." She wrapped both arms around him and looked in his eyes. "What would you do if I was no longer in your life?"

"I'd hunt you down, cut out your heart and eat it." Thomas didn't smile.

Rachel pushed back from him. "I didn't mean that I would physically leave you. I meant, if I died."

Thomas could see that she was shaken. He walked over and held her from behind. "I'm sorry. I didn't mean to frighten you. I would never hurt you, because I know you would never leave me." He held her tightly.

Rachel tuned to face him. "Security is important to me. Saying things like that doesn't help. Please don't do that again."

"I won't. Let's never discuss anything about leaving. It makes me insecure. You wouldn't like me when I'm insecure." Thomas pulled her close and hugged her. She couldn't see the wild look that covered his face. He was a hand grenade waiting to explode.

On Thursday morning Rachel drove Thomas to Baltimore's Inner Harbor to catch a cruise ship to Bermuda. The beard, baseball cap and dark glasses were enough to prevent anyone from recognizing him.

Standing with Rachel on the pier, Thomas handed her a check. "Here, take this and go get a new car. We can't keep driving what you've got now. It's not reliable."

Rachel took the check. "You can't keep giving me money like this. I'm going to get spoiled."

"It's my money and I can do with it as I please. Get a Mini Cooper, I like those." He smiled and kissed her. "When I get home we're going to look for a house."

"Thomas. A vacation, a car, a house, I don't know what to say."

"You've earned it. What you had to endure while growing up, was hell. It's your turn to live now." Thomas blew her a kiss and walked to the boarding gate.

◆

Rachel drove back to Georgetown. She had a list of tasks that needed to be completed. After watching Thomas board a cruise ship, first on her agenda was the travel agent's office.

◆

February was a week away and Schaffer was in DC assisting Renita's team in shagging leads on the case. For the past three weeks everything was quiet; no other murders fitting their profile were reported.

Drawings of the now infamous 'Thomas the Tiger' were being circulated worldwide.

Additional follow-up stories in the *Post* failed to produce any further response from Thomas. He seemed to have vanished from the face of the earth.

Schaffer parked near Georgetown University to visit the travel agent he'd used for the past fifteen years. He got out of the car and saw Rachel walk into the travel agent's office. He walked in behind her. "Rachel?"

She turned towards the voice. "Schaffer!" She was excited to see him and hugged and kissed him.

"You really look good." Schaffer held her arm. "Something seems to be agreeing with you."

She spun around showing him the entire package. "It's good to see you too. I guess I've owed you a phone call for some time now."

"Yes you have." He looked at the brochure in her hand. "Are you planning a trip?"

"Yes. I came in here to get some ideas. What brings you in?"

"We need a getaway."

Rachel looked surprised. "We? Who's we? I don't remember you having a girlfriend."

"Well I do. As a matter of fact, you two met the last time I saw you." He noticed the quizzical look on her face. "You ran into her getting off the elevator at the Four Seasons."

"Yes, I remember. She's a very beautiful lady." Rachel set the brochure down. "I've got to tell you what's happened to me since then. You won't believe it."

"I can't wait. Let me get this trip booked and I'll buy you lunch. You can tell me all about it then." Schaffer pulled out his wallet.

"Where are you going?"

Schaffer smiled. "St. Johns. I need some warm weather. I want to hear waves rolling in, smell the salt air and not worry about a single thing."

Rachel snapped her fingers. "That's a good idea. We'll go too. Maybe we could have dinner one night while we're all there. When are you going on your trip?"

"Valentines day. We're going to stay the weekend." Schaffer turned to the travel agent. "Hi, Jenny. Can you book dinner reservations for Friday night during our trip?"

"Sure. I take it from the conversation there will be for four of you?" Jenny looked at Schaffer and Rachel.

Schaffer nodded. "Please. Why don't you choose a nice romantic location?"

Jenny looked at Rachel. Should I book you on the same flight as Mr. O'Grady? He's leaving on Wednesday and returning the following Monday."

"No. We can't leave until Friday morning. We want to spend a week there."

Jenny typed in the information and the tickets printed on her computer. "Mr. O'Grady, you leave the Wednesday before Valentines at 8 a.m. Your golf outing and dinner reservations for Asolare Restaurant are in your package." She handed him a folder and then did the same for Rachel.

Schaffer opened the door for Rachel. "Let's get some lunch. I'm dying to hear your story."

They went to Billy Martin's in Georgetown for lunch. Rachel was more relaxed than Schaffer ever remembered her being. "So, tell me your story. What's got you riding so high?"

Rachel couldn't possibly hide her smile. "I've met someone. He really believes in me. He's putting me through college, Georgetown no less. He's wonderful."

"He must be. I'm happy for you. When did you two meet?"

"The day I saw you at the Four Seasons. I thought he was weird at first, but then the check cleared. My life hasn't been the same since." Rachel took a sip of her wine.

Schaffer began to show his concern. "What do you mean, the check cleared?"

Rachel looked more serious. "I was completely out of cash. I hadn't eaten in a week, so I fell back on what I know. Honestly Schaffer, I had just gone out on the street." She looked around to make sure no one was listening to their conversation. "I had not been out there since you took me off two years ago. I promise. Anyway, I wasn't out there ten minutes when he showed up."

"I can see why he chose you. You're still young and attractive." Schaffer swirled his wine glass. "Rachel, you are very smart. There's no reason you had to go out on 14th Street again."

She put her hand on his. "Let me finish. He took me to dinner at a very nice restaurant, Mendocino Grille and Wine Bar. We must have been there two hours or more. Then yes, we did go back to his hotel room. He went to take a shower and I fixed us a drink. The next thing I remember is waking up the next morning." She frowned still trying to fill in the blanks. "He hadn't touched me."

"He must have been impotent, or a fool. I'm not sure I could have kept my hands off of you all night." Schaffer winked.

Rachel blushed. "Listen to you. You know very well we've spent the night together before and you never even came close to me."

"That was different." Schaffer touched his chest. "I was working."

"So was I." Rachel held her glass close to her face. "I even tried to give you something for the money you were paying me, but you refused. To which of those two categories you mentioned, do you belong?"

Schaffer smiled and looked into Rachel's eyes. "You most certainly did give me something. You served as my consultant for the story."

"You know what I mean." She returned his gaze. "Back to my story before one of us gets into trouble. Thomas left me a note. Inside was a check for forty thousand dollars. He told me to go to school."

At the mention of the name Thomas, the hair stood up on the back of Schaffer's neck. "Have you seen him since then?"

"Sure. I dropped him off in Baltimore earlier today. He had to go out of town on business."

Schaffer frowned and began flipping a knife in his hand. "Did he ever ask you to take any type of personality test?"

Rachel could see the concern radiating across Schaffer's face. "What's wrong? Your face is filled with tension."

Schaffer dropped the knife from his hand. "What about a test? Did he ever give you one, or ask you to complete some type of survey?"

"Schaffer, he's never asked me to do anything, except pick out a place to go on vacation and buy a new car." She pulled the check from her purse. "He gave me this, just this morning."

Schaffer took the check and read the name. "Thomas Brothers." He sat it down, but kept his hand on it. "So, to date he's given you seventy five thousand dollars and he's asked for nothing in return?"

Rachel began to look sad, dropping her eyes to the table. "Nothing more than that I go to school and become a psychologist. I start this summer."

Schaffer stared at the check for a long time. "This guy must be some kind of savior. I guess stranger things have happened. With all you've been through, you deserve some kindness in your life. If I were you, I'd have taken it too."

"Thank you." Rachel spoke into her wine glass. She took a sip before continuing. "I just don't want to seem like I'm taking advantage of anyone." Rachel paused as if reflecting. "He's got the kindest eyes. You'll see when you meet him in two weeks."

Schaffer was still holding the check. "Do you mind if I make a copy of this and check him out for you? Just to be sure."

"As long as you don't try to cash it." Rachel laughed. "I'm glad I've got you looking out for me."

"I just don't want anyone hurting you again."

Chapter
51

Schaffer and Renita drove back from Richmond together and the rest of the team followed in another car. They completed a sweep of Dirk's house looking for clues that might lead to the location of his body.

Schaffer handed the file to Renita. "Was Dr. Gerard staying in DC the entire time we investigated the case?"

"No. He only used the hotel room for one week. I guess he enjoyed commuting." Renita looked at the file and thought about what she'd just said. "No one likes commuting to DC. What could I have been thinking?"

"If he was driving back and forth he must have spent a great deal of time eating out. All the food in his refrigerator had expired long before he disappeared." Schaffer poked out his tongue and wrinkled his face. "The green hamburgers were the worst."

Renita changed the subject. "I've been meaning to ask you, why did you want me to take off next week?" She smiled knowing that he had something planned.

"I guess it's close enough that I can tell you." Schaffer reached into his jacket pocket and pulled out the travel folder. A red ribbon was tied around the outside. "Happy Valentines day."

Renita clapped her hands together. "Oh boy. Let me see." She took the ribbon off and opened the folder. "We're going to St. Johns? God, I need a get away. Can we leave now?"

"I wish we could. I can smell the sea air from here." Schaffer noticed a golf course beside the interstate and realized that he had never asked her whether she played. "You do golf don't you?"

"I play in the FBI Charity tournament every year. That is the extent of my golfing experience." Renita looked at the other papers in the folder. "I see you have a tee time set up. We'd better get there early so I can take a lesson. What's this dinner reservation for four all about?"

"You remember the day we first met, a young lady ran into you getting off the elevator?" He looked for Renita's positive recollection. "Well, she and her new boyfriend are going to be in St. Johns the same time as we are, so I suggested we all have dinner together. I hope you don't mind."

"Not at all, it should be fun." Renita closed the folder.

"You'll never guess what her boyfriend's name is."

Renita cut her eyes in his direction. "Don't tell me it's—"

"That's right, it's Thomas. Thomas Brothers."

Renita grunted. "His mother must have had a twisted sense of humor."

Schaffer's brow wrinkled. "Why do you say that?"

"Don't you know what Thomas means?" Renita shook her head.

Schaffer's frown remained. "I always thought it was just one of the Apostles' names."

Renita put her hands in the air. "Did you ever pay attention in church? Thomas means 'twin.' So his mother named him Twin Brothers."

"That's interesting. Now you can do something for me." Schaffer flashed his best shit-eating grin.

"I should have known this was a setup. What do you need?"

He pulled out the copy of the check Rachel gave him. This guy has given Rachel seventy five thousand dollars since we ran into her. I just think she needs to know more about his background. You have the credentials to find out, I don't."

Renita looked at the check. "I'll do what I can."

♦

Schaffer was out on the deck smoking an Hemmingway Masterpiece watching Gretchen scare up her favorite family of quail. The day was unusually warm for February in Virginia. Temperatures had climbed into the seventies earlier, allowing him to be outside in a polo shirt.

The phone rang and Schaffer found it hard to pull himself away from the outdoors. Reluctantly, he went in to answer the call. He glanced at the caller ID and was glad he'd come in for the call. "Hello gorgeous."

"That's the kind of greeting that makes a girl glad she took the time to call." Renita put down the papers in her hand. "I've got the information you wanted. Thomas Brothers is a corporation set up to help underprivileged students attend college."

"In order to do that, they would have to have a large sum of money on deposit somewhere earning interest for their funding. Did they list an owner?"

Renita looked at the fax. The only person listed is a lawyer in Orange County. But, he's not the owner, just the legal counsel."

"Someone must have set up the account at the bank in person. Did you find out who did that? Schaffer took a long puff from his cigar, filling the room with blue smoke.

"It was all handled by phone. The bank officer has never seen anyone other than the lawyer."

"Who's listed on the Board of Directors?"

"The papers came in just before I called you; I haven't had a chance to look yet." Renita flipped through the pages. "Oh my God."

"What did you find?" Schaffer puffed even harder on the cigar.

"Dirk Gerard M.D. is listed as the Chairman of the Board."

Schaffer didn't speak right away. "Orange County is just a few miles down the road. I think we should pay a visit to the lawyer tomorrow morning. Can you get here tonight?"

"You'll do anything to get me alone. Let me call Nina. I'll be there as soon as I can."

Chapter
52

Renita and Schaffer reached the office of Gill Tannenbaum Esq. at 8 a.m. Tuesday. Fifteen minutes later, Gill's assistant arrived and was immediately flustered by the FBI's request to see her boss.

Schaffer knew that Gill was a 'hands-on' boss, the minute he saw his assistant. She was no older than twenty-seven or twenty-eight and stood five feet, ten inches tall. She wore a mini skirt that showed every possible inch of her legs, which were as long as a racehorse's. Her low-cut blouse removed any need to use one's imagination when confronted with her generous breast.

"I'll check to see if Mr. Tannenbaum is in. Sometimes he uses the back door." She leaned across the desk to get the key to Gill's office.

Once she was out of sight, Renita poked Schaffer in the side. "Did you enjoy the view?"

"The only way I could have missed that thong was if I were blind. I'm sure she's practiced her technique at Tannenbaum's insistence. Now you know what to expect when we see him."

"I expect you'll punch his lights out if he eye-gropes me."

Schaffer made a fist. "No problem. I'll just hurt him a little."

Nervously, the assistant came back to the reception area. "Mr. Tannenbaum is not available at the moment. He must have an appointment elsewhere." Her eyes darted from side to avoiding direct eye contact when she spoke.

Maybe you could call him on his cell phone and tell him we're waiting." Schaffer grabbed the phone on her desk and held it out to her.

The assistant stuttered. "H-He doesn't have one. You may just have to come back at another time, after you've made an appointment."

Renita stood, walked to the edge of the assistant's desk and leaned forward placing both hands on it. "Listen honey, there're three cars in the parking lot of a one office building. We came in one car, you came in one and the Benz, with the car phone antenna was here when we arrived. We're going to wait here until he comes out, even if it takes all night. In the mean time, my partner over there is going to call in the license plate of that Benz and wait beside it to see if it belongs to Tannenbaum. If he tries to go out and get in it, I'm going to arrest both of you for obstruction of justice."

A voice came from behind Gill's door. "Good morning, Jessie. I was at the service station getting us some Krispy Krems." Gill walked out with half a box of donuts and brushed the evidence of the other half from his mouth and chest. He looked over at Renita and Schaffer. "I'm sorry. I didn't realize we had clients in. Would you like a donut?"

Renita flashed her FBI creds. "No thank you. But we would like you to fill us in on a few things. Shall we go in your office?"

Gill waved. "Surely, surely. Come right in. I'm never too busy to help any of our fine members of law enforcement." He turned to Jessie. "Hold my calls. I'm sure we'll be finished shortly."

Schaffer leaned to Renita and pointed out the sweat that dripped from beneath Gill's hairpiece. "It's not hot in here, what do you think could make him sweat that badly?"

"Let's not jump to any conclusions. At least until after we turn up the heat."

Renita and Schaffer sat directly in front of Gill. Schaffer pulled out his recorder and handed it to Renita.

"We want to ensure that nothing you tell us can be misinterpreted by any involved parties." Renita nodded towards Gill.

"Please feel free. I have nothing to hide." Gill sat back in his chair and put his fingers in front of his face forming a steeple.

Schaffer locked stares with Gill. "We are simply looking for some clarity on a corporation you formed."

Gill never moved his hands. "I'm sure both of you are aware that any information pertaining to a client is protected as a sacred bond between lawyer and client."

Renita drew Gill's attention from the standoff brewing between him and Schaffer. "We're not here to have you divulge any privileged information. Corporations are a matter of public record. All of our questions will focus in that arena. Shall we begin?"

"As you say, corporations are a matter of public record. All such records are readily available and are self-explanatory. I don't see how I can help any further." Gill let his hands fall to his lap.

Renita smiled. "I think you underestimate your abilities. For example, the corporation lists you as corporate counsel. I assume then, that you prepare all the company's filings."

"That's correct."

Renita reached in her bag and pulled out a copy of the corporation's filings. "We noticed the names of your Board of Directors. How are they selected?"

"They're hand picked." Gill's hands came back to his face.

"By whom?" Renita asked.

"By the owner of the corporation."

"That's interesting. You see, I couldn't determine the name of the owner in any of the filings, or on the tax records for that matter. Surely, that isn't the normal course of business."

"Thomas Brothers Inc. is not your normal company." Gill wiped away a drop of sweat that ran down the side of his face.

"I should say not. Not many corporations are formed for the sole purpose of helping the underprivileged attend college. That is a noble cause, one that is seldom questioned. From what we've gathered the corporation is extremely generous. One recipient has received seventy five thousand dollars in the past four months alone. That is nothing short of amazing, wouldn't you agree? How does a company like that stay in business?" Renita held out her hand, giving Gill the floor.

"Thomas Brothers Inc. is a very generous corporation. We assist a variety of people who have different needs. We simply attempt to meet the needs of those we serve."

Renita rested her hand on top of the documents. "You all should be publicly commended."

Gill put his hand in the air. "That's the last thing we want. Public attention would upset the quality of services we provide. Then, where would these poor students be? Our founder was helped in his time of need and now he is giving back to the community. Seeing these students become successful is the only reward, or acknowledgement he seeks."

Renita nodded in agreement. "Back to the Board of Directors for a moment. Has a replacement been named to fill Dr. Gerard's seat since his untimely death?"

"It's my understanding that a name has been selected. However, as of yet, I have not received that name." Gill shifted in his seat.

"How long was Dr. Gerard on the Board?" Renita looked Gill directly in his eyes.

"Since the company's inception twelve years ago."

Renita stood. "I'm sure Dr. Gerard will be sorely missed. Thank you for your help, Mr. Tannenbaum." She gathered her things and Schaffer rose to leave with her. About half way to the door, she turned around. "One more question." Renita reached in her bag. "Have you ever seen this man?" She sat the drawing of Thomas in front of him.

Gill's sweat returned, covering his forehead and upper lip. He looked over the picture with apparent care. "I don't believe I have."

"Are you completely certain?"

Gill looked at it again. "It could be anybody, I'm just not sure."

Renita left the picture and walked out of the office with Schaffer.

Chapter
53

"I think it's time we look a little closer into Dr. Gerard's background. That may lead us where we want to be." Schaffer looked over at Renita. "Why don't you find out where he went to school?"

"I'm one step ahead of you. He did his undergrad work at Virginia Union University, his medical school at Tulane in New Orleans, and his residency at the Medical College of Virginia." Renita slid the paper back in her bag.

"In that case, we're heading to Richmond. We'll be there before 10:30 a.m. We can begin at Virginia Union to see if the administration or any instructors can shed light on Dirk's background."

♦

At Virginia Union, Renita and Schaffer went to the administration building and questioned the registrar. Renita scanned through several documents before she spoke. "According to your records, anything relating to Dirk Gerard was directed to the President of the University. Can you explain that?"

"The only man who could have explained that died last year. Edward was always taking in 'stray dogs.' He called them his special projects. A dog is a dog and sometimes they'll bite you in the ass." She raised the folder. "These are copies of what we were allowed to keep. The originals and everything else were probably buried with Edward."

"Why was there so much secrecy surrounding one student?" Schaffer looked over the papers.

The registrar sighed heavily. "I am not capable of answering these questions. You should ask Helen. If she doesn't know, chances are you'll never find out."

"Helen? You mean the President's wife?" The registrar nodded and Renita continued. "Where can we find her?"

"She is a very private person. After Edward died, she moved. She doesn't want her location revealed. Let me contact her and see what she wants to do."

"We're investigating multiple murderers here. We don't have time for games." Renita's tone reflected both her frustration and determination.

"Helen is my dearest friend. I don't want to see her hurt. She has already suffered too much. She hasn't heard from her daughter in two months. Victoria finally left her husband and both she and Helen are terrified of him. That's a terrible way to live."

"We can help her. Who is her son-in-law?" Schaffer asked.

The registrar looked at Renita and then at Schaffer. As if she were receiving some twisted pleasure from the knowledge, a wicked smile crossed her face. "I'm surprised you don't already know. I think it's best if Helen tells you. I've already gotten more involved than I should have."

Schaffer cocked one eyebrow. "You mean Thomas?"

The registrar tilted her head to one side. "Helen's the person you need to talk to."

Renita reached in her bag and pulled out the drawing. She looked at it before handing it to the registrar. "Is this the man you're talking about?"

The registrar hung her head. "She's going to kill me for this. You can find Helen Richards in Blackstone, Virginia. The Catholic Church there has a very large residence; she rents the upper portion of the house. She has all the answers you're looking for. Please don't tell her I told you where to find her."

Renita touched the registrar's arm. "You may have just saved her life."

♦

Renita looked over at Schaffer. "You seem to know just where you're going."

"I should. I grew up one town over. My family was the only Black Catholic family that attended the church that we're going to. I know every square inch of that house."

Renita flipped through the papers she had on the case. "I hope Mrs. Richards can shed some light on this case. We need to put this one to bed, now."

"We sure do. Tomorrow we're supposed to be in the Virgin Islands. We both need the break."

"It would be nice to be able to enjoy ourselves while we're there. Getting Thomas off the streets would help. She looked around at the scenery. "Where the hell are you taking me? I haven't seen this many cows or this much wooded area in a long time. This has to be some type of short cut."

"No, this is the way to reach Blackstone. There are a lot of dairy farms out this way. You should be thankful that it's not warm enough to have the windows down, bovine methane can kill with one deep breath." Schaffer pushed the button and cracked her window a little.

"Alright you." She put the window back up. "Remind me not to come this way with you in the summer."

Twenty minutes later, they arrived at the only Catholic Church in Blackstone. Schaffer drove to the back of a large house attached to a small church. "Here we are."

Renita looked at the house. "Wow. This place must be about three or four thousand square feet. How did the church get it?"

Schaffer laughed. "Rumor has it the place is haunted. A doctor owned the house at one time. The story that I've always heard is that the doctor had cancer and committed suicide. Some parishioners have reported vacuum cleaners running on their own and lights coming on in the attic by themselves. When we were kids we used to play all over the house, especially in the attic. We never saw anything weird, but who knows? Maybe the doctor liked kids."

"Mrs. Richards must be a brave woman, or she hasn't heard the rumors yet." Renita rang the doorbell.

A small, gray-haired lady looked through the glass next to the door. "The church is closed right now. The hours are posted on the door." She pointed to the side where they hung.

"That's okay Mrs. Richards. We're here to see you." Renita held up her FBI creds.

Mrs. Richards slowly opened the door. "Please, won't you come in? I was just about to fix some coffee. Would you like some?"

"Yes, please." Renita answered and followed her into the kitchen. "We won't take up very much of your time. We just want to ask you a few questions."

"How did you find me?" Mrs. Richards asked as she pulled the coffee from the shelf.

Schaffer filled the coffee pot with water. "We ran into a friend of yours who was concerned about your safety. She told us where to find you."

"You must have been very convincing to get Noreen to tell you where I was. Have you found Victoria and the children as well?" Mrs. Richards sat the coffee can on the counter and burst into tears. "I'm so worried about them."

Renita walked over and held Mrs. Richards. "We'll do everything we can to find them. When was the last time you heard from them?"

"It's been about two months. She was terrified that Dirk may find them. Just before Victoria left him he swore he would rather see them all dead before seeing them separated."

Schaffer's head snapped around catching Renita's gaze. She put up her hand to stop him from talking. He put the coffee in the filter and started it brewing. "Dr. Gerard is dead. What makes you afraid of him?"

Mrs. Richards dabbed her eyes with the back of her hand. "Have you all found a body yet?" It only took a glance at the faces of both Schaffer and Renita's for her to know the truth. "I didn't think so. I read the article in the paper about the suspect. I even saw the picture. If you'd ever seen Dirk up close you would have to have noticed the slight resemblance."

Renita handed Mrs. Richards another tissue. "We worked side by side with Dr. Gerard on this case, until he was supposedly abducted."

Mrs. Richards blotted the tears from her eyes. "Dirk was very good at his work. Anyone with his qualifications, that knew how to find the minutest evidence, surely knew how to avoid leaving any damning evidence behind at his own crime scenes."

Renita walked with her to the table and sat down. "If you felt so strongly about Dr. Gerard, why didn't you contact the FBI?"

"I tried after reading the article, but I couldn't bring myself to say anything. I was afraid if I did you might start looking for Victoria and inadvertently lead him to her. I wasn't willing to take that kind of chance with my daughter's life."

Schaffer moved to the table. "That's understandable." He sat down. "Believe me; we don't want to see Victoria hurt. Maybe you can tell us something that may help us locate Dirk, if he's still alive."

Mrs. Richards looked at Schaffer and then let her eyes fall back to the table. "I promised my husband that I would take their secret to my grave. I've never broken a promise to him."

Renita rubbed Mrs. Richards' back. "That was before you were concerned with the lives of your daughter and grandchildren. We can only help if you let us."

Schaffer got up to get the coffee and Mrs. Richards retrieved the cream and sugar. She sat them on the table and took her seat. "Dirk Gerard was not always Dirk Gerard."

Renita stopped pouring her cream and sat the decanter down. "I'm afraid I'm not following you."

Mrs. Richards took a sip of her coffee and slowly pulled the cup from her face. "Almost twenty years ago a young man came to my husband looking for odd jobs around the house. Edward was always trying to uplift the younger members of the community, so he hired the boy. As it turns out, he only wanted access to the house to steal from us. Edward caught him before he got away."

Schaffer looked at Mrs. Richards. "So, this young man was Dirk Gerard?"

"Not at that point, let me explain." Mrs. Richards took another sip of her coffee. "The young man's name was Thomas Walker. Edward was taken in by Thomas' obvious intelligence. The sheriff was a good friend of Edward's, so he convinced the sheriff to lock Thomas up in isolation for a few days. Edward wanted to give the boy time to think." Mrs. Richards shook her head and gave a weak smile. "Edward went by to visit that boy every day. On the third day he told the boy, Jesus rose from the dead in three days, so he was going to give Thomas a chance to rise above his troubles. He offered him jail or college. Naturally, Thomas chose the latter."

Renita slid her coffee cup from hand to hand listening to the story. "That took an incredible leap of faith on your husband's part. But, how did it involve Dr. Gerard?"

Mrs. Richards appeared even more troubled. "Thomas excelled his first year in college. Edward was elated; said all he needed was someone to care. From that point forward he practically made Thomas a part of the family. Thomas told Edward after his first year of school that he wanted to become a doctor, but his arrest record was standing in the way. Edward was very connected politically. He pulled in a few favors from some of his friends and they had Thomas declared dead. They even issued a death certificate. Somehow, they came up with the name of a baby boy that had died the same year Thomas was born. Thomas assumed the dead boy's name, Dirk Gerard."

Schaffer shook his head from side to side. "That's a very elaborate scheme. Since he had already completed his freshman year, how did they avoid everyone at school that already knew Thomas?"

Mrs. Richards looked into her coffee cup. "Edward had all the bases covered. He concocted a story that went along with the name change; it was just as involved. They told everyone that Thomas had been adopted at a very young age, because his father went off to Viet Nam and never returned. His mother just couldn't be around anything that reminded her of her husband, so she put him up for adoption. Then, after twenty-three years his father, whom everyone presumed was dead, returns, locates

Thomas, and tells him his real name is Dirk Gerard. The story made him very popular at the school."

"Is that when he and Victoria became an item?" Renita asked.

"No, it wasn't until their junior year. Dirk is five years older than Victoria, but they started school together. By the end of their junior year it was fairly certain that Dirk would be going to medical school. That's when Victoria found him totally irresistible. Dirk had been dating Victoria's best friend, Ava Hayes at the time, but she wouldn't let that stop her."

Renita almost leapt from the chair. "Ava Hayes, the victim Ava Hayes?"

"Precisely. When she was killed, Victoria broke off all contact with me. Before she disappeared she made me promise not to contact the authorities. She was certain that they would lead Dirk to her. I had to protect my daughter."

Mrs. Richards started crying again. Renita patted her hand. Schaffer sat back in his chair. He looked drained as if the story was sucking away his life. "Mrs. Richards. Do you know anything about a corporation that Dirk started?"

"You're talking about Thomas Brothers. Dirk said he found a private investor to put up most of the money. The company helps underprivileged children attend college. He said he did it because Edward helped him. He named the company Thomas Brothers because he said he and Thomas Walker were twins. Thomas means twin, you know, so the company is essentially, Twin Brothers."

Renita winked at Schaffer and pulled out the papers on the company. "Did he ever say who the investor was who funded the company?"

"He told Edward some guy died and left him the money for the company. Edward saw no need to investigate it further."

"Mrs. Richards if you hear from your daughter, please call me right away." Renita handed her a business card. "My cell phone number is on here too. Call me anytime day or night."

Schaffer leaned on the table. "Mrs. Richards, before your daughter left, were she and Dirk living in Richmond?"

"No. They sold that house and moved to Fredericksburg. They bought a house on the Rappahannock River with a lot of land. I told them it was wrong to isolate those children on a place like that. As usual, they didn't listen. After Edward died, I never went back."

"Would you happen to have the address?" Schaffer slid a pad and pen to her.

"Let me get my address book." She left to get the book and stopped before she left the room. "You don't think he's still there do you?"

Renita stood up. "It would be a blessing for all of us if he was."

Chapter
54

Schaffer looked back as they pulled out of the church's driveway. He pounded the steering wheel several times. "Holy shit. I almost pissed on myself when Mrs. Richards said Victoria was married to Dirk who is actually Thomas the Tiger. We had that son of a bitch within our reach from the beginning."

"You know we should be worried about your friend, Rachel. Dirk is unpredictable. Since Dirk and Thomas are the same person if she tells him that we're getting together in St. Johns he may snap and kill her for booking the trip. Remember, we can tie him to at least three of the murders once we get a DNA match." Renita called headquarters. "We need to have a team in place in the Virgin Islands by Thursday evening. It's got to be new faces, none that have been involved in this case before."

"That's not fair. You're taking people that haven't worked on the case. Why do they deserve a vacation and not me?" The agent asked.

"Because, we know who 'Thomas the Tiger' is and he knows each of us on the team." Renita paused. "We're having dinner with him on Friday."

"Wait a minute. You're having dinner with the son of a bitch we've been hunting for the past four months?"

"Yes. Pass the word that our target is Dr. Dirk Gerard, A.K.A. 'Thomas the Tiger,' Thomas Walker and God knows who else he's pretended to be." Renita let her words hang.

The agent took a while to respond. "This is going to blow the Director away."

Renita added quickly. "Tell him not to tell Virginia's governor yet. We need to keep this close to the vest, no one outside the Director and the team should know. While you're at it, pull everything on a Thomas Walker, originally from Orange County, Virginia. He's got an arrest record and a death certificate."

The agent frowned and momentarily pulled the phone from his ear. "Why am I looking up a dead man?"

"I'll explain all that later. Also have Virginia send up Dr. Gerard's prints and state employee file. Finally, get several teams to Baltimore. Station them at the airport, train station, bus station, and any other place that brings people in or out of the city. Dr. Gerard should be coming back to Baltimore on Thursday. Pick him up then if possible. I want to enjoy my vacation."

"I'm on it. Are you coming back to the office before tomorrow?"

"I don't think there'll be enough time. Make sure you e-mail me with the new team members. I'll see you when we get back." Renita ended the call.

Schaffer began talking the second she hung up. "Why didn't you tell them to meet us in Fredericksburg? We may need their help."

"Don't tell me you, Mr. Marine ex-re-con, are afraid of one little man with a gun." Renita teased. "Actually, we're almost there. It would take them too long to get here. If we encounter anything we can't handle, I'll call in the Cavalry. I don't expect to find him though."

Schaffer followed Mrs. Richards' directions to Dirk's house in Fredericksburg. The driveway was one of the longest he could remember. Schaffer stopped the car before he could see the house. "Are you sure we shouldn't call for backup?"

"It's too late for that. The bump you hit just before stopping was a pressure plate. If he's in the house he already knows we're here."

Schaffer pulled his gun from his side and racked it, chambering the first round. "I guess we'd better be ready for anything."

"I can't believe you waited until now to do that. Your weapon should always be ready. It's not like the movies where you get to rack it during a firefight. They would have you believe you can rack the damn thing five or six times before you shoot. If you did that half your bullets would be on the ground." Renita pulled out her Glock. "If he meets us at the door we're ready. Get the shotgun out of the trunk when we stop. We may need the extra firepower."

There were no external signs of life at the house. Renita rang the doorbell and no one answered. Schaffer looked through the windows. "There's nothing here at all, no furniture, no people, nothing. The house is completely empty."

Renita turned the doorknob. "The door is open. He didn't bother to lock it." She didn't open the door; she only confirmed that it was not locked. "We've got to get a warrant before going in. I don't want Dr. Gerard walking on a technicality."

"He's smart enough to set a trap for us too. He knows you want him real badly. If he's sophisticated enough to use pressure plates to detect someone's arrival, he would likely know if we we'd been in his house before too. We don't want to spook him and send him deeper into hiding. We'll just have to wait until we get that warrant." Schaffer was holding Renita's arm as if he were trying to hold her back.

She looked at her watch. "It's already 5 pm. I guess you're right. Let's get back to DC. With the rush hour traffic it'll be 8 pm before we get back to D.C. I want to spend some time with Tina before leaving tomorrow.

♦

Thursday night after Asolare Restaurant closed the 'Tony the Tiger' Task Force met there to prepare for Friday. They painstakingly scrubbed the area for their meeting. By the time they were finished there wasn't a latent print on a piece of furniture or a speck of dust embedded in the carpet. Collecting trace and DNA evidence is much simpler when the area starts out pristine. Hidden microphones were placed under and around the table Renita picked out for their dinner and live feed digital video cameras were set up to capture the meeting from all angles.

Renita addressed the team. "I don't want anything to happen here in the restaurant. We'll take him down elsewhere. The first thing we have to do is confirm we're dealing with the right guy." She turned to another black female agent. "Your job will be to get fingerprints from his glass, or even better, a hair from the back of his chair. How's the accent coming?"

"Great mon. I grew up 'ere, don't you know. Evryting is ire."

Schaffer walked over to the window that exposed the entire back wall of the restaurant to the surf outside. He watched the waves rolling in. "Let's not forget this isn't your ordinary criminal. He'll be expecting something. He's been several steps ahead of us since we started and he's eluded capture by preventing us from finding any evidence. He's not going to make it easy for us now."

"Schaffer's right. We still have to tie him to the actual crimes. If we can secure a DNA match between the tissue sample we collected and his hair, we can take him off the streets permanently." Renita looked at the other female agent, who was just starting to appreciate the gravity of her upcoming assignment.

The agents paid the restaurant what the table would ordinarily make in three days to keep it free from customers until Friday night. A small army of agents were given their SOG, or Surveillance Operations Group assignments, to monitor Dirk's movements around the Island. An agent was even going to be on the flight from DC to St. Thomas, his seat assignment put him directly across from Rachel and Dirk. Dirk would not be alone for a single second from the moment he left the Dulles airport till he was safely in FBI custody.

The team moved to the hotel where Rachel and Dirk would be staying. There, they set up digital transmitters and cameras in the suite. Renita avoided discussing with Schaffer that she felt Rachel was actually being used as bait, since it was possible that Dirk may try to kill her if he felt threatened. She wanted to be ready just in case.

At 1 a.m. Friday morning the team was ready in place. Renita's phone rang just as they finished the hotel room. She recognized the number as the team leader from the Baltimore detail. "We haven't seen anyone resembling Dr. Gerard, or the drawing of the suspect. If he came back to this city, I don't know how he got here. I guess we'll have to wait until tomorrow at Dulles."

"Call me as soon as you confirm he's boarded. According to the airline ticket he was issued, he's traveling under the name Thomas Richards." Renita hung up the phone and turned to Schaffer. "All we can do now is wait."

Chapter

55

Schaffer used the down time to call Bacchus. Even though the FBI planned on taking Dirk down in the Virgin Islands, he knew someone had to be prepared back home just in case.

"Yo, Tree, you asleep?"

Bacchus rubbed his beefy hand across his face. "What the fuck do you think? What the hell time is it anyway?"

"It's about one in the morning. What I've got to tell you should wake you up."

"You'd better have a goddamned big ass check for me after this thing is all over." Bacchus sat up and turned on a light. "What's so damned important?"

"Seems you know your stuff, Dr. Dirk Gerard is our guy. He is also 'Thomas the Tiger' and God knows who else. His wife left him a few months ago. I guess that's what triggered his killing spree."

Bacchus cleared his throat. "I told you those smart-ass fuckers are crazy as shit."

"I'll tell you this; he's not the typical serial killer. He worked right beside us day in and day out without even flinching. Many serial killers freak out when they are confronted with things from the site of their crime. This guy is as cool as a January polar bear." Schaffer slid out a cigar and held it inches from his lips.

"Typical or not, somebody needs to put this guy out of his misery. I hope you find him before I do; I don't need to know why he's preying on innocent women."

Schaffer slipped the uncut cigar between his teeth. "Then this is really going to knock your socks off. Renita and I are having dinner with him tonight."

Bacchus' irritation flowed out. "Have you lost your mind? How can you even sit at the same table with the devil?"

"Calm down. He has no clue what we know or that Renita and I will be there. The other reason I called is because I want you to go to his house in Fredericksburg, VA. See what you can find there, but be careful, he's smart, paranoid, and unpredictable. Watch out for traps."

Bacchus was wide awake but just as angry. "What about a

warrant? You don't want this guy to get off."

Schaffer pinched off the end of his Hemmingway Masterpiece and put a flame to it. "Renita got a warrant before we left, but she didn't want to tip him off by having anyone go in before we had the chance to take him into custody. I want you to check things out in an unofficial capacity. Don't disturb anything; just let me know what's there."

"I can be there in a couple of hours. You might want to let your girlfriend know that I'm there. I don't feel up to dodging bullets today."

Schaffer took a puff from the cigar. "If she dispatches any team, I'll let her know. I haven't told her anything about you yet. I don't anticipate having to reveal anything about you at this point."

Bacchus grunted. "Everybody should have a friend like you—always willing to stick their necks out for you."

Chapter
56

2 a.m. Friday morning Thomas used his key to enter Rachel's apartment. He went to the bedroom and silently slid in bed with her. Rachel stirred, but didn't open her eyes. "I was expecting you earlier. When did you get in?"

"I had to finish a few things before returning. We can talk about it in the morning, go back to sleep." For two hours he felt her naked body against his. Sleep was the last thing on his mind.

The alarm clock rang at 4 a.m. Thomas reached up and turned it off. He slid back beneath the covers and cupped both of Rachel's breasts from behind.

She let him play for a moment, but soon said. "We've got to get up so we can get to Dulles on time."

"Oh, I've been up for some time now." Without another word he slid easily into her and their bodies began to rock in rhythm. "There's always time for me to make love to you." He whispered letting his lips brush against her ear.

The intensity and speed of their movements increased until a force reached deep inside them, exploding. Their bodies' jerked uncontrollably and guttural noises more primal than time rose to express their pleasure.

Rachel leaned back to kiss Thomas. What she saw forced her to leap from the bed, grabbing the covers to shield her naked body. "Who the fuck are you and what the fuck do you think you're doing?"

"Take it easy, Rachel. It's me, Thomas. Don't you recognize my voice?" The expression on her face never eased. He kept talking, trying to ignite a spark of recognition. "We went to Mendocino Wine Bar and Grill for our first date. You called me two days ago on my cell phone, (540) 555-8282 to tell me we were going to St. Johns. You called it our paradise getaway."

Rachel blinked hard trying to force the sleep from her eyes and the cobwebs from her brain. "What did you do to yourself?" She sat on the bed and touched his face.

He let her run her hands over his face and through the long hair that covered his head. Gently, he reached for her hand and kissed her softly on the palm. "When I was out of town a friend of mine called to let me know he had an opening. He's a plastic surgeon in Rio. I had been putting off a procedure to fix my nose for a very long time. Since he was going in, I had him take out a few lines in my face and put the dimple in my chin as well."

She ran her fingers through his hair again. "Where did this come from? You look ten years younger."

Thomas smiled. "You know how badly I was thinning. My friend found a guy who was willing to sell over half the hair on his head. We did a transplant from his head to mine. It cost me about fifteen thousand and was worth every penny. What do you think?"

"Will it stay? It's beautiful." Rachel continued to play with his new hair.

"There's no way to be sure. I'm taking prednisone to keep my body from rejecting the transplant. I haven't had hair this long since college." Thomas tilted his head letting some of the hair fall to his face.

"How did everything heal so quickly? I don't see any scars." Rachel turned on the lights. She brought her hand over her mouth, protecting Thomas from the smile on her face. "You have two slightly black eyes."

Thomas shrugged. "Modern plastic surgery is miles ahead of what it used to be, but no one has learned to prevent the bruising yet. The hair was done using micrographs so it healed in a week. Everything else needs two weeks to heal. I'll be as good as new before we finish our trip. You're looking at the new and improved me."

"I didn't see anything wrong with the old you. This will take some getting used to, but I'll manage. I love the hair."

"Just remember this is our little secret. I don't ever want anyone else to know. I'm starting a new life. The less we involve others the better off we'll be."

Rachel reached under the covers. "I can tell you one thing your friend didn't change." She grabbed him. "I'd say right now he has a lot of new life. He's standing at attention again." She pushed Thomas back on the bed and climbed on top.

◆

United Airlines flight 443 touched down in St. Johns right on time. The agent sitting across from Thomas and Rachel watched them carefully throughout the entire flight. He kept his seat, letting them deplane first. When they reached the first class section he radioed the waiting agents. "They're on their way out. It doesn't look like our guy. He doesn't resemble the composite or Dr. Gerard's work photo at all. The girl's wearing a short purple sundress and he's got oatmeal colored linen pants on and a teal shirt. They both have coats draped across their arms."

Another agent stationed as a greeter welcoming people to the island, spoke into a microphone hidden behind his collar. "I see them now. They're coming down the ramp."

The tag team of agents passed Rachel and Thomas off so often, it would have been difficult to detect that they were being watched at all. Even the driver of the hotel shuttle was an agent, complete with accent and dreadlocks.

By the time they reached the hotel, Rachel and Thomas had been photographed twelve times without their knowledge. Thirty minutes later, an agent delivered twelve eight by ten glossy photographs to Renita and Schaffer's room.

Schaffer studied each of the pictures. "That's Rachel, but I've never seen the guy with her."

Renita examined the photos carefully. "He's got a tan line on his ring finger. I don't remember Dr. Gerard wearing a ring, do you?" She showed the picture to Schaffer.

"It's not the type of thing I look for. I can't say I recall seeing one." Schaffer handed the pictures back to Renita.

"I wish I could see his eyes. Dr. Gerard's eyes were striking. They were predominantly a hazel color, but streaks of tan were dispersed throughout." She flipped through the photos, but none revealed his eyes, only mirrored sunglasses.

"And just why were you looking at his eyes?" Schaffer asked.

"In my job, you notice everything, especially the minute details. It's what I'm trained to do."

There was nothing left to do until dinner. Renita and Schaffer used the time to try to relax a bit and to pick up souvenirs for Tina, Nina and Joe. They monitored all radio transmissions to prevent any chance encounters before dinner. If Rachel didn't tell Thomas who they were meeting for dinner, surprise would be on the FBI's side. Any advantage in dealing with Thomas was a plus.

Renita and Schaffer went back to the hotel at 3 p.m. to prepare for dinner. Renita stepped across the hall where three agents were monitoring all transmissions from the rest of the team as well as, Rachel and Thomas' room. "What's the latest?" She asked.

"Things have been quiet on this front. They've done some of the tourist stuff, but not much else. They walked in just before you came in."

The agent pointed to the monitor.

Renita watched Rachel and Thomas in their room. "Thomas, I forgot to tell you we're having dinner a friend of mine tonight." Rachel laid a dress on the bed.

"Who's the friend?" Thomas asked.

"You don't know him. He's from DC. I ran into him at the travel agency, we were booking the same trip."

"But, it's Valentine's Day. We should be alone. It's more romantic."

Rachel walked up behind him and rubbed his shoulders. "They're only going to be here a couple of days. We've got the whole week. Sharing dinner with them will be fun. Let's see how much we can get away with sitting right at the table with them watching."

"In that case, leave your panties here." Thomas turned and faced Rachel. Her suggestion produced instant results and the FBI got an eye full.

The agent watching the screen leaned back in his chair. "I hope I don't have to watch this shit all night."

Renita looked at the screen. "What's wrong? I thought all guys liked porn. At least they'll be nice and relaxed when they get to dinner. Buzz me if anything significant happens." She turned and left the room.

A black limousine with deeply tinted windows picked Renita and Schaffer up at 4:15 p.m. Six other agents waited inside the vehicle. They had mobile devices set up inside to track Rachel and Thomas as soon as they left the hotel.

Renita stepped inside and saw the other agents focusing on the viewing screen. "Don't tell me the show is still going on."

"No, we're just watching her get dressed." One of the agents said. "He's going to miss her when he goes to prison."

"Let's not get ahead of ourselves; we have to lock him up first." Renita reached for a bottle of water.

Another of the agents began to focus more on Renita from the moment she entered the car. Her hair loosely held her face. The white top she was wearing stopped just below her breast line, exposing her muscular abdomen. Her white linen flair-legged pants flowed easily around her frame. What little sun she saw since Wednesday gave her skin a warm golden glow against the white clothing. The agent pointed towards her. "It amazes me that you can hide a gun wearing something as sheer as that."

Renita lifted her pant leg revealing the gun. "A well placed holster usually does the trick."

The agent looked at Schaffer. "I'll give you five hundred dollars to switch places with me."

Schaffer raised a hand and waved it around the car. "Do I hear a thousand?"

Renita punched him in the side. "For a thousand dollars I'll let you boys watch me take my shoe off. We need to hurry and finish this case so you all can get home. Watching that monitor has brought your horns out."

The limousine parked at the side of the restaurant. Everyone remained inside waiting for Rachel and Thomas to arrive. The wait wasn't long.

Rachel and Thomas made their way to the restaurant fifteen minutes early. They were immediately seated. Rachel slid her chair back as soon as she was seated. "I'm going to the ladies room. I'll be right back."

Thomas stood when she did. "I'll order a bottle of Champagne for our celebration, hurry back."

Renita and Schaffer waited until Rachel returned before entering Asolare's. They walked across the lobby, lead by an agent pretending to be the restaurant's host.

Thomas' mirrored Ray-Ban sunglasses made it impossible for anyone to gauge his level of surprise when he saw Renita and Schaffer approaching the table.

Rachel stood and waved. She tapped Thomas' shoulder. "Here they are now."

Thomas greeted them with a cheery smile, while Rachel made the introductions all around. The game of 'Cat and Mouse' began. What was not clear was who would ultimately wind up in which role.

"This is great isn't it? Getting together with friends on Valentine's Day." Thomas poured Champagne for everyone and raised his glass. "To old farts and the beautiful women they love."

Their glasses met in the middle of the table with a clink. "This is really great." Schaffer looked across the table. "Rachel, you did say dinner was on you, right?"

"I recall the offer for dinner came from those lips." Rachel pointed to Schaffer and slid her free hand down Thomas' leg.

"That's the impression I got from Rachel." Thomas' hand went across her legs parting them slightly. "She said that you wanted us to spare no expense, so I ordered a two hundred dollar bottle of Dom Perignon. What's a little money between friends? Since you seem to have a palate for better wines, I'll pay for the first bottle. Consider it a Valentine's Day gift."

Schaffer put his arm around Renita. "He must be talking about you. My normal brand is Champale."

Thomas laughed heartily. "You could have fooled me Mr. O'Grady. I see you as the type of guy that appreciates the finer things in life."

"Only as fine as my budget allows." Schaffer took another drink.

The first bottle of champagne was empty. Their waitress walked over and stood behind Thomas. "Would you like another bottle?"

"Absolutely, this is a celebration of life and love." Thomas said to the waitress. "As long as you're here, you might as well take our food orders."

She looked down at the back of Thomas' chair. Two or three loose hairs lay across the back. The waitress scooped them up and placed them between the sheets of her order pad. Thomas had also been the only one to handle the champagne bottle. After everyone placed their orders, she lifted the ice bucket and took the bottle along with the hairs to an agent waiting in the kitchen.

The two pieces of evidence were carried to the evidence van to be processed. The agents there worked feverishly to complete testing on the evidence. They used an alternative light source to check for latent prints. Finding none, they processed it with ninhidren, which yielded the same conclusion. "This is really freaky. There's not a print on this bottle."

"There's got to be. I watched him lift the bottle several times." The agent acting as the waitress looked at the bottle.

"Did you get a look at his hands, was he wearing gloves?"

"Not that I can tell." She looked at the hair in a Petri dish. "We won't have the DNA results from the hairs for a few days at best; we need to do something else."

"Why don't you run out there and stab him. His blood could put us a lot closer. One thing's for damn sure; if we can't get the evidence tonight we could be months away from making an arrest."

Chapter
57

Thomas suggested they all take a walk on the beach after dinner. They strolled through the sand close to the edge of the water. "I'm a big fan of yours Mr. O'Grady. Your series on that serial killer was very revealing."

"Thanks. I only wish the FBI could catch the bastard. He's a demented fuck." Schaffer kicked the sand.

Thomas looked out across the ocean. "Perhaps, on the other hand he must be fairly intelligent to evade capture for so long."

"We're closer to him than he thinks." Renita looked at Thomas for a reaction. "It's only a matter of time before he slips, we'll be waiting."

"I wonder how he could get close to so many women. Anyone who kills like that can't have any charm or appeal." Rachel moved a little closer to Thomas.

"Let's go over there by those rocks. We'll be away from prying eyes there." Thomas led the way.

An agent walking in the opposite direction radioed in after he passed them. "We're about to loose visual contact. Are agent Duplechain or Mr. O'Grady wired?"

"Negative." Another voice broke in. "We'll have to rely on the two of them. I'll send another team out to try and get closer."

One of the agents in the lab came on. "Gentlemen we've got a bigger problem. Two of the champagne glasses showed traces of GHB. Anything could be getting ready to go down. But this probably confirms that he's our man. If organophosphate and LSD were present too there'd be no doubt. I don't think he was willing to risk having people pass out at their table."

Renita sat on one of the rocks. "This was a good time to take a break; I'm feeling a bit lightheaded."

"I thought it was just me." Rachel added, putting her hand to her head.

"Too bad we don't have a blanket. We could lie out here all night." Thomas reached out and pulled Rachel against him. They started rubbing each other uninhibited by the other eyes on them.

Renita lay in Schaffer's arms and started rubbing her hand across his chest. She pulled his head near her mouth. "I'm feeling frisky myself.

I don't want to just sit here and watch them."

Schaffer stood and helped Renita from the sand. "We're going in. Thanks for dinner."

Rachel was in the process of freeing Thomas from his pants. He looked over to Schaffer with a big smile and responded. "You have fun the rest of the night Mr. O'Grady. I hope you took your vitamins, it's Valentine's Day."

Schaffer got Renita back to the limousine. "Get us back to the hotel. That asshole must have slipped her something."

"It's GHB Mr. O'Grady. We found it in two glasses. We thought it was yours and agent Duplechain's, but you look okay."

"I am. He must have given it to Renita and Rachel. She whipped his Johnson out right in front of us. She didn't give a damn that we were there." Schaffer put Renita in the car.

Renita kissed Schaffer but he grabbed her hands to prevent anything further. "Why don't we dump these guys and go back to the room?"

"That's what we're doing, Renita. That bastard drugged you, but you'll be okay." Schaffer held her tightly.

"You should get some. I feel good as shit and a whole lot horny. I think we should release a little of our own sexual tension." Renita put her hands in the air and started singing Marvin Gay's *Sexual Healing*.

Schaffer looked at the other agents in the car, who were having a hard time keeping straight faces. "Did you guys video anything at the table?"

"Yes. There were some still shots taken as well. We can look through all of it to see if we can determine when he slipped the drugs. If we can confirm that we can make an arrest."

"With what Renita told me earlier about the session in their room, I'm surprised he gave Rachel anything. Unless—" A look of horror started to cross Schaffer's face. "He might try to kill Rachel. Somebody needs to get back there."

"It's already covered. We had a team on their way over before you two came out of the sand."

Saturday morning Renita startled awake and looked around the room. Schaffer was nowhere to be seen. She found him in the lounging area of the suite. "Aren't you coming to bed?"

"How do you feel this morning?" He asked.

"Morning? What are you talking about? We just got in. I must have fallen asleep waiting for you."

Schaffer stretched and yawned. "I'm glad I didn't take you up on any of your offers last night."

"What are you talking about?" Renita put her hands on her hips and canted her head to one side.

Schaffer knew she meant business. "Our dinner guest slipped you a dose of GHB last night. During the ride home you told everyone in the limousine how horny you were. I had to restrain your hands to stop them from roving."

Renita's face was buried in her hands. "I can't face any of them this morning, or ever."

"They were the ones who detected the GHB in your glass. Don't feel so all alone, he slipped Rachel one too. She was humping him before we were even off the beach. I think Dirk, Thomas, or whomever he is thought he was doing me a favor."

Renita kept her head down. "Did we—"

"No. I wouldn't have felt right. But after we're married if you come home like that, look out; I had to practically tie you up to keep you in the room last night. As soon as we shower we should go across the hall to see what else went on last night. We left them on the beach. I want to make sure Rachel's alright."

Renita and Schaffer entered the room across the hall. Several agents were waiting. "How are you feeling this morning? We felt so bad about what happened that we wanted to get you a little something." An agent handed her a box.

"Thanks guys. I'm fine though, you didn't have to do this." She opened the box and pulled out a frog that had spikes coming off its skin.

"It's a horny toad." The agents and Schaffer clapped.

Renita's face turned red. "I should have known you guys weren't capable of genuine affection." She pulled it from the box and showed it to everyone. "I guess this will have to go on my desk."

Schaffer turned to the agent at the screen. "Did he bring her home last night?"

"Yeah, after the action on the beach I'm surprised either of them could walk. They were getting' busy."

A knock at the door hushed the room. "See who's there." Renita directed an agent.

"It's just the guys from the lab." The agent opened the door.

The agent from the lab entered and walked over to Renita. "This shouldn't be a great surprise since Dr. Gerard was bald a few weeks ago." He held out the papers. "He's gone to great lengths to hide his identity.

The DNA from his hair doesn't match the DNA from the skin we found in the dog."

"What about the saliva from the glass or fork?" Renita sounded desperate.

"All wiped clean."

"That's impossible…Damn!" Renita took the papers. "He was toying with us last night. He enjoyed being so close. He thinks we can't find anything on him, which makes him feel superior, but that will prove to be his biggest mistake."

"He's already made it." Everyone in the room looked at Schaffer. "We need to isolate him from Rachel. She has the missing piece of the puzzle. If I can get her alone I can get what we need."

Chapter
58

Thomas and Rachel were out until early Saturday afternoon. They went straight to the bedroom to quench their insatiable thirst for each other's bodies. Their session was shorter than what either of them had grown accustomed to.

Rachel was restless today. But after three days on a total of six hours sleep, Thomas fell into a deep sleep. Rachel wrote him a note and left to go shopping.

Renita and Schaffer were both in the monitoring room following the latest encounter. Renita saw Rachel prepare to leave. "We've got to catch her."

Schaffer stopped her. "Let me go on my own. I can talk to her and get her to help us."

"We've got to get her to give us a sample of what she's carrying. It's our only chance to prove his identity and pull that psycho off the streets."

Schaffer grabbed both of Renita's shoulders. "That's why I have to go alone. Put a transmitter on me with an ear piece, you'll be able to hear the conversation and send me any messages you need to."

Renita pointed to an agent. "Wire him up, quickly."

Schaffer bolted down the stairs. Rachel was walking from the hotel lobby just as he came running through the stairwell door. He ran onto the street and an agent pointed him in the right direction. "Rachel. Wait up." He caught up and fell into stride alongside her.

"Where are you going?" She asked taking his arm.

"I'm going wherever you are. I hoped I would catch you alone today. And here you are."

Rachel continued to hold his arm as they walked. "I was hoping for the same thing. I've wanted to talk to you since you've had the chance to meet Thomas. What do you think so far?"

Schaffer was looking at the ground as they walked. He didn't answer her question right away. "From what I've seen, he seems okay, I guess. What I want to know is how well do you really know Thomas?"

"We've known each other for four months." She looked at Schaffer's face. "He's treated me better than anyone ever has in my life. Why do you look so concerned?"

Schaffer didn't answer. "What does he do for a living?" His head never rose.

"He's involved in medical research. Why are you asking these questions?" Rachel stopped walking and forced Schaffer to look at her. "I thought you'd be happy for me."

"I have to ask you these questions. I'll explain in a moment." Schaffer put his arm around her back. "Come on. Let's keep walking. A few steps later he looked over at Rachel. "Have you ever been to his house?"

"No I haven't. But, that doesn't mean anything." Rachel's demeanor and facial expression changed. "Please God, don't mess this up for me." She looked at Schaffer. "You're not going to tell me he's married are you?"

"I'm not sure. He might be. I did some background work on him after you gave me a copy of the check. There are some things that don't add up."

"Like what." Rachel crossed her arms defensively.

"Rachel, you've trusted me for a long time now. That's because I've never let you down. I need you to trust me now; I only have your best interests at heart."

Rachel couldn't breathe. She tried to force the tears back down into their ducts, but it was useless, they had a will of their own that was much too strong. "Oh God, here it comes." She collapsed into Schaffer's arms.

He held her tightly. "It's okay. Things may be better than you think." He glanced over to a large rock on the beach. "Let's go over there and sit down."

"If you're asking me to sit down then I know things are about to get real bad." Rachel held his arm for support.

"That may not be entirely true." He sat on the rock next to Rachel and held her. "There is a possibility that Thomas is not who he says he is. Believe it or not, you actually hold the key to finding that out."

"How could I possibly do that? Thomas is the best person that I've ever known. He gave me a life when hope was fading fast. If he had not rescued me when he did I wouldn't have made it out this time, I'd completely lost hope. I can't betray him."

"There may be no need for you to." Schaffer held her like he would a frightened child. "Did you read about the serial killer case I uncovered?"

"I read a couple of your articles. The story was all over the news after Thanksgiving; it would have been hard to miss. What does that have to do with Thomas?"

Schaffer stroked her hair. "Hopefully, nothing. That's what we need to find out."

Rachel wiped her tears. "You've said *we* a couple of times. Who are you talking about?"

Schaffer sighed. "I'm working with the FBI. We've had you guys under surveillance since you left DC. We're surrounded by agents right now."

Rachel sat up and looked around. "Where are they?"

"Renita is an agent. She's been leading the charge to catch the killer. When we had dinner the other night we tried to make a positive ID, but Thomas left no fingerprints— on anything. He didn't look like what we expected. Renita tried to see his eyes; she said the ones she remembered were an unmistakable hazel color. Of course, Thomas didn't remove his sunglasses all night. Are his eyes hazel?"

Rachel nodded slowly. "A lot of people have hazel colored eyes."

Schaffer sat up and looked Rachel in the eyes. "Did you know he drugged you and Renita at dinner last night? You started having sex with him right in front of us on the beach."

Rachel struggled to remember. "I don't remember much after dinner. I don't even remember you leaving the restaurant, or us getting back to the hotel."

"That's because you were under the influence of GHB. They call it the date rape drug. It makes you very horny and you forget what you did after taking it. He gave that to you to control your actions and so you wouldn't remember anything." Schaffer paused a second to let his words sink in. "Have you noticed any changes in Thomas since you've known him? Have there been wide mood swings?"

Rachel's face held a hint of anger. "Why would Thomas give me drugs? He didn't need to; I would have done anything he asked."

"It's a form of control. It's as bad as what caused you to leave home in the first place. He took advantage of you." Schaffer could see his words struck a nerve.

Rachel thought about what Schaffer said for a long time. Her head fell back to his shoulder. "When Thomas went out of town he had surgery to repair a problem with his nose. Putting the dimple in his chin and having his skin tightened, I thought it was his way of trying to look younger, since I'm so much younger than he is. He even had a hair transplant using someone else's hair."

Schaffer felt his excitement grow. "Did he tell you before he made any of these changes?"

"No. He almost scared me to death when he came back." Rachel remembered the moment when she saw Thomas' face. "I thought it was odd, but I didn't want to question it. I didn't want to change what we've had."

"He's lied, or withheld the truth from you on several occasions. Something's wrong with that. What happened to trusting the person you love? Will you help us?" Schaffer could feel the weight of his question.

"What can I do?" Rachel's voice was filled with pain.

Schaffer held her even tighter than before. His words came out very slowly. "Right before you came out here you made love to Thomas. We need a specimen."

Rachel hit him in the chest and tears burst from her eyes. "Goddamnit! You watched me?" Her tears rolled out in waves and her chest heaved up and down. "I can't believe you did that. That's a violation no better than any other I've had to endure." Her sobs were heavy; she pulled away from him, wrapped her arms around herself, and rocked.

"I had to make sure he didn't try to kill you. I know all this hurts, but there was no other way to ensure your safety. If he's who we think he is, he's a very dangerous criminal. He's already killed eleven people and he's become more and more violent in the last killings. We've got to get him locked up. I promise the FBI will stand behind you and I will personally make sure your dreams of becoming a psychologist are fulfilled. You can count on me Rachel." He kissed her forehead and held her as she rocked and cried.

Rachel's crying eventually slowed. "You've hurt me Schaffer. You've destroyed my vacation and came close to destroying my life." Her tears fell silently. "I don't know why horrible shit always seems to find me. What did I ever do to deserve this type of pain?"

"You didn't do anything to deserve any of this. I'll be by your side, helping you to recover from this ordeal. Whatever it takes, I'll make sure you get it." Schaffer kissed her again.

"You'd better be right about Thomas. If you're wrong, I'll never forgive you." Rachel's body felt as if the effects of gravity had just doubled for her, she felt too heavy to move.

Schaffer helped her up. "Come on, the van is waiting for us."

Chapter
59

Renita helped Rachel into the van and turned to Schaffer. "Why don't you wait here? I'll see you in a few minutes."

Rachel tapped Renita's shoulder. "If he's not coming, neither am I."

"I was just concerned about your privacy." Renita assured Rachel.

Rachel looked at the other agent in the van. "I remember her. She was our waitress at dinner last night. I guess you're an agent too. From what Schaffer tells me you've all been watching my home movies, so everyone here has already seen what I've got, including Schaffer. At least I know I can trust him."

Renita reached out to him. "If the lady wants you aboard, then you're aboard."

Schaffer stepped in the van and it pulled off. "It's going to be okay, I promise."

Rachel rested on a cot in the van while Renita and the other female agent waited to retrieve a specimen. She held Schaffer's hand and looked in his eyes. She sat up abruptly. "I can't do this. Not until I look in Thomas' eyes when I ask him about it. He can't lie to me."

"That's too dangerous. If you say something about what we expect, he may snap and kill you before we have a chance to stop him." Schaffer held her hand tightly as if he wouldn't let her move.

"Let me go!" She jerked her hand from Schaffer. "You can't make me do this if I don't want to."

Renita took over. "It will only take a few minutes to get a search warrant, but I don't want to do that. Your life is in danger, this is the way we can prove it to you."

"Thomas has never raised a hand to me. He has only been kind, considerate and trusting, which is more that I can say about any of you. None of you care about my feelings." Rachel looked at Schaffer in an accusatory fashion. "Stop this car. I want to get out."

Schaffer touched her shoulder. "Come on, I'll walk with you. I want you to think about things a while."

"I don't want you anywhere around me. I feel violated by you the most. You have no idea how disappointed I am." Rachel pounded her fists on the cot. "Stop this van now."

"Rachel, don't you care about the eleven other people who died by his hands?" Renita pleaded, trying to ease her back onto the cot.

"You have no proof that Thomas had anything to do with those killings. If you did, you wouldn't be asking me for anything." Rachel looked Renita in her eyes.

Renita put her hands on her hips. "Don't you want to know for sure?"

"I will know when I ask Thomas." Rachel reached for the door. "I'm getting out of here whether you stop or not."

The van pulled over and Rachel got out. She turned and looked at Schaffer, who was sitting in the doorway. "Don't even waste your breath to speak. I'm not sure I will ever want to speak to you again."

He watched as Rachel walked away disappearing into the shopping village. "Never underestimate the blindness caused by love."

Renita had her arms folded across her chest. "That's okay. We've got a warrant for the room. When she takes a shower we'll pick up her underwear. They'll contain all the evidence we need."

What if she's not wearing any?" The agent asked.

"Then find me something with some evidence on it."

◆

Rachel got back to her suite and Thomas was in the shower. She poured a stiff drink of Vodka and drank it straight down. She walked into the shower. "I'm back."

"What did you get?" Thomas yelled from behind the curtain.

"I got some things for a few friends back home. I found you a nice pair of shorts." She laid them in the bathroom and started walking out. She turned at the door. "I ran into Schaffer in one of the shops."

Thomas slid the curtain back. "What did he have to say?"

Rachel detected the coldness in his voice. "He talked about dinner last night and what a good time he had with us. Maybe we should get together with them again before they leave on Monday."

"I don't think so. I've seen enough of people for a while. I just want to be with you." Thomas' words were hollow. "I'm going out for a swim. Would you like to come?"

"I think I'm going to shower and lay around for a while, if you don't mind." Rachel yelled from the other room as she refilled her Vodka glass.

Thomas walked in with his towel around him. "What did Schaffer say about me?"

She took a sip of the drink. "Not much. Just that you seemed to be an okay guy and that you reminded him of someone."

Thomas charged over and grabbed Rachel by the side of her arms shook her and yelled. "Who did he say I reminded him of?"

Rachel jerked back. "That hurt. What the hell is wrong with you? He said you reminded him of someone he grew up with."

Thomas hugged her. "I'm sorry. I didn't mean to act like that. I guess the lack of sleep it catching up to me. Do you forgive me?"

Rachel looked at the floor. She was thinking about who Schaffer suggested Thomas might be. She felt drained, but knew she had to keep up the act. "I forgive you; just don't let anything like that happen again."

"It won't. Just stay away from Schaffer. I don't like him. He always seems like he's up to something. If I didn't know you better I would say he was trying to take you away from me. I'll fight him to the death if he ever tries."

"Schaffer has someone special. He's just a good friend that looked out for me when no one else cared. I'll always owe him for that." Rachel listened to herself and realized she felt the same way about Thomas.

Thomas went to his bag and pulled out an envelope. "I was going to give you this last night, but I wanted to wait until we were alone."

Rachel smiled. She still enjoyed surprises, regardless of the circumstance. "What is it?"

Thomas handed it to her. "It's the deed to a house I bought for you. It's nestled in the country in Fredericksburg, VA. With the high-speed train you can be at Georgetown in less than an hour. I figured it would give us the added privacy we need."

Rachel took the envelope and sat down and cried. She wanted to hug him but couldn't move. "Thank you."

Thomas slid on his new shorts and left the room with another envelope in his hand. He gave it to the attendant at the front desk and was given another small manila envelope. He turned it upside down and a new pair of keys fell into his hand. He put them into the pocket of his shorts and headed to the beach.

Agents watched him closely as he walked to the far end of the beach to a boat pier. He got on a forty-five foot Sea Ray 460 Sundancer. He cranked it with the keys from his shorts and roared away. The agent read the name on the side, *D8 with V*. He radioed in. "Agent Duplechain, we've got a problem. The suspect just got on a boat. 'D8 with V' was on the side. He could be going somewhere to kill again."

"Is Rachel in her room?" Renita asked.

"Yes. She's in the shower." The agent monitoring the screen said.

"Get someone down there. Take the underwear she was wearing before she got in the shower. Then, get out of there before she realizes you're there."

"That's going to be a problem. She flushed the only thing she had on under that sundress."

"Damnit! We'll just have to forget it for now; we've got to get after Thomas. Have someone call for a chopper." Renita barked her orders. "It's time we take Thomas down. When Rachel comes out of the shower pick her up and move her to the safe house. Sit on her until I get back."

Chapter
60

Renita waited on the beach with three other agents, for the Coast Guard helicopter. Schaffer stood nearby, concerned by their late start. "He'll be in international waters in a matter of minutes. What happens once he's there?"

"Article 23 of the United Nations' *Convention on the High Seas* allows us to continue pursuit of a suspect once engaged. This time we're bringing him in. He has nowhere to run." Renita looked out at the water. She knew the ocean offered no cover for Thomas. "Stay with Rachel, she's going to need your support."

"I hope you find him quickly." Schaffer looked at his watch, confirming what he already knew. "There's only a little sunlight left today." "Call me as soon as you arrest him."

"I may not have time. Get a radio from the monitoring room. You'll be able to hear everything on it." The helicopter's noise filled the air. Renita kissed Schaffer. "I've got to go. I love you."

Schaffer helped her onto the helicopter and walked back to the hotel. FBI agents were everywhere. He stopped by the room Rachel and Thomas once shared. The agents sweeping the suite invited him in.

Schaffer was careful where he stepped. "You guys have any luck finding anything yet?"

"It's what we haven't found that is the most shocking. All of the suspect's luggage and clothing are gone."

"Shouldn't someone have seen luggage leaving the room?" Schaffer pointed towards one of the overhead cameras.

"They should have, but anything could have happened. I suspect it would have only taken a few seconds to hand bags to a bellman. If you switched cameras to check another room, or got up to get a cup of coffee you could have missed the whole thing. We're reviewing the tapes and interviewing the bellmen on duty. We should know something soon.

Schaffer left for his room. On the way to his room he stopped by the monitoring room and got a radio to listen to any action. He had to pack their things, he and Renita would be moving to the safe house with Rachel until they returned to the mainland on Monday.

The Coast Guard 270 foot Cutter spotted Thomas' boat and engaged pursuit. "This is Crow's Nest. We have the boat in sight and are initiating chase."

The radio crackled. "Roger, Crow's Nest. We should be joining you in approximately fifteen minutes. We've been advised that the suspect should be considered armed and dangerous, approach with caution."

"Roger, Eagle's Wing. We'll treat the boat as hostile."

The Sea Ray 460 Sundancer was no match for the much larger Coast Guard ship. The Coast Guard Cutter caught up to Thomas' boat minutes later. "This is the United States Coast Guard. Cut your engines and prepare to be boarded." The Captain demanded over the loudspeakers.

The warning was ignored and the Sundancer continued on its path. The Coast Guard Captain gave an order and several rounds from a 50cal machine gun flew across the bow of Thomas' boat. The Captain then repeated his command.

The Sundancer began to slow as the engines ceased their thrusting. A crew of twenty men stood on the deck of the Cutter with their M-16 rifles pointed at the Sundancer. They pulled along side the boat and deployed.

A young boy about seventeen or eighteen stepped from the helm with his hands raised. "Don't shoot. He paid me to pilot the boat out here."

The Coast Guard crew never lowered their weapons. "Where is he now?"

The boy shrugged his shoulders. "I don't know. I came from below after we left and he told me to maintain the direction. He said if I looked back he would take the money he gave me. I saw him in a wetsuit and heard him walk to the back of the boat. I haven't seen or heard him since."

The Coast Guard crew checked every square inch of the boat and found nothing. The helicopter landed on the deck of the Cutter as the men completed their search.

Renita jumped from the helicopter wearing a bulletproof vest and carrying her gun. "Is he in custody?" She yelled to the men on the Sundancer.

"No, ma'am. This boy is the only one on the boat. He said the suspect had a wetsuit on, my guess is he's in the water somewhere."

"Damnit!" Renita holstered her gun, but wanted to fire it several times into the side of the boat. "Were you supposed to come back and pick him up?" She asked the boy.

"All he told me to do was to come out here as far as I could before someone stopped me. He gave me a thousand dollars and told me I could keep the boat until he came back."

A seaplane flew past the boats off in the distance. Renita watched it then summoned an agent. "Get on the radio to the base. Have them shut down all travel from the island until we're able to check for Thomas. Make sure they shut everything down, private and public aircraft as well."

From his seat on the seaplane, Thomas looked through binoculars at the boats in the water. By the time anyone knew he had left St. Johns he would be in Costa Rica.

CHAPTER
61

Thomas was only in Costa Rica long enough to charter a jet to take him back to Fredericksburg. The proper amount of cash erased the pilot's memories and flight log documents as well.

His final act as an American citizen would be the elimination of the man who brought him the unwanted attention. Thomas knew that Renita would be with Schaffer when they arrived in Fredericksburg. Killing her would be a bonus.

The note Thomas left for Rachel at the desk was ultimately for Schaffer. He gave her specific instructions to give it to O'Grady no more than an hour before landing in D.C. In it he hinted at surrendering at his home in Fredericksburg, providing Schaffer and Renita came alone to get him. Thomas was in a rush to get to Fredericksburg first so that he could prepare for his grand finale.

During the flight from Costa Rica, Thomas wrote a letter to Rachel. In an eight by ten envelope he placed the insurance policy for the house in Fredericksburg. Both the house and insurance policy had been transferred to her name. He also included bank account information for an account in the Grand Caymans. During his trip three weeks ago, Thomas transferred the Thomas Brothers account to one he'd established in the Caymans. He left Rachel instructions in his letter.

My Dearest Rachel,

I realize things are very confusing right now. I won't begin to try and explain anything today. There will be time for that later.

The documents in this envelope are for you. I have established an account in your name in the Grand Caymans. No one but you can get to this money. I'll tell you the same thing my dad told me in a letter almost twenty years ago. The money is invested to maximize its growth. Never use more than half the interest this account generates per year and the six million will double in ten years.

I want you to promise me you will finish school at Georgetown. Once you become a licensed psychologist, publish it in the Washington Post and I will send for you. I'll miss you until then.

Thomas
    Thomas addressed the envelope and mailed it once he was on the ground.

♦

    Renita, Rachel and Schaffer flew from St. Johns on an early flight Sunday morning.

    Two hours into the flight Rachel handed Schaffer the envelope Thomas left at the front desk. She closed her eyes and lay back in her seat.

    "What's this?" Shaffer asked taking the unopened envelope.

    Rachel tilted her head in his direction. "I don't know. I was told to give it to you today at this time."

    Schaffer ripped it open and read the note.

Mr. O'Grady,

    You started this mess we find ourselves in. Only you can end it.

    As a reporter you are a prisoner to your curiosity. You require resolution of those stories that have baffled you, such as the one you've covered for the past four months. I commend your efforts that have delivered you to your current level of understanding. That however, is only part of the story. I will answer your remaining questions tonight at my home in Fredericksburg.

    Of course, I must make a few stipulations for your visit. First, I know you won't come without your sidekick, Agent Duplechain. She's welcome, however, no one else is to come with you two. The consequences of disobeying these restrictions will be grave. I have taken measures to ensure the death of anyone who does not heed my warning.

    Your plane will touch down at Dulles at 3 p.m. You've got until 5 p.m. to reach my home. You know the way as you've already been here last Tuesday. I'm W8ing. Don't miss your D8 with F8.

Ex-8-cutioner

    Schaffer tapped Renita, who was trying to sleep. "You need to see this."

    Renita sat up and read the letter. "I'll get on the phone and have a team meet us at Dulles. We're going to need a full strike force in place when we get to Fredericksburg."

Schaffer checked his watch. "We land in thirty minutes. Is that going to be enough time to put a strike force together?"

"You'd be surprised what we can put together in a short period of time." Renita pulled the phone from the back of the seat in front of her and called FBIHQ.

The plane touched down at 3 p.m. Three unmarked cars and a van waited for Renita, Rachel, and Schaffer on the tarmac.

Rachel was whisked away in one car, taking her to a safe location until Thomas was in custody. Even though she didn't fear for her life, the FBI did.

Renita and Schaffer were put into bulletproof vests and FBI raid jackets and hats. Blue lights came on as the van and two cars sped from the tarmac heading to Fredericksburg.

Renita lifted the radio. "This is Special Agent Duplechain. No one is to enter the grounds of the suspect's house before we arrive. He has issued specific threats to anyone trying to enter other than Mr. O'Grady and me. He is capable of anything and shouldn't be taken lightly. There's an open field across from the turn to his house. The helicopter can set down there. We will arrive in forty five minutes."

In the van Renita and Schaffer were wired with hands-free microphones and transmitters. They would use them to communicate with the rest of the team.

Schaffer slid a 9mm Uzi into a holster and strapped it on. "I feel like I'm back in Re-con carrying all this heat."

"We need to be ready for war with this sonofabitch. He's not going to give up without a fight." Renita strapped her Glock onto her chest in addition to the Uzi on her hip.

"Mr. O'Grady, would you like a spare sidearm?" An agent asked him.

"No. If I can't get it done with this one, I doubt the extra will help."

Renita lifted her cell phone. "I've got to call Tina. I haven't talked to her since we got to St. Johns."

"That's a good idea. Let me speak to Joe when you're finished." Schaffer knew the call was more than touching base; it was a contingency in case they didn't make it out alive.

"Hi baby. Mommy's going to be late getting in. I've got something to deal with at the office first." Renita could feel a lump rise in her throat.

"Are you chasing some bad people again? You always come home first if you aren't." Tina showed no fear talking to Renita.

"You're too smart for me. I can never pull anything over on you. I love you baby. I'll see you soon."

"I'll be fine mommy. You make sure you're careful. Can I speak to Schaffer?"

Renita handed Schaffer the phone. "She wants to talk to you."

"What's my girl up to? Did you miss me?" Schaffer asked.

Tina was direct getting to her point. "Are you going to be with mommy?"

"Every step of the way."

"Don't let anything bad happen to her. I need her to come home." Tina couldn't hide the fear in her voice now.

Schaffer swallowed hard trying to maintain his composure. "I'll take good care of her. We'll be home soon. I love you little girl."

"Me too." Tina said and hung up the phone.

Chapter
62

Bacchus dialed Schaffer's cell number for nearly the hundredth time; just as before, it went unanswered. He had visited Dirk's house in Fredericksburg. He'd found the lab in which Dirk had prepared the drugs he'd used on his victims, but he'd found nothing else. The house filled Bacchus with a persistent uneasy feeling.

Since he had not heard from Schaffer, Bacchus was trying to make contact. He didn't know if Dirk had been taken into custody, which added to his unease. Bacchus didn't like leaving not knowing if they had been successful at bringing in a killer.

The last time he'd felt this unsettled, his life had been ripped apart. Though, Schaffer was not Bacchus' family, he was as close a friend as Bacchus had allowed himself. If he didn't act on his feelings and something happened to Schaffer, he could never forgive himself.

Bacchus had already left Schaffer about twenty messages. He knew that Schaffer was scheduled to return today; according to what Schaffer had told him, the plane should have been on the ground twenty minutes ago.

Bacchus fumbled with his cell phone trying to send a text message to Schaffer. Finally, he remembered he could send one easier by using his computer. His anxiousness grew waiting for the computer to boot up. As quickly as he could, Bacchus sent Schaffer a text message. Impatiently, he waited for his cell phone to ring, but nothing ever happened.

Bacchus' restlessness transformed to irritation. He couldn't sit by and wait any longer; what he was feeling wasn't right. He opened his closet, reached up, and retrieved his M24 sniper rifle. The uncomfortable feeling Dirk's house had given Bacchus had stayed with him. In his mind, that was where the problem would be.

Bacchus jumped on I-95 north heading to Dirk's house in Fredericksburg, VA. If he pushed it, he could be there in about and hour and a half. As he began the trip he had no way of knowing that the FBI already had a team in place.

♦

Bacchus rounded a curve way too fast for the road he was on and had to break aggressively in order to avoid hitting the FBI team blocking the road. The FBI team trained their M-16s on Bacchus' car as it skidded to a stop.

On of the agents approached the car. "Sir, we're closing this area. Do you live around here?"

Bacchus didn't hesitate. "Yeah, about a mile or so down the road."

The agent looked over at other members of the team. Receiving a nod from the team leader, he bent down to Bacchus' window. "Okay, you can go through. Slowly this time, I wouldn't want you to run into anyone."

Bacchus attempted a weak smile, but his lips never made it past a straight line. "Thanks."

Bacchus' mind was working overtime. He knew that the FBI would have every inch of the area covered. Before pulling off, he signaled to the agent still standing next to his window.

"Sir, I need you to move along."

Bacchus flashed the DEA creds that he'd never bothered to return when he resigned. "You boys seem as if you're about to tangle with someone. Is it something we neighbors should know about?"

The agent looked closely at Bacchus' creds. "Everything is under control. Just make sure you keep your family inside. We should be finished here soon."

Bacchus took his creds back rolled the window up and pulled off. Immediately, he began looking for somewhere he could set up. About a quarter mile away, he pulled the car over and climbed to the top of a hill. He donned his Guilly suit and dug in using leaves and branches to conceal his position. Then he brought the M24's scope to his eye to locate the FBI agents positioned as snipers.

Bacchus switched his cell phone to 'silent' and positioned it next to him on the ground. He prayed Schaffer would call to let him know what was going on. Whatever it was, he knew it couldn't be good.

Chapter
63

The FBI van and cars arrived at the makeshift command center set up in the field near Thomas' house. Renita and Schaffer met the agent in charge of the operation.

"Mr. O'Grady, I can't let a civilian go into a situation like this."

Schaffer turned to him. "You don't have a choice. I'm the only person he is willing to communicate with. I understand the risks involved. Let's just get it over with."

Renita confirmed Schaffer's statement. "He's right. He's our best hope of resolving this case and bringing Thomas to justice."

"We're not even sure he's in there. This whole setup could be a trap. I don't like it one damn bit." The agent's face was crimson with concern. He turned around. "Put that chopper in the air. I want it over the house at all times."

Renita and Schaffer entered the lead car. She rolled down the window. "Wish us luck."

Schaffer pulled the car into the driveway and slowly proceeded towards the house. When the car hit the pressure plate blinding floodlights came on, quickly followed by a loudspeaker.

"Stop." Thomas yelled. "Only the car carrying Mr. O'Grady and Agent Duplechain can come forward. Anyone else who attempts to come onto the grounds is taking their lives into their own hands. I promise you, they will not survive. The car that is sitting on the pressure plate has just activated enough C-4 to blow you all to hell. Be my guest if you think this is a bluff."

Renita spoke into her mouthpiece. "Back off, guys. We'll be fine."

The SAC pulled his men back and formed two groups on either side of the driveway. "After they're in we'll approach on foot through these trees."

Schaffer stopped the car in front of the house. Before he got out of the car he leaned over and kissed Renita. "I love you. Now let's get this bastard."

They walked in the front door and Thomas' voice could be heard over an intercom. "Welcome. Lock the deadbolt and toss the key into the living room fireplace on your right.

Schaffer locked the door and tossed the key. "That fireplace would be hard to miss. It's the largest one I've ever seen."

"Thank you, Mr. O'Grady. I had it and two others designed after some I saw in a castle in Europe. I'm sure your friends outside are listening to our conversation so this is for their benefit. The deadbolt has just activated additional explosives at all the entry points to the house. If anyone tries to enter everyone inside dies." He turned his attention back to Schaffer. "If you two would be so kind, look around the windows and doors."

Renita spoke into her mike. "He's telling the truth. Everything is wired with what appears to be packs of C-4."

An explosion outside startled Renita and Schaffer. "What the hell was that?" Schaffer asked.

The loud speakers outside came on again. "I see you have found one of my land mines. If there is another explosion, I'll blow this house up with everyone in it. Now back the fuck up!" Thomas was yelling. "Why must you people continue to doubt my resolve?"

"Would you just keep everyone back?" Schaffer yelled into his mike. The stress in his voice was evident.

"Let's hope they take your advice Mr. O'Grady. Now, continue down the foyer. There's a door to your right just as you come to the family room. Open it and come down to the basement. There, we can solve any dilemmas you have."

Schaffer lead the way. On the stairwell he pulled the Uzi from its holster. Renita did the same. "I don't like this. It looks eerie down there." Renita noticed the flickering lights.

The basement was lit by candles, which were all over the floor. "Sorry there's no place for you to sit. Victoria saw to it that nothing remained when she left."

"What did you do with Victoria?" Schaffer asked.

"What will I do to Victoria once I find her is a better question. If I had found her first, none of the other women would have died. They were surrogates for Victoria because they had the same Enneagram personality type."

Renita started to probe. "You had everything, a good job, millions of dollars in a corporation you controlled and a beautiful young woman who loves you. Why would you give all that up by killing these innocent women?"

"Turn to your left and walk into my lab." Thomas began to sound irritated. "I didn't have shit. Dr. Gerard had it all. He thought he could control me by making me live in one of these damn things."

Renita and Schaffer stepped into the lab. Mirrors surrounded them. The room had the feel of a carnival attraction. They could see Thomas' reflection in several of the mirrors and knew he was close by.

Schaffer spoke to one of the reflections. "You are Dirk Gerard, Thomas, so he couldn't control you; you're one and the same person."

"I thought you were better than that Mr. O'Grady. Dirk made me live in here." Thomas pointed to a mirror. "Any time I wanted to talk to him he demanded I only approach him as a reflection. As long as my image came out of a mirror, a piece of glass, or water he allowed me to talk. He said that was his way of keeping me under control, as if letting me out would upset the universe. Did you ever notice that Dirk wore two cell phones? That's because one was mine, it was the only way he could hear me and he let me call whenever I wanted to. But, after that bitch left him, I started getting out of the mirrors. Before he knew what had happened, I was back inside his body. I let him think he was in charge by letting him suppress me when he needed to interact with people like you two. Ultimately, there was only room in this body for one master so I killed Dr. Gerard and took over, assuming my rightful position. He declared me dead once before, but he was wrong. Thomas lives!"

Renita and Schaffer looked at each other. "He's come full circle; back to the person he started out as years ago." Schaffer watched the reflection and looked for its origin. "Thomas, answer another question for me. Why did you kill both Black and White women?"

"You're slipping Mr. O'Grady. Your investigative skills need some polishing. You're spending too much time around the FBI."

"We know about Thomas Walker." Renita said.

"So, you've found the old bitch. Tell me where she is and maybe we'll all get out of here alive. She can give me who I really want."

"You haven't answered my question yet." Schaffer said.

"If you know about Thomas Walker, then you should already know that my mother abused me as a child and you should also know that dad killed her. I'm simply following his lead, except I'm taking a more proactive approach." Thomas stopped to reflect. "I've let two women abuse me, Victoria and my whore of a mother. I'm not giving anyone else the chance to do it again. Now, where is she?" Thomas' body tensed.

"She's safely tucked away where you'll never find her you sick fuck." Renita yelled at one of the reflections. She grew restless waiting for something to happen. "Why haven't you killed Rachel yet?"

"You leave her out of this." Thomas pointed the octagon-barrel rifle.

"I can't, she's an accessory. Besides, she withheld evidence. She'll probably do some jail time." Renita said to provoke a reaction.

"If you hurt her I'll fucking kill you." Thomas was in a rage. He lifted the rifle to his shoulder and fired.

Schaffer fell to the ground knocking Renita down as well. One of the mirrors shattered sending shards of glass raining down. In their ears they heard someone cry. "Shots fired, shots fired."

The SAC's voice came on next. "Get the HRT in there now."

Schaffer kept his body over Renita's and whispered. "Now we know his Achilles heel. He really is in love with Rachel."

"Yes, and she feels the same way about him. We've got to try and use it to flush him out." Renita positioned her microphone in front of her mouth. "Chief, don't forget the bombs on all the windows and doors."

"A team's on the way in. We'll cut through the walls."

The helicopter hovered near the house and a team of men repelled down fast ropes. A buzzing sound could be heard, followed by the unmistakable sound of a chain saw cutting through the side of the house.

Thomas' voice came over the loudspeakers. "You stupid fuckers have refused to listen to reason. Now you will pay for your insolence." Thomas ran past the mirrors.

Renita caught a glimpse as he ducked behind one of the ceiling length mirrors. "There he is." She fired the Uzi from a prone position, shattering the mirrors.

Thomas darted into a door on the back wall of the basement. He pressed a series of buttons on a control panel in the hidden room and explosions began outside. The pressure plate was the first, blowing bits of metal high into the air. Then the land minds exploded knocking down trees in their path. The house was last. Packets on the windows and doors exploded. Thomas had not used C-4 on them, but a combination of chemicals that started a brilliant fire. All the exits were cut off, including the stair well leading from the basement upstairs.

Schaffer pulled Renita from the floor. "Come on. We've got to get out of here." They could hear screams above the roar of the fire, from men that had tried to reach them but would never make it.

Everywhere they attempted, fire challenged their escape. "We're in a lot of trouble down here. This place is going up fast." Renita moved closer to Schaffer.

He looked around desperately for any sign of hope. "Over there." Schaffer pointed to the connecting room. "That's our way out." He tugged Renita's arm and ran to the fireplace. He bent down and looked up. "We're lucky. It's got rungs inside. Get in, up you go."

They climbed into the fireplace chimney and Schaffer closed the flue behind them. The chimney narrowed near the top so they could only climb up about half way. Above their heads they could see the flames lapping around the top of the chimney.

Renita pointed to the opening. "If that fire continues to burn around there we could loose all our oxygen."

"We'll be okay if we don't bake in the heat first. The chimney's fairly thick, that should help insulate us. Loosen your belt and attach it to a rung. If you pass out it will keep you from falling."

They both fastened their belts around rungs. "I hope the fire department gets here fast. It's starting to get hot as hell in here." Renita wiped away sweat from her head.

Oxygen levels grew low and both Renita and Schaffer passed out, leaving their belts to keep them in place. They hung precariously, with their heads and arms loosely dangling.

The fire department worked furiously to put out the fire, but it refused to give an inch. Within thirty minutes the house burned to the ground leaving only the two chimneys standing on either side of the foundation. The firemen dumped water onto the smoldering coals, most of which sizzled into the hole that was once the basement.

A host of FBI agents stood by helplessly, as the steam rose from the charred hole in the ground. Many, who worked closely with Renita and Schaffer, openly wept at the apparent loss of their friends.

"We don't stand a chance of recovering the bodies until morning." The SAC said as he looked on in disbelief. "I'll have to wait until then before telling her daughter. That's one call I wish I never have to make."

♦

Working late into the night under the powerful illumination of floodlights the fire department located the remains of three charred bodies in the rubble. The FBI agent that stayed behind with the firemen was Renita's closest associate. When the first body was pulled from the coals he broke down, falling to his knees in tears.

"I wish I knew which of these bodies is Thomas'. I'd piss on it before I stomped his bones to dust." Through his tears and pain he called the SAC with the news as the remains were placed in body bags.

Chapter
64

The sun rose around the smoldering ashes at 5:45 a.m. Schaffer's hand twitched and slowly his eyes opened. His body hurt all over from the intense heat he endured during the fire. Both he and Renita were covered in soot.

He reached up and shook Renita, but she didn't move. Frantically, he unhooked his belt and climbed up to her. He took her belt off the rung and carried her limp body down the chimney. When he reached the flue he had to kick it several times before it opened.

As quickly as he could he carried Renita across the coals and made his way to the grass near the stairs leading down the cliff to the boat ramp. He felt for a pulse. "Come on babe, you've got to be alright." Schaffer lightly slapped the sides of her face.

He heard something moving quickly near the edge of the trees about twenty-five yards from where he knelt next to Renita. Thomas bolted from the bushes carrying the octagon-barrel rifle. "Goddamnit, what does it take for you two to die?" He grabbed Schaffer by his hair from behind, jerking him from Renita's side.

"You killed her. Now it's your turn to die." Schaffer scrambled to his knees.

Thomas lowered the rifle pressing it against Schaffer's head. "I don't think so Mr. O'Grady. I'm already dead, for the second time, I might add. At least that's what the FBI believes. I had an escape tunnel put in the house years ago. I didn't even tell Victoria. I didn't want that bitch to escape harm. I never knew when I would need a quick escape. The damn thing finally came in handy."

"You're a sadistic, sick fuck! Someone will kill you before it's all over. You can't run forever." Schaffer wanted to spit, but his mouth was coated with thick black soot.

"Get on your feet. You're about to have an accident over this cliff." Thomas held the rifle at Schaffer's chest. "I'll give you a choice. You can dive onto the pier below, or I can shoot you first."

One thought constantly pulsed through Schaffer's head; Master Po's three foot rule. He remembered what his Kung Fu instructor had told him twenty years earlier. *Never let a guy with a gun kill you if he's less than three feet away.* He reached out and grabbed the barrel of the rifle spinning away from the barrel. A shot rang out splitting the silence of the morning.

The bullet exploding through the rifle barrel made it too hot for Schaffer to hold on to. He released it and Thomas stumbled a few steps away.

"So, Mr. O'Grady, the mouse wants to toy with the cat. Don't you know, the cat always wins." Thomas took his time raising the rifle to his shoulder. "For good measure, I want to ensure the bitch is dead first."

Schaffer jumped to block Thomas' line of fire to Renita. Two quick shots rang out. Schaffer spun towards Renita. His heart fell. He wanted to lunge at Thomas, tearing his throat from his body. But he slipped in the wet grass, causing him to land beside Renita.

During his fall, Schaffer did not notice any explosion of blood, or the invariable signs of pain that came along with being struck by a bullet. Schaffer hit the ground and spun with cat-like agility, expecting to see the barrel of Thomas' gun trained on him. Instead, Thomas was gone.

Renita moaned, raising her head as if she was trying to sit up.

"Renita! You're okay." Schaffer rushed to her side.

Renita fell back to the wet grass. "I'm alive. Okay remains to be seen." Her hand went to her head. "I've got one hell of a headache."

Schaffer kissed Renita's soot covered face. "How'd you get those shots off?"

Renita managed to roll her head to one side and open one eye. "I didn't shoot, I thought it was you."

Schaffer looked back to where Thomas had been standing. "He must have stepped backwards and fell over the cliff. I guess the shots we heard came from the rifle he was holding."

Renita gripped Schaffer's shoulder to sit herself up. "Even as out of it as I was, I know those shots didn't come from a rifle. That was a handgun."

Schaffer was the first to hear the approaching footsteps. He slid his hand to Renita's leg holster gripping her Glock.

"I hope you don't plan on pulling that gun out to use it on me."

Schaffer relaxed his grip. His head fell to Renita's shoulder and he welled with emotion. "Tree."

Bacchus' monstrous hand gently gripped Schaffer's shoulder. "I don't think he'll be bothering anyone again."

Renita looked up to Bacchus' face. He was on one knee beside them and she still had to lean back to see his face. "I guess 'Tree' is a reference to Redwood."

Schaffer laughed and for the first time in years, Bacchus smiled. Schaffer hugged his friend and they both helped Renita to her feet. "No, not Redwood; Tree refers to the size of his arms because everyone used to say they're the size of tree trunks."

Bacchus held Renita gently. "The name's Bacchus Jones, ma'am."

Renita rolled her eyes a little. "There's got to be a story behind that."

Bacchus smiled for the second time. "Yes, ma'am, I'll tell you when you're well enough to share a drink with me."

"May I ask you one question now though?"

"Shoot."

"How did you just happen to be out here to ride to our rescue?"

Bacchus looked at Schaffer for help and quickly decided on the truth. "I've kinda been helping O'Grady here with the case. I knew you guys were scheduled to be back last night and I was calling him like crazy. The problem was, he didn't call me back. I'd been here to the house while you guys were in St. Johns and to tell you the truth, I just had a bad feeling about this place."

Renita cut her eyes sharply at Schaffer. "I guess it's lucky for us that Schaffer never told me about you. I surely would have told him to keep you away from the case."

"Bacchus is trained." Schaffer knew he'd better speak up. "He spent years with the DEA, but now he's private. We were having such a tough time that I thought an extra pair of eyes could help. Damn glad I did too."

Renita's eyes maintained their severe tilt in Schaffer's direction. "When did you happen to arrive on the scene?"

"I got here right after the first wave of your team arrived. I told them I lived just down the road and flashed my DEA creds, so they let me go." Bacchus pointed to a hill about a quarter mile away. "I set up over there. When the house went up and everyone left after pulling three bodies from the rubble, the nagging feeling just wouldn't let go of me. I started slowly making my way to the house last night."

Schaffer couldn't believe it. "You stayed out here all night?"

Bacchus hunched his shoulders. "Yeah, man. When I saw you run out with your girlfriend a few minutes ago, I knew I'd done the right thing. Shit, you weren't out of that heap of ashes three seconds before I heard that sick bastard moving. When he pointed the gun at you guys I knew I had to act quickly. Sorry, I know you wanted him alive."

Renita looked around. "Where is he?"

Bacchus nodded. I hit him with two, one in the shoulder and the other dead center. He went over the cliff."

"Good for you, now let me make sure that bustard's dead." Schaffer walked to the side of the cliff and looked over. "He's not going anywhere. He looks like a pretzel covered in ketchup."

Renita pointed to her car. "My cell phone is in there. Call for help."

Schaffer got the phone from the charred car, it was destroyed as well. Bacchus was already handing his to Schaffer, who dialed 911. After requesting an ambulance he called the Hoover Building. "This is Schaffer O'Grady. Agent Duplechain and I are headed to the hospital."

"Who the hell is this?" The agent asked. "It's a federal offense to lie to an agent. If you're playing some kind of sick joke, I'll personally see to it that you have a long visit to one of our nastier federal prisons."

"Renita, you'd better talk to them. They don't believe me." Schaffer handed her the phone.

"Who's the bonehead on the line?" She said to the agent on the other end.

The agent turned to the others in the room. "It's agent Duplechain, she's alive." Cheers went up in the background. "How did you manage that? That fire was brutal."

"I'll tell you later. Did everyone make it away okay yesterday?"

"We lost three agents last night and two are in critical condition in a burn unit. He paused. "The SAC just left Joe DeApuzzo's house. He went by to tell them about you two."

"I've got to go. Tina is probably a wreck." Renita hung up and dialed Joe's number.

Nina answered the phone. "This is really a bad time. May we call you back?" Renita could hear her sniffing and the crying in the background. Tears came to her eyes. "But, Nina, you didn't even ask who it was."

Nina fell to her knees. "Renita? Oh my God, is that really you?"

"Thanks to the guardian Angel you introduced me to and a good friend of his. If it hadn't been for Schaffer's foresight to bring Bacchus in, we'd both be dead."

Nina sat the phone down. "Tina, Joe, it's Renita. They're alive, both of them!"

Tina ran to the phone. "Mommy?"

"Yes baby, it's me. Tell Uncle Joe to bring you to Bethesda Naval Hospital in an hour. We are headed there now."

Tina hung up the phone without another word. She turned to Joe. "We've got to go now. Mommy is on her way to the hospital. I've got to be there when she arrives, she needs me."

Sirens wailed as an ambulance and police cruiser made their way to Thomas' house. Schaffer and Renita walked down the driveway. The ambulance, police, and FBI arrived at the scene together. Their vehicles couldn't get past the crater Thomas made last night, so the agents, police and EMTs jumped from their cars to help Renita and Schaffer.

Schaffer helped Renita onto the stretcher and turned to the agents. "Thomas the Dead Tiger is just over the cliff back there." Schaffer pointed the direction where the house used to stand. "He's on the pier at the bottom. Shoot him a few more times. I want to be sure that fucker's dead."

◆

Bacchus left when he heard the approaching sirens. He didn't want to have any more interaction with law enforcement than was necessary. So Renita promised that she would cover him for killing Thomas. She knew that Bacchus was a valuable asset and she may need him again if things ever got as crazy as they had been on this case.

Bacchus felt human for the first time in years. He'd saved a friend, keeping his budding family in tact. He longed for his family, knowing he would never seen them again, but saving Schaffer and Renita somehow eased his pain a bit. The warm feeling in his chest brought tears, not for his loss, but because finally felt alive again.

Chapter

65

Renita and Schaffer arrived at Walter Reed. Tina, Nina and Joe were waiting in the emergency room for them. Schaffer climbed out of the ambulance and Tina ran through the doors to meet them.

Schaffer took Tina's hand to prevent her from climbing onto the stretcher with her mom. "She's going to be fine. She's too tough and ornery to die."

Renita raised her head. "If I wasn't tied down here I'd kick you." She smiled at Tina. "Hey baby. I'm okay, just a little crispy." Renita had to laugh at her unintended joke. She was covered with soot and appeared more blackened than fried.

The SAC met the stretcher just inside the emergency room. He looked at Renita and Schaffer. "Damn, it's good to see the two of you. I'm afraid I've got some bad news though. When our agents got to the pier they didn't find a body. There was a blood smear leading to the water. He must have gone in. We've got agents in the water dragging the river now."

Renita let her head fall back to the stretcher. "Somebody find that motherfucker and put a hole through his head."

Tina was in Schaffer's arms. She put her hands over her ears and looked at Schaffer. "She's going to have to get a spanking when she's better."

Schaffer hugged Tina. "She's just frustrated, but that doesn't excuse her language. I think you'll have to have a discussion with her."

"We'll find him, Renita. From the amount of blood we saw he can't be alive." The SAC held her stare.

"Don't believe it until you find and identify the body. As a matter of fact, maybe you should chop the body into four pieces and take them as far away from each other as possible. I don't even trust Dr. Gerard to die like a human."

"I don't think any of us will feel comfortable until he's spread out in our morgue."

♦

Wednesday morning Renita and Schaffer were released from the hospital. All their tests came back negative the day before and they were issued a clean bill of health. The SAC insisted that the hospital keep them an extra day just to let them catch up on sleep and keep Renita from the crime scene.

Thomas' body still had not been recovered. Renita and Schaffer knew that meant trouble. There were no reports of any injured person being treated for a gunshot wound in any hospital or doctor's office within a three-hundred mille radius. Thomas had once again disappeared.

Joe picked them up from the hospital and took them to his house. After Renita settled in, Schaffer decided to leave. "I've got to get back to Charlottesville. I haven't seen Gretchen in over a week. She probably thinks I've abandoned her."

Nina protested. "Why don't you just stay with us? Gretchen will be fine another couple of days."

"I need the peace and solitude, but thanks for the offer. I've got to complete a follow-up story on this case. I'll be fine. All of you can come over to the house on Saturday. President's day is Monday so we can have a long weekend together." He walked over and kissed Renita and Tina.

"They don't understand people like us, or our need to carry on. I'll see you this weekend." Renita walked him to the door.

Two hours later Schaffer arrived home. He pulled into the garage and left it open while he went to get the mail. As he walked back to the garage, his IPhone rang.

"I see you made it home alright." Renita said.

"Yeah, it's good to be back."

"I'm afraid I've got some more bad news. John Cordell, the man that tried to kill you at the naval base in Florida a couple of years ago, escaped from prison earlier today."

"Great. Another lunatic who hates me is running loose on the streets." Schaffer flipped through his mail.

Renita's voice became more solemn. "It gets a bit worse. In his cell they found pages of writings, all swearing that he would find you and finish the job he should have done years ago. He wants you dead. Just be careful."

"I don't even live in the same place as I did when he was locked up. Hell, I'm not even in the same city; I should be fine."

"Revenge is one of the strongest motivators I've ever seen. You've got to remember, Cordell is trained by the FBI."

"I'm not going to sit around worrying about it. My sidekick will alert me to any oncoming danger." Schaffer reached the garage and was about to walk in when he saw Gretchen running across the field. "Here comes my girl—"

Renita heard an explosion, but Schaffer's cell phone didn't disconnect. She could hear Gretchen whining and Donna screaming as she crossed the field. Renita's heart dropped as she screamed into the phone. "Schaffer, Schaffer."

Made in the USA
Middletown, DE
14 August 2020

15339133R00191